THE COLLECTED SHORT STORIES OF
NOËL COWARD

The Collected
Short Stories of
Noël Coward

HEINEMANN : LONDON

William Heinemann Ltd
10 Upper Grosvenor Street, London W1X 9PA

LONDON MELBOURNE TORONTO
JOHANNESBURG AUCKLAND

First published in one volume 1962
Reprinted 1965
This edition 1969
Reprinted 1971, 1980

434 14701 X

Printed and bound in Great Britain by
Fakenham Press Limited, Fakenham, Norfolk

FOR NATASHA AND JACK

Contents

Introduction

THE stories in this book have been selected from *To Step Aside*, published in 1939, and *Star Quality*, published in 1951. Having been asked to write this preface re-introducing them to the reading public I decided, with a certain reluctance, to re-read them carefully and try to assess their worth as objectively as possible. I say 'with a certain reluctance' because it is frequently a saddening experience for a writer to turn back to his earlier efforts. He is liable to find them either outmoded and inept, or so good that he feels, with a pang of despair, that he can never do so well again. In either case he is likely to wish to God that he had never written them.

In this particular instance I am happy to say I was most pleasantly surprised. These stories strike me as being neither outmoded nor inept, nor indeed so perfect that I feel I can never better them. In fact I enjoyed reading them very much and hope, before my day is done, to write several more.

The short story, like its cousin the one-act play, is regarded by some people with a certain irritated tolerance. It is not quite fish, flesh nor fowl, nor even, except in rare instances, good red herring. The rare instances, the good red herrings, have been provided by the masters of the craft such as de Maupassant, Maugham, Katherine Mansfield, O. Henry, Saki, etc. This is not to say that other writers have not occasionally produced masterpieces in this particular genre, but the great ones have remained constant and consistent and, as a general rule, have concentrated on this one form of creative activity rather than dally with any others. True, Somerset Maugham has written plays, novels and autobiographies, but I think that it is as a short story writer that he will chiefly be remembered. The same applies to de Maupassant and Saki, both of whom wrote excellent novels, but it was undoubtedly in the short story that their true genius shone.

In my own case, being primarily a dramatist, short stories have been an absorbing experiment in form, lying somewhere between a play and a novel. I found them fascinating to write, but far from easy. They demand perhaps a little less rigid self-discipline than a play, and a great deal more than a novel. In a novel there is room for divergencies and irrelevancies, in a play there is none; in a short story, just a little, but it must be strictly rationed. In a play the delineation of character must of course be limited to dialogue, and occasional dialogue at that. The author knows at the outset that all he has is two and a half hours of playing time at the most in which to develop his characters, unfold his plot and arrive at some sort of conclusive ending by eleven-fifteen. Naturally I am not suggesting that these arbitrary rules apply to some of our present-day playwrights to whom the idea of a plot or a conclusive ending at any time of night is beneath contempt. I am merely rambling on in my quaint old-fashioned way about how a play *should* be written and constructed. The same abyss of years lies between me and the sort of modern short story which begins in the middle of a sentence, wanders on for a while through a jungle of confused word-images and psychological abstractions, and comes to an end in the middle of another sentence. Like Mr Maugham, who is admittedly no chicken, I prefer my plays and stories and even novels to have a beginning, a middle and an end. A modern novel of course can be forgiven anything providing only that it is long enough and this, on the American market at least, has been triumphantly proved. Acres of words, regardless of their content, closely printed on seven to eight hundred pages and bound handsomely in heavy cloth, can hardly fail to remain on the best-seller lists for several months. I may add modestly that even shorter novels can occasionally achieve this distinction, but I digress.

Although in most of the stories in this volume a certain amount of personal experience is involved, only one, 'What Mad Pursuit?', could really be described as autobiographical. This was written many years ago in a white heat of retrospective fury shortly after I had spent one of the most uncomfortable week-ends of my life in a gracious home on Long Island. I have of course altered the characters and the appearance of my hostess, and exaggerated here and there the general atmosphere of hectic fatuity into which I was unwittingly plunged, but in essence the story is true. It was a valuable experience taken all in all, for it taught me a sharp lesson. I have made it a hard and fast rule ever since it happened to me never to accept invitations for 'restful' social week-ends when I am working. It is all very well to take a breather in the country after a week of eight strenuous performances in the theatre, but it must be on the strict understanding that the house you visit is conditioned to the vagaries of Theatre people. You must be allowed to sleep as late as you like, slouch about in a dressing-gown for as long as you want to, meet as few strangers as possible, and relax thoroughly in an atmosphere that is familiar, comfortable and without strain. This can only be achieved in the houses of loving, theatre-minded friends. Happily for me I have always had several of these havens to which I can turn. The hospitality of 'civilians', however well-intentioned, is too alien and strenuous for hard-working actors.

The only other story in this collection which in any way concerned me personally is 'Mr and Mrs Edgehill'. These two lovable and, to me, enchanting characters I met when I was weatherbound on a small island in the South Pacific on my way home from New Zealand in 1941. I have changed their names and also the name of the island: I have even changed myself, for the purposes of the story, into a kindly, world-weary English society woman. But the essentials of the episode are true and the Queen (now Queen Elizabeth, the Queen Mother) *did* most graciously accede to my request and send an official photograph of herself and His Majesty to the British Resident of a far-away coral atoll. Unfortunately, however, 'Mr and Mrs Edgehill' had left the island and never received it.

The rest of the stories are more or less imaginary. Aunt Tittie is a complete invention and I love her dearly. Mrs Radcliffe, also an invention, I proudly detest. The description of the air flight from London to Jamaica in 'This Time Tomorrow' was written in the early nineteen-fifties before the introduction of jet planes, so therefore may appear to be a trifle dated.

'A Richer Dust' and 'Star Quality' are both satires and both entirely fictional. I sincerely hope that anyone reading these stories for the first time will derive as much pleasure from them as I did on reading them for the second time.

                                                    NOËL COWARD

Traveller's Joy

LEROY STREET started high up in the social scale, just off Vernon Square where the Boots' Cash Chemists was, and the Kardomah Café and the new Regal Cinema, but it deteriorated just about in the middle, where the houses, although the same size as those further up, seemed to lose caste subtly, like respectable women who are beginning to take to drink. Towards the end of the street all pretensions died, and it wandered inconclusively in squalor out into the waste land behind the town among slag heaps, piles of rubbish, broken bits of Ford cars rusting in the weather, and marshy ponds lying stagnant by the side of the canal.

The Theatre Royal was in the High Street, and although it backed practically on to the garden of Number Fourteen, you had to walk right up into Vernon Square and round and down again before you got to it. Herbert Darrell could actually see into his 'combined' on the first floor if he turned his head while he was making up. It irritated him sometimes to see Miss Bramble fussing about among his things; he had to repress an impulse to yell at her from the dressing-room window, but, he told himself, these sudden bursts of annoyance were only liver, and so he controlled himself and took an extra sip of Guinness as a nerve soother. He generally had a little rule by which he limited himself to only one glass before the first act. It was a game he played, resisting small temptations, and he had it all laid out beautifully. Two or three gulps before starting to make up, two or three more after the foundation had been put on (Numbers Five, Three, and Nine, Leichner always), then a nice long draught before he put on his eyes and mouth, leaving just a little at the bottom of the glass to give a final tickle to the gullet before going down on to the stage.

Not having much imagination, the signs of age in his face depressed him rarely. On the whole it seemed to him to look much the same as it always had. Of course there were more lines and the eyes were a bit puffy underneath, but there was still a glint in them all right. He sometimes winked archly in the glass just to prove it and also, when dressing alone, he occasionally indulged in his 'Passion' face. This was one of his triumphs of the past. A slight projection of the head, half-closed eyes swimming with desire, and an almost imperceptible dilating of the nostrils. In the garden scene in *Lady Mary's Love Affair* in nineteen hundred and four, that particular expression had caused a considerable sensation. He had been hailed, for a time, as one of the great lovers of the stage. Now, in nineteen thirty-four, he still used it, but with a deliberate slackening of intensity, a gallant middle-aged mellowness. He was no fool, he often told himself, none of that painful mutton-dressed-as-lamb business for him! Why, he had voluntarily given up playing Juveniles years ago when he was a bare forty-five.

Just before the end of the performance every night, during his wait in the last act, he usually gave way to a little misty retrospection. Misty, owing to the fact that his fourth Guinness was standing at his elbow. It was pleasant to review the past without anger or bitterness, although God knows he had cause enough for bitterness; the Theatre going to the dogs as it was and all these inexperienced muttering young actors playing leading parts in the West End. But he was all right, pretty contented on the whole, generally in work and with enough money saved to tide him over the bleak periods between tours. Just every now and then, quite unaccountably, in the middle of the night, or riding along on the top of a bus, awareness of failure plunged at him like a sword; twisting in his consciousness cruelly as though it had been lying in wait to murder his self-respect and puncture and wound his pleasure in himself. These searing moments were fortunately rare and passed away as swiftly as they came. There was always something to do, some amiable method of passing the time. Life was full of small opportunities of enjoyment; the sudden meeting of an old friend on a train call for instance, the hurried furtive Guinness in the pub opposite the station with one eye on the clock. Hashing over the past lightly enough not to rumple the dust of illusion, which, more and more as the years advanced, was settling deeper upon it. Every gay episode was, by now, over-coloured into vivid relief, magnified beyond all proportion of its actual happening. Every bad moment was trodden into the lower darkness. Short runs. Bad Press notices. The losing of jobs after perhaps a week's rehearsal. 'I'm afraid, Mr Darrell, you are really not quite suited to this part.' Agonies such as these had been too swift and sudden to be dodged immediately. Egos, however strong and truculent, must be allowed a little time to summon their forces, and the moments between the actual shock and the soothing palliative of a drink, were frequently unbearably long, little grey eternities stretching from the stage door to the nearest pub, with the head averted so that passers-by should not catch the glimmer of unmanly, mortified tears. These happenings lay low in his mind, fathoms deep, like strange twisted creatures that inhabit the depths of the sea; blind and unbelieved and only horrible when some unforeseen tidal disturbance brings them to the surface. In these awful moments Herbert Darrell turned tail and ran, stumbling, panic-stricken and breathless until exhaustion outstripped pursuit and he could relax with some acquaintance, not even a friend was necessary, and preen his draggled feathers; fluffing them out bravely and crowing a little, weakly at first, until the second or third drink gurgled smoothly into his stomach and drowned his fears.

His digs in Leroy Street were really very good. Better and cleaner than Mrs Blockley's in Nottingham that everyone went on so much about. They were cheaper too. Mrs Blockley was too bloody grand, and even if the Martin Harveys had stayed there once there was no need to make such a song and dance about it. Here, at Number Fourteen there were no star memories. No eminent ghosts in Shakesperean tights leered down from the mantelpiece. There were, in point of fact, very few photographs, which was a relief. Only one group of Miss Bramble's mother and father and elder sister, and a tinted enlargement of Miss Bramble herself as a girl. A very pretty girl she must have been too, sitting down on a sofa with her humped back cunningly obscured by a jagged cloud of pink tulle. It was only a very slight hump, anyhow, poor thing. Herbert Darrell regarded her with a pity that he was careful not to let her see, his manner to her being occasionally quite brusque in consequence. She must be, he thought, round about the middle-forties now. Her eyes and skin were still young and her mouth, at certain moments, attractive but over full, with a lift of the upper lip which might have denoted sensuality in anyone else but Miss Bramble; poor dear, what chance had she had for that sort of thing with her deformed back and little spindly legs. He wondered if she minded. Minded as much as he would have under the circumstances. His imagination baulked at the idea of himself, Herbert Darrell, not being physically attractive. It was difficult to conceive a life utterly devoid of 'That sort of thing'. Poor Miss Bramble!

When remembering his past loves he allowed his face to slide into a whimsical smile. Women, many of them nameless, held out their arms to him across the years. He could still recapture the sensation of their smooth bodies in his arms; hear the echo of their small whimpering cries under his lips. A procession of incompletely identified bedrooms passed slowly before his mind's eye, like rather foggy lantern slides

projected on to a screen. Dressing-tables. Wardrobes. Chintz
curtains. Lace curtains. Silk and velvet curtains. Small tables.
Scent bottles. Little feminine clocks ticking away complacently, unmoved by desire or fulfilment or ecstasy. Beds of
all shapes and sizes. Doubles. Singles. With canopies. Without
canopies. One with a little naked Cupid dangling a light just
above his head. Another with a gilt bird catching up mauve
taffeta in its claws. That must have been Julia Deacon's, either
hers or Marion Cressal's. Funny how he always got those two
muddled up. They had both been high spots, definite
triumphs for him. Both well kept and difficult to attain. Then
there was Minnie. Here his mind shied in the darkness
because he had married Minnie and memories of her were
clearer and less glamorous. The first two years had been all
right. Quite a nice little flat they had had in New Cavendish
Street. He had been playing *Captain Draycott* then, his last
success in the West End. Then things had begun to slide,
gradually at first, then three failures on top of one another,
forcing him out into the provinces with the tour of *Captain
Draycott*, starting with the number one towns and finishing,
the following year, with an undignified scamper through the
number threes. Penarth had been the worst, he remembered.
So near Cardiff and yet so far. The reason that it had been the
worst had been because of Minnie. It was in Penarth that he
had seen her strongly and clearly for the first time as a bitch.
His memory lifted its skirts over this patch and hurried convulsively, like an old lady picking her way barefoot across a
shingly beach. The digs just near the pier. Billy Jenner's party
at the hotel on the Thursday night to celebrate his having fixed
a job at Wyndham's for the autumn. Then suddenly feeling
ill and going home early and hearing Minnie's 'Oh Christ!' as
he turned the handle of the bedroom door.

Herbert Darrell turned over heavily in Miss Bramble's
'combined' room bed and went to sleep.

        ·   ·   ·   ·

On Sunday morning the alarum clock dragged Miss Bramble out of a deep tranquil dream at seven o'clock precisely, and she lay for a while blinking at the ceiling and trying to locate a pain somewhere in her inside. Not a physical pain; not even a pain at all really, more a sensation of loss, vague and undefined, as though someone she loved had died and she couldn't quite remember who it was. Sleep still pulled at her eyes, and she turned her head sharply on the pillow; staring at the room until the worn familiarity of everything in it wakened her to reality and sent the last cling-ing vestiges of her dream sliding back into the night. The acorn knob on the end of the blind cord rapped intermittently against the wainscotting because the window was open a little at the top, and the chintz strip on her dressing-table twitched irritably in the draught. She had left the top off her box of Houbigant powder and the edges of stiff paper sticking up inside it looked like a face, somebody lying down asleep, or perhaps dead. A beam of light shooting from behind the blind caught the bristles of her hair-brush showing a few fuzzy hairs with a surprisingly blonde glint on them, and she noticed, with a pang, that the small framed photograph of her mother had fallen over on its face. This got her out of bed with a jerk, and when she had set it upright again and caught sight of herself in the glass, full and complete memory of last night struck at her savagely. Just as a flash of lightning sears against the sky every detail of a landscape, she saw, in an instant, the bright wallpaper of the 'combined' room and the heavy blue-and-white stripes of Mr Darrell's pyjamas.

Still looking in the glass she put out her hand to steady her-self and noted, mechanically, a red flush creeping up from under her Celanese nightgown and suffusing her face. Then she sat down suddenly on the dressing-table chair and felt sick. After a little she went over to the bed again and sat on the edge of that, feeling the linoleum ice-cold under her bare toes. The bland Woolworth clock announced six minutes past seven. At a quarter to eight he was to be called, with a cup of tea and a boiled egg, because the company was going on to Derby and the train went at nine. At a quarter to eight she would be in that room again. She would open the door, after a discreet knock, and walk in as though nothing had happened at all. Just as last night she had walked in in answer to his bell bringing him nothing but her starved and stunted little body; this morning she would bring him a cup of tea and a boiled egg.

She got up from the bed and started to dress feverishly; the cold water splashed over the edge of the basin as she poured it out of the jug and she whimpered a little, making a clucking noise with her tongue against her teeth. A lot of things went wrong with her dressing. Her hair pulled and wouldn't stay up properly. She put her blouse on inside out and had to struggle out of it and into it again, and the button came off one of her strap shoes. Her face looked redder than ever in the glass, and even when she had rubbed in a lot of Icilma vanishing cream and dabbed it generously with the puff, it still flamed shamefully. Finally she got herself downstairs to the kitchen with her loose shoe-strap flapping on every step.

At twenty minutes to eight she absent-mindedly ate one of the bits of toast she had made and had to do another piece hurriedly. He liked his egg done four minutes, and she stood over the gas-stove watching it bobbing about in the saucepan jumping up and down again and rolling over and over impudently as though it were mocking her. Nellie wouldn't arrive to do the rooms until nine-thirty, if then, it being Sunday; she would have the house to herself for a bit when he'd gone, when the taxi had rattled him out of her life together with his two fibre suit-cases, his bulgy Gladstone bag and his dark blue Aquascutum mackintosh with the grease marks on the inside of the collar. She glanced at it hanging up in the hall as she passed along with the tray. It looked tired and depressed, and one of the little sockets at the side was broken, causing the belt to hang down on to the floor like a snake.

She mounted the stairs slowly and carefully; the geyser snorted at her as she passed the bathroom door and one of the stair-rods rattled loose as her feet touched it, nearly tripping her up. At last she stood outside his door waiting for a moment for the courage to knock, and listening to the beating of her heart, the only sound in the silent house. It was lucky there weren't any other lodgers this week. She couldn't have borne that; other rooms to enter, other breakfasts to get. It was very silly, she felt, just to go on standing there outside the door letting his tea and his egg get cold; she balanced the tray in her right hand and lifted her left to knock, then she lowered it again and with a little shiver, sat down on the top step of the stairs putting the tray carefully down beside her. The blind of the landing window was not drawn, and she could see out across the roofs to where the spire of St Catherine's stood up against the grey sky. It was raining a little. She remembered the very first time she had seen that view, from the small room at the top of the house which she had always had when she came to stay with Aunt Alice. She was fifteen then and Aunt Alice, although rather grim and domineering, had been very kind on the whole. Now she was dead and lying in St Catherine's churchyard, possibly tormented by the knowledge that her clean, respectable boarding-house had dwindled slowly, in the hands of her niece, from gentility and social pride into theatrical lodgings. Miss Bramble often thought of this. She often regretted the hard circumstances and lack of stamina which had caused her to deal so shabbily with Aunt Alice's bequest. Theatrical people, according to Aunt Alice, were a worthless lot, possessing little or no moral sense and seldom any religion whatsoever. Miss Bramble wondered dimly what Aunt Alice would say if she knew that her favourite niece, deformity or no deformity, had become so lost to all sense of what was right and proper as to allow herself to be seduced, at the age of forty-four, by an elderly actor in the second floor back. Again she shivered, this time with the sudden chill of clear realisation that she wanted him again, that every nerve in her body was tingling with an agony of desire. She recaptured, behind her closed eyes, the strength of his arms round her; the roughness of his face against her neck and the weight of his body crushing her down deep into an ecstasy sweeter than any she had ever dreamed. It was the 'being in love' of all the people in the world. The essence of every love scene from every movie and play she had ever been to, concentrated miraculously in her. And now, now the moment had gone, no more of it, no more of it ever again in her life probably. The ordinary way of things would continue: shopping, cooking, washing up, welcoming lodgers, saying 'good-bye' to lodgers. . . . This very afternoon Mable Hodge was coming and a new couple, Mr and Mrs Burrell, whom she had never had before. They were all in the same show at the Royal, *Disappearance*, Direct from the Shaftesbury Theatre, London. The Burrells would have the ground floor front with sitting-room, and Mabel Hodge, the 'combined'. She had had it several times before; her silly face had greeted Miss Bramble many a morning when she had gone in with her glass of hot water – 'It must be fraightfully, fraightfully hot, Miss Bramble dear, with just the teeniest slaice of lemon' – She remembered thinking once that Mabel Hodge's face was like one of the fancy cakes in Jones's window in the High Street, one that had been there for a long time until the sugar had melted a bit at the edges, and being ashamed of herself afterwards for being so uncharitable. It was because of Mabel Hodge that she had had the gas-fire put in. She had always grumbled so about the cold, and Nellie letting the fire out, and one thing and another. . . .

Once more a surge of pain engulfed her. The gas-fire had been on last night. In the first moment of putting the light out it hadn't been noticeable at all, and then, gradually, the warm glow of it had spread, throwing a vast shadow of the armchair against the wall. She had opened her eyes to that shadow just once or twice and then closed them again.

The Town Hall clock struck the quarter and, a few seconds later, the clock downstairs did the same, a feeble little noise it made with a convulsive whirr before and after as though it had a cold. Miss Bramble rose to her feet, picked up the tray and walked into the 'combined,' forgetting, in the sudden urgency of her decision, to knock at all.

Herbert Darrell was lying on his back with his head turned away towards the wall. His mouth was open and he was breathing stertorously; the top button of his pyjama jacket was undone, and a tangle of wipsy, greyish hairs rose and fell languidly with the movement of his chest. Miss Bramble put the tray on the table and jerked the blind; the cord escaped her fingers and it went flying up with a tremendous clatter, whirling round and round itself at the top.

Herbert Darrell moved uneasily and opened his eyes, and he had said 'good morning' huskily before she could detect any memory in them. She said quite firmly, but in somebody else's voice, that she was sorry that she was a bit late but that the fire had refused to light properly. He sat up at this, and then she saw him frown and look at her suddenly, blinking. No kind intentions, not all the practised graces of the world could have concealed that expression in time. It was the look she was waiting for and when it came, cutting straight through her heart and out through her hump at the back, she greeted it with an excellent smile. 'I'll go and light the geyser,' she said, and went jauntily out of the room.

Aunt Tittie

I

ONCE upon a time in a small fishing village in Cornwall there lived a devout and angry clergyman named Clement Shore. He was an ex-missionary and had a face almost entirely encircled by whiskers, like a frilled ham. His wife, Mary, was small and weary, and gave birth to three daughters, Christina, Titania, and lastly Amanda, with whose birth she struggled too long and sadly, and died, exhausted by the effort. Amanda was my mother. On Christmas Day 1881, Grandfather Clement himself died and my Aunt Christina, then aged sixteen, having arranged for what furniture there was to be sold, and the lease of the house taken over, travelled to London with several tin trunks, a fox terrier named Roland, and her two younger sisters aged respectively thirteen and eleven. They were met, dismally, at Paddington by their father's spinster sister Ernesta, a grey woman of about fifty, who led them, without protest, to Lupus Street, Pimlico, where with a certain grim efficiency she ran a lodging house for bachelors. Once installed they automatically became insignificant but important cog-wheels in the smooth running machinery of the house, which was very high and respectable. The three of them shared a small bedroom with Roland, from whom they refused to be parted, and lived two years of polite slavery until in the spring of 1883 Christina suddenly married James Rogers, Ernesta Shore's first-floor-front tenant, and went with him to a small house in Camberwell, taking with her Titania and Amanda.

James Rogers was a good man and a piano tuner at the time of his marriage, later he developed into a travelling agent for his firm, so that during my childhood in the house I didn't see much of him; but he was mild-tempered and kind when he did happen to be at home and only drank occasionally, and then without exuberance.

Aunt Christina was formidable, even when young, and ruled him firmly until the day of his death. She was less successful however with Aunt Titania and my mother. Aunt Titania stayed the course for about a year and then eloped to Manchester with a young music hall comedian, Jumbo Potter, with whom she lived in sin for three years to the bitter shame of Aunt Christina. At the end of this liaison she went on to the stage herself in company with three other girls. They called themselves 'The Four Rosebuds' and danced and sang through the music halls of England. Meanwhile my mother, Amanda, continued to live in Camberwell, helping with the housework and behaving very well until 1888, when Titania reappeared in London, swathed in the glamour of the Theatre, and invited her to a theatrical supper party at the Monico. Amanda climbed out of her bedroom window and over the yard fence in order to get there and never returned. Titania on being questioned later by Christina stated that the last she'd seen of Amanda, she was seated on the knee of an Argentine with a paper fireman's cap on her head, blowing a squeaker. Titania's recollections were naturally somewhat vague as she had been drinking a good deal and left the party early on the strength of an unpremeditated reunion with Jumbo Potter. Christina anxiously pursued her enquiries, but could discover nothing about the Argentine; nobody knew his name, he had apparently drifted into the party, entirely uninvited. Finally when two days had elapsed and she was about to go to the police, a telegram arrived from Amanda saying that she was at Ostend and that it was lovely and that nobody was to worry about her and that she was writing. A few weeks later she did

write, briefly, this time from Brussels, she said she was staying
with a friend, Madame Vaudrin, who was very nice and there
were lots of other girls in the house, and it was all great fun,
and nobody was to worry about her as she was very, very
happy.

For five years after that, neither Titania nor Christina heard
from her at all until suddenly, just before Christmas 1893, she
appeared at Christina's house in Camberwell in a carriage and
pair. She was dressed superbly and caused a great sensation in
the neighbourhood. Christina received her coldly but finally
melted when Amanda offered to pay off all the instalments on
the new drawing-room set and gave her a cheque for twenty-
five pounds as well. Titania by this time had married Jumbo
Potter and Amanda gave a family Christmas dinner party at
the Grosvenor Hotel where she was staying, and as a *bonne
bouche* at the end of the meal, produced an Indian Prince who
gave everybody jewellery. She stayed in London for six weeks
and then went to Paris, still with her Prince, and spent a
riotous month or two, until finally she accompanied him to
Marseilles where he took ship for India leaving her sobbing
picturesquely on the dock with a cabuchon emerald and a
return ticket for Paris. It was while she was on the platform
awaiting the Paris train that she met my father, Sir Douglas
Kane-Jones. He was a prosperous-looking man of about
fifty, returning on leave from Delhi to visit his wife and
family in Exeter. However he postponed his homecoming
for three weeks in order to enjoy Paris with Amanda. Finally
they parted, apparently without much heart-break, he for
England, and she for Warsaw, whither she had been invited
by a Russian girl she had met in Brussels, Nadia Kolenska.
Nadia had been living luxuriously in Warsaw for a year as the
guest of a young attaché to the French Embassy. Upon arrival
in Warsaw, Amanda was provided with a charming suite of
rooms and several admirers, and was enjoying herself greatly

when, to her profound irritation, she discovered she was going to have a child.

She and Nadia, I believe, did everything they could think of to get rid of it but without success, and so Amanda decided to continue to enjoy life for as long as she could and then return to England. Unfortunately, however, she left it rather late, and on a frozen morning in January, I was born in a railway carriage somewhere between Warsaw and Berlin. The reason for my abrupt arrival several weeks earlier than was expected was the sudden jolting of the train while my mother was on her way back from the lavatory to her compartment. She fell violently over a valise that someone had left in the corridor, and two hours later, much to everyone's embarrassment and discomfort, I was born and laid in the luggage rack wrapped in a plaid travelling rug.

A week later Aunt Christina arrived in Berlin in response to a telegram, just in time to see my mother die in a hospital ward. With her usual prompt efficiency she collected all my mother's personal effects, which were considerable, and having ascertained that there were no savings in any bank, took me back to England with her and ensconced me in her own bedroom in her new house, Number 17, Cranberry Avenue, Kennington.

2

My life until my Uncle James Rogers' death in 1904 was as eventful for me as it is for most children who are learning to walk and talk and become aware of things. A few incidents remain in my memory. Notably, a meeting with my Aunt Titania when I was about three. She smelt strongly of scent and her hair was bright yellow. She bounced me gaily on her knee until I was sick, after which she seemed to lose interest in me. I remember also, when I was a little older, my Uncle

Jim came into my room late at night. I awoke just in time to see him go over to the mantelpiece and throw two green china vases on to the floor. I cried a lot because I was frightened, Aunt Christina cried too and finally soothed me to sleep again by singing hymns softly and saying prayers.

When I was five I was sent to a kindergarten on week-days, and a Sunday School on Sunday afternoons. A Miss Brace kept the kindergarten. She wore shirt blouses with puffed sleeves, and tartan skirts. Her hair was done up over a pad. Twice a week we had drawing lessons and were allowed to use coloured chalks. I didn't care for any of the other children, and disliked the little girls particularly because they used to squabble during playtime, and pull each other's hair, and cry at the least thing.

I enjoyed the Sunday School much more because we used to stand in a circle and sing hymns, and the teacher had a large illustrated Bible which had a picture of God the Father throwing a hen out of Heaven, and another one of Jesus, with his apostles, sitting at a large table and eating india-rubber rolls. Everybody had beards and white nightgowns, and looked very funny.

When I was nine, Uncle Jim died. All the blinds in the house were pulled down, and we walked about softly as though he were only asleep and we were afraid of waking him. Iris, the servant, who had only been with us for two weeks, trailed up and down the stairs miserably with woebegone tears streaking her face. Perhaps she cried as a natural compliment to bereavement, however remote from herself, or perhaps she was merely frightened. Even the cat seemed depressed and lay under the sofa for hours at a time in a sort of coma. Aunt Christina took me in to see Uncle Jim lying in bed covered with a sheet up to his chin, his eyes were closed, and his face was yellow like tallow, his nose looked as though someone had pinched it. Aunt Christina walked firmly up to the bed, and having straightened the end of the sheet, bent down and kissed him on the forehead so suddenly that I'm sure he would have jumped if he had been alive. Then she looked across at me and said that his spirit had gone to heaven. Outside in the street a barrel organ was playing and there were some children yelling a little way off, but these sounds seemed faint and unreal as though I were listening to them from inside a box.

I went to the funeral with Aunt Christina and Aunt Titania in a closed carriage which smelt strongly of horses and leather. On the way Aunt Titania wanted to smoke a cigarette but Aunt Christina was very angry and wouldn't let her; I sat with my back to the horse and watched them arguing about it, sitting side by side jogging slightly as the carriage wheels bumped over the road. Finally Aunt Christina sniffed loudly and shut her mouth in a thin line and refused to say another word, whereupon Aunt Titania leaned a little forward and looked grandly out of the window until we reached the Cemetery. I stood under a tree with her while the actual burial was going on and she gave me some peppermints out of her muff. When we got home again we all had tea and Iris made some dripping toast, but the atmosphere was strained. After tea I went down to the kitchen to help Iris with the washing up and we listened to the voices upstairs getting angrier and angrier until finally the front door slammed so loudly that all the crockery shook on the dresser. Presently we heard Aunt Christina playing hymns and I didn't see Aunt Titania again for many years.

Soon after this I went to a day school in Stockwell, it wasn't very far away and I used to go there in a bus and walk home. There was an enormous horse chestnut tree just inside the school gate and we used to collect the chestnuts and put them on strings and play conkers. They were rich shiny brown when we first picked them up, like the piano in our front room, but afterwards the shine wore off and they weren't nearly so nice. I hated the Headmaster who was stout and had a very hearty laugh. He insisted on everybody playing football and used to keep goal himself, shouting loudly as he jumped about. One of the under masters was freckled and kind and used to pinch my behind in the locker room when I was changing. Much as I disliked school, I disliked coming home in the evenings still more, my heart used to sink as I stood outside the front door and watched Aunt Christina wobbling towards me through the coloured glass. She generally let me in without saying a word and I used to go straight upstairs to my bedroom and read and do my home-work until supper time, because Iris left at six and there was nobody to talk to. Aunt Christina always said grace before and after meals, and regularly, when we'd cleared away the supper things and piled them up in the kitchen, she used to play hymns and make me sing them with her. Sunday were particularly awful because I had to go to Church morning and evening, as well as to Sunday School in the afternoons. The Vicar was very skinny and while I listened to his throaty voice screeching out the sermon I used to amuse myself by counting how many times his Adam's Apple bobbed up and down behind his white collar. The woman who always sat next to us had bad feet and the whole pew smelt of her.

I used to ask Aunt Christina about my mother but all she'd say was that Satan had got her because she was wicked, and whenever I asked about my father she said he was dead and that she had never known him.

At the beginning of 1906 when I was eleven, things became even gloomier. Aunt Christina bought a whole lot of modelling wax and made a figure of Jesus lying down, then she put red ink on it to look like blood, but it soaked in. It wasn't a very good figure anyhow; the face was horrid and the arms much too long, but she used to kiss it and croon over it. Once she tried to make me kiss it but I wouldn't, so she turned me out into the yard. I stayed all night in the shed and caught cold. After that she wouldn't speak to me for days; I was unhappy and made plans about running away, but I hadn't any money and there was nowhere to run.

One evening in April, I came home from school and she was in bed with a terrible headache; the next morning when I went in to her room, she was gasping and saying she couldn't breathe, so I ran out and fetched a doctor. He said she had pneumonia and that we must have a nurse, so we did, and the nurse rattled about the house and clicked her tongue against her teeth a good deal and washed everything she could. Three days later Mr Wendell, the vicar, came and stayed up in Aunt Christina's room for a time, and a short while after he'd gone the nurse came running downstairs and said I was to fetch the doctor. Just as I was leaving the house to fetch him, I met him at the gate on his way in. He went upstairs quickly and an hour later he and the nurse came down and told me that my aunt had passed away.

He asked me for Aunt Titania's address, so we looked through Aunt Christina's davenport and found it and sent her a telegram. Late that afternoon Uncle Jumbo Potter arrived and interviewed the nurse, and then took me round to the doctor's house, and he talked to him for ages while I sat in the waiting-room, and looked at the people who had come to be cured; one little boy with a bandage round his head was whimpering and his mother tried to comfort him by telling him stories. Presently Uncle Jumbo came out and took me home with him in a cab. He lived in rooms near Victoria Station. He told me that Aunt Titania wasn't living with him any more and that she was in Paris singing at a place called the Café Bardac, and that he was going to send me to her the next day. That night I went with him to Shoreditch where he was doing his turn at the Empire. I sat in his dressing-room and watched him make up and then he took me down on to the stage and let me stand at the side with the stage manager. Uncle Jumbo was a great favourite and the audience cheered and clapped the moment he walked on to the stage. He wore a

very small bowler hat and loose trousers and had a large red
false nose. His songs were very quick indeed until it came to
the chorus, when he slowed down and let the audience join in
too. The last thing he did was a dance in which his trousers
kept nearly falling off all the time. At the end he had to go
before the curtain and make a speech before they'd let him
go. He took me upstairs with him and undressed, still very
out of breath. He sat down quite naked and smoked a
cigarette, and I watched the hair on his chest glistening with
sweat as he breathed. He asked me if I liked his turn and I said
I loved it and he said, 'Damned hard lot down here, can't get a
bloody smile out of 'em, pardon me.' After he'd taken his
make-up off and powdered his face and dressed we went to a
bar just opposite the Theatre and he drank beer with two
gentlemen and a woman with a white fur, then we went home
first in a tram and then a 'bus. I went to sleep in the 'bus.
When we got to his rooms he gave me a glass of soda water
and made up a bed for me on the sofa.

The next morning Uncle Jumbo took me back to Aunt
Christina's house. The nurse was still there, and Mrs Harrison
from next door, who kissed me a lot and told me to be a brave
little man and asked me if I would like to come upstairs and
see my dear Auntie; but Uncle Jumbo wouldn't let me, he
said he didn't hold with kids looking at corpses because it was
morbid. He helped me pack my clothes and then we got a cab
and drove back to his rooms. In the afternoon he went out
and left me alone and I amused myself by looking at some
magazines and a large album of photographs and press
cuttings about Aunt Titania and Uncle Jumbo. When he came
back he had a friend with him, Mrs Rice, who he said would
take me to the station, as the train went at eight o'clock and he
would be in the Theatre. Mrs Rice was pretty and laughed a
lot. We all made toast, and had tea round the fire. Mrs Rice sat
on Uncle's knee for a little and he winked at me playfully over
her shoulder and said, 'You tell your Aunt Tittie how pretty

Mrs Rice is, won't you?' whereupon she got up and said, 'Leave off, Jumbo, you ought to be ashamed,' and looked quite cross for a minute. Uncle Jumbo went off to the theatre at 5.30; he gave me five pounds and my ticket and said that he had telegraphed to Aunt Tittie to meet me at the station. He kissed me quite affectionately and said, 'Fancy me being fatherly!' Then he laughed loudly, tickled Mrs Rice under the arms, and went down the stairs whistling. When he'd gone Mrs Rice and I went back and sat by the fire. She asked me a lot of questions about Aunt Titania but as I hadn't seen her since Uncle Jim's funeral I couldn't answer them very well. After a while she went to the cupboard and poured herself a whisky and soda, and while she was sipping it she told me all about her husband who used to beat her and one night he tied her to the bed in their rooms in Huddersfield and kept on throwing the wet sponge at her until her nightgown was soaking wet and the landlady came in and stopped him. She said she'd met Uncle Jumbo in Blackpool in the summer and that they used to go out after the show and sit on the sand dunes in the moonlight, and then her husband found out and there was an awful row, and Jumbo knocked her husband down on the pier and brought her to London on the Sunday and she hadn't seen her husband since, but she believed he was still on tour in *Miss Mittens* and hoped to God he'd stay in it and not come worrying her. She had several more whiskies and sodas before it was time to go and showed me a scar on her thigh where a collie bit her during her honeymoon in Llandudno. I looked at it politely and then she pulled her skirts down and said I was a bad boy and how old was I anyhow? I said I was eleven and she laughed and asked me if it made me feel naughty to see a pretty girl's bare leg. I said no and she said, 'Get along with you. I must put some powder on my nose.' After a minute she came out of the bedroom, put her hat on and said we must go. We took a cab to the station on account of my trunk and Mrs Rice told the porter to register it through to Paris. She bought me some buns and chocolate and two magazines and put me in the train and waited to tell the guard to keep his eye on me before she kissed me and said good-bye. I waved to her all the way up the platform until she was out of sight and then sat back in my corner feeling very grown up and excited and waiting for the train to start.

That journey to Paris was momentous for me. I was alone and free for the first time, my going was in no way saddened by memories of people I'd left behind. I had left no one behind whom I could possibly miss; my school friendships were casual and I had definitely grown to hate poor Aunt Christina during the last few years of her life. I pressed my face against the cold glass of the carriage window and searched for country shapes in the darkness, trees and hills and hedges, and felt as though I should burst with joy. There were two other people in the carriage with me; a man and a woman who slept, sitting up, with their mouths open. When we reached Newhaven, the guard came and led me to the gangway of the ship and gave me in charge of one of the men on board who offered me a ham sandwich and showed me a place in the saloon where I could put my feet up and go to sleep, but I couldn't begin to sleep until the ship started although I was dead tired, so I went up on deck and watched the lights of the town receding, and the red and green harbour lamps reflected in the water and I looked up at the clouds scurrying across the moon, and, suddenly, like a blow in the face, loneliness struck me down. I was chilled through and through with it – I wondered what I should do if when I got to Paris Aunt Titania was dead too. I tried very hard not to cry but it was no use, I had a pretty bad fit of hysteria and everyone crowded round me and patted me and tried to comfort me with eatables, until finally one kind woman took me in charge completely and gave me some brandy which made me choke but pulled me together. Then she put me to sleep in her private cabin and I didn't wake up until we got to Dieppe. I was all right from then on, the woman's name was Roylat and she was on her way to Ceylon to visit her son who was a rubber planter. I had some tea with her in the station buffet at Dieppe and travelled with her to Paris, sleeping most of the way.

When we arrived at the Gare St Lazare Aunt Titania was waiting at the barrier wearing a sealskin coat and a bright red hat with a veil floating from it. I said good-bye to Mrs Roylat who kissed me, bowed to Aunt Titania and disappeared after her luggage. Aunt Titania and I had to go and sit in the Customs room for three-quarters of an hour until my trunk came in. She was pleased to see me but very cross with Jumbo for having sent me by night instead of day. She said it was damned thoughtless of him because he knew perfectly well that she never got to bed before four o'clock in the morning and to have to get up again at six-thirty was too much of a good thing; then she hugged me and said it wasn't my fault and that we were going to have jolly times together.

At last, when the Customs man had marked my trunk, we got a cab and drove out into Paris. It had been raining and the streets were wet and shiny. The shutters on most of the shops were just being put up and waiters in their vests and trousers were polishing the tables outside the cafés. We drove across the river and along the quai Voltaire with the trees all glistening and freshly green; our cab horse nearly fell down on the slippery road as we turned up the rue Bonaparte. Aunt Tittie talked all the way about everything she'd been doing and her contract at the Café Bardac which they'd renewed for another month. She asked me if Aunt Christina had left me any money and I said I didn't know, but I gave her a letter that Jumbo had told me to give her. She pursed up her lips when she read it and then said, 'It looks like I shall have to find a job for you, duckie, you'd better come along with me and see Monsieur Claude but there's no hurry, we'll talk about that later on.' Finally the cab drew up before a very high house, and a little

man in a shirt and trousers ran out and helped the driver down
with my trunk. Aunt Tittie said something to him in French
and took me up four flights of dark stairs and opened the door
into a sitting-room which had a large bedroom opening out of
it on one side with a feather mattress on the bed that looked
like a pink balloon, and a tiny room on the other side which
she said I was to have. There were lots of coloured bows on
the furniture and hundreds of photographs, lots of them fixed
to the blue-striped wallpaper with ordinary pins. There was a
small alcove in her bedroom with a wash-hand stand in it and
a gas ring, and on the sitting-room table was a tray with some
dirty glasses on it and a saucer full of cigarette-ends. Aunt
Tittie took off her hat and coat and threw them on the sofa,
then she ran her fingers through her hair and said, 'Well, here
we are. Home Sweet Home with a vengeance.' Then she went
out on to the landing and screamed, 'Louise!' very loudly and
came in again and sat down. 'We'll have some coffee and rolls,'
she said, 'then we'll go to bed until lunch time, how does that
suit you?' I said it suited me very well and we lapsed into
silence until Louise came. Louise was about seventeen with a
pallid face, a dirty pink dress turned up under an apron, and
green felt slippers, her hair was bristling with curl-papers.
Aunt Tittie had a long conversation with her in French and
then the little man came clambering upstairs with my trunk
and put it in my room. Then Louise and he both disappeared
and I was left alone with Aunt Tittie. I felt rather strange and
oddly enough a little homesick, not really homesickness for
that dreary house in Kennington, but a longing for something
familiar. Aunt Tittie must have sensed that I wasn't feeling
too happy because she put her arm round me and hugged me.
'It's funny, isn't it?' she said, 'you arriving suddenly like this?
You must tell me all about poor Aunt Christina and what
you've been learning at school and everything, and you
haven't got any cause to worry about anything because you're
going to be company for me and I shall love having you here.'

Then she held me close to her for a moment and surprisingly burst out crying, she fumbled for her handkerchief in her belt and went into the bedroom and shut the door. I didn't know what to do quite, so I started to unpack my trunk. Presently Louise returned with a tray of coffee and rolls and butter; she plumped it down on the table and screamed something at Aunt Tittie through the door and went out again. I sat at the table and waited until Aunt Tittie came out of the bedroom in a long blue quilted satin dressing-gown, with her hair down. She looked quite cheerful again. 'I can't think what made me burst out like that,' she said as she seated herself at the table. 'It came over me all of a sudden about you being all alone in the world and your poor mother dying in childbirth and now Christina. We're the only ones left out of the whole lot and that's a fact. Two lumps?' She poured out coffee for us both and talked volubly all the time, a stream of scattered remarks, beginnings of stories, references to people I'd never heard of, all jumbled together incoherently, but somehow all seeming to fit into a sort of pattern.

She must have been about forty then, her hair had been re-dyed so often that it was entirely metallic, as bright as new brass fire-irons. Her face was pretty with a slightly retroussé nose and wide-set blue-grey eyes, her mouth was generous and large and gay when she laughed. She talked of Jumbo a good deal, irritably, but with underlying tenderness, I suspect that she always loved him more than anyone else. She asked me if I'd seen Mrs Rice and said that she was sorry for any man that got tangled up with a clinging vine of that sort. After breakfast, and when she'd smoked two or three cigarettes, she said she was going to bed until one o'clock and that I could do what I liked, but that she strongly advised me to go to bed too as I was probably more tired after my journey than I thought I was.

I went into my little room and when I'd finished unpacking I sat and looked out of the window for a while. It was at the back of the house looking down into a courtyard, the sun was shining into the rooms on the other side of the court, in one of them I saw an old woman in a blue dressing-gown working a sewing machine, the whirr of it sounded very loud, and every now and then there was the noise of rattling crockery far down on the ground floor, and somebody singing.

There were lots of grey roofs and chimney-pots and several birds flying about and perching on the telegraph wires, which stretched right across into the next street and then were hidden by a tall many-windowed building that looked like some sort of factory. I felt very drowsy and quite happy so I went and lay down on the bed and the next thing I knew was that it was lunch time and Aunt Tittie was shaking me gently and telling me to get up. She was still in her dressing-gown, but her head was done up in a towel because she'd just washed her hair.

We had hot chicken and vegetables and salad for lunch and fresh crusty bread and coffee. When we'd finished Aunt Tittie stretched herself out on the sofa and then moved her legs so as to make room for me on the end of it.

'Now we'd better talk a bit,' she said. 'I had a good think while I was washing my head and if you'll listen carefully I'll tell you just how things stand and then we'll decide what's best to be done.' I settled myself more comfortably and handed her the matches off the table which she was reaching out for. 'To begin with,' she said, 'I haven't got any money except what I earn, but we can both live on that if we're careful anyhow for a bit, until you start to make a little on your own. I know I ought to send you to school really but I can't; it's none too easy living in this damned town, because you've got to look smart and have nice clothes otherwise nobody will take any notice of you. Now I've got an idea which I'll have to talk over with Mattie Gibbons, she's my partner. We do a parasol dance, and then she does her skipping rope speciality which is fine; then I sing a ballad, one verse and chorus in English and the second verse and chorus in French and then we do a number together called "How would you like a rose like me?" and go round to all the tables giving the men paper roses out of a basket. My idea was that you should be dressed up as a little dandy with a silk hat and a cane and gloves, you know the sort of thing, and flirt with us during the parasol dance and bring on our props for us all through the act. If Mattie agrees we'll ask Monsieur Claude about it. I think he'll say yes because he's a bit keen on me if you know what I mean and you ought to get about fifteen francs a week which would be a help to begin with. Would you like that?'

I said eagerly that I'd love it better than anything in the world and flung my arms round her neck and kissed her and she said, 'Here wait a minute, it isn't settled yet, we've got to talk to Mattie and Monsieur Claude and arrange hundreds of things. I shall have to tell you a whole lot you're really too young to know, before I let you loose in the Café Bardac; to start with, how much do you know?' This was rather a difficult question to answer so I sat looking at her without saying anything. 'You know about men and women having babies and all that, don't you?' she said with an obvious effort.

I said 'Yes,' and blushed.

'Well, that's a good start anyway,' she said. 'Now then——' she stopped short and blushed herself, and then giggled nervously. 'Oh, my God, I don't know how the hell to begin and that's a fact, well——' she pulled herself together. 'Take the plunge, that's always been my motto, so here goes.' She crushed out her cigarette and sat up and spoke very fast. 'Now listen, Julian, it's a strange world, and it's not a bit of good pretending it isn't. You're only a kid and you ought to have a nice home and go to a nice school and learn history and geography and what not and get to know all about everything gradually, so it wouldn't be a shock to you, but as it happens you haven't got a nice home, you haven't got a home at all, you're alone except for me and Christ knows I'm no Fairy Godmother, but I've got to tell you everything I can so that you don't go and get upset by things and led away through

not realising what it's all about. To begin with, dear, you're a
bastard, which sounds awful but isn't so bad really, it only
means that your mother wasn't married to your father, they
just had an affair and that was that, no obligations on either
side and then you were born and your mother died and
nobody knew who your father was anyhow, except by
rumour, and what Nadia Kolenska, who was your mother's
friend, wrote to your Aunt Christina. You were brought up
on the money that your mother's jewels fetched when your
Aunt Christina sold them, and now she's dead too and here
you are, alone in Paris with your Aunt Tittie who's not a
"good" woman by any manner of means, but she's all you've
got so you'd better make the best of her.' Here she leant back
and the cushion fell over the end of the sofa on to the floor, so
I picked it up and put it behind her head and sat down again.

'When I say I'm not a good woman,' she went on, 'I mean
I'm not what your Aunt Christina would call good. I take life
as I find it and get as much as I can out of it. I always have been
like that, it's me all over and I can't help it, tho' many's the
row I've had with Christina because she never would see that
what was good for her wasn't necessarily good for me. I'm
more like your mother I think really, only not quite so reckless.

'Now if you're going to live with me here, there's a lot of
goings on you'll have to open your eyes to wide and then shut
'em tight and not worry, and you mustn't be upset by Mattie's
swearing, her flow of language is something fierce when she
gets going, but she's a really good friend and you'll like her.
As far as the Café Bardac goes you'll have to look out and not
be surprised by anything; it's none too refined there after one
in the morning. People of all sorts and sizes come and drink at
the bar, and sometimes there's a fight and you'll get a good
laugh every now and again to see the way those old tarts
shriek and yell and carry on. You know what tarts are, don't
you?'

I said I wasn't sure, but I thought I did.

'Well,' she continued, 'they're women who have affairs with men professionally, if you know what I mean. They take 'em home and cuddle up with 'em and the men pay them for it, though when you've had a look at some of them you'll wonder how the hell they get as much as fourpence. But they're quite decent sorts, most of them. Then there are young men who dance around and get paid by the women, they're called "macros" and aren't much use to anyone except that they dance well and keep the rich old American ladies happy. Then there are lots of boys and young men who make up their faces like women, they're tarts too, only male ones as you might say. Heaps of men like cuddling up with them much better than women, though I should think personally it must feel rather silly, but after all that's their look-out and no business of mine. They're awfully funny sometimes, you'd die laughing to see them have a row. They scream and slap one another. There's one at the Bardac called Birdie, always in trouble, that one, but he's awfully sweet so long as he doesn't get drunk. If any of the old men ever come up and ask you to drink or go out with them don't you do it, and if they catch hold of you and start getting familiar just wriggle away politely and come and tell me. I'll let 'em have it all right. It's a queer world and no mistake, and you'd much better get to know all you can about it as soon as maybe and then you can stand on your own feet and not give a damn for anyone.'

She finished up with rather a rush and then looked at me anxiously. I felt slightly bewildered but I said I'd try to remember all she'd told me and not be surprised at anything whatever happened; then we talked about other things. She asked me to tell her all the details of Aunt Christina's death which I did and she sighed and shook her head sadly and looked for a moment as if she were going to cry, but fortunately just then there was a loud banging on the door and Mattie Gibbons came in. She was shorter and plumper than

Aunt Tittie and very dark, she had a grey dress with grey laced-up boots which showed when she sat down, and a bright green blouse with a small diamond watch pinned on it; her hat was grey felt with a blue bird on it. She was very nice to me and shook hands politely and said she didn't know I was going to be such a big boy. She had a deep husky voice, and I liked her at once.

Aunt Tittie said they wanted to talk privately for a while and would I like to go for a walk. I said I would, and after she'd warned me about looking to the left first when crossing the road, and told me to mark well the number of the house and street so that I wouldn't get lost, she kissed me and waved me out of the door. I felt my way carefully down the dark stairs and when I got to the front door it wouldn't open. After I'd struggled with it for a long time, a woman put her head out of a door and screamed something at me and then there was a click and the door opened of its own accord. The street was very narrow and filled with traffic. I walked down it slowly looking into all the shop windows; pastry-cooks with the most beautiful-looking cakes I'd ever seen; several artists' shops with easels and paints and boxes of coloured pastels, and wooden jointed figures in strange positions; and a toy shop with hundreds of cheap toys jumbled up in cardboard boxes. There were also grocers and greengrocers and one big shop filled with old furniture and china. This was on the corner and half of it faced the river. I crossed over carefully and walked along the other side past all the little boxes on the parapet filled with books and coloured prints and thousands of back numbers of magazines, very tattered and dusty and tied together in bundles with string.

There were lots of people fingering the books and hurrying along the pavement, nearly all the men had long beards and some of them went into round iron places covered with advertisements on the outside, and then came out again doing up their trousers. I was very puzzled by this so I peeped into one of them and saw what it was. After that it amused me a lot, looking at the different kinds of feet standing round underneath.

I crossed over a bridge and leant on the stone rail, the water was very green and there were several steamers puffing up and down, occasionally a larger one would come along and its funnel would bend in half as it went under the bridge. The river divided a little way further up, leaving an island in the middle with houses on it coming out almost into a point, and there were trees everywhere all along the edges. Everything looked much clearer and cleaner than London and the shadows of the houses stretched right across the road, sharp and definite.

I felt excited and adventurous and went across to the other side and walked for a long way under the trees; every now and then a noisy yellow tram came along. The lines were more like railway lines than tram lines, and grass was growing between them. By the time I got back to the house the sun was setting and all the windows along the quay looked as though they were on fire.

That evening Mattie came round at about nine o'clock and we all three of us went and had dinner at a café. Our table was right on the pavement and there was a little red-shaded lamp on it. Mattie and Aunt Tittie were very gay and talked very fast in French to the people that they knew and in English to each other and to me. Aunt Tittie told me what lots of things were in French and said I'd better learn to speak it as quickly as I could as it was very useful. They had had a long talk about me being a 'dandy' in their turn and Mattie was pleased with the idea; they said they'd take me that night to the Café Bardac with them and interview Monsieur Claude right away.

After dinner we walked along the boulevard to another café where we had coffee in glasses and they had brandy as well, then we went home and Aunt Tittie made me lie down for an hour while she dressed. She said that as I was going to be up late I'd better get as much rest as possible. At about half-past eleven Mattie called for us, she and Aunt Tittie were both in sparkling evening dresses and cloaks and then we all got into a cab and drove a long way through brightly-lighted streets. In the cab Aunt Tittie gave me a latch-key and some money and made me repeat the address over and over again, and said that I should always have to come home by myself, even when I was actually acting in the turn with them, because they generally had to stay on and talk to people sometimes nearly all night. She told me how much the cab would cost and then very slowly and clearly what I was to say to the driver. When I repeated it she and Mattie both laughed and said I spoke French like a native. Mattie said she wondered if it was all right to let me wander about Paris alone at night, and Aunt Tittie said I was very sensible for my age and that it was much better for me to get used to managing for myself and learn independence.

When we arrived at the Café Bardac nobody was there but a lot of waiters and a man behind the bar. We all went upstairs and sat in a small dressing-room which Mattie and Aunt Tittie shared. Their dresses were hanging up on pegs and there were two chairs, two mirrors on a shelf, and a very small wash-basin in the corner with a jug without a handle standing on the floor by the side of it.

Mattie took a bottle out of the cupboard and they both had a drink. Presently Aunt Tittie went downstairs to see Monsieur Claude and left me to talk to Mattie.

Mattie asked me if I didn't feel strange and I said 'yes' but that I was enjoying it. She said, 'It's a bloody awful life this really, you know, but it has its funny moments. This café's not so bad as some I've been in. I was dancing with a troupe in Antwerp once and they made us dress in a lavatory on the third floor, and the smell was enough to knock you down I give you my word; this is a little peep at Paradise compared to that and no error!'

Then she took out the bottle again and had another swig and said would I like a taste. I said 'yes' and she said 'My God, here I go corrupting you already,' but she let me have a sip and laughed when I made a face. 'It's raw gin, ducks, and don't let anybody ever tell you it's water, but it does make you feel fine, all ready to go out and fight someone, and believe me or believe me not you need that feeling in this Pavilion d'Amour!'

Aunt Tittie came back, looking very pleased and said Monsieur Claude wanted to see me, so down we went to the next floor into a little room with a desk in it and a lot of photographs of naked women stuck on the walls. Monsieur Claude was fat and excitable; he kissed me on both cheeks and then held me by the shoulders and pushed me away from him and looked at me carefully, talking all the time very quickly in French. Then he whispered a lot to Aunt Tittie, gave her a smacking kiss on the lips and ushered us out into the passage. Just as I went through the door, he fumbled in his pocket and gave me three francs. Aunt Tittie was frightfully pleased and said didn't I think he was a dear. 'Kind as can be, you know, of course he gets a bit excited now and again but he's never downright nasty except when he's had a couple, which isn't often, thank God.'

We went upstairs to the dressing-room again and told Mattie all about it. I was to get ten francs a week to begin with and fifteen later on if I was good. Mattie said the mean old bastard might have come across with a bit more, but Aunt Tittie reminded her that after all he did have to think of his business. We all three went downstairs after a little while. Aunt Tittie introduced me to the barman. He spoke English and gave me a high stool to sit on in a corner behind the bar where I could watch all the people. I sat there for ages until my eyes prickled with the smoke. Every now and then Mattie or Aunt Tittie would come and see if I was all right, then they came down dressed as shepherdesses with bare legs and after they'd had a little port at the bar they did their parasol dance. Nobody seemed to watch it very much, but they all applauded and cheered when it was finished. I watched their turn all through and then felt so tired that I decided to go home, so I went upstairs to the dressing-room to fetch my hat. I knocked and went in thinking Aunt Tittie and Mattie were downstairs, but they weren't – at least Aunt Tittie wasn't. She was in there with Monsieur Claude. She was sitting on his knee with hardly any clothes on at all and he was kissing her. They both had their eyes closed and neither of them saw me, so I closed the door again very quietly and went out without my hat. I got a cab quite easily and he drove me home and when I paid him, had a long conversation with me which I didn't understand, so I bowed and said *bon soir* and he drove away.

I lay in bed for a long while without sleeping. I felt strange, as though none of the things that were happening to me were real. I wondered whether Aunt Tittie liked being kissed by fat Monsieur Claude, and then all the faces of the people I'd seen at the café seemed to go across my eyes very fast until they were all blurred and I fell asleep. I woke up just for a second in the early morning; a cold grey light was showing through the shutters and I heard Aunt Tittie's voice in the next room. Then her bedroom door slammed and I turned over and went to sleep again.

3

When I first appeared with Aunt Titania and Mattie Gibbons at the Café Bardac in Paris, I had a great personal success; all the tarts made a tremendous fuss of me and said I was *très gentil* and *très beau gars* and gave me sweet cakes, and Monsieur Claude raised my salary from ten francs to fifteen francs a week, quite soon. When the engagement came to an end Mattie and Aunt Tittie had a row and parted company. I think the row somehow concerned Monsieur Claude and it was terrible while it lasted. Aunt Tittie cried a lot and said Mattie was a dirty double-faced bitch and Mattie just sat there laughing until Aunt Tittie completely lost control and threw a vermouth bottle at her, which missed her and went flying through the open door into my bedroom and broke the looking-glass over my wash-basin. After that Mattie stopped laughing and chased Aunt Tittie round the table, swearing loudly. They were both drunk and I got rather frightened so I ran outside and sat on the stairs with my fingers in my ears. Presently Mattie came rushing out and fell over me; she smacked my face and went on downstairs screaming. I heard her wrestling with the front door and swearing at it, finally she got it open and slammed it behind her so hard that a large bit of plaster fell off the ceiling into a slop pail on the landing. When I went back into the sitting-room Aunt Tittie was lying on the sofa crying; her hair was down and her nose was bleeding, making stains all down the front of her dress. When I came in she got up and stumbled into her bedroom where I heard her being very sick. I shut the door and locked it and opened the shutters to see what the day looked like. It was raining hard and the gutters were gurgling loudly so I went back to bed and slept.

Soon after this Aunt Tittie and I packed up everything and went to Ostend. We appeared at a Café Concert in a side street which led down to the Plage. Aunt Tittie did three songs and I learnt a speech in French to introduce her. Everybody used to laugh and clap when I came on with my silk hat and cane and white gloves. Aunt Tittie thought it would be a good thing if I wore a monocle, but I couldn't keep it in my eye until we stuck it in with spirit gum, then it was a great success. We stayed there for six weeks and I used to play about on the Plage during the day.

We lived in a cheap hotel kept by a very thin woman called Madame Blücher; she was half German and sometimes made chocolate cakes with whipped cream on them which were delicious. She had a lot of sons and used to show me photographs of them. One was a sailor and he was photographed holding an anchor and sticking his chest out. He had the biggest behind I've ever seen.

When we'd finished our engagement in Ostend we went to Brussels and were out of work for nearly five weeks. We used to go and sit in the waiting-room of an agent's office with lots of other people wanting jobs. The walls were plastered with posters of celebrated stars very vividly coloured and there was a signed photograph of Sarah Bernhardt looking like a sheep in white lace.

We had to move out of the hotel we were in and go to a still cheaper one. Aunt Tittie got more and more depressed, but one day she met an Austrian officer in some café or other and came home late looking much more cheerful. He was very handsome and took us both to dinner at an open air restaurant one night; he joked with me a lot and pinched my ear which hurt, but I pretended I liked it. After dinner he put me in a cab and told it to go to the hotel, and gave me the money to pay it, but I stopped the driver when we'd got round the corner and paid him a little and walked home; it was further than I thought but I was three francs to the good. About a week after this Aunt Tittie got a contract to go to Antwerp for three weeks. After that we went to Amsterdam and then back again to Brussels, where we stayed for two months and played for some part of the time at the Mercedes Music Hall.

It was strange at first, doing our turn on an actual stage, but I liked it much better. It wasn't really a proper theatre because most of the audience sat at tables, but it had footlights and scenery and a drop curtain.

Aunt Tittie taught me a song which I did dressed as a pierrot while she changed her dress. It was called 'Keep Off the Grass' and was out of a musical comedy in England. Nobody seemed to pay very much attention to it but I enjoyed doing it enormously.

After this we got a long contract and travelled all over France playing a week in each place, ending up with Lyons and Nice and Marseilles and then we went over to Algiers where we stayed for three weeks. There was a conjuror on the bill with us who took a great fancy to me. He asked me to have supper with him one night and we sat in a café with lots of Arabs wearing fezzes. I think he was half an Arab himself. Then we went for a drive along by the sea and he said I was 'very nice boy' and 'very pretty and had naughty eyes'. He held my hand for a little and I knew what was coming so I said I felt very sick and started retching. He took me back to the hotel at once. His turn came on after ours and I always used to wait and watch it; he did card tricks and shot pigeons out of a gun and then to finish up with he used to walk down to the front of the stage and say very solemnly, 'Mesdames, Messieurs, maintenant je vous monterai un experiment très, très difficile, une expérience de vie,' whereupon he would take off his coat and shirt and stand stripped to the waist in dead silence for a moment, then, with great deliberation, he'd take a sharp-pointed dagger from a table, test it and bend it slightly with his long thin fingers, and then proceed, amid a breathless hush from the audience, to carve out his left nipple. It was very realistically done even to a dark stream of blood which ran down over his ribs. Then suddenly, with a quick jerk, he'd throw the dagger away, whip out a handkerchief, and staunch the blood and cry 'Voilà' and the curtain fell. He had, I think, a small rubber squeezer filled with red solution concealed in his hand, and then having made up his own nipple with flesh colour, he stuck a false red one over the top of it. It always brought forth thunders of applause.

After Algiers we went on to Tunis which was very much the same except that the weather was warmer. Then we had a week's engagement in Genoa which was a great failure – all the young Italian men made such a noise that we couldn't make ourselves heard, so we worked our way back to Paris by slow degrees, playing in Geneva and Montreux on the way.

We tried to get the same rooms we'd had before but they were occupied, so we went to a small hotel behind the Invalides and stayed for a few weeks until Aunt Tittie fixed up an autumn contract. Then to fill in the time we went and stayed at a farm near Bordeaux with an old friend of Aunt Tittie's, Madame Brinault. She had been a dancer and had married and retired; she was fat and kind and had three grown-up step-daughters and a step-son, who looked after the vines. They were all very vivacious and talked at the top of their voices all through meals. They had a monkey which bit every now and then but could be very affectionate when it liked. We used to fish in the pond for eels and small mud fish, and walk all along through the vines and pinch the grapes to see if they were coming along all right.

We stayed there for six weeks, and it did us a lot of good. Aunt Tittie got quite fat from drinking so much milk and cream and she let her hair go for the whole time without dyeing it so that it looked very odd, yellow at the ends and brownish-grey at the roots.

We spent most of the next year in Germany playing in Frankfurt, Hamburg, Dresden, Nuremberg, Munich, Hanover, Heidelberg and Berlin, where Aunt Tittie met Arthur Wheeler, an acrobat, and fell violently in love with him. We stayed on there for several months, playing sometimes in suburban halls and sometimes in cafés in Potsdam and Berlin itself. Arthur Wheeler was a thick-set bad-tempered little man and he used to beat Aunt Tittie often, but I don't think she minded. He came with us in the summer to a place called Achensee in the Tyrol and we stayed in a pension hotel and used to go out for picnics on the lake. He taught me to swim and dive. The lake water was ice cold even with the hot sun on it, but I got used to it and often swam seven or eight times a day. Wheeler used to lie on the grass by the side of the water with a towel tied round his middle, and do acrobatics, frequently with such violence that the towel would fall off and Aunt Tittie would laugh until she cried and say, 'That's it, Arthur, give the poor Germans a treat!'

Every evening we used to sit outside the pension and have dinner. The tables were set almost in the road and processions of German families would march by, very hot and tired from their climbing. Even the young men had fat stomachs and they all wore shorts, and embroidered braces and small hats.

Every evening at about six o'clock we had beer at an open-air restaurant just by the water. We liked watching the steamer come puffing across the lake and then stop at the pier and land the passengers.

One evening when Wheeler had paid for the beer and we were about to walk back to the pension, he suddenly stood still, clutched Aunt Tittie's arm and said, 'Jumping Jesus, that's my wife!'

I looked up and saw a thin woman in a brown dress walking down the pier and staring fixedly at us. We all stood where we were until she came up to us. She looked very angry and was biting her lips nervously.

'Arthur,' she said, 'I want to talk to you.' Her voice was grating and hard, and completely determined.

Arthur Wheeler started to bluster a bit: 'Now look here, Amy——' he began, but she cut him short by taking his arm and leading him to the other end of the garden where they sat down at a table. I looked at Aunt Tittie who was very white, she hadn't said a word.

'Shall we go back to the pension?' I said. She shook her head. 'No, we'll stay here,' so we sat down again at the table we'd just got up from, and waited. The steamer gave a sudden hoot of its siren which made me jump, then it went churning away up the lake. It was twilight and the mountains looked jagged against the sky as though they had been cut out of black paper. On the other side of the lake, lights were already twinkling in the villages. The steamer hooted again a good

way off and a flock of birds flew chattering out of the big
trees behind the restaurant. I looked at Aunt Tittie. She was
staring straight in front of her and her face was set and still
except for two little pulses twitching at her temples.

Presently Mrs Wheeler came over to us. Aunt Tittie stood
up.

'Arthur's leaving with me on the first boat tomorrow
morning,' said Mrs Wheeler. 'He's going back to your hotel
now to pack his things. I've engaged a room here for us for
tonight.'

'Oh,' said Aunt Tittie. 'That will be nice, won't it?'

'If you haven't any money,' went on Mrs Wheeler, 'I'm
sure Arthur'll give you enough to get you back to wherever
you come from.'

Aunt Tittie gave a little gasp. 'Thank you for nothing,' she
said, her voice sounded high and strained. 'I don't want
Arthur's money and you know it.'

'You're a low woman,' said Mrs Wheeler. 'I don't wish to
exchange words with you.'

'I'm not so low as to live on a man's earnings for fifteen
years and not give him anything in return.'

'Your sort couldn't hold a man fifteen years,' said Mrs
Wheeler.

'I wouldn't want to hold anyone who didn't want to stay,'
said Aunt Tittie. 'He loves me more than he does you, otherwise he wouldn't be here, would he? And you can put that in
your pipe and smoke it.'

Mrs Wheeler trembled. 'You're nothing but a low class
prostitute,' she said hoarsely, whereupon Aunt Tittie gave
her a ringing slap on the face which knocked her hat on one
side and left a pink stain on her cheek.

Arthur came running up looking very frightened. 'Leave
off you two, for Christ's sake,' he said. 'Everyone's looking at
you.'

'I'm sorry I hit her,' said Aunt Tittie. 'I never did know

when to control myself. Come on home, Arthur, and pack
your bag.' She turned and walked away. Arthur followed her
rather uncertainly and I came last. I looked back at Mrs
Wheeler who was standing quite still where we'd left her with
her hat still on one side. I know she was crying because the
lamp by the gate showed wet streaks on her face.

We all walked back to the pension in silence. When we got
there I stayed outside and let them go in by themselves. I went
and sat on the wall by the lake. The water was completely still
and lay along the shore like a glass sheet. Presently Arthur
Wheeler came out of the house carrying his suit-case, he
waved to me half-heartedly and then walked away quickly.

When I went back into the pension, Aunt Tittie was sitting
at the window with her head buried in her arms, sobbing. She
didn't take any notice of me so I sat on the bed and said
nothing. Presently she pulled herself together and got up and
looked in the glass. 'I'm a pretty sight and no mistake,' she
said huskily, and tried to smile, then she put on her hat and
went out. I watched her from the window wandering along in
the opposite direction from the village. I waited up until she
came back at about half-past ten. She seemed glad I was there
and made a great effort to be cheerful. She took off her hat and
fluffed out her hair and we made tea on the gas-ring and ate
biscuits with it.

She talked a lot but didn't mention Arthur once. She said
she'd been thinking things out and had decided to go to
Vienna; she said she knew an agent there called Max Steiner
and that we'd probably get work right away. She said Vienna
was a lovely place and she was longing to see it again, she'd
been there once before with Mattie several years ago. When I
said good night she suddenly hugged me very tight and said,
'Well, dear, we're on our ownsome again now, so let's enjoy
it!'

After this, poor Aunt Tittie was terribly dispirited and unhappy for weeks. We went to Vienna and found that Max

Steiner was away so we trudged around to several other agents until we had no more money left. Then I got a job in the Prater Amusement Park at a Houp-la Booth. I had to jerk the hoops on to a stick after the people had thrown them and then sling them back to the proprietor who was a brass-throated fat little man but quite kind. I made enough money that way to get us food, and Aunt Tittie managed to pay for our rooms in a very dirty little hotel, by picking up men every once in a while; it wasn't really too easy for her because there were so many young and attractive professionals who knew the best cafés and resented intrusion on their beats. I used to be dreadfully tired when I got home every night and I got awful blisters on my feet from standing about all day.

In October, Aunt Tittie met a very rich old man who took her to Budapest. When she'd been gone about a week she telegraphed me some money to come at once so I gave a day's notice to the Houp-la Booth and went. Aunt Tittie met me at the station in a smart motor-car; she was well-dressed and looked much happier. She said she had a small flat overlooking the river and that if only her old man could live for a little longer we'd be on velvet, but that he was very, very old indeed, and she was afraid he wouldn't keep through the winter. We laughed a lot and were delighted to be together again. Her flat really was quite nice and I slept in a little servant's room at the back. There was a Hungarian cook who came in by the day and we did the housework ourselves. The old man didn't trouble us much, he only came to dinner two or three times a week and then didn't stay very late. I used to go out when he came and walk in the town, which was beautiful, and sit about in cafés drinking coffee and listening to the Tziganes.

After we'd been there a few weeks Aunt Tittie met an old friend of hers from Paris in the Hungaria Hotel. He was a Frenchman, and was running a small café on the other side of the river. He came to tea at the flat two days later and we did our turn for him and he said he would engage us. Aunt Tittie was really looking very well just then and had a lot of nice clothes. We started work the following Monday and stayed there the whole winter, we changed our songs every fortnight, and saved quite a lot of money.

In April, Aunt Tittie's old man had to go and do a cure at Baden-Baden. He decided to go quite suddenly and wrote a letter to her saying good-bye and enclosing enough money to pay the last month's rent and a bit over besides. We were both very relieved really and never saw him again. A year later we read in the paper that he had died.

We left Budapest in May and went back to Vienna where we stayed a few days, then went to Prague where we played in an open-air café for six weeks. Then we came back to Paris with enough money to keep us for the summer at least, if we lived cheaply.

That autumn we started again on our travels, we got return engagements in some of the towns we had played before. I was now fourteen and getting very tall. For the next two years our lives went along pretty evenly. We met Arthur Wheeler once in Nice on the Promenade des Anglais; he looked spruce and well and was wearing a straw hat, which he lifted politely, but Aunt Tittie cut him dead, and as we were leaving the next day we didn't see him again. In the summer of 1911 we were back in Paris. Aunt Tittie wasn't well and complained of pains inside. We didn't work for a few weeks and they went away.

In the January following, I had my seventeenth birthday. It came on a Sunday and we were travelling to Spain where we'd neither of us been before. We got out at Bayonne and bought a bottle of champagne and had a celebration all to ourselves in the compartment. We finished the bottle between us and I got drunk for the first time in my life and went shouting up and down the corridor; Aunt Tittie was too weak with laughter to stop me.

We played in a Café Chantant in San Sebastian; it had only

just opened and was new and gaudy and smelt of paint. The
proprietor was a fat Belgian Jew who wore an enormous
diamond and sapphire ring on his little finger. We had been
recommended to him by Demaire, our agent in Paris, as a
novelty. He didn't seem to think we were very novel and was
rude to Aunt Tittie when she asked for the band to play more
quietly, but it mattered little as hardly anybody came to the
café anyhow and we were paid our salary and dismissed after
the first week. We played in several different places in Spain
but without much success. The Spaniards were polite and
applauded our turn perfunctorily and that was all; there was
no enthusiasm, and when Aunt Tittie went from table to table
singing 'How would you like a little rose like me?' they
generally sat quite silently and looked at her, and very seldom
even held out their hand for the paper roses, so poor Aunt
Tittie had to put them down on the table and go on to the next
one. It was very discouraging for her; of course, she was
beginning to look rather old, and her smile lacked the gaiety it
used to have.

When we got to Barcelona we played in a very dirty music
hall which was a bit better because the floor of the auditorium
was uncarpeted wood and the people stamped their feet
instead of clapping, which made a tremendous noise and
made everything we did seem like a triumphant success. We
went to a big bull fight one afternoon which upset us both
horribly; Aunt Tittie cried all the way back to the hotel,
thinking about the horses, and how they trotted into the ring
so amicably with a bandage over one eye to prevent them
from seeing the bull coming. Some of them screamed dreadfully when they were gored and the memory of it haunted us
for days.

We sat outside a café on the way home and had Ochata
which is an iced sweet drink made of nuts, and looks like very
thick milk. Aunt Tittie kept on bursting into tears and then
laughing at herself hysterically, altogether she was in such a

state that she had to have some brandy and lie down before the show. Two nights after that when we had finished our turn and I was waiting outside the dressing-room under the stage, while Aunt Tittie dressed, there was suddenly a terrific crash up above and a loud scream and the orchestra stopped dead. I rushed up on to the stage to see what had happened. Everyone was running about and yelling. One of the big limelight lamps had exploded and fallen down and set fire to the curtains, which were blazing.

A conjuror who had been doing his turn when the thing fell came rushing past me and knocked me against the wall; his wife, who was his assistant, was shut up in his magic cabinet in the middle of the stage and was hammering on the inside of it to be let out. The stage manager ran towards it to open it, but before he could reach it a whole length of blazing curtain fell right across it.

I ran quickly downstairs to fetch Aunt Tittie and met her coming up in her dressing-gown with grease all over her face. We heard the conjuror's wife shrieking horribly as the cabinet started to burn, but there was no chance of rescuing her because by this time the whole stage was blazing. We tried to beat our way through the thick smoke to the stage-door. Aunt Tittie was choking, and a stage hand, mad with fright, knocked her down and stumbled right over her; one of his boots cut her face. I helped her up and we finally got out into the alley. There was a terrific crash behind us as part of the roof fell in. Aunt Tittie gave a little gasp and collapsed, so I grabbed her under the arms and dragged her along the alley with her heels scraping over the cobblestones. There were hundreds of people running about screaming and I was terrified that we'd be thrown down and trampled to death. When I got Aunt Tittie out of the alley into the street I suddenly thought of the conjuror's wife trapped inside the cabinet, and I laid Aunt Tittie on the ground and was violently sick in the gutter.

When I'd finished, I sat down on the kerb by her side. Then I noticed that her face was bleeding, so I dabbed it with my handkerchief and she opened her eyes. The fire engines had arrived by this time. I could hear them in the next street. A man came up and we both helped Aunt Tittie to her feet; she stood swaying for a moment with our arms supporting her and then gave a scream and clutched her side and fainted again. I didn't know what to do, the man couldn't speak French or English, and I only knew a few words of Spanish. He helped me carry her along to the street corner and I signed to him to wait with her while I got a taxi. I ran very fast but couldn't see one anywhere. Suddenly I saw a motor ambulance coming out of a side street, I stopped it and directed it back to where I'd left Aunt Tittie. The two ambulance men lifted her into it and I said good-bye to the strange man and thanked him very much, and he raised his bowler hat and bowed and we drove away to the hospital leaving him standing there.

When we arrived at the hospital they took Aunt Tittie into the emergency ward and I sat by her for ages before anyone came near us. She came to after a little and started to cry; she said she had a terrible pain in her stomach at the side! Her voice sounded very weak and husky. There were lots of other people lying on beds and groaning. One man's face was almost black and all the hair on the top of his head was burnt away leaving mottled red patches. He kept on giving little squeaks like a rabbit, and clutching at the sheet with his hands which were dreadfully burned.

Presently two Sisters of Mercy came in and went round to all the beds and tried to make people a little more comfortable. Finally two doctors came with several nurses; and they went from bed to bed and talked a lot, in low voices. When they got to us I stood up and explained in French about Aunt Tittie's pain. Fortunately one of them understood all right and felt her stomach with his fingers, then he sent one of the nurses away and she came back in a few minutes with a stretcher on wheels. We all got Aunt Tittie on to it and I walked behind it with the doctor through miles of passages.

Eventually we got to a very quiet ward with only a few beds occupied. A Sister of Mercy was sitting reading at a table with a shaded lamp on it. She got up when we came in. Then the doctor took me downstairs to the waiting-room and said that he was afraid Aunt Tittie had a very bad appendix but that he was going to give her a thorough examination and make sure and that I'd better go home and come back in the morning. I said I'd rather stay in case Aunt Tittie wanted me, so he said 'very well' and left me. I lay on a bench all night and slept part of the time. In the early morning two cleaners came in and clattered about with pails. I got up and found my way to the main entrance and finally found a nurse who spoke a little French. She said it was too early to find out anything and that I'd better have some coffee and come back, so I went out into the street and found a café that was just opening and drank some coffee and ate a roll. When I got back I met the doctor coming down the steps, he took me into an office and a Sister of Mercy took down particulars about Aunt Titania which I gave her in French, and the doctor translated into Spanish. When that was done he told me that the only chance of saving Aunt Tittie's life was to operate immediately; I asked if I could see her and he said no, that she was almost unconscious and that if I was agreeable he would operate right away. I said he'd better do what he thought best and that I'd wait, so I went back to the waiting-room. A lot of people had come in, several were relatives of people who had been in the fire, most of them moaned and wailed and made a great noise. About three hours later a nurse came and called out my name. I stood up, and she took me into the office again. After a minute or two the doctor came in looking very serious. He told me that there was scarcely any hope of Aunt Tittie living, as when they operated they discovered that the appendix had burst. He said she hadn't come to yet from the anæsthetic, but that I could see her when she did. I asked when that would be and he said he couldn't tell for certain, but that I'd better wait. They let me stay in the office which was nicer than the waiting-room, and the Sister of Mercy gave me some dry biscuits out of a tin on her desk. She had a round face, and glasses, and peered at me through them sympathetically. Presently a nurse appeared and signed to me to follow her. We went several floors in a lift. There was a wheel stretcher in it with a man lying on it and an orderly standing by the side. The man didn't move at all and his head was covered with bandages.

This time Aunt Tittie was in a private room which was very dim and there was a screen round the head of the bed and another near the door. When I went in I could hardly see for a minute; the nurse drew up a chair and I sat down by the bed. Aunt Tittie was lying quite still with her eyes closed. Her face was dead white and she had a nightdress on of thick flannel which was buttoned up to the chin. She looked terribly, terribly tired and every now and then her mouth gave a little twitch. I felt a longing to put my arms round her and hold her tight and tell her how much I loved her, but when I thought about that I wanted to cry, so I looked away for a moment and tried to control myself. Presently she opened her eyes and moved her head to one side; she saw me and said 'Hello, dearie,' in a whisper. Then she frowned and closed her eyes again, I took her hand which was outside the coverlet, and held it. It felt dry and hot. After a little while she moved again and tried to speak, her hand clutched mine very hard and then relaxed. I put my head down close to hers and she said, 'Take care of yourself.' I started crying then, hopelessly, but I was careful not to make any noise and her eyes were still shut so she couldn't see. Suddenly she gave a little moan and the nurse came out from behind the screen and motioned me to go out of the room. I disengaged my hand from Aunt Tittie's very gently; she didn't seem to notice, and I went out into the passage. There was a window at the end and I stood and looked out across the hospital grounds to the town. It was a very windy day and there was a flagstaff upon the hill with the flag standing straight out from it looking as though it were made of wood. Every now and then it fluttered and subsided for a moment and then blew out straight again.

I waited about all day in the hospital, but they wouldn't let me in to see Aunt Tittie again, because they said she was unconscious, and in the evening at about seven o'clock she died. I went back to the hotel and lay on my bed, trying to be sensible and think things out, but I wasn't very successful and finally gave way and cried for a long time until I dropped off to sleep. When I woke up it was about eleven o'clock and I felt better, but I couldn't sleep any more so I went out and wandered about the town. I walked right down to the harbour and watched the ships. There was a big liner, standing a little way out, all the decks were brilliantly lighted and I could hear music faintly. I suddenly realised that I hadn't had anything to eat all day, so I went into a restaurant which was filled with sailors, and had a plate of stew and some coffee; everything was very greasy and I couldn't eat much of it.

The next day I went through all Aunt Tittie's things and discovered that she had twenty sovereigns locked in her jewel-case, also a brooch with diamonds and two rings, one with very small rose diamonds, and the other plain gold. I myself had fourteen pounds saved, mostly in francs. I went back to the hospital and interviewed the doctor about the operation and funeral expenses. He was very kind, and when I told him how much I had, said that he wouldn't charge for the operation. In spite of this, however, I had to pay out a good deal and when the whole business was over I had about seventeen pounds left. Aunt Tittie was buried two days later. An English clergyman appeared and did it all. He was officious, and kept on asking me questions about her. I bought a bunch of flowers and put them on the grave, then I went back and packed up everything and bought a ticket for Paris.

The Paris train was crowded, and I sat in the corridor all night and thought about Aunt Tittie, until my heart nearly burst with loneliness and I pressed my head against the window and longed to be dead, too.

What Mad Pursuit?

I

EVAN LORRIMER'S celebrity value was unquestionably high. In the course of twenty years he had written no less than eleven novels; a volume of war poems, tinged with whimsical bitterness; one play which had been much praised by the London critics and run nearly two months; a critical survey of the life and times of Madame de Staël entitled *The Life and Times of Madame de Staël*; sundry essays and short stories for the more literary weeklies, and an autobiography. The autobiography had been on the whole the least successful of his works, but he in no way regretted having written it. For years he had been aware that incidents, journeys, and personal experiences had been accumulating in his mind until it had come to a point when he could no longer feel free to pursue his historical researches. He felt himself to be congested, or, to put it more crudely, constipated, and that unless he could get rid of this agglomeration of trivia, his real genius, which was writing graphically of the past in terms of the present, would atrophy. The autobiography, therefore, was a sort of cathartic and as such achieved its object. Hardly had the corrected and revised manuscript been delivered to the publishers before he was at work again, drafting out with renewed energy and clarity of thought his great novel of the Restoration, *A London Lady*. There was no doubt in his mind that if *My Steps Have Faltered*, which was the title of the autobiography, had not been written when it was, *A London Lady* would never have been written at all. The success of *A London Lady* transcended by far everything else he had ever written. It went into several editions within the first few weeks of its publication. It was elected, without one dissentient vote, as the Book Society's choice for the month of February. The most important moving picture company in Hollywood acquired the film rights of it at an even higher price than they had paid for *The Life of Saint Paul*, which had been awarded the Pulitzer Prize for the year before, and in addition to all this, its sales in America surpassed those of England a hundredfold before it had been out six weeks. It was on the suggestion of Evan's New York publisher, Neuman Bloch, that he had agreed to do a short lecture tour in the States. He had been naturally apprehensive of the idea at first, but after a certain amount of coaxing, and tempted by the prospect of visiting America for the first time in such singularly advantageous circumstances – full expenses there and back, a tour of only eight weeks visiting the principal towns, and a guaranteed fee for each lecture that appeared to be little short of fantastic – he gathered his courage together, made exhaustive notes on the subjects on which he intended to speak, and set sail in the *Queen Mary*.

Now it would be foolish to deny that Evan Lorrimer enjoyed publicity. Everyone enjoys publicity to a certain degree. It is always pleasant to feel that your name is of sufficient interest to the world to merit a prominent position in the daily newspapers. For many years past, Evan had been privately gratified to read such phrases as 'Of course Evan Lorrimer was there, suave and well-groomed as usual,' or 'That inveterate first-nighter, Evan Lorrimer, arrived a few minutes before the curtain rose and was seen chatting laughingly to Lady Millicent Cawthorne in the foyer,' or 'Evan Lorrimer whose new novel, *A London Lady*, has caused such a sensation, was the guest of honour at the Pen and Pencil Club on Sunday evening.' Such allusions, guileless and dignified, are immensely agreeable. Unimportant perhaps in their essence, but in their implication very important indeed.

Just as millions of little coral animals in so many years construct a barrier reef against the sea, so can these small accolades, over a period of time, build, if not quite a barrier reef, at least a fortification against the waves of oblivion. Evan felt this very strongly. His reviews he read as a matter of course, regarding them rightly as part of the business. Naturally he was pleased when they were good and pained when they were bad, but the gossip columns were different. They were both unprejudiced and uncritical; they contented themselves with the simple statement that he was here or there with so-and-so, or accompanied by such-and-such, and by their repetitious banality did more to consolidate his reputation than all the carefully phrased opinions of the literati put together. But Evan, well used as he was to being photographed and interviewed and occasionally signing a few autograph books, was certainly unprepared for the violence of his reception in New York. From the moment the ship paused at Quarantine turmoil engulfed him. He was belaboured with questions by over a dozen reporters at the same time, photographed waving to mythical friends by no less than fifteen cameras simultaneously, hurried on to the dock where he was met by Neuman Bloch, Mrs Bloch, the firm's publicity agent, several more reporters and, most surprisingly, a man who had been at school with him and whom he hadn't clapped eyes on for twenty-six years. In the flurry of Customs examination, interviews, and the effort to sustain a reasonably intelligent flow of conversation with the Blochs, he was completely unable to recall the man's name; however, it didn't matter, for after wringing his hand warmly, and standing by his side in silence for a few minutes, he disappeared into the crowd and Evan never saw him again.

Evan Lorrimer at the age of forty-three was, both in appearance and behaviour, a model of what an eminent Englishman of letters should be. He was five-foot-ten, his figure was spare but well-proportioned, he had slim, expressive hands, dark hair greying slightly at the temples, deep-set grey eyes, a small, neat moustache and an urbane smile. Perhaps his greatest asset was his voice which was rich in tone and, at times, almost caressing, particularly when, with his slyly humorous gift of phrase, he was describing somebody a trifle maliciously. Lady Cynthia Cawthorne, who in Lowndes Square had achieved the nearest approach to a London salon since Lady Blessington, was wont to say, with her loud infectious laugh, that had she only been younger she'd have married Evan Lorrimer out of hand if only to hear him repeat over and over again his famous description of being taken, at the age of fifteen, to the Musèe Grevin by Marcel Proust.

Evan, like so many people who have attained fame and fortune by their own unaided efforts, was a firm self-disciplinarian. He apportioned his time with meticulous care: so many hours for writing, so many for reading. He ate and drank in moderation and indulged in only enough exercise to keep himself fit. He contrived, although naturally of a highly-strung, nervous temperament, to maintain an agreeable poise both physically and mentally and to derive a great deal of enjoyment from life, admittedly without often scaling the heights of rapture, but also without plumbing the depths of despair. This self-adjustment, this admirable balance, was dependent upon one absolute necessity and that necessity was sleep. Eight solid hours per night minimum, with a possible snooze during the day, was his deadline. Without that he was lost, his whole organism disintegrated. He became jumpy and irascible, unable to concentrate. In fact on one occasion, owing to an emotional upheaval when the pangs of not sufficiently requited love gnawed at his vitals for nearly four months, he became actively ill and had to retire to a nursing home. Realising this one weakness, this Achilles heel, he arranged his life accordingly.

At home, in his small house in Chesham Place, his two

servants had been trained to a mouse-like efficiency. Until he was called in the morning the house was wrapped in the silence of death. The knocker had been taken off the front door, and both bells, front and back, muffled down to the merest tinkle; the telephone by his bed was switched off nightly and rang in the basement, and even there, after a series of dogged experiments by Albert his valet, it had been reduced to nothing more than a purr. Naturally, taking all this into consideration, the first few nights in New York were a torture to him. He had, of course, been warned that the sharpness of the climate and the champagne quality of the air would enable him to do with less sleep than he was accustomed to in the older, more stagnant atmosphere of England, and although he discovered this to be true to a certain extent, he was unable to repress a slight feeling of panic. If only, he reflected, he could get away into the country for two or three days, to relax, to give himself time to adjust himself, he might come to view the so much swifter tempo of American life with more equanimity.

It was on the fourth day after his arrival, towards the end of a strenuously literary cocktail party given in his honour by the Neuman Blochs that he met Louise Steinhauser. He was introduced to her by his hostess and immediately taken out on to the terrace to look at the view. This had already happened to him five times, and although he had been deeply impressed by the view the first two times, it was now beginning to pall a little; however Louise was adamant. 'Look at it,' she said in a husky, rather intense voice. 'Isn't it horrible?'

Evan gave a slight start of surprise. Louise went on, 'Every time I look at New York from a height like this, I positively shudder. All those millions of people cooped up in those vast buildings give me such a feeling of claustrophobia that I think I'm going mad. If I didn't live out in the country most of the time I really should go mad. My husband, poor darling, comes in every day of course, and we have an apartment at the Pierre – you can just see it from here behind that tower that looks like a pencil with india-rubber on top – but really I hardly ever use it unless I happen to come in for a late party or an opening night or something, and even then I often drive down home afterwards, however late it is.'

'How far away is your home in the country?' enquired Evan.

'About an hour in the automobile; at night of course, it's much quicker and I can't begin to tell you how lovely it is to arrive at about two in the morning and smell the sea – my house is right on the sea – and just go to sleep in that wonderful silence – you'd think you were miles away from anywhere, and yet it's actually only a little way from New York. There are no houses near us, we're completely isolated—— You really must come down for a week-end, except that I warn you there isn't a thing to do except lie about and relax. Bonwit, that's my husband, plays golf occasionally or a little tennis, but I don't play anything. I find at my age – I shall be forty-four next month, imagine!' – she laughed disarmingly, 'I never try to hide my age, it's so silly, after all what *does* it matter. Anyhow, as I was saying, at my age I find that all I want are my comforts, nice books, a few real friends, not just acquaintances, and good food. I'm afraid that's all I can offer you, peace and good food, but if you would like to slip away from all this,' she indicated the remainder of the cocktail party milling about inside with a wave of her hand, 'and really lead the simple life for a couple of days, you don't even have to bring dinner-clothes if you don't want to. Please come, both Bonwit and I would be absolutely enchanted.'

Evan had been looking at her carefully while she was talking, carefully and critically. Being a writer, he was naturally observant, his mind was trained to perceive small indicative details. Being a celebrity he was also cautious. He noted Louise's clothes first; they were obviously expensive, the ruby and diamond clip in her small cloche hat could only have come from Cartier. Her pearls might or might not be real, but the clasp most certainly was. In addition to these external advantages he liked her. She was vivacious, humorous and friendly. She also seemed to have a sensible appreciation of the values of life.

'You're most kind,' he said. 'There's nothing I should like better.'

'Now isn't that lovely,' cried Louise. 'How long are you going to be here?'

'Alas, only until next Wednesday, then I have to lecture in Chicago.'

'I suppose you're booked up for this next week-end?'

Evan shook his head. He had been tentatively invited to the Neuman Blochs' house at Ossining, but he hadn't definitely accepted. 'I was supposed to go to the Blochs',' he said, 'but I can get out of it.'

'Then that's settled,' said Louise gaily. 'I'm coming in on Saturday to go to *Starlight*, that's a musical comedy that Lester Gaige is in. He's one of my greatest friends, you'll adore him. Why don't you dine with me and come too, and we'll all three drive down afterwards. He's the only person I've invited for this week-end. I daren't have a lot of people when he comes because he insists on being quiet. He says he gives out so much at every performance during the week that he's damned if he'll give a social performance on Sundays. He really is divine, and he certainly won't bother you because he does nothing but sleep.'

As they rejoined the cocktail party, Evan felt that the much-vaunted American hospitality was a very genuine and touching trait.

2

Lester Gaige was certainly amusing. At first, watching him on the stage, Evan had been unsure as to whether or not he was going to like him; he seemed to be too debonair, almost arrogant in the manner in which he moved through the bewildering intricacies of *Starlight*. True, he danced beautifully, sang, with no voice but compelling charm, and dominated by sheer force of personality every scene he was in; but there was a something about him, a mocking veneer that made you a trifle uneasy as to what you might discover underneath. However, in the car driving down to the country, he was much more human. His clothes were inclined to be eccentric. He had on suède shoes, thin silk socks, very pale grey flannel trousers of exquisite cut, a bois de rose sweater with a turtle neck, a tweed sports jacket of extravagant heartiness and a fur-lined overcoat with an astrakhan collar. In addition he wore a small beret basque and a pair of the largest horn-rimmed glasses Evan had ever seen. The conversation between him and Louise was stimulating if a little local in allusion. They referred to so many people in such a short space of time that Evan became quite confused; but he sat back in the corner of the luxurious Packard and gave himself up to being agreeably soothed and entertained. It was obvious that Louise and Lester had been intimate friends for several years; their talk, generally in a gaily reminiscent vein, jumped from London to Paris, from Antibes back to New York, from New York to Venice and from Venice to California. 'That amazing party of Irene's when Broddie got blind and had that awful scene with Carola.' 'That terrible night in Salzburg when Nada refused to go home and finally disappeared into the mountains with Sonny Boy for three days.' Occasionally Evan, not wishing to appear out of it, ventured a question as to who So-and-so was, and was immediately rewarded by a vivid, if not always entirely kind, description of So-and-so's life, activities and morals. On the whole he enjoyed himself very much. To begin with, they had all three had a Scotch Highball (ridiculous expression) in Lester's dressing-room before they started and then another one at Twenty One where they had had to stop for a moment because Lester had to give some message to Ed Bolingbroke, who had been apparently too drunk to understand it, then not long after they had crossed the Fifty-ninth Street Bridge, Lester had produced a bottle of Scotch from his overcoat pocket, and they had all had a little extra swig to keep them warm. It was necessary to keep warm for the night was bitterly cold; there had been a blizzard the day before and the snow was several inches thick and freezing over.

When they finally reached the Steinhauser home Evan got out of the car, stretched his cramped legs and gave an exclamation of pleasure. It really was most attractive. A large low white house built on three sides of a square and looking out over Long Island Sound. It was a clear moonlight night and far away on the Connecticut coast lights twinkled across the water. Behind the house was nothing but snow, and a few bleak winter trees. Above all, there was silence, complete and soul-satisfying silence, broken only by the soft lap of the waves on the shore.

Inside, the house was the acme of comfort, a large fire was blazing away in a wide open fireplace in the main living-room; before it was set a table laid for supper. A pleasant, coloured butler in a white coat met them at the front door. Evan sighed a deep sigh of relief. This was even better than he had imagined.

They sat up until very late over the fire talking. The supper had been delicious, a simple but tasty dish of spaghetti, tomatoes and eggs, a well-mixed green salad with cream cheese and Bar le Duc and further Scotch Highballs. Evan had had two since his arrival and although he was far from intoxicated, he felt enjoyably mellow. Lester, who was really a great deal more intelligent than one would expect a musical comedy actor to be, displayed a flattering interest in Evan's work. He had read *A London Lady*, and been thrilled with it, he was also one of the few people who had read and enjoyed

My Steps Have Faltered. Evan dismissed his praise of this with a deprecatory laugh, but he was pleased none the less. Louise was a good hostess and, more than that, Evan decided, an extremely good sort. She talked with vivacity and her sense of humour was true and keen. She appeared to be one of those rare types, a rich woman who is completely unaffected by her wealth. She was downright, honest, and withal very attractive. She alluded to her husband frequently, and it was apparent that although they might not quite see eye to eye over certain things, she was deeply attached to him. They had a son at Harvard to whom they were both obviously devoted. Louise showed Evan a photograph of him dressed in the strange robotish armour of an American footballer. He was a husky, fine-looking lad. Lester was highly enthusiastic about him. 'That boy is fantastic,' he said, 'you'd never believe it to look at him, but he paints the most remarkable water-colours! He gave me one when I was playing Boston in *And So What*. It's a seascape, rather Japanesey in quality, almost like a Foujita.' Evan looked again at the photograph, slightly puzzled. Really Americans were most surprising. It was difficult to imagine that six feet of brawn and muscle painting demure seascapes, and even more difficult to understand how Lester Gaige playing in *And So What* in Boston could ever have heard of Foujita. Perhaps there was something to be said after all for that American culture that Europeans referred to with such disdain.

It wasn't until nearly four o'clock that Louise suddenly jumped up from the sofa on which she had been lying and cried, 'Really this is terrible – I bring you down here to rest and keep you up to all hours talking. We simply *must* go to bed.' She led the way through the hall and along a little passage. 'I've given you the quietest room in the house,' she said over her shoulder, 'it's on the ground floor and you'll have to share a bathroom with Lester. I would have given you a room upstairs with a bath to yourself but it isn't nearly so shut away and you might be disturbed by Bonwit getting up early or the servants or something.' She opened the door leading into a charmingly furnished bedroom. 'This is Lester's,' she said, 'you're along here.' They passed through a gleaming, well-equipped bathroom, along another little passage and there was Evan's room. It was large, with two beds and decorated in a pale, restful green. In addition to the two beds there was a chaise-longue piled with cushions in front of the fire which, although it must have been lit hours ago, was still burning cosily. Evan smiled with pleasure. 'What a perfect room,' he said gratefully. Louise gave the fire a poke. 'I know how English people loathe central heating,' she said, 'and I've told them to have a fire for you all the time you're here, but if you'll take my advice you'll have the heat on a little bit as well, because the weather's really freezing.'

After Louise had said good night and gone up to bed, and Lester and Evan had smoked one more cigarette and exchanged the usual politeness as to which of them should use the bathroom first, Evan, at last alone, opened the window, and, cold as it was, stood for a moment looking up at the stars and listening to the silence. He sniffed the icy air into his lungs, and with a sigh of utter contentment climbed into bed and was asleep in five minutes.

3

Evan woke at ten-thirty, which was rather early considering how late he had gone to bed. He counted up in his mind, four-thirty to ten-thirty, only six hours, but still it didn't matter, he could easily make up for it that night. He lay there idly looking at the reflection of the sea on the ceiling and contemplating, with a slight sinking of the heart, his lecture on Monday night. It was drawing very near and he was naturally nervous, but still he had certainly been wise to give himself this breathing

space immediately before it. He planned to go over his notes
sometime during the day. He was aware, of course, that he
spoke well and that his subject 'History and the Modern
Novel' was pretty certain to interest his American audience.
He intended to start with the middle ages, the period of his
first two novels, then jump to French eighteenth century,
bringing in his *Porcelaine Courtesan, Madame is Indisposed* and
The Sansculotte, then to the Directoire and *Madame de Staël*,
leaving the Restoration and *A London Lady* to the last. He was
determined, in spite of the cautious advice of Neuman Bloch,
to deliver a few well-deserved slaps at some of the more
successful American writers who so impertinently twisted
European history to their own ends. Evan detested slang and
the use of present-day idiom in describing the past. Not that
he was a believer in the 'Odd's Boddikins' 'Pish Tushery'
school of historical writing; he himself eschewed that with
the greatest contempt, but he did believe in being factually
accurate insofar as was possible, and in using pure English.
Had not the exquisite literacy of *A London Lady* been one of
the principal reasons for its success with the Book Society?
And not only the Book Society, with the reviewers of both
continents and with the general public. One of Evan's most
comforting convictions was that the general public had a good
deal more discrimination and taste than it was given credit
for, and that all this careless, slipshod, *soi-disant* modern style
with its vulgarity of phrase and cheap Americanisms would,
in a very little while, be consigned to the oblivion it so richly
deserved.

At this point in his reflections he broke off to wonder
whether or not he should ring for some fruit juice and coffee.
He remembered from last night that the only entrance to his
room was through Lester's and the bathroom and it would be
inconsiderate to wake Lester if he were still sleeping. Evan,
with a little sigh not entirely free from irritation, decided to go
and see. He tiptoed out into the passage and into the bath-

room and opened the door leading to Lester's room very quietly. Lester *was* still sleeping in a pair of pastel blue silk pyjamas with his head buried in the pillow. Evan stood there regarding him uncertainly for a moment. It would, of course, be unkind to wake him, and yet on the other hand he might possibly sleep until lunch-time and Evan would have to wait nearly three hours for his coffee. He retired into the bathroom, closing the door softly after him, and pondered the situation. Presently, renouncing indecision once and for all, he flushed the toilet and then listened carefully with his ear to the door. He was rewarded by hearing a few grunts and then the creaking of the bed. Quick as a flash he darted across to the lavatory basin and turned the tap on full, once embarked he intended taking no chances. After a few moments he opened the door again and peeped in. Lester was sitting up looking, he was glad to observe, quite amiable. Evan coughed apologetically. 'I'm awfully sorry,' he said, 'I'm afraid I woke you up. I'd no idea the tap would make such a row.'

'It wasn't the tap,' said Lester without rancour, 'it was the Lulu.'

'How does one get coffee, do you suppose?'

'Let's ring,' said Lester. 'We can either have it here or put on our dressing-gowns and go into the sun porch – which do you prefer?'

'I don't mind a bit.' Evan, his plan having succeeded so easily, was feeling a little guilty and determined to be amenable at all costs.

'I think the sun porch is nicer.' Lester jumped out of bed, rang the bell and went into the bathroom to brush his teeth.

While they were breakfasting on the sun porch, an agreeable glass-enclosed room at the side of the house commanding a wide view of the sea and the drive, Bonwit Steinhauser appeared in elaborate plus-fours. He was a red-faced, rather dull-looking man, with a large body that had once been muscular but was now just fat. He said 'good morning' affably and after a little desultory conversation went away. When he had gone Lester pushed his coffee-cup out of his way and leant across the table almost furtively.

'You know I like Bonwit,' he whispered as though by such a confession he was straining credulity to the utmost. 'There's something really awfully kind about him. Of course everyone says he's a bore and I suppose he is in a way, but when he's had a few drinks, my dear!' He did one of his characteristic gestures of pawing the air with his right hand. 'He can be terribly, terribly funny! I shall never forget when I was up here one week-end with Ida Wesley, she's dead as a door-nail now, poor sweet, and Bonwit, who shall be nameless, got so fried——' Here he broke off abruptly and said, 'My God!' Evan turned round to see what had startled him and saw a car coming slowly up the drive. He jumped to his feet. Lester got up too, and, after looking out carefully for a moment, gave a laugh. 'It's all right,' he said, 'it's only Irene and Suki and Dwight and Luella – I thought for a minute it was strangers.'

'Are they coming for lunch?' asked Evan apprehensively.

'I expect so,' replied Lester, sitting down again. 'But you'll love Irene, she's divine, but *divine* – you've heard her sing, haven't you?'

Evan shook his head.

'You've never heard Irene Marlow sing!' Lester was horrified. 'You haven't lived, that's all, you just haven't lived! We'll make her sing after lunch, Suki's with her fortunately, he always plays for her. It really is the most lovely voice and there's somebody with an amazing sense of humour! I mean, she really gets herself, which is more than you can say for most prima donnas, and if you could hear her when she's in a real rage with Dwight, – that's Dwight Macadoo who shall be nameless – my God! it's wonderful: bang goes the Italian accent and out pops Iowa!'

'We'd better go and dress, hadn't we?' suggested Evan, feeling unequal to greeting a famous Iowan prima donna in his pyjamas.

'You go and dress,' said Lester. 'And you might turn on a bath for me when you've finished. I'll go and deal with the visiting firemen.'

Evan retired to his room, shattered. It was really appalling luck that these people should have selected today of all days to come to lunch. How cross Louise would be. But still, he comforted himself, she'd be sure to get rid of them all as soon as possible.

When he emerged, bathed, shaved and dressed in perfectly cut English country clothes, he found everybody in the large living-room. Apparently, while he had been dressing, some more people had arrived. Bonwit was mixing cocktails behind a little bar in the far corner of the room. There was no sign of Louise.

Seeing Evan come in, Lester, who was sitting on the sofa with a fattish little man and two women, jumped up. 'This is my friend,' he cried, 'I don't think you know my friend! who shall be nameless,' he added with a light laugh. Evan smiled sheepishly, he was unused to being nameless, but Lester came over and took him affectionately by the arm. 'I must introduce you to everybody,' he said. 'We'd better begin right here and work round the whole God-damned circle.' He raised his voice. 'Listen, everybody – this is Evan Lorrimer, one of the greatest living English novelists, he's my friend and I'm mad about him!' He turned enquiringly to Evan. 'Aren't I, honey?'

Evan summoned up enough poise to give a little smile and say, 'I hope so,' whereupon Lester, holding him firmly by the arm, walked him round the room. A slight hush fell while this tour was in progress. Evan shook hands with everyone and responded pleasantly to their assurances of how glad they were to know him, but he was unable to catch more than a few names as he went along, and finally sat down feeling rather confused, in the place on the sofa that Lester had vacated. The fattish little man, he discovered, was Otis Meer, who wrote a famous gossip column for one of the daily papers, and the two women were Irene Marlow and Luella Rosen. Irene was flamboyant, but attractively so, she was dressed in a scarlet sports suit, with a vivid green scarf, her brown hair was done in clusters of curls and her hat – it couldn't have been anyone else's – was on the mantelpiece. Luella Rosen was sharp and black, like a little Jewish bird, she also was wearing sports clothes, but of a more sombre hue.

Irene smiled, generously exposing a lot of dazzlingly white teeth. 'Lester had been telling us all about you,' she said – her voice had a trace of a foreign accent – 'and you've no idea how thrilled we are to meet you. I haven't read your book yet, but I've got it.'

'Mr Lorrimer has written dozens of books, dear,' said Luella.

Irene sat back and closed her eyes in mock despair. 'Isn't Luella horrible?' she said. 'I'm never allowed to get away with a thing – anyway, I meant your last one, and I know it couldn't matter to you whether I've read it or not; but I really am longing to, particularly now that I've met you.' She winked at Evan, a gay, confiding little wink and nudged him with her elbow. Luella gave a staccato laugh. 'Irene's our pet moron,' she said. 'She's never read a book in her life except *Stories of the Operas*. She's just an Iowa girl who's made good, aren't you, darling?'

'Listen, lamb pie,' said Irene, 'you leave Iowa out of this. What's the matter with Iowa, anyway?'

'Nothing apart from Julia de Martineau,' said Otis Meer, and went into a gale of laughter. Irene and Luella laughed too. Evan was naturally unaware of the full piquancy of the joke. At this point an exceedingly handsome man came up and handed him an 'old-fashioned'.

'This is my dream prince,' said Irene. 'Dwight, you know Mr Evan Lorrimer, don't you?'

'We've met already,' said Evan, nodding to Dwight who nodded back with a grin and sat down on the floor at their feet, balancing his own drink carefully in his right hand as he did so. 'Where the hell's Louise?' he asked.

'Louise has never been known to be on time for anything,' said Luella.

Irene turned to Evan. 'Isn't Louise a darling? You know she's one of the few really genuine people in the world. I can't bear people who aren't genuine, can you?' Evan made a gesture of agreement and she went on. 'Being a writer must be just as bad as being a singer in some ways, having to meet people all the time and look pleased when they say nice things about your books.'

'Tough,' said Luella. 'My heart goes out to you both.' She got up and went over to the bar.

'You mustn't pay any attention to Luella,' said Irene, comfortingly, observing that Evan looked a trifle non-plussed. 'She always goes on like that, she's actually got the kindest heart in the world, sometimes I really don't know what I'd do without her, she's one of our few really genuine friends, isn't she, Dwight?' Dwight looked up and nodded and then stared abstractedly into the fire. At this moment, Louise came into the room with a scream.

'I'm so terribly sorry, everybody——' she wailed. 'I over-slept.' While she was being swamped with greetings, Evan looked at her in horror. She seemed to be a totally different person. Could this be the same woman whose friendly tranquillity and wise, philosophical outlook had so charmed him last night? Could she have known all these people were coming or was she merely masking her dismay at their appearance and trying to carry everything off with a high hand? If so, she was certainly doing it very convincingly. She seemed to be wholeheartedly delighted to see them. Her eye lighted on him and she came over with her arms round a red-haired woman in black and a small fair man. 'My dear,' she said, 'you really must forgive me – I do hope you slept all right——' She broke off and turned to the red-haired woman. 'He's a sleep maniac just like me,' she said. Then to Evan again: 'You have met everyone, haven't you, and been given a drink and everything?' Evan held up his glass in silent acknowledgment, he was bereft of words, whereupon she snatched it out of his hand. 'You must have another at once,' she cried. 'That looks disgusting,' and led him vivaciously to the bar.

During the next half an hour, which Evan spent leaning against the bar, he managed to sort out people a little in his mind. The red-haired woman in black was the Countess Brancati, she had been a Chicago debutante a few years back and had married into the Italian aristocracy. The thin grey man by the window talking to Luella Rosen was her husband. The little fair man was Oswald Roach, commonly known as Ossie. Ossie was a cabaret artist whose speciality was to sing rather bawdy monologues to his own improvisations on the ukelele. The source of this information was Bonwit, who, although sweating copiously from the efforts of mixing different sorts of drinks for everybody, was willing, almost grateful, for an opportunity to talk. 'Who is the thin boy with the pale face?' Evan asked him. Bonwit shook the cocktail-shaker violently. 'That's Suki,' he said with obvious distaste. 'He's a Russian fairy who plays the piano for Irene, he's all right until he gets tight, then he goes cuckoo.'

Evan was regarding this phenomenon with interest, when there was a loud commotion in the hall, and two enormous Alsatians sprang into the room followed by a neatly-dressed girl in jodhpurs and a fur coat. 'I came just as I was,' she said, as Louise advanced to kiss her. 'I was riding this morning and Shirley wouldn't wait, she's gone into the kitchen to see about food for Chico and Zeppo.' She indicated the Alsatians who were running round the room wagging their tails and barking. 'I do hope you didn't mind us bringing them, but we couldn't leave them all alone in the apartment for the whole day.' Louise gaily assured her that she didn't mind a bit and brought her over to the bar. 'Here's someone who's been dying to meet you,' she said to Evan. 'Leonie Crane, she's written three plays herself, she's one of my closest friends and she's read everything you've ever written.' Leonie Crane blushed charmingly and wrung Evan's hand with considerable force. 'Not quite all,' she said in a well-modulated deep voice. 'Louise always exaggerates, but I did think *A Lady of London* was swell. Shirley and I read it in Capri in the summer.'

'*A London Lady*,' Evan corrected her gently and she blushed again. 'That's typical of me,' she said. 'I'm so vague that Shirley says she wonders how I've lived as long as I have without being run over – Hallo, Bonny,' she leant over the bar and patted Bonwit's wet hand. 'What about a little hard liquor – I'm dying!'

Leonie was undeniably attractive, she radiated health and a sort of jolly schoolboyish vitality; her canary-coloured silk shirt was open at the neck and her curly brown hair was cut close to her head. She was a little shy and tried to conceal it with a certain lazy gaucherie. Evan found her most sympathetic, and they talked for several minutes and then Shirley appeared. Leonie presented her to Evan with brusque matter-of-fact despatch.

'This is Evan Lorrimer, Shirley – Shirley Benedict.' They shook hands. Shirley was on the same lines as Leonie but older and a little more heavily built. She had jet black hair, clear blue eyes, and was wearing a perfectly plain grey flannel coat and skirt. She wore no jewellery except a pair of pearl button earrings. Both girls were singularly free from trifling adornments.

Presently Lester reappeared dressed in an entirely new colour scheme so far as tie and sweater went, but with the same strong, garish sports coat that he had worn the night before. He kissed Leonie and Shirley affectionately, and told Evan that they were both angels and that when he'd got to know them a little better he'd worship them. They all four had an 'old-fashioned' on the strength of this prophecy and Evan began to feel a little drunk. It was not part of his usual routine to drink three tumblers of practically neat whisky in the middle of the day on an empty stomach, but he had now become sufficiently light-headed not to care. After all, there was no sense in just sitting about in corners looking sulky, just because some rather odd people had happened to come over for lunch. It would be both disagreeable and silly. Everyone seemed disposed to be most gay and friendly, why not relax and enjoy himself. Comforted by this successful disposal of his conscience, he agreed with cheerful resignation when Louise suggested that they should all go over to the Hughes-Hitchcocks for one more tiny drink before lunch. He had not the remotest idea who the Hughes-Hitchcocks were, but it was apparent from the enthusiastic assent of everyone present and from Lester's glowing description of them that they were an entrancing young married couple who lived only just down the road. Evan accepted an offer to go in Leonie's car and together with her and Shirley and Lester – the Alsatians were left behind – he went.

Lester's assurance that the Hughes-Hitchcocks lived only just down the road proved to be inaccurate. Evan, wedged between Shirley, who was driving, and Leonie in a small Dusenberg roadster, with Lester on his lap, suffered cramp and terror simultaneously for a full half an hour's fast going. Shirley drove well, there was no doubt about that, if she had not they would all have been dead within the first five minutes; but it was the sort of driving that is liable to react unfavourably on the nerves of anyone who happens to drive himself. Evan had driven for years. He owned a sedate Studebaker in far-away green England and frequently conveyed himself back and forth through the country in it, but not at a pace like this, not at seventy miles an hour over an ice-covered road that had frozen so hard that it was like glass. The fact that he was also unaccustomed to a right-hand drive added considerably to his agony. His instinct time and time again was to seize the wheel and swerve over to the left to avoid what seemed to be imminent destruction. Fortunately, however, he restrained himself and sat in frozen misery until at last they turned into a large driveway under tall trees.

On the terrace outside the Hughes-Hitchcocks' house, which was a vast grey structure built on the lines of a French chateau, stood several cars. It was obviously quite a large party. Once inside, his legs felt so shaky after Lester's weight and the rigours of the drive that he accepted with alacrity the first drink that was offered to him, which was a dry Martini in a glass larger than the cocktail-glasses he was used to. After a little he relaxed sufficiently to look about him. There were at least twenty people in the room apart from his own party which was arriving in groups. His host, a good-looking hearty young man, brought up a fair girl whom he introduced as Mrs Martin. Evan, as he shook hands with her, was unable to avoid noticing that she was in an advanced stage of pregnancy. She seemed quite unembarrassed over the situation and looked at him with vague brown eyes. He observed that her fragile young hand was clasping a highball. 'Don't be frightened,' she said with a simper, 'it's not due until Wednesday, and if it doesn't come then I'm going to have a Cæsarian.' Evan felt at a loss to know how to reply to such compelling candour, so he smiled wanly. She gave a slight hiccough and said, 'Excuse me.' Evan fidgeted awkwardly.

'Is that necessary?' he asked, and then flushed to the roots of his hair at the thought that she might imagine he was referring to the hiccough, but she either hadn't noticed or was too drunk to care. 'Not necessary,' she replied with a little difficulty, 'not exactly necessary, but nice work if you can get it,' then she drifted away. Presently Lester came up and they went over and sat down together in a window seat. 'It's always like this in this house,' he said. 'Thousands of people milling around – I can't think how they stand it. They're such simple people themselves too, and grand fun, you know, there's no chichi about them, that's what I like and Hughsie——' Here Lester chuckled – 'Hughsie's a riot, my dear, if you get Hughsie alone sometimes and get him to tell you some of his experiences in the Navy, he'll slay you; of course he's settled down now, and mind you he adores Sonia, and they've got two of the most enchanting children you've ever seen, but still what's bred in the bone comes out in the what have you. . . .'

At this moment Otis Meer joined them. 'Christ,' he whispered to Lester, 'Charlie Schofield's still trailing round with that bitch. I thought they were all washed up weeks ago.'

'You should know,' replied Lester, 'if anybody should.'

Evan asked for this interesting couple to be pointed out to him.

'That man over by the fireplace, the tall one with the blonde. He's Charlie Schofield, one of our richest playboys. She's Anita Hay, she used to be in "The Vanities". Otis hates her,' he added, Evan thought, rather unnecessarily.

'She's one of these high-hatting dames,' said Otis. 'She'd high hat her own father if she knew who he was.'

'Is she invited everywhere with Mr Schofield?' enquired Evan, who was puzzled by the social aspects of the situation.

'If she's not he just takes her,' replied Lester laconically. 'He's been crazy about her for years.'

Presently Louise came up with Luella Rosen. 'I must apologise for dragging you over here,' she said to Evan, 'but I absolutely promised we'd come, and they're such darlings really, but I'd no idea there was going to be this crowd – have another drink and we'll go in five minutes.'

'Can I drive back with you?' asked Evan wistfully.

'Of course,' said Louise. 'We'll meet in the hall in about five minutes.'

During the next hour Evan was forced to the conclusion that the time sense, in the wealthier strata of American society, was lacking. Louise showed no indication of wanting to leave. Almost immediately after she had promised to meet Evan in the hall in five minutes, she sat down with Mr Hughes-Hitchcock and began to play backgammon; her laugh rang out several times and Evan wondered bleakly if 'Hughsie' were retailing some of his experiences in the Navy.

Lester had disappeared. Otis Meer, Ossie and the Russian pianist were sitting in a corner engrossed in an intense conversation. Irene Marlow was entertaining a large group of people with a description of her first meeting with Geraldine Farrar – a few disjointed sentences came to Evan's ear – 'That vast empty stage——' 'My clothes were dreadful, after all I was completely unknown then, just an ambitious little girl from Iowa——' 'She said with that lovely gracious smile of hers "My child——" ' What Miss Farrar had said was lost to Evan for at that moment Charles Schofield came and spoke to him.

'We haven't been formally introduced,' he said amiably, 'but I think you know a great friend of mine, the Prince of Wales?' Evan, endeavouring not to betray surprise, nodded casually. 'Of course,' he said, 'although I fear I don't know him very well.' Actually he had met the Prince of Wales twice, once at a charity ball at Grosvenor House and once at a supper party at Lady Cynthia Cawthorne's. On both occasions he had been presented and the Prince had been charming, if a trifle vague; neither conversation could truthfully be said to have established any degree of intimacy.

'He's a grand guy,' went on Charlie Schofield, 'absolutely genuine. I've played polo with him a lot. Do you play polo?'

'No – I don't ride well enough.'

'It's a grand game,' said Charlie. 'I used to play on Boots Leavenworth's team – you know Boots Leavenworth, of course?'

Evan did not know the Earl of Leavenworth except by repute, but he felt it would sound churlish to go on denying everything. 'Rather,' he said, 'he's awfully nice.'

'I suppose you don't know what's happened about him and Daphne?'

'I think things are much the same,' hazarded Evan.

'You mean Rollo's still holding out?'

'When I left England,' said Evan boldly, 'Rollo was still holding out.'

'God!' said Charlie with vehemence. 'Aren't people extraordinary! You'd think after all that business at Cannes last summer he'd have the decency to face facts and come out into the open. As a matter of fact, I've always thought he was a bit of a bastard, outwardly amusing enough you know, but something shifty about him. As a matter of fact poor Tiger's the one I'm sorry for, aren't you?'

'Desperately,' said Evan.

'Where is Tiger now?'

'I don't know.' Evan wildly racked his brains for an appropriate place for Tiger to be. 'Africa, I think.'

'Jesus!' cried Charlie aghast, 'you don't mean to say he's thrown his hand in and left poor Iris to cope with everything?'

The strain was beginning to tell on Evan. He took refuge in evasion. 'Rumours,' he said weakly. 'One hears rumours, you know how people gossip!'

Fortunately at this moment Shirley and Leonie came up and asked him if he'd like to play table-tennis. 'We can't play at all,' said Shirley, 'we're terrible, but it's good exercise.' Evan smiled affably at Charlie and went with them into an enormous room glassed in on three sides, furnished only with the table, a few garden chairs and some large plants in pots. It was hotter than a Turkish bath. On the way he confided to them that he didn't play, but would be enchanted to watch them. He sat down, lit a cigarette and they started. They hadn't been playing a minute before he realised how wise he had been to refuse. They played like lightning, grimly, with an agility and concentration that was nothing short of ferocious. He watched them amazed. These two attractive young women, smashing and banging, occasionally muttering the score breathlessly through clenched teeth. Sometimes Leonie gave a savage grunt when she missed a shot, like a prize fighter receiving a blow in the solar plexus. Presently, they having finished one game and changed round and started another, Evan began to feel drowsy. The hypnotic effect of following the little white ball back and forth and the monotonous click of the wooden bats lulled him into a sort of coma. Vague thoughts drifted through his mind. He wondered who Rollo was and why he was probably holding out, and what Tiger might have left poor Iris to cope with – Poor Iris – Poor Tiger – Evan slept.

4

At ten minutes past four precisely the Steinhauser party rose from the lunch table and Evan went to his bedroom and shut the door. Lunch had not started until after three. There had been a certain amount of delay while Louise and Lester were rounding everybody up at the Hughes-Hitchcocks'. Then several arguments as to who should drive back with whom. Evan, with commendable tenacity, considering that he had just been awakened from a deep sleep, had clung to Louise like a leech despite all efforts of Shirley and Leonie to persuade him to go back with them, and finally succeeded in being brought home at a more reasonable speed in Louise's Packard. Lunch had been rather a scramble and consisted principally of clam chowder which he detested and veal cutlets which, not surprisingly, were so overdone as to be almost uneatable. Evan, whose head was splitting, took two aspirin, divested himself of his shoes, trousers and coat, put on his dressing-gown and lay thankfully on the bed pulling the eiderdown up to his chin. If he could get a real sleep now, he reflected, not just a doze in a chair, and get up at about seven and bath and change, everyone would have assuredly gone. They must all have dinner engagements in New York, and he would be able to dine peaceably with Louise and Bonwit and Lester, allow a polite hour or so for conversation, and go to bed firmly at ten-thirty. The warmth of the eiderdown stole round him, his legs began to congeal pleasantly with a prickling sensation, the throbbing of his head gradually diminished and he fell asleep.

About an hour later he felt himself being dragged to consciousness by somebody shaking him rhythmically. With intense reluctance he opened his eyes and beheld Lester bending over him. He moaned slightly and tried to evade that inexorable hand.

'You must wake up now, honey,' said Lester. 'You've had over an hour and Irene's going to sing.' Evan's mind, still webbed with sleep, tried unsuccessfully to grapple with this announcement. 'Who's Irene?' he muttered.

'Don't be silly,' said Lester. 'Irene Marlow; she's mad about you, she says she won't so much as open her trap unless you're there – we've been trying to persuade her for twenty minutes – she says she'll sing for you or not at all – come on.' He flicked the eiderdown off the bed and pulled Evan into a sitting posture. It was no use trying to go to sleep again now, even if Lester had allowed him to. Once wakened up like that he was done for. He went drearily into the bathroom and sponged his face, then came back and put on his trousers, coat and shoes. Lester, while he did so, lay on the chaise-longue and discoursed enthusiastically upon the quality of Irene's voice, her passion for Dwight Macadoo and the fact that leaving all her success and glamour aside she was really completely genuine. 'It's amazing about that boy,' he said apropos of Dwight. 'Really amazing – she's absolutely nuts about him and although he may be the biggest thing since *Ben Hur* I must say I think he's just plain dumb! Of course, you can't expect him to be anything else really, he was only a cowboy in Arizona when she met him, galloping about on a horse all day in "chaps", and rounding up all those God-damned steers – who shall be nameless – well, anyway, she met him out on Grace Burton's ranch and gave her all, if you know what I mean, and since that she's taken him everywhere – mind you, I'm not saying he isn't sweet, he is, but he just doesn't utter.'

Lester led the way into the living-room. The party was sitting round expectantly. Irene was standing by the piano while Suki, with a cigarette dangling from his lips, was playing a few introductory chords. When Lester and Evan came in everybody said 'Shhh' loudly. They sank down on to the floor by the door, Irene flashed Evan a charming smile and started off on 'Vissi d'Arte'. She sang beautifully. Evan, whose understanding of music was superficial to say the best of it, recognised at once that the quality of her voice and the charm with which she exploited it was of a very high order indeed. When she had finished 'Tosca' everyone gave little groans and cries of pleasure, and someone called for 'Bohème'. Irene sang 'Bohème'; then Ossie implored her to sing the waltz from *The Countess Maritza*. She started this and forgot the words half-way through, so she stopped and sang three songs of Debussy in French, and then some Schumann in German. Evan, being by the door in a draught, wished that she'd stop, the floor was beginning to feel very hard and he was afraid of catching cold. Irene, blissfully unaware that even one of her audience wasn't enjoying her performance to the utmost, went on singing for over an hour. When she finally left the piano and sat down, amid ecstasies of admiration, Evan rose stiffly and went over to the bar. Otis was leaning against it with Shirley and Leonie, Bonwit was still behind it.

'Isn't that the most glorious voice you've ever heard?' cried Ossie. 'Frankly I'd rather listen to Irene than Jeritza, Ponselle and Flagstad all together in a lump.' Evan, repressing a shudder at the thought of Jeritza, Ponselle and Flagstad all together in a lump, agreed wholeheartedly and asked Bonwit for a drink.

'Martini, "old-fashioned", Daiquiri, rye and ginger ale, Scotch highball, pay your dime and take your choice,' said Bonwit cheerfully. Evan decided on a highball, not that he wished to drink any more for the pleasure of it, but he was chilled by the draught from the door. Bonwit mixed him a strong one, and after a while he began to feel more cheerful. Louise came over, Evan noticed that she looked very flushed, and dragged Ossie away from the bar. 'Darling Ossie, you must,' she insisted, 'everybody's screaming for you – Lester's gone to get your ukelele, you left it in the hall.' Ossie, after some more persuasion, sat down in the middle of the room with his ukelele which Lester had handed to him, and began to tune it. Otis shouted out, 'Do "The Duchess",' and Irene cried, 'No, not "the Duchess", do "Mrs Rabbit".' Louise cried, 'No, not "Mrs Rabbit", do "Ella goes to Court".' Several other people made several other suggestions, and there was pandemonium for a few moments. Shirley whispered to Evan, 'I do hope he does "Ella goes to Court", you'll adore it.'

Ossie silenced the clamour by striking some loud chords; then he sang 'Mrs Rabbit'. 'Mrs Rabbit' was a description, half-sung and half-spoken, of the honeymoon night of an elderly lady from Pittsburg. It was certainly amusing, while leaving little to the imagination. Ossie's rendering of it was expert. He paused, raised his eyebrows, lowered and raised his voice, and pointed every line with brilliantly professional technique. Everyone in the room shouted and wept with laughter. When he had finished with a vivid account of the death of Mrs Rabbit from sheer excitement, the clamour started again. This time he sang 'The Duchess'. It was rather on the same lines as 'Mrs Rabbit' although the locale was different. It described a widow from Detroit who married an English Duke and had an affair with a Gondolier during their honeymoon in Venice. Evan permitted himself to smile tolerantly at Ossie's somewhat stereotyped version of an English Duke. Finally, when he had sung several other songs, all of which varied only in the degree of their pornography, he consented to do 'Ella goes to Court'. Evan, having finished his highball and noticing another close to his elbow, took it hurriedly and braced himself for the worst. 'Ella goes to Court' was, if anything, bawdier than the others had been. It was a fanciful description of a middle-aged meat packer's wife from Chicago who, owing to the efforts of an impecunious English Countess, is taken to a Court at Buckingham Palace and becomes intimately attached to a Gentleman-in-Waiting on her way to the Throne Room. The whole song was inexpressibly vulgar, and to an Englishman shocking beyond words. Fortunately the references to the Royal Family were comparatively innocuous; if they had not been Evan would undoubtedly have left the room, but still, as it was, the whole thing, with its sly implications, its frequent descents to barroom crudeness, and above all the ignorance and inaccuracy with which Ossie endeavoured to create his atmosphere, irritated Evan profoundly. Aware that several people were covertly watching him to see how he would take this exhibition, he debated rapidly in his mind whether to look as disgusted as he really felt or to pretend to enjoy it. He took another gulp of his highball and forced an appreciative smile on to his face. A diversion was caused by the noisy entrance of four newcomers. 'My God!' cried Lester. 'It's Carola!' There was a general surge towards a smartly-dressed woman with bright eyes and still brighter hair who walked in a little ahead of the others. Lester kissed her, Louise kissed her, everybody kissed her except Evan, who was formally introduced a little later by Otis Meer.

Her name was Carola Binney and she was, according to Leonie and Shirley, the most famous and gifted comedienne on the New York stage. Evan vaguely remembered having heard of her at some time or other. She certainly possessed abundant vitality and seemed to be on the most intimate terms with everybody present. The people with her, Evan learned, were Bob and Gloria Hockbridge who were scenario writers from Hollywood, and Don Lucas. There was probably no one in the world, even Evan, who had not heard of Don Lucas. Evan looked at him and really experienced quite a thrill. He was even handsomer in real life than he was on the screen. His young finely-modelled face healthily tanned by the sun; his wide shoulders and long curling lashes; his lazy, irresistible charm. There it all was. 'It was exactly,' thought Evan, 'as tho' some clear-eyed, vital young God from the wider spaces of Olympus had suddenly walked into a night club.' Lester brought him over. 'This is Don Lucas,' he said exultantly. 'He's just a struggling boy who's trying to make a name for himself and got side-tracked by somebody once saying he was good-looking.'

'Nuts, Les!' said the clear-eyed Olympian as he shook hands. 'Glad to know you, Mr Lorrimer.'

Lester, Don and Evan drifted over to the bar where Bonwit, after greeting Don, gave them each a highball. Evan tried to refuse but Lester insisted. 'Phooey!' he cried, placing his arm round Evan's shoulders. 'This is a party and life's just one big glorious adventure – which shall be nameless!'

Don, it appeared, was on a three weeks' vacation from Hollywood; he had just completed one picture, 'The Loves of Cardinal Richelieu', and was going back on Thursday to start another which was to be called 'Tumult', and was based on Tolstoi's *War and Peace*. The Hockbridges were writing it and had apparently done a swell job. Evan glanced across at the Hockbridges. Mr Hockbridge was a plump bald man in the early forties, while his wife was much younger, possibly not more than twenty-five, with enormous wide blue eyes and platinum blonde hair done in the style of Joan of Arc. Evan tried to imagine them sitting down together and writing the story of *War and Peace* and gave up. After three strong whiskies and sodas such fantasy was beyond him.

Don, within the first few minutes of their conversation, pressed him warmly to come and stay with him when he lectured in Los Angeles. 'It's a very simple house,' he said. 'None of that Spanish crap – all loggias and whatnot, but I can let you have a car and an English valet.' 'Simple house!' Lester gave a shriek. 'It's about as simple as Chartres Cathedral. It's the most gorgeous place in California.' He turned to Evan. 'You really must go,' he went on. 'Seriously, I mean it – it's an experience, if you know what I mean, and when I say experience, well!——' He laughed and dug Don in the ribs.

'It would be grand to have you if you'd come,' he said. 'You mustn't pay any attention to the way Les goes on – we happened to have a party when he was there and Oh boy!' He shook his handsome head and sighed as though shattered by the memory of it. 'But if you came you wouldn't be disturbed. I shall be working all day anyhow – you could do exactly as you liked.'

Evan thanked him very much, and said it sounded delightful. Lester went off into further eulogies about the magnificence of Don's house but was interrupted by Louise who came up and placed one arm round Don's waist and the other round Evan's.

'We're all going over to the Grouper Seligmans for just ten minutes,' she said. 'Carola's longing to see their house; I must say it's unbelievable what they've done with it.' Evan gently disentangled himself. 'I don't think I'll come if you don't mind,' he said. 'I've got to go over my notes for my lecture tomorrow night.'

There was a shocked silence for a moment, then Louise gave a wail of distress. 'Oh my dear,' she cried, 'please come, just for a few minutes. The Grouper Seligmans will be so bitterly disappointed, they're pining to meet you and they're such darlings.'

Evan shook his head. 'I'd really rather not,' he said firmly.

'Then I won't go either,' said Lester.

'Neither will I,' said Louise. 'We'll none of us go.'

Don Lucas patted Evan's shoulder encouragingly. 'Come on,' he coaxed. 'Be a sport.'

'They're divine people,' said Lester. 'They really are, you'll love them, and old Bernadine's a riot; she's Jane Grouper Seligman's mother, you know; you can't go back to Europe without having seen Bernadine Grouper.'

'Only for just ten minutes,' said Louise. 'I shall really feel terribly badly if you don't go – it's quite near, just down the road and the house really is lovely, the most perfect taste, they've spent millions on it——'

'Don't worry him if he'd rather not,' said Don. 'Let's all have another drink.'

Evan, touched by the sympathy in Don's voice and embarrassed by Lester's and Louise's obvious disappointment, gave in. 'Very well,' he said, 'but I really must get back in time to go over my notes before dinner.'

Louise's face lit up with pleasure. 'Of course you shall,' she cried. 'You're an angel – the four of us shall go in my car – come on everybody.'

5

It was nearly an hour's drive to the Grouper Seligman's house, and in the car Lester suggested playing a word game to pass the time. Evan didn't care for word games but as he couldn't very well sit in morose silence he capitulated with as good a grace as possible. They played 'Who am I?' and 'Twenty Questions' and 'Shedding Light'. Evan acquitted himself favourably and, owing to his superior knowledge of history, won reverent praise for his erudition in 'Twenty Questions'.

'Shedding Light' bewildered him, but he was glad to see that it bewildered Don Lucas even more. As a matter of fact everything bewildered Don Lucas; his contributions consisted mainly of the names of obscure baseball players and movie directors, but he persevered with naïve charm in the face of the most waspish comments from Lester. Suddenly the games were interrupted by the chauffeur taking a wrong turning and arriving, after a few minutes of violent bumping, on to the edge of a swamp. Louise, who had been too occupied in trying to think of a Spanish seventeenth-century painter beginning with M to notice, leant forward, slid back the glass window and shouted a lot of instructions, most of which Lester contradicted. 'We ought to have turned to the left by the bridge, I know we ought,' she said.

'If we'd done that we should have arrived at the Witherspoons',' said Lester. 'And God forbid that we should do that.'

'Nonsense,' cried Louise. 'The Witherspoons are right over on the other side near the Caldicotts.'

'If,' said Lester with a trace of irritation, 'we had gone up that turning just past the Obermeyers' gate and then on over the hill we should have got into the high-way and been able to turn right at the cross roads.'

'Left,' said Louise. 'If you turn right at the cross roads, you come straight to the golf course, and that's miles away, just next to the Schaeffers.'

'You'd better back,' said Lester to the chauffeur. 'And when you get into the main road again stop at the first petrol station and ask.'

Presently after some more bumping and a frightening moment when the frozen surface of the ground nearly caused the car to skid into a ditch, they emerged again on to the main road. About a quarter of an hour later, having followed the instructions of a negro at a petrol station, and gone back the way they had come for a few miles, they turned up a small lane and arrived at the Grouper Seligmans'. The rest of their party had naturally arrived some time before and everybody was playing skittles in a luxurious skittle alley with a bathing pool on one side of it and a bar on the other. Mr and Mrs Grouper Seligman came forward to meet them both grasping large wooden balls. They were a good-looking young couple in bathing costume. 'This is wonderful,' cried Mrs Grouper Seligman. 'We thought you were dead, we're just going to finish this game, have one more drink and then go in the pool – go and talk to mother, she's stinking!'

Mr Grouper Seligman led them to the bar where the members of his own house-party were sitting on high stools apparently having relinquished the joys of the alley and the pool to the invaders. Old Mrs Grouper, elaborately coiffed and wearing a maroon tea-gown and a dog-collar of pearls, greeted Evan warmly. 'You may or may not know it,' she said in a harsh, bass voice, 'but you're my favourite man!'

Evan bowed politely and tried to withdraw his hand, but she tightened her grasp and pulled him towards her. 'That book of yours,' she said portentously, and cast a furtive look over her shoulder as though she were about to impart some scurrilous secret, 'is great literature – No, it's no use saying it isn't because I know – Henry James used to be an intimate friend of mine and I knew poor Edith Wharton too, and believe me,' her voice sank to a hoarse whisper, 'I *know*.' She relaxed Evan's hand so suddenly that he nearly fell over backwards. At that moment his host gave him an 'old-fashioned' with one hand and piloted him with the other up to an emaciated dark woman in a flowered dinner dress.

'Alice,' he said, 'you English ought to get together – this is a countryman of yours – Mr Lorrimer – Lady Kettering.' Lady Kettering shook hands with him wearily and gave an absent smile. 'How do you do,' she said. The sound of an English voice comforted Evan, he hoisted himself on to a vacant stool next to her. Mr Grouper Seligman having done his duty as a host, left them. 'What a lovely house,' said Evan. Lady Kettering looked at him in surprise and then glanced round as though she were seeing it all for the first time. 'I suppose it is,' she replied, 'if you like this sort of thing.'

Evan felt a little crushed. 'Of course I haven't seen much of it, I've only just arrived.'

'I've been here for three months,' said Lady Kettering, 'and I must say it's beginning to get me down. I'm going to Palm Beach next week. I think Palm Beach is bloody, don't you?'

'I've never been there,' said Evan.

'Well, take my advice and don't go. It's filled with the most frightening people.'

'I shan't be able to anyhow,' said Evan. 'I'm over here to do a lecture tour.'

'How horrible,' said Lady Kettering. 'Whatever for?'

'My publishers were very insistent that I should.' Evan was slightly nettled. 'And after all I think it will be interesting to see something of America. This is my first visit.'

'You ought to go to Mexico,' said Lady Kettering. 'That's where you ought to go.'

'I'm afraid I shan't have time.'

'That's the one thing you don't need in Mexico – Time doesn't exist – it's heaven.'

'Why don't you go to Mexico instead of Palm Beach?'

'I've promised to join the Edelstons' yacht and go on a cruise in the Bahamas,' said Lady Kettering. 'Do you know the Edelstons?'

'No,' replied Evan.

'Well, take my advice,' she said, 'and give them a wide berth. They're bloody.'

At this moment Don Lucas came and prised Evan gently off his stool. 'Come and swim,' he said.

The idea of swimming on a Sunday evening in mid-February seemed fantastic to Evan. 'I don't think I will.'

'Come on, be a sport.'

'I'd rather watch you.'

'Nuts to that,' cried Don. 'Everybody's going to swim, it'll be swell.'

Evan allowed himself to be led over to the pool, inwardly vowing that no power on earth would get him into the water. Leonie and Shirley were giving an exhibition of fancy diving from the highest board, while Louise, Lester, Carola Binney, Irene Marlow and Ossie, who were already in bathing suits, sat round the edge and applauded. 'Isn't that amazing?' cried Lester as Leonie did a spectacular Jack knife. 'I'd give anything in the world to be able to dive like that, but everything, if you know what I mean!'

Don took Evan firmly into a richly appointed men's dressing-room and handed him a pair of trunks. 'Now undress,' he ordered.

Once more Evan protested. 'Really I'd rather not——'

'What the hell——' said Don. 'The water's warm and we'll all have fun – come on, be a pal——'

'Honestly——' began Evan.

'Now listen here,' Don sat down on a bench and looked at Evan reproachfully, 'this is a party and we're all having a good time and you're just bent on spoiling the whole shooting match.'

'Why should you be so anxious for me to swim?' asked Evan almost petulantly.

'Because I like you,' said Don with a disarming smile. 'I liked you from the word go and you like me too, don't you? Come on, be frank and admit it.'

'Of course I like you,' said Evan. 'I like you very much.'

'Very well then,' said Don triumphantly. 'Do we swim or don't we?'

'You do and I don't.'

'You wouldn't like me to get tough now, would you?' said Don in a wheedling voice, but with an undertone of menace. 'I could, you know!'

'I'm sure you could, but I fail to see——'

'Come on now, quit stalling.' Don advanced towards him and forcibly removed his coat. For one moment Evan contemplated screaming for help, but visualising the ridiculous scene that would ensue he contented himself with struggling silently in Don's grasp. 'Please let me go,' he muttered breathlessly, 'and don't be so silly.'

Don had succeeded in slipping Evan's braces off and was endeavouring to unbutton his shirt when Lester came in. 'Boys, boys,' he cried admonishingly, 'do try to remember that this is Sunday – which shall be nameless,' and went into gales of laughter. Don released Evan immediately.

'This guy's a big sissy,' he said. 'He won't swim.'

'I don't blame him,' said Lester. 'The water's like Bouillebaise. It's got more things in it than Macy's window.'

'To hell with that, I'm going to swim if it kills me.'

'It probably will on top of all that liquor.' Lester went over and took a packet of cigarettes out of the pocket of his coat which was hanging on a peg. Then he came and sat on the bench next to Evan who, with a flushed face, was adjusting his clothes. 'Relax, honey,' he said, 'Don always goes on like this when he's had a few drinks. Have a camel?'

Evan took a cigarette, meanwhile Don was tearing off his clothes with ferocious speed. When he was completely naked he stood over Lester and Evan with arms folded and regarded them with scorn. Lester looked up at him. 'It's all right, Puss,' he said, 'we've seen all that and it's gorgeous, now go jump in the pool and sober up.'

'I don't know what's the matter with you guys,' he grumbled, and went towards the door.

'You'd better put on some trunks,' said Lester, 'or have I gone too far?'

Don came slowly back and put on a pair of trunks. 'Funny, hey?' he said bitterly and went out. A moment later they heard a loud splash and a shriek of laughter.

'What about another little drinkie?' said Lester.

6

About an hour later Evan found himself in a car sitting between Carola Binney and Luella Rosen whom he hadn't spoken to since before lunch. Don and Lester were squeezed together in the front seat next to Dwight Macadoo who was driving. The car apparently belonged to Irene Marlow. Evan had had two more 'old fashioneds' since his struggle with Don and was drunk, but in a detached sort of way. He had lost all capacity for resistance. From now on, he decided, he would drink when he was told to, eat when he was told to and go where he was taken. There was no sense in fighting against overwhelming odds. He lay back, quite contentedly, with his head on Luella's shoulder and listened to Carola describing a man called Benny Schultz who had directed a play she had tried out in Boston last September——

'Never again——' she was saying vehemently, 'would I let that rat come within three blocks of me—My God – you've no idea what I went through – he comes prancing into my dressing-room on the opening night after the first Act – the first Act! believe it or not, and starts giving me notes – "Listen, Benny," I said, "you may have directed *Crazy Guilt* and *Mother's Day* and *The Wings of a Dove*, and you may have made Martha Cadman the actress she is, and Claudia Biltmore the actress she certainly isn't, but you're not coming to my room on an opening night and start telling me that my tempo was too fast and that I struck a wrong note by taking my hat off at my first entrance. To begin with I had to take that God awful hat off which I never wanted to wear anyway because the elastic band at the back was slipping, and if I hadn't it would have shot up into the air and got a laugh in the middle of my scene with Edgar; in the second place if you had engaged a supporting company for me who could act and a leading man who had some idea of playing comedy, and at least knew his lines, I wouldn't have had to rush through like a fire engine in order to carry that bunch of art-theatre hams and put the play over, and in the third place I should like to remind you that I was a star on Broadway when you were selling papers on the East side, and I knew more about acting than you when I was five, playing the fit-ups with *The Two Orphans*. And what's more, if you think I'm going to tear myself to shreds trying to get laughs in the supper scene in the pitch dark – well, you're crazy——" ' She paused for a moment, Luella gave a barely audible grunt.

'You've got to have light to play comedy,' she went on, 'and all the phoney highbrow directors in the world won't convince me otherwise.'

'For all that I think Benny's pretty good,' said Luella.

'He's all right with Shakespeare. I give you that,' said Carola. 'His Macbeth was fine, what you could see of it, but comedy never – look at the flop he had with *Some Take it Straight*.'

'*Some Take it Straight* was the worst play I ever sat through,' Luella admitted.

'It needn't have been,' cried Carola. 'I read the original script. They wanted me to do it with Will Farrow, it really wasn't bad apart from needing a little fixing here and there – then that rat got hold of it and bitched it entirely.'

Lester let the window down. 'What's Carola yelling about,' he enquired.

'Benny Schultz,' said Luella.

'I wouldn't trust him an inch, not an inch,' said Lester. 'Look what he did to Macbeth.'

'Are we nearly home?' asked Evan.

'We're not going home – we're going to Maisie's.'

Evan lifted his head from Luella's shoulder. 'Who's she?' he asked sleepily.

'She's divine,' replied Lester. 'You'll worship her – I mean she's a real person, isn't she, Luella?'

'It depends what you call real,' said Luella. 'Personally she drives me mad.'

At this point the car turned into a gateway and drew up before a low, rather rambling white-walled house. Everyone got out and stamped their feet on the frozen snow to keep warm, while they waited for the door to be opened, which it presently was by a large forbidding-looking Swedish woman who regarded them suspiciously. Lester embraced her. 'It's all right, Hilda,' he said, 'it's only us.'

She stood aside and they all trooped in, shedding their coats in the hall. Lester led the way into a sort of studio panelled in pitch pine with wide bow windows and an immense log fire. The room was luxuriously furnished in a style that Evan supposed was early American. Anyhow in spite of its being extremely over-heated, its simplicity was a relief after the other houses he had visited. He felt as though he had been going from house to house all his life. A grizzled woman with fine eyes and wearing a riding habit greeted them brusquely and introduced the other people in the room. There were two girls called Peggy and Althea, one fat and the other thin, a very pale young man in green Chinese pyjamas called George Tremlett, and a statuesque Frenchwoman with raven hair who appeared to be dressed as a Bavarian peasant. The only two members of their own party present were Leonie and Shirley who were lying on the floor playing with a Siamese cat. There was a large table of drinks along one of the windows. Don Lucas made a bee-line for it. 'Donny wants some fire water,' he said. 'Donny wants to get stinking.'

'You were stinking at the Grouper Seligmans',' said Luella.

'Isn't he beautiful,' said the Frenchwoman.

When everyone had helped themselves to drinks Evan found himself sitting on a small upright sofa with George Tremlett.

'You arrived in the middle of a blazing row,' whispered George with a giggle. 'Suzanne and Shirley haven't spoken for two years and suddenly in she walked with Leonie——'

'Which is Suzanne?'

'The dark woman, Suzanne Closanges. She writes poetry either in French or English, she doesn't care which, and she lives here with Maisie.'

'Maisie who?' asked Evan.

'Maisie Todd, of course,' said George with slight irritation. 'This is Maisie Todd's house – I did it.'

'How do you mean "did it"?'

'Designed it,' George almost squealed. 'I'm George Tremlett.'

'How do you do?' said Evan.

'It was lovely doing this house,' went on George, 'because I had an absolutely free hand – Maisie's like that – we had the grandest time driving all over New England and finding bits and pieces here and there. I found this very sofa we're sitting on tucked away in a fisherman's bedroom at Cape Cod.'

'How extraordinary,' said Evan – he felt overpoweringly sleepy.

Leonie came over with the Siamese cat and placed it on Evan's lap. 'Isn't he adorable?' she said. 'I gave him to Maisie for a Christmas present in 1933 and he's grown out of all knowledge.'

The cat arched its back, dug its claws into Evan's leg and with a loud snarl hurled itself to the floor. 'They're very fierce,' went on Leonie picking it up again by the nape of its neck so that it hung spitting and kicking in the air. 'And the older they grow the fiercer they get, but Dante isn't fierce though he's older than hell – are you, my darling?' she added affectionately, kissing it on the side of the head. The cat gave a sharp wriggle and scratched her cheek, from her eye, which it missed by a fraction, to her chin. She screamed with pain and dropped it on to a table where it knocked over and smashed a photograph of a lady in fencing costume framed in glass, jumped down and disappeared behind a writing-desk. Evan started to his feet, everyone came crowding over.

'The son of a bitch,' wailed Leonie. 'He's maimed me for life.' With that she burst into tears. Maisie Todd took charge with fine efficiency. She produced a large white handkerchief to staunch the blood, dispatched George to fetch some iodine from her bathroom. Shirley flung her arms round Leonie and kissed her wildly. 'Don't darling, don't cry,' she besought her. 'For God's sake don't cry, you know I can't bear it.'

'There's nothing to cry about,' said Maisie, 'it's only a scratch.'

'It may only be a scratch,' cried Shirley, 'but it's terribly deep and it's bleeding.'

'Don't fuss,' said Maisie.

'It's all very fine for you to say "don't fuss",' Shirley said furiously, 'but it might very easily have blinded her – you oughtn't to keep an animal like that in the house, it should be destroyed.'

'Leonie gave it to Maisie herself before she knew you,' put in Suzanne with a little laugh.

'Mind your own business,' snapped Shirley.

Leonie dabbed her eyes and her cheeks alternately with the blood-stained handkerchief.

'For God's sake shut up, everybody. I'm all right now, it was only the shock.'

'Drink this, darling,' said Lester, handing her his glass.

'We should never have come – I knew something awful would happen,' said Shirley.

'There is nothing to prevent you going.' Suzanne spoke with icy dignity. There was a horrified silence for a moment. Shirley left Leonie and went very close to Suzanne.

'How dare you,' she said softly. Evan noticed that she was trembling with passion. 'How dare you speak to me like that——'

Maisie intervened. 'Now listen, Shirley,' she began. Shirley pushed her aside. 'I've always disliked you, Suzanne, from the first moment I set eyes on you, and I wish to say here and now that you're nothing but a fifth-rate gold-digger sponging on Maisie the way you do and making her pay to publish your lousy French poems, and you're not even French at that – you're Belgian!'

Suzanne gave a gasp of fury, slapped Shirley hard in the face and rushed from the room, cannoning into George Tremlett who was coming in with the iodine and knocking the bottle out of his hand on to the floor. 'Oh, dear!' he cried, sinking on to his knees. 'All over the best Hook rug in the house!'

From then onwards everybody talked at once. Maisie dashed out of the room after Suzanne; Leonie started to cry again. The two girls, Althea and Peggy, who had been watching the whole scene from a corner, decided after a rapid conversation to follow Maisie and Suzanne, which they did, slamming the door after them. George was moaning over the Hook rug and trying to rub out the iodine stains with a silk scarf. Lester joined Luella and Carola by the fireplace, Carola was protesting violently at Suzanne's behaviour, while Luella smiled cynically. Lester, genuinely distressed, was sympathising with Shirley and Leonie, while Don added to the din by strolling over to the piano with Dwight Macadoo and playing 'Smoke Gets in your Eyes' with one hand. Presently he desisted. 'This piano stinks,' he said. 'No tone – where's the radio?' Before he could find it Luella, to Evan's intense relief, suggested that they should all go, and led the way firmly into the hall. While they were struggling into their coats and wraps the large Swedish woman watched them silently with a baleful expression. The freezing night air struck Evan like a blow between the eyes; he staggered slightly. Don quickly lifted him off the ground and deposited him in the car with infinite tenderness.

'You were wrong about that swim,' he said affectionately. 'It was swell, made me feel like a million dollars. Now we'll go home and have a little drinkie.'

7

They had no sooner got inside the Steinhausers' front door when Irene came rushing out of the living-room. 'Where the hell have you been?' she cried angrily to Dwight. 'I looked for you all over and when I came out you'd gone off in my car.'

'Now don't be mad at me, darling——' began Dwight.

'Mad at you! I've never been madder in my life – come in here.' She dragged him into the library and banged the door.

'Well,' said Lester, 'isn't she the cutest thing – My dear!' He waved his hand benevolently after them. 'These Prima Donnas – who shall be nameless——'

Louise appeared with a great cry and flung her arms round Evan. He was dimly aware that she had changed into a long flowing tea-gown. '*There* you are,' she said, 'I couldn't think what had happened to you – you must be starving.' Still holding him tightly she pulled him into the living-room which had undergone a startling change. All the furniture had been pushed out on to the sun porch with the exception of the chairs which were arranged round the walls. An enormous buffet loaded with hams, turkeys, salads, bowls of fruit, bowls of cream, two large cakes and piles of plates, stood along one side of the room. Another smaller table for drinks was joined on to the bar behind which Bonwit was still officiating, assisted by a Japanese in a white coat. There were at least fifty people in the room and the noise was deafening. Evan, dazed as he was, distinguished the Grouper Seligmans, Lady Kettering, and several of the people he had seen at the Hughes-Hitchcocks', including the young expectant mother who was sitting on the floor with her back against one of the piano legs, and a large plate of variegated food on her lap, apparently in a stupor, while Suka played an unending series of complicated syncopation in her ear.

Louise led Evan to the table and gave him a plate on which she piled, with professional speed, a turkey leg, Virginia ham, baked beans, a fish cake, potato salad, lettuce, a wedge of Camembert cheese and a large slice of strange-looking brown bread. 'There,' she said, 'now sit down quietly, and eat, you poor dear.' With that she whisked away from him and rushed across to Carola and Luella. He looked round for a vacant chair but there wasn't one, so he stayed where he was and ate standing against the table. The food was certainly good although there was far too much of it on his plate. He was about to slide the cheese and one of the slices of ham into an empty bowl that had held salad when he was arrested by Charlie Schofield putting his hand on his shoulder. He jumped guiltily as though he'd been caught in the act of doing something nefarious.

'I told Alice Kettering what you said about Tiger being in Africa,' said Charlie, 'and she's in an awful state – she was crazy about him for years you know.'

Before Evan could reply Don came up and forced a glass into his hand. 'I promised you a little drinkie,' he said genially, 'and a little drinkie you're going to have.'

A big woman in yellow put her arm through Charlie Schofield's and led him away. Evan saw out of the corner of his eyes that Lady Kettering was drifting towards him. He retreated on to the sun porch followed by Don looking very puzzled.

'What's the idea?'

'Just somebody I don't want to talk to,' said Evan with as much nonchalance as he could muster.

'Listen, Pal,' said Don. 'If there's anyone you don't like just you tip me off and I'll sock 'em.'

Evan, shuddering inwardly at the thought of Don socking Lady Kettering, muttered that it was of no importance really, and leant against the window. Outside the moon had come up and the sea shone eerily in its light like grey silk; far away in the distance a lighthouse flashed. It all looked so remote and quiet that Evan felt inclined to weep. Don squeezed his arm reassuringly. 'You know I like you,' he said, 'I like you better than any Englishman I've ever met. Most Englishmen are high hat, you know, kind of snooty, but you're not high hat at all, you're a good sport.'

'Thank you,' said Evan dimly.

'I hope you weren't sore at me for trying to make you go in the pool,' Don went on. 'I wouldn't like to have you sore at me. It isn't often I get a chance to talk to anyone really intelligent – not that you're only just intelligent, you're brilliant, otherwise you wouldn't be able to write all those God-damned books, would you now?'

'Well,' began Evan, feeling that some reply was demanded.

'Now don't argue.' Don's voice was fierce. 'Of course you're brilliant and you know you are, don't you?'

Evan smiled. 'I wouldn't exactly say——'

Don patted his hand tolerantly. 'Of course you do – everybody knows when they're brilliant, they'd be damned fools if they didn't. Jesus, the way you played that question game in the car – if that wasn't brilliant I should like to know what is? But what I mean to say is this: I'm just a simple sort of guy, really, without any brains at all – I've got looks, I grant you that otherwise I shouldn't be where I am today should I? But no brains, not a one. Why, the idea of sitting down and writing a letter drives me crazy let alone a book. Sometimes when I look at something beautiful like all that,' he indicated the view, 'or when I run across someone really brilliant like you are I feel low – honest to God I do——'

'Why?' said Evan.

'Because I'm such a damn fool of course. I couldn't write down what that looks like to me, not if you paid me a million dollars I couldn't. I couldn't paint it either, I couldn't even talk about it. What do I get out of life I ask you? Money, yes – I make a lot of dough and so what – Happiness, no – I'm one of the unhappiest sons of bitches in the whole world,' he broke off.

'Cheer up,' said Evan as cheerfully as he could. He was feeling depressed himself.

'It gets me down,' murmured Don, pressing his forehead against the glass of the window. 'It just gets me down.'

Evan was pained and embarrassed to observe that he was crying. A concerted scream of laughter came from the living-room. Evan peeped in. Everyone was grouped round Carola who, with a man's Homburg hat perched on her head, was doing an imitation of somebody. Evan glanced back at Don, who was still staring out into the night; his shoulders were heaving. Now was the moment to escape, everyone was far too occupied to notice whether he was there or not; if he could get into the hall without Louise seeing him, the rest was easy; he could get into his room, lock the door and go to bed. He crept along behind the buffet, avoiding Mr Hockbridge, who was asleep on a chair, and reached the hall in safety. From behind the closed door of the library came sounds of strife, apparently Irene's fury at Dwight had in no way abated. Evan paused long enough to hear her scream angrily – 'It was Luella's fault, was it – we'll see about that!' – then he darted down the passage, through Lester's room and the bathroom

and reached his own room with a sigh of relief. He switched on
the lights by the door and started back in horror. Stretched
out on his bed was a woman in a heavy sleep. On closer
examination he recognised the Countess Brancati. Her black
dress was rumpled and her hair was spread over the pillow like
pink hay.

A great rage shook Evan to the core. He seized her by the
shoulder and pushed her backwards and forwards violently;
she continued to sleep undisturbed. He knelt down on the
floor by the bed and shouted 'Wake up – please wake up' in
her face to which she replied with a low moan. He shook her
again and one of her ear-rings fell off; he picked it up and put
it on the bed table and stood there looking at her, his whole
body trembling with fury and frustration. He gave her one
more despairing shove but she paid no attention. Then, with
an expression of set determination he marched back to the
living-room. On his way he met Bonwit emerging from the
library. 'My God,' Bonwit said, 'there's all hell breaking
loose in there,' and then, noticing Evan's face, 'what's
happened to you?'

'There's a woman on my bed,' Evan almost shouted.

'I'll bet it's Mary Lou Brancati,' said Bonwit. 'She
always passes out somewhere – come on – we'll get her
out.'

They went back together. The countess had turned over on
to her face. Bonwit slapped her behind; she wriggled slightly
and he did it again harder. Presently, after several more
whacks, she turned over and muttered, 'G'way and leave me
alone——' Bonwit whereupon hoisted her up on to the side
of the bed and shook her. She opened her eyes and looked at
him malevolently. 'Get the hell away from me,' she said.
'What d'you think you're doing!'

'Come on, baby,' said Bonwit, 'you're missing everything.
There's a party going on.'

'To hell with it,' she replied. 'G'way and leave me alone.'

'Take her other arm,' ordered Bonwit. Evan obeyed and they hauled her struggling and protesting into the bathroom. There Bonwit dabbed her face with a wet sponge; she gave a scream and tried to hit him. Finally they got her into the hall and deposited her in a chair. Bonwit slapped his hands together as though he had just felled a tree and said, 'Now you're Okay, fellar.'

At that moment the hall suddenly filled with people. Louise came out of the library with her arms around Irene who was sobbing. Dwight followed them miserably. Unfortunately Luella and Otis Meer came out of the living-room at the same instant followed by Lester, Lady Kettering and the Grouper Seligmans. Irene, catching sight of Luella, wrested herself from Louise's arms. 'So you're still here,' she said harshly. 'I'm surprised you have the nerve!'

Luella looked at her coolly. 'You're tight, Irene,' she said. 'You'd better go home.'

'You're a snake!' cried Irene, breathing heavily. 'A double-faced, rotten snake!'

Lester tried to calm her. 'Look here, honey,' he said, 'there's no cause in getting yourself all worked up.'

Irene pushed him aside. 'You shut up – you're as bad as she is – you're all of you jealous of Dwight and me and always have been – Luella's been trying to get him for years, and if you think I'm so dumb that I haven't seen what's been going on you're crazy.'

'Really,' murmured Lady Kettering. 'This is too bloody – we'd better go——'

'Go and be damned to you!' said Irene.

Louise gave a cry of distress. Lady Kettering turned and tried to make a dignified exit into the living-room, but was prevented by Ossie, Suki, the Hughes-Hitchcocks and Mrs Hockbridge, who had crowded into the doorway to see what was happening.

Luella seized Irene by the arm in a grip of steel. 'Behave

yourself,' she hissed. 'What do you mean by making a disgusting scene like this about nothing?'

'Nothing!' Irene screamed and writhed in Luella's grasp. Otis Meer gave a cackle of shrill laughter. Dwight tried to coax Irene back into the library. Louise wept loudly and was comforted by Lester and Ossie. Lady Kettering struggled valiantly through the crowd to try to find her cloak. Carola, who had joined the group with Shirley and Leonie, announced in ringing tones that in her opinion the possession of an adequate singing voice was hardly sufficient excuse for behaving like a Broadway floosie. Lester turned on her and told her to shut up and not make everything worse, and in the indescribable pandemonium that ensued, Evan fled.

8

About an hour later, Evan, sitting up rigidly in his bed, began to relax. He had brushed his teeth, taken three aspirins, undressed, tried to lock the door but discovered there was no key, and read four chapters of *Sense and Sensibility* which he always travelled with as a gentle soporific. He had left no stone unturned in his efforts to drag his aching mind away from the horrors he had endured. He had turned out the light twice and attempted to sleep but to no avail. Incidents of the day, people's names, unrelated scraps of conversation crowded into his brain, making even the possibility of lying still out of the question let alone sleep. Sleep was aeons away, he felt that it was well within the bounds of probability that he would never sleep again. The thought of the lecture he had to give that very night, it was now three a.m., tortured him. He felt incapable of uttering one coherent phrase and as for talking for an hour, his mind reeled at the very idea of it. The continual noise, the endless arrivals and departures, the impact of so many different atmospheres and personalities, the unleashing of vulgar passion he had witnessed, to say nothing of the incredible amount of alcohol he had drunk, had lacerated his nerves beyond bearing. He was outraged, shamed, exhausted and bitterly angry.

Now at last he was beginning to feel calmer. The three aspirins he had taken had made his heart thump rather, his maximum dose as a rule being two, but it was apparently taking effect. He glanced at his watch, ten minutes past three, if he could manage to sleep until eleven he would have had nearly his eight hours and probably be able to get in an extra hour at his hotel before his lecture if he wasn't too nervous. 'I'll give myself another ten minutes,' he reflected, 'and then turn out the light, by that time it ought to be all right.'

He lay there still as a mouse, resolutely emptying his mind and concentrating on gentle, peaceful things, the waves of the sea, a vast four-poster bed in some remote English country house, the cool, soft lavender-scented sheets, the soughing of the wind outside in the elms—— At this moment the door opened and Bonwit came in on tiptoe. He was in his pyjamas and carrying a pillow and an eiderdown. He looked relieved when he saw that Evan wasn't asleep.

'I'm awfully sorry, fellar,' he said, 'but I've got to come and use your other bed – there's been all hell going on. Irene drove off in her car with Dwight, leaving Suki and Luella behind, the Brancatis went too, leaving Ossie and Otis, and we've only just found Don Lucas – he's in the living-room on the sofa. Ossie and Otis are in with Lester, Luella's in with Louise and Suki's in my room. I've got to get up at seven to go into town but don't be afraid I'll disturb you – I've left my clothes in the bathroom so as I can dress in there.'

'Oh,' said Evan hopelessly, the blackness of despair made further utterance impossible.

Bonwit clambered into bed and switched off his light. 'I'm all in,' he said. 'Good night, fellar.'

Evan switched off his light too, and lay staring into the darkness.

In a remarkably short space of time Bonwit began to snore. Evan groaned and tried to fold the pillow over his ears, but it was no good, the snores grew louder. They rose rhythmically to a certain pitch and then died away. Occasionally the rhythm would be broken by a grunt, then there would be silence for a moment, then they'd start again. Evan, after a half an hour of it, suddenly leapt up on an impulse of pure blinding rage, switched on the light and went over to Bonwit's bed and stood looking at him. Bonwit was lying on his back with his mouth wide open – the noise issuing from it was incredible. Evan, flinging all gentleness and consideration to the winds, seized him violently by the shoulders and turned him over. Bonwit gave a terrific snort, turned back again almost immediately and went on snoring louder than ever. Evan began to cry, tears coursed down his cheeks and fell on to his pyjamas – panic assailed him – if this went on he would definitely go mad. He walked up and down the room fighting to prevent himself from losing control utterly and shrieking the house down. He went over to the window and looked out. The night was crystal clear, there wasn't a cloud in the sky. Suddenly he knew what he was going to do, the idea came to him in a flash. He was going away, that's what he was going to do. He was going to dress, telephone for a taxi and leave that horrible house for ever. It was idiotic not to have thought of it before. He would leave a note for Louise in the hall asking her to bring his suitcase into New York with her. He tore off his pyjamas and began to dress. Bonwit stopped snoring and turned over, Evan switched off the light and stood still hardly daring to breathe. If Bonwit woke up and caught him trying to escape, he'd obviously try to prevent him – there would be arguments and persuasions and protests, probably ending in the whole house being roused.

Bonwit started to snore again and Evan, with a sigh of

relief, finished dressing. Holding his shoes in his hand he crept down the passage, through the bathroom and into Lester's room. He could dimly make out two forms in one bed and one in the other. He banged against a chair on his way to the door and immediately lay down flat on the floor. Lester moved in his sleep but didn't wake; finally, on hands and knees, Evan crawled out into the other passage and into the hall. Once there, he put on his shoes and went cautiously in search of the telephone; just as he was about to go into the library he remembered that it was in the bar, he had heard Bonwit using it before lunch. He went into the living-room. The curtains were not drawn and moonlight was flooding through the windows. Don was sleeping soundly on a sofa, he looked rather debauched but extraordinarily handsome. Poor Don. Evan shook his head at him sorrowfully and went over to the bar. There was a shutter down over it which was padlocked. This was a terrible blow, Evan thought for a moment of going back and waking Bonwit; but decided against it. If there was no taxi he'd walk and if he didn't know the way he'd find it, at all events he knew he would rather die in the snow than spend one more hour in that house. He scribbled a note to Louise in the library. 'Dear Mrs Steinhauser——' He debated for a moment whether or not to address her as Louise, she had certainly kissed him several times during the day and called him Darling frequently, also he knew her to be a kindly, well-intentioned woman, although at the moment he could cheerfully have strangled her. On the whole he felt that 'Mrs Steinhauser' better expressed the manner in which he was leaving her house. 'Dear Mrs Steinhauser—— Finding myself unable to sleep I have decided to go back to New York. Please forgive this unconventional departure, but it is essential, if I am to lecture with any degree of success, that I relax for several hours beforehand. Please don't worry about me, I am sure I shall find my way to the station quite easily, but if you would be so kind as to have my suitcase packed and bring it in with you tomorrow, I should be more than grateful. With many thanks for your delightful hospitality I am, yours sincerely, Evan Lorrimer.' He signed his name with a flourish. 'She can stick that in her damned visitors' book,' he said to himself. He left the note in a prominent position on a table in the hall, found his hat and coat in a cupboard and let himself quietly out of the front door. The cold air exhilarated him. It was odd, he reflected, how the excitement of escape had completely banished his nervous hysteria. He felt surprisingly well, all things considered. The snow shone in the moonlight and the country lay around him white and still. He noticed a glow in the sky behind a hill. That must be a village, he thought, and set off jauntily down the drive.

About an hour later, when he had walked several miles and his adventurous spirit had begun to wilt a trifle, he was picked up by a milk van. The driver was rugged and friendly and agreed to take him to the nearest station. They had some coffee together in an all-night lunch room when they got there; the next train for New York wasn't due for three-quarters of an hour, and the driver talked freely about his home and domestic affairs with an accent that Evan found, at moments, extremely difficult to understand. Finally he drove away in his van having allowed Evan to pay for the coffee, but refused to accept two dollars.

'Nuts to that,' he said with a laugh. 'I like you – you're not high hat and kind of snooty like most Englishmen—— So long, buddy.'

Buddy, warmed by this tribute, went on to the platform and waited for the train.

When he arrived in New York it was daylight. The night-porter at his hotel greeted him in some surprise and handed him a pile of telephone messages and a letter. When he got to his room he opened the letter first. 'Dear Mr Lorrimer,' he read, 'Although we have never met, your books have given me so much pleasure that I am taking this opportunity of welcoming you to Chicago, where I understand you are going to talk to us next week on "History and the Modern Novel". My husband and I would be so pleased if you would come out to us for the week-end after your lecture. Our home is on the edge of the lake and we flatter ourselves it is the nearest approach to an English country house that you could find in the whole of the Middle West. It is peaceful and quiet, and no one would disturb you, you could just rest. If you have anyone with you we should, of course, be delighted to receive them, too. My husband joins me in the hope that you will honour us by accepting. Yours very sincerely, Irma Weinkopf.' Evan undressed thoughtfully and got into bed.

Cheap Excursion

Jimmy said, 'Good night, Miss Reed,' as she passed him in the passage. He did it ordinarily, no overtones or undertones, not the slightest indication of any secret knowledge between them, not even a glint in his eye, nothing beyond the correct subservience of an assistant stage-manager to a star. She answered him vaguely, that well-known gracious smile, and went on to the stage door, her heart pounding violently as though someone had sprung at her out of the dark.

In the car, she sat very still with her hands folded in her lap, vainly hoping that this very stillness, this stern outward quietness might help to empty her mind. Presently she gave up and watched herself carefully taking a cigarette out of her case and lighting it. 'I am Diana Reed. *The* Diana Reed, lighting a cigarette. I am Diana Reed driving home in my expensive car to my expensive flat – I am tired after my performance and as I have a matinée tomorrow it is sane and sensible for me to go straight home to bed after the show. I am having supper with Jimmy tomorrow night and probably Friday night, too – there are hundreds of other nights and there is no reason whatsoever for me to feel lonely and agonised and without peace. I am Diana Reed – I am celebrated, successful, sought after – my play is a hit – my notices were excellent – except the *Sunday Times*. I am Diana Reed, famous, nearing forty and desperate. I am in love, not perhaps really in love like I was with Tony, nor even Pierre Chabron, but that was different, because it lasted such a little time and was foreign and mixed up with being abroad and everything, but I am in love all right and it's different again, it's always different and always difficult, and I wish to God I could be happy with it and give up to it, but there's too much to remember and too much to be careful of and too many people wanting to find out about it and gossip and smear it with their dirty fingers.'

She let down the window and flicked her cigarette on to the pavement. It fell at the feet of a man in a mackintosh and a bowler hat, he looked up quickly and she drew herself back guiltily into the corner of the car. When she let herself into her flat and switched on the lights in the sitting-room its smug tidy emptiness seemed to jeer at her. It was a charming room. The furniture was good, plain and luxuriously simple in line. There was the small Utrillo that Tony had given her so many years ago – it had been in her flat in Cavendish Street for ages, and she had even taken it on tour with her. That sharp sunny little street with the pinkish-white walls and neat row of plane trees making shadows across the road. The only other picture in the room was a Marie Laurencin of a woman in a sort of turban. It was quite small and framed in glass. That she had bought herself a couple of years ago when she was in Paris with Barbara and Nicky. Nicky said it looked like a very pale peach with currants in it.

She pitched her hat on to the sofa where it lay looking apologetic, almost cringing, and went over and opened the window. Outside it was very quiet, only dark roof tops and an occasional light here and there, but there was a glow in the sky over Oxford Street, and she could hear the noise of traffic far away muffled by the houses and squares in between. Just round the corner in George Street she heard a taxi stop, the slam of its door and the sharp ping as the driver shut off the meter. It might so easily be Jimmy, knowing that she was coming home alone, knowing how happy it would make her if he just came along for ten minutes to say good night. The taxi with a grind of its gears started up and drove away, she could hear it for quite a while until there was silence again. It might still be Jimmy, he wouldn't be so extravagant as to keep a taxi waiting – he might at this very moment be coming up in the lift. In a few seconds she would hear the lift doors opening and then the front-door bell. She listened, holding her breath. He might, of course, come up the stairs in order not be seen by the lift man. Jimmy was nothing if not cautious. She waited, holding on to the window-sill tight to prevent herself from going to the front door. There was no sound, and presently her tension relaxed and, after rather a disdainful glance at herself in the glass over the mantelpiece, she went and opened the front door anyhow. The landing was deserted. When she came back into the room again she discovered, to her great irritation, that she was trembling.

She sat on a chair by the door, bolt upright, like somebody in a dentist's waiting-room. It wouldn't have surprised her if a bright, professionally smiling nurse had suddenly appeared and announced that Doctor Martin was ready for her. Again she folded her hands in her lap. Someone had once told her that if you sat still as death with your hands relaxed, all the vitality ran out of the ends of your fingers and your nerves stopped being strained and tied up in knots. The frigidaire in the kitchen suddenly gave a little click and started whirring. She stared at various things in the room, as though by concentrating, identifying herself with them she could become part of them and not feel so alone. The pickled wood Steinway with a pile of highly-coloured American tunes on it; the low table in front of the fire with last week's *Sketch* and *Bystander*, and the week before last's *New Yorker*, symmetrically arranged with this morning's *Daily Telegraph* folded neatly on top; the Chinese horse on the mantelpiece, very aloof and graceful with its front hoof raised as though it were just about to stamp on something small and insignificant. Nicky had said it was 'Ming' and Eileen had sworn it was 'Sung' because she had once been to China on a cruise and became superior at the mention of anything remotely oriental.

There had been quite a scene about it culminating in
Martha saying loudly that she'd settle for it being 'Gong' or
'Pong' if only everybody would bloody well shut up arguing
and give her a drink.

Diana remembered how Jimmy had laughed, he was sitting
on the floor next to Barbara. She looked at the empty space in
front of the fireplace and saw him clearly, laughing, with his
head thrown back and the firelight shining on his hair. That
was during rehearsals, before anything had happened, before
the opening night in Manchester and the fatal supper party at
the Midland, when he had come over from his party at the
other end of the French restaurant to tell her about the rehearsal for cuts the next afternoon. She remembered asking
him to sit down and have a glass of champagne, and how
politely he had accepted with a rather quizzical smile, almost
an air of resignation. Then the long discussion about Duse
and Bernhardt, and Jonathan getting excited and banging the
table, and Jimmy sitting exactly opposite her where she could
watch him out of the corner of her eye, listening intently to
the conversation and twiddling the stem of his wine-glass.
They had all been dressed, of course. Jonathan and Mary had
come up from London especially for the first night, also
Violet and Dick and Maureen. Jimmy was wearing a grey
flannel suit and a blue shirt and navy blue tie; occasionally the
corners of his mouth twitched as though he were secretly
amused, but didn't want to betray it. Then he had caught her
looking at him, raised his eyebrows just for the fraction of a
second and, with the most disarming friendliness, patted her
hand. 'You gave a brilliant performance tonight,' he said. 'I
felt very proud to be there.' That was the moment. That was
the spark being struck. If she had had any sense she'd have
run like a stag, but instead of running, instead of recognising
danger, there she had sat idiotically smiling, warmed and
attracted. Not content with having had a successful first night
and having given a good performance, not satisfied with the

fact that her friends, her close intimate friends had trailed all the way from London to enjoy her triumph with her, she had had to reach out greedily for something more. Well, God knows she'd got it all right. Here it was, all the fun of the fair. The fruits of those few weeks of determined fascination. She remembered, with a slight shudder, how very much at her best she had been, how swiftly she had responded to her new audience, this nice-looking, physically attractive young man at least ten years younger than herself. How wittily she had joined in the general conversation. She remembered Jonathan laughing until he cried at the way she had described the dress rehearsal of *Lady from the East*, when the Japanese bridge had broken in the middle of her love scene. All the time, through all the laughter, through all the easy intimate jokes, she had had her eye on Jimmy, watching for his response, drawing him into the circle, appraising him, noting his slim wrists, the way he put his head on one side when he asked a question, his eyes, his thick eyelashes, his wide, square shoulders. She remembered saying 'good night' to him with the others as they all went up in the lift together. Her suite was on the second floor, so she got out first. He was up on the top floor somewhere, sharing a room with Bob Harley, one of the small part actors. She remembered, also, looking at herself in the glass in her bathroom and wondering, while she creamed her face, how attractive she was to him really, or how much of it was star glamour and position. Even then, so early in the business, she had begun to doubt. It was inevitable, of course, that doubt, particularly with someone younger than herself, more particularly still when that someone was assistant stage-manager and general understudy. A few days after that, she had boldly asked him to supper in her suite. She remembered at the time being inwardly horrified at such flagrant indiscretion; however, no one had found out or even suspected. He accepted with alacrity, arrived a little late, having had a bath and changed his suit, and that was that.

Suddenly, the telephone bell rang. Diana jumped, and with a sigh of indescribable relief, went into her bedroom to answer it. Nobody but Jimmy knew that she was coming home early – nobody else would dream of finding her in at this time of night. She sat on the edge of the bed just in order to let it ring once more, just to give herself time to control the foolish happiness in her voice. Then she lifted the receiver and said 'Hallo,' in exactly the right tone of politeness only slightly touched with irritation. She heard Martha's voice at the other end, and the suddenness of the disappointment robbed her of all feeling for a moment. She sat there rigid and cold with a dead heart. 'My God,' Martha was saying, 'you could knock me down with a crowbar, I couldn't be more surprised. I rang up Jonathan and Barbara and Nicky, and finally the Savoy Grill – this is only a forlorn hope – I never thought for a moment you'd be in.' Diana muttered something about being tired and having a matinee tomorrow, her voice sounded false and toneless. Martha went on. 'I don't want to be a bore, darling, but Helen and Jack have arrived from New York, and they're leaving on Saturday for Paris, and they've been trying all day to get seats for your show, and the nearest they could get was the fourteenth row, and I wondered if you could do anything about the house seats.' With a great effort Diana said, 'Of course, darling. I'll fix with the box-office tomorrow.' 'You're an angel – here are Helen and Jack, they want to say Hullo'.' There was a slight pause, then Helen's husky Southern voice, 'Darling——'

Diana put her feet up and lay back on the bed, this was going to be a long business. She was in command of herself again, she had been a fool to imagine it was Jimmy, anyhow; he never telephoned unless she asked him to, that was one of the most maddening aspects of his good behaviour. Good behaviour to Jimmy was almost a religion. Excepting when they were alone together, he never for an instant betrayed by the flicker of an eyelash that they were anything more than casual acquaintances. There was no servility in his manner, no pandering to her stardom. On the contrary the brief words he had occasion to speak to her in public were, if anything, a trifle brusque, perfectly polite, of course, but definitely without warmth. Helen's voice went on. She and Jack had had a terrible trip on the *Queen Mary*, and Jack had been sick as a dog for three whole days. Presently Jack came to the telephone and took up the conversation where Helen had left off. Diana lay still, giving a confident, assured performance, laughing gaily, dismissing her present success with just enough disarming professional modesty to be becoming. 'But, Jack dear, it's a marvellous part – nobody could go far wrong in a part like that. You wait until you see it – you'll see exactly what I mean. Not only that, but the cast's good too, Ronnie's superb. I think it's the best performance he's given since *The Lights Are Low*, and, of course, he's heaven to play with. He does a little bit of business with the breakfast-tray at the beginning of the third act that's absolutely magical. I won't tell you what it is, because it would spoil it for you, but just watch out for it—— No dear, I can't have supper tomorrow night – I've a date with some drearies that I've already put off twice – no, really I couldn't again – how about lunch on Friday? You'd better come here and bring old Martha, too – all right – it's lovely to hear your voice again. The seats will be in your name in the box-office tomorrow night. Come back-stage afterwards, anyhow, even if you've hated it – good-bye!'

Diana put down the telephone and lit a cigarette, then she wrote on the pad by the bed, 'Reminder fix house seats, Jack and Helen.' Next to the writing-pad was a thermos jug of ovaltine left for her by Dora. She looked at it irritably and then poured some out and sipped it.

Jimmy had probably gone straight home. He generally did. He wasn't a great one for going out, and didn't seem to have many friends except, of course, Elsie Lumley, who'd been in repertory with him, but that was all over now and she was safely married, or was she? Elsie Lumley, judging from what she knew of her, was the type that would be reluctant to let any old love die, married or not married. Elsie Lumley! Pretty, perhaps rather over-vivacious, certainly talented. She'd be a star in a year or two if she behaved herself. The picture of Elsie and Jimmy together was unbearable – even though it all happened years ago – it *had* happened and had gone on for quite a long while, too. Elsie lying in his arms, pulling his head down to her mouth, running her fingers through his hair—— Diana put down the cup of Ovaltine with a bang that spilt a lot of it into the saucer. She felt sick, as though something were dragging her heart down into her stomach. If Jimmy had gone straight home he'd be in his flat now, in bed probably, reading. There really wasn't any valid reason in the world why she shouldn't ring him up. If he didn't answer, he was out, and there was nothing else to do about it. If he was in, even if he had dropped off to sleep, he wouldn't really mind her just ringing up to say 'Good night.'

She put out her hand to dial his number, then withdrew it again. It would be awful if someone else was there and answered the telephone, not that it was very likely, he only had a bed-sitting room, but still he might have asked Bob Harley or Walter Grayson home for a drink. If Walter Grayson heard her voice on the telephone it would be all over the theatre by tomorrow evening. He was one of those born theatrical gossips, amusing certainly, and quite a good actor, but definitely dangerous. She could, of course, disguise her voice. Just that twang of refined cockney that she had used in *The Short Year*. She put out her hand again, and again withdrew it. 'I'll have another cigarette and by the time I've smoked it, I shall decide whether to ring him up or not.' She hoisted herself up on the pillow and lit a cigarette, methodically and with pleasure. The ache had left her heart and she felt happier – unaccountably so, really; nothing had happened except the possibility of action, of lifting the receiver and dialling a number, of hearing his voice – rather sleepy, probably – saying, 'Hallo, who is it?' She puffed at her cigarette luxuriously watching the smoke curl up into the air. It was blue when it spiralled up from the end of the cigarette and grey when she blew it out of her mouth. It might, of course, irritate him being rung up, he might think she was being indiscreet or tiresome or even trying to check up on him: trying to find out whether he'd gone straight home, and whether he was alone or not.

How horrible if she rang up and he wasn't alone: if she heard his voice say, just as he was lifting the receiver, 'Don't move, darling, it's probably a wrong number,' something ordinary like that, so simple and so ordinary, implying everything, giving the whole game away. After all, he was young and good-looking, and they had neither of them vowed any vows of fidelity. It really wouldn't be so surprising if he indulged in a little fun on the side every now and then. Conducting a secret liaison with the star of the theatre in which you work, must be a bit of a strain from time to time. A little undemanding, light, casual love with somebody else might be a relief.

Diana crushed out her cigarette angrily, her hands were shaking and she felt sick again. She swung her legs off the bed and, sitting on the edge of it, dialled his number viciously, as though she had found him out already; caught him redhanded. She listened to the ringing tone, it rang in twos – brrr-brrr – brrr-brrr. The telephone was next to his bed, that she knew, because once when she had dropped him home he had asked her in to see his hovel. It was a bed-sitting-room on the ground floor in one of those small, old-fashioned streets that run down to the river from John Street, Adelphi ... brrr brrr – brrr-brrr – she might have dialled the wrong number. She hung up and then re-dialled it, again the ringing tone, depressing and monotonous. He was out – he was out somewhere – but where could he possibly be? One more chance, she'd call the operator and ask her to give the number a special ring, just in case there had been a mistake.

The operator was most obliging, but after a few minutes her voice, detached and impersonal, announced that there was no reply from the number and that should she call again later? Diana said no, it didn't matter, she'd call in the morning. She replaced the receiver slowly, wearily, as though it were too heavy to hold any longer, then she buried her face in her hands.

Presently she got up again and began to walk up and down the room. The bed, rumpled where she had lain on it, but turned down, with her nightdress laid out, ready to get into, tortured her with the thought of the hours she would lie awake in it. Even medinal, if she were stupid enough to take a couple of tablets before a matinée, wouldn't be any use tonight. That was what was so wonderful about being in love, it made you so happy! She laughed bitterly aloud and then caught herself laughing bitterly aloud and, just for a second, really laughed. Just a grain of humour left after all. She stopped in front of a long glass and addressed herself in a whisper, but with clear, precise enunciation as though she were trying to explain something to an idiot child. 'I don't care,' she said, 'I don't care if it's cheap or humiliating or unwise or undignified or mad, I'm going to do it, so there. I'm going to do it now, and if I have to wait all night in the street I shall see him, do you understand? I shall see him before I go to sleep, I don't mind if it's only for a moment, I shall see him. If the play closes tomorrow night. If I'm the scandal of London. If the stars fall out of the sky. If the world comes to an end! I shall see him before I go to sleep tonight. If he's alone or with somebody else. If she's drunk, sober or doped, I intend to see him. If he is in and his lights are out I shall bang on the window until I wake him and if, when I wake him, he's in bed with man, woman or child, I shall at least know. Beyond arguments and excuses I shall *know*. I don't care how foolish

and neurotic I may appear to him. I don't care how high my
position is, or how much I trail my pride in the dust. What's
position anyway, and what's pride? To hell with them. I'm in
love and I'm desperately unhappy. I know there's no reason
to be unhappy, no cause for jealousy and that I should be
ashamed of myself at my age, or at any age, for being so un-
controlled and for allowing this God-damned passion or
obsession or whatever it is to conquer me, but there it is. It
can't be helped. No more fighting – no more efforts to behave
beautifully. I'm going to see him – I'm going now – and if he is
unkind or angry and turns away from me I shall lie down in
the gutter and howl.'

She picked up her hat from the sofa in the sitting-room,
turned out all the lights, glanced in her bag to see if she had her
keys all right and enough money for a taxi and went out on to
the landing, shutting the door furtively behind her. She
debated for a moment whether to ring for the lift or slip down
the stairs, finally deciding on the latter as it would be better on
the whole if the lift man didn't see her. He lived in the basement and there was little chance of him catching her unless by
bad luck she happened to coincide with any of the other
tenants coming in. She got out into the street unobserved and
set off briskly in the direction of Orchard Street. It was a fine
night, fortunately, but there had been rain earlier on and the
roads were shining under the lights. She waited on the corner
of Orchard Street and Portman Square for a taxi that came
lolling towards her from the direction of Great Cumberland
Place. She told the driver to stop just opposite the Little
Theatre in John Street, Adelphi, and got in. The cab smelt
musty and someone had been smoking a pipe in it. On the
seat beside her, something white caught her eye; she turned it
over gingerly with her gloved hand, and discovered that it
was a programme of her own play, with a large photograph of
herself on the cover. She looked at the photograph critically.
The cab was rattling along Oxford Street now, and the light

was bright enough. The photograph had been taken a year
ago in a Molyneux sports dress and small hat. It was a three-
quarter length and she was sitting on the edge of a sofa, her
profile half turned away from the camera. She looked young
in it, although the poise of the head was assured, perhaps a
trifle too assured. She looked a little hard too, she thought, a
little ruthless. She wondered if she was, really. If this journey
she was making now, this unwise, neurotic excursion, merely
boiled down to being an unregenerate determination to get
what she wanted, when she wanted it, at no matter what
price. She thought it over calmly, this business of being
determined. After all, it was largely that, plus undoubted
talent and personality, that got her where she was today. She
wondered if she were popular in the theatre. She knew the
stage hands liked her, of course, they were easy; just remembering to say 'thank you', when any of them held open a
door for her or 'good evening', when she passed them on the
stage was enough – they were certainly easy because their
manners were good, and so were .hers; but the rest of the
company – not Ronnie, naturally, he was in more or less the
same position as herself; the others, little Cynthia French, for
instance, the ingenue, did she hate her bitterly in secret? Did
she envy her and wish her to fail? Was all that wide-eyed,
faintly servile eagerness to please, merely masking an implacable ambition, a sweet, strong, female loathing? She
thought not on the whole, Cynthia was far too timid a
creature, unless, of course, she was a considerably finer
actress off the stage than she was on. Walter Grayson, she
knew, liked her all right. She'd known him for years, they'd
been in several plays together. Lottie Carnegie was certainly
waspish at moments, but only with that innate defensiveness
of an elderly actress who hadn't quite achieved what she
originally set out to achieve. There were several of them
about, old-timers without any longer much hope left of
becoming stars, but with enough successful work behind

them to assure their getting good character parts. They all had their little mannerisms and peculiarities and private fortresses of pride. Lottie was all right really, in fact as far as she. Diana, was concerned she was all sweetness and light, but, of course, that might be because she hated Ronnie. Once, years ago apparently, he had been instrumental in having her turned down for a part for which he considered her unsuitable. The others liked her well enough, she thought, at least she hoped they did; it was horrid not to be liked; but she hadn't any illusions as to what would happen if she made a false step. This affair with Jimmy, for example. If that became known in the theatre the whole of London would be buzzing with it. She winced at the thought. That would be horrible. Once more, by the light of a street lamp at the bottom of the Haymarket, she looked at the photograph. She wondered if she had looked like that to the man with the pipe to whom the programme had belonged; whether he had taken his wife with him or his mistress; whether they'd liked the play and cried dutifully in the last act, or been bored and disappointed and wished they'd gone to a musical comedy. How surprised they'd be if they knew that the next person to step into the taxi after they'd left it was Diana Reed. Diana Reed herself, the same woman they had so recently been applauding, as she bowed and smiled at them in that shimmering silver evening gown – that reminded her to tell Dora at the matinée tomorrow that the paillettes where her cloak fastened were getting tarnished and that she must either ring up the shop or see if Mrs Blake could deal with it in the wardrobe.

The taxi drew up with a jerk opposite to the Little Theatre. Diana got out and paid the driver. He said, 'Good night, Miss,' and drove away down the hill, leaving her on the edge of the kerb feeling rather dazed, almost forgetting what she was there for. The urgency that had propelled her out of her flat and into that taxi seemed to have evaporated somewhere between Oxford street and here. Perhaps it was the photograph on the programme, the reminder of herself as others saw her, as she should be, poised and well-dressed with head held high, not in contempt, nothing supercilious about it, but secure and dignified, above the arena. Those people who had taken that taxi, who had been to the play – how shocked they'd be if they could see her now, not just standing alone in a dark street, that wouldn't of course shock them particularly, merely surprise them; but if they could know, by some horrid clairvoyance, why she was here. If, just for an instant, they could see into her mind. Diana Reed, that smooth, gracious creature whose stage loves and joys and sorrows they had so often enjoyed, furtively loitering about in the middle of the night in the hope of spending a few minutes with a comparatively insignificant young man whom she liked going to bed with. Diana resolutely turned in the opposite direction from Jimmy's street and walked round by the side of the Tivoli into the Strand. Surely it was a little more than that? Surely she was being unnecessarily hard on herself. There was a sweetness about Jimmy, a quality, apart from his damned sex appeal. To begin with, he was well-bred, a gentleman. (What a weak, nauseating alibi, as though that could possibly matter one way or the other and yet, of course, it did.) His very gentleness, his strict code of behaviour. His fear, so much stronger even than hers, that anyone should discover their secret. Also he was intelligent, infinitely more knowledgeable and better read than she. All that surely made a difference, surely justified her behaviour a little bit? She walked along the Strand towards Fleet Street, as though she were hurrying to keep an important appointment. There were still a lot of people about and on the other side of the street two drunken men were happily staggering along with their arms round each other's necks, singing 'Ramona'. Suddenly to her horror she saw Violet Cassel and Donald Ross approaching her, they had obviously been supping at the Savoy and decided to walk a little before taking a cab. With an instinctive gesture she jammed her hat down over her eyes and darted into Heppell's, so quickly that she collided with a woman who was just coming out and nearly knocked her down. The woman said, 'Christ, a fugitive from a chain gang?' and waving aside Diana's apologies, went unsteadily into the street. Diana, faced with the enquiring stare of the man behind the counter and slightly unhinged by her encounter in the doorway and the fact that Donald and Violet were at that moment passing the shop, racked her brains for something to buy. Her eyes lighted on a bottle of emerald green liquid labelled 'Ess Viotto for the hands'. 'I should like that,' she said, pointing to it. The man, without looking at her again, wrapped it up and handed it to her. She paid for it and went out of the shop. Violet and Donald were crossing over further down. She walked slowly back the way she had come. An empty taxi cruising along close to the kerb passed her and almost stopped. She hailed it, gave the driver her address, got in and sank thankfully back on to the seat. 'A fugitive from a chain gang.' She smiled and closed her eyes for a moment. 'What an escape!' She felt utterly exhausted as if she had passed through a tremendous crisis, she was safe, safe as houses, safe from herself and humiliation and indignity. No more of such foolishness. She wondered whether or not she had replaced the stopper in the thermos. She hoped she had, because the prospect of sitting up, snug in bed, with a mind at peace and a cup of Ovaltine seemed heavenly. She opened her eyes as the taxi was turning into Lower Regent Street and looked out of the window. A man in a camel-hair coat and a soft brown hat was waiting on the corner to cross the road. Jimmy! She leant forward hurriedly and tried to slide the glass window back in order to tell the driver to stop, but it wouldn't budge. She rapped on the glass violently. The driver looked round in surprise and drew into the kerb. She was out on the pavement in a second, fumbling in her bag. 'I've forgotten something,' she said breathlessly. 'Here' – she gave him a half a crown and turned and ran towards Jimmy. He had crossed over by now and was just turning into Cockspur Street. She had to wait a moment before crossing because two cars came by and then a bus. When she got round the corner she could still see him just passing the lower entrance to the Carlton. She put on a great spurt and caught up with him just as he was about to cross the Haymarket. He turned his head slightly just as she was about to clutch at his sleeve. He was a pleasant-looking young man with fair hair and a little moustache. Diana stopped dead in her tracks and watched him cross the road, a stream of traffic went by and he was lost to view. She stood there trying to get her breath and controlling an overpowering desire to burst into tears. She stamped her foot hard as though by so doing she could crush her agonising, bitter disappointment into the ground.

A passing policeman looked at her suspiciously, so she moved miserably across the road and walked on towards Trafalgar Square, past the windows of the shipping agencies filled with smooth models of ocean liners. She stopped at one of them for a moment and rested her forehead against the cold glass, staring at a white steamer with two yellow funnels; its decks meticulously scrubbed and its paintwork shining in the light from the street lamps. Then, pulling herself together, she set off firmly in the direction of the Adelphi. No use dithering about any more. She had, in leaving the flat in the first place, obeyed an irresistible, but perfectly understandable impulse to see Jimmy. Since then, she had hesitated and vacillated and tormented herself into a state bordering on hysteria. No more of that, it was stupid, worse than stupid, this nerve-racking conflict between reason and emotion was insane. Reason had done its best and failed. No reason in the world could now woo her into going back to that empty flat without seeing Jimmy. Fate had ranged itself against reason. If Fate hadn't dressed that idiotic young man with a moustache in Jimmy's camel-hair coat and Jimmy's hat, all would have been well. If

Fate had arbitrarily decided, as it apparently had, that she was to make a fool herself, then make a fool of herself she would. Jimmy was probably fast asleep by now and would be furious at being awakened. She was, very possibly, by this lamentable, silly behaviour, about to wreck something precious, something which, in future years, she might have been able to look back upon with a certain wistful nostalgia. Now of course, after she had observed Jimmy's irritation and thinly-veiled disgust, after he had kissed her and comforted her and packed her off home in a taxi, she would have to face one fact clearly and bravely and that fact would be that a love affair, just another love affair, was ended. Not a violent break or a quarrel or anything like that, just a gentle, painful decline, something to be glossed over and forgotten. By the time she had reached the top of Jimmy's street there were tears in her eyes.

She walked along the pavement on tiptoe. His windows were dark, she peered into them over the area railings. His curtains were not drawn, his room was empty. She walked over the road to where there was a street lamp and looked at her wrist-watch. Ten past two. She stood there leaning against a railing, not far from the lamp, for several minutes. There were no lights in any of the houses except one on the corner. On the top floor, a little square of yellow blind with a shadow occasionally moving behind it. On her left, beyond the end of the road which was a cul-de-sac, were the trees of the gardens along the embankment; they rustled slightly in the damp breeze. Now and then she heard the noise of a train rumbling hollowly over Charing Cross bridge, and occasionally the mournful hoot of a tug on the river. Where on earth could he be at this hour of the morning? He hated going out, or at least so he always said. He didn't drink much either. He wouldn't be sitting up with a lot of cronies just drinking. He was very responsible about his job too and in addition to a matinée tomorrow there was an understudy rehearsal at eleven – she knew that because she had happened to notice it on the board. He couldn't have gone home to his parents; they lived on the Isle of Wight. She sauntered slowly up to the corner of John Street and looked up and down it. No taxi in sight, nothing, only a cat stalking along by the railings. She stooped down and said 'Puss, puss' to it but it ignored her and disappeared down some steps. Suddenly a taxi turned into the lower end of the street. Diana took to her heels and ran. Supposing it were Jimmy coming home with somebody – supposing he looked out and saw her standing on the pavement, watching him. Panic seized her. On the left, on the opposite side of the road from the house where he lived, was a dark archway. She dived into it and pressed herself flat against the wall. The taxi turned into the street and drew up. She peeped round the corner and saw a fat man and a woman in evening dress get out of it and let themselves into one of the houses. When the taxi had backed and driven away she emerged from the archway. 'I'll walk,' she said to herself out loud. 'I'll walk up and down this street twenty times and if he hasn't come by then I'll – I'll walk up and down it another twenty times.' She started walking and laughing at herself at the same time, quite genuine laughter; she listened to it and it didn't sound in the least hysterical. I'm feeling better, she thought, none of it matters nearly as much as I think it does, I've been making mountains out of molehills. I'm enjoying this really, it's an adventure. There's something strange and exciting in being out alone in the city at dead of night, I must do it more often. She laughed again at the picture of herself solemnly setting out two or three times a week on solitary nocturnal jaunts. After about the fifteenth time she had turned and retraced her steps she met Jimmy face to face at the corner. He stopped in amazement and said, 'My God – Diana – what on earth——'

She held out to him the parcel she'd been holding.

'I've brought you a present,' she said with a little giggle. 'It's Ess Viotto – for the hands!'

The Kindness of Mrs Radcliffe

I

MRS RADCLIFFE always awoke on the dot of half-past seven. It was a habit of years and from this regularity she derived a certain pride. It signified a disciplined mind in a disciplined body, and Mrs Radcliffe was a great one for discipline. Life was a business that had to be handled with efficiency and despatch otherwise where were you? She had a poor opinion of those, and alas there were all too many of them, who allowed themselves to be swayed this way and that by emotions and circumstances over which they had little or no control. To have little or no control over emotions and circumstances was, to Mrs Radcliffe, anathema. Not only did she consider it was foolish to succumb to the manifold weaknesses inherent in our natures, and after all there are many of these in even the sternest of us, it was downright dangerous. Mrs Radcliffe could quote several instances of people of her acquaintance, occasionally even relatives, who, owing either to self-indulgence, lack of sense of responsibility or, in some cases, wilful stubbornness – such as Cousin Laura for example – had completely degenerated and failed. It must not be imagined that Mrs Radcliffe, who heaven knows was a broad-minded and kindly woman, referred to failure merely in the worldly sense; many of those who from her point of view had 'Failed' had, on basely materialistic counts, done exceedingly well for themselves. Failure was a hydra-headed monster. You could be shrewd and business-like, marry well and become a senior partner in no time and still fail. You could bear children, bring them up firmly, embark them on promising careers, keep your figure, wear smart clothes and play Bridge as well as Mrs Poindexter and still fail. On the other hand you could be poor and of no account, an insignificant cog in the great wheel of life and succeed, succeed triumphantly, for surely success in the eyes of God is of more ultimate importance than the glittering transient satisfaction of success in the eyes of the world. This, to sum it up briefly, was Mrs Radcliffe's philosophy and she was delighted with it. She felt herself to be on a footing with the Almighty which was, to say the least of it, cordial. She referred to Him frequently in her mind and even more frequently in her conversation, not, it must be understood, with the slightest trace of sanctimoniousness. Hers was far too healthy and sane a character for that; rather more in a spirit of reverend friendliness. Occasionally she even blasphemed mildly to the extent of saying 'Good Lord' or 'My God' in moments of light stress. This, she considered in her secret heart, to be rather amusingly racy provided she didn't allow it to become a habit.

On this particular morning in early April Mrs Radcliffe awoke as usual and lay for a few moments in dreamy awareness of the comfort of her bed, the translucent greenish charm of her bedroom, and the fact that it was a sunny day. This was apparent from the bars of strong light shining through the venetian blind and making stripes on the corner of the dressing-table and the chaise-longue by the window. Presently she heard Mildred approaching with her early tea; a swift glance at the clock on the table by her bed informed her that Mildred was four and a half minutes late. She decided, however, not to mention it this time. Mildred's unpunctuality was, unfortunately, the least of her defects; in fact there were moments when Mrs Radcliffe genuinely regretted her generous impulse in taking her from the orphanage when she might quite easily have found a girl from the Registry Office with a certain amount of previous training in domestic service. The training of Mildred presented many problems and showed every sign of being an uphill struggle. But still Mrs Radcliffe in her capacity as one of the esteemed Vice-Presidents of the Orphanage Committee had felt it her bounden duty to set an example to some of the other members, who, although volubly free with suggestions for the future of their charges when the moment came to launch them on to the world, were singularly unresponsive when it came to the point of doing anything practical about it themselves. Mrs Radcliffe often smiled whimsically as she recalled the various expressions on the faces of the committee when she had burst her bombshell. 'I will take Mildred myself,' she had said, quite simply, without undue emphasis on the magnanimity of her gesture; just like that, 'I will take Mildred myself!' She remembered that Mrs Weecock, who was over-emotional and effusive, had risen impulsively and kissed her, and that Doctor Price had immediately proposed a vote of thanks which had been carried unanimously with the greatest enthusiasm.

Mildred, after several months of strenuous effort, had, as yet, only managed to scrape the surface of what was ultimately expected of her; however she was willing, sometimes almost too eager to please, all of which was natural enough, poor little thing; nobody could accuse Mrs Radcliffe of being unable to recognise pathetic, overwhelming gratitude, however nervous.

At this moment the object of her reflections entered the room. She was an uncouth girl of eighteen. Her abundant sandy hair straggled widely away from her neat cap, giving it the appearance of a small white fort set in the middle of a desert. Her hands were large and pink and her feet, encased in cotton stockings and strap shoes, were larger still. Her face, however, apart from a few freckles, was pleasing. She had a generous mouth and well-set greyish-green eyes. She said 'Good morning, 'um,' in a breathy voice and, having deposited the tray temporarily on the chest-of-drawers, went over and pulled up the blind. She also closed the window, which during Mrs Radcliffe's slumbers had been open a fraction at the top, rather too sharply, so that the panes rattled.

'Gently, Mildred, gently,' said Mrs Radcliffe as she hoisted herself up on her pillows preparatory to receiving the tea-tray. Mildred, by drawing in her breath and then clicking her tongue against her teeth several times, made a noise which, although intended to express bitter self-reproach, merely succeeded in being irritating. Mrs Radcliffe winced and waited for her tray in silence. The tray was a complicated affair designed for the comfort of invalids. By pressing lightly with the hands, two pairs of wooden legs shot out from each side thereby forming a neat little bridge across the patient's knees. This was one of the banes of Mildred's life. If the eiderdown were rumpled or Mrs Radcliffe had not arranged herself in a completely symmetrical position, the whole thing was liable to tip sideways causing everything on it to slide alarmingly and hover on the brink of disaster. This morning, aware that she had transgressed over the window shutting, Mildred was even more nervous than usual. Her large hands were trembling and she breathed heavily. She set the tray across Mrs Radcliffe's legs with laborious care; so far so good, only a few drops slopped out of the milk jug. She straightened herself with a sigh of relief and in that moment of triumph God struck her down. The corner of her apron, unbeknownst to her, had been caught by the left legs of the tray and the straightening of her body jerked it free with just sufficient force to over-balance the tea-pot. It was one of those moments in life when Time ceases to exist, years of fear and agony are endured in the passing of a brief instant. Mildred watched, with dilating eyes, the fat blue tea-pot with the willow-pattern design on it wobble from side to side and then slowly, slowly, with the slowness of protracted death, fall off the tray, roll over twice on the smooth slope of the counterpane, shedding its lid on the way, and finally crash to the floor, emptying its contents with devilish exultance into Mrs Radcliffe's ostrich feather bedroom slippers. In the deadly silence that ensued a train whistled in the cutting a mile away, causing Mildred to jump violently as though the last trump had sounded for her.

Mrs Radcliffe, who as a rule could be relied upon to assume an attitude of splendid calm in any crisis, for once lost control and fairly let fly. Mildred stood before her wretchedly twisting her hands, dumb with misery, too frightened even to take in half of what was being said to her. Disjointed words flashed across her consciousness like those moving electric light signs which tell of immediate events but which, if your attention is not wholly concentrated on them, become a series of meaningless phrases. A few invectives like 'Idiot', 'Fool', 'Clumsy' and 'Stupid' seared her mind for a moment and then were gone with the rest, leaving her shivering in a void of hopelessness and shame.

Presently Mrs Radcliffe regained control and, after a slight pause, spoke with icy precision, 'Pick it up,' she said, and then again, 'PICK IT UP!' using each word as a sword. Mildred stooped and picked up the tea-pot and stood with it in her hands, only vaguely aware of its heat. 'The tray,' said Mrs Radcliffe. 'Take the tray.' Mildred put the tea-pot down on the floor again and took the tray.

The next ten minutes was devoted, in so far as was possible, to restoring order to chaos. Mildred, galvanised suddenly into feverish activity, flew down to the kitchen, blurted out the disaster in a few stumbling words to Cook, flew upstairs again with a cloth, rubbed and scrubbed with hot water out of the silver-plated jug to erase the tea-stains from the carpet amid a hail of frigidly patient directions from her mistress. Finally, when the best that could be done had been done, she blurted out, 'I'm sure I'm very sorry, 'um, it was an accident,' and made for the door. Mrs Radcliffe halted her.

'Just a moment, Mildred.'

Mildred waited, standing first on one foot then on the other. Mrs Radcliffe's voice was cold and just, she was now in full command again and sailing to victory.

'To explain that it was an accident, Mildred,' she said, 'was unnecessary. I should hardly have imagined that you had done such a thing on purpose. But what I wish to point out to you is that the accident would never have occurred if you had not been both careless and slovenly. I have spoken to you, Heaven knows often enough, about your clumsiness, and if you don't try to improve I very much fear I shall have to give you your notice. This time, however, and it is the last time, I shall excuse you.' Mildred's heart leapt with relief like a bird in her breast. 'But,' continued Mrs Radcliffe, 'in order that this shall be a lesson to you, in order that you shall think and be more careful in future, I intend to punish you.' There was a slight pause. The small gilt clock on the mantelpiece gave a little whirr and struck eight. Mrs Radcliffe waited portentously until it had finished. 'I understand that today is your afternoon out?' The bird in Mildred's breast dropped like a stone to the earth and through the earth into deep caverns of despair. 'Yes, 'um,' she said huskily. 'Well,' went on the voice of doom, 'you will stay in this afternoon and help with the silver. That is all, thank you.' A tear coursed down the side of Mildred's nose. 'Very good, 'um,' she said in a voice so low as to be almost unaudible, and went out of the room.

The fact that every minute of every hour of every day of Mildred's week had been concentrated on the anticipatory bliss of that afternoon out was of course hidden from Mrs Radcliffe. How could she possibly know that Fred, thrilling wonderful Fred, assistant to Mr Lewis the chemist in the High Street, had arranged to meet Mildred at two-thirty outside Harvey Brown's and take her to see Spencer Tracy, Clark Gable and Myrna Loy in *Test Pilot*? How could she possibly know that Messrs Tracy and Gable and Miss Loy would be up and away by next Thursday and their sacred screen occupied by an English historical picture featuring Sir Cedric Hardwicke? How also could she guess that as Fred would be out on his rounds all the morning there was no possible way of letting him know that Mildred would be unable to meet him and that, after waiting for a half-an-hour or so on the pavement outside Harvey Brown's, he would probably be so furious that he would never speak to her again?

Fortunately for Mrs Radcliffe's peace of mind she was ignorant of all this and in consequence, her sense of exhilaration at having handled a difficult and annoying domestic drama with her usual consummate calm and decision, was in no way impaired.

2

Mr Stanley Radcliffe stood five foot six inches and a half in his socks which, no matter with what fickleness the weather might change, were invariably of austere grey worsted. His hair, thin on the top but happily bushy at the sides, was of the same colour as his socks. As a character he was amiable, temperate and industrious but, if criticise we must, a trifle lacking in spirit. This defect, however, could be understood, if not altogether excused, by the fact that he had been married to Mrs Radcliffe for thirty-three years. It is a well-known sociological truism that two dominant personalities become ill-at-ease when compelled by force of circumstance to inhabit the same house for a long period of time. It is possible that Mr Radcliffe wisely realised this early on in his married life and, being a man of peaceful and sensible disposition, relinquished the ever dubious joys of domestic authority to his wife. It must not be supposed, however, that outside his home he was anywhere near as weak as he was in it. On the contrary, in his office – he was a partner in the firm of Eldridge,

Eldridge and Black, Solicitors-at-Law – in his office he was
often a veritable martinet. Times out of number Miss Hallett,
his secretary, would emerge from taking the morning letters
with pursed lips and a spread of scarlet stretching from her
neck up to her ears that spoke volumes.

On the morning of the tea-pot tragedy he was feeling cheerful. It was a cheerful day. The birds were twittering in the
garden. He had received a letter from Henry Boulder, a more
or less private client, that is to say a client who combined the
transaction of legal business with a pleasant personal relation-
ship, inviting him to visit him that afternoon at his house near
Bromley to discuss the details of a new building contract that
Eldridge, Eldridge and Black were drawing up for him, and
perhaps play a round of golf afterwards. A game of golf to
Stanley Radcliffe was as steel is to a magnet, or rather a
magnet to steel. He loved golf deeply and truly with all the
passion of his nature. He was also fond of Mrs Boulder, not in
any way lasciviously, Mr Radcliffe's sex impulses had
atrophied from neglect at least fifteen years ago, but with a
warm sense of comradeship. She was a gay, vivacious creature
in the early forties, given to telling rather risqué stories, and
she had a loud, infectious laugh. Life at the Boulders' home
seemed to consist of one long joke. Henry Boulder laughed a
lot too, and frequently said the most outrageous things, but
with such an air of worldly geniality that no offence could
possibly be taken.

Mr Radcliffe looked at his wife sipping her coffee and
opening letters at the other side of the table. She had her
glasses on and appeared to be in a tranquil mood. He
wondered if the moment was at last ripe for him to suggest
what he had been longing to suggest for weeks. Why not take
the plunge? He cleared his throat. Mrs Radcliffe looked up.
'Such a nice letter from Mrs Riddle,' she said. 'They've just
come back from a cruise to the Holy Land.'

A fleeting vision of Mrs Riddle, a formidable woman of

vicious piety, blustering through the Church of the Holy Sepulchre, flashed across Mr Radcliffe's mind for a moment and was obliterated. Now or never.

'How nice, dear,' he said. 'I wanted to——'

'They bathed in the Dead Sea,' went on Mrs Radcliffe, glancing at a closely written page of thin notepaper. 'And it was so salt that they couldn't sink.'

'I shouldn't have thought,' said Mr Radcliffe with a bold chuckle, 'that they would have wished to.'

Mrs Radcliffe looked at him suspiciously and then smiled, but without mirth, and went on reading the letter. Humour was not her strong suit and flippancy definitely irritated her.

Mr Radcliffe, realising that he had made a tactical error, cleared his throat again. 'Adela,' he said, 'I have just had a letter from Henry Boulder.' This, he realised the moment the words were out of his mouth, was another tactical error implying as it did that a letter from Henry Boulder was on a par with a letter from Mrs Riddle. Mrs Radcliffe ignored him completely and went on reading. Then Mr Radcliffe, in a determined effort to get what was in his mind out of it, committed the gravest blunder of all. He advanced recklessly into the open. 'I thought of inviting the Boulders to dinner tonight,' he said.

Mrs Radcliffe slowly lowered her letter and stared at him. If he had suggested inviting two naked Zulus to dinner she could not have expressed more shocked surprise. 'My dear Stanley!' she said in the exasperated tone one might use in addressing a particularly fractious invalid. 'The Dukes are coming.'

'I don't see that that would make any difference,' he said suddenly.

Mrs Radcliffe, scenting mutiny, decided to scotch it once and for all. She leant across the table and smiled. 'I fully appreciate,' she said, 'that they are great friends of yours,' the emphasis on the word 'yours' implied just enough subtle contempt, 'but they are certainly not great friends of mine, in fact I barely know them. Also, my dear, although I am sure they are very useful to you in business, they are hardly' – here she gave a little laugh – 'hardly the sort of people I would invite to meet the Dukes!'

Mr Radcliffe opened his mouth to speak, to speak sharply, to say with firmness and conviction that the Reverend Francis Duke, vicar or no vicar, was an overbearing, pretentious bore, and his wife a giggling fool, and that for good humour and pleasant company and making a dinner-party a success Mr and Mrs Henry Boulder could knock spots off them any day of the week. All this and more was bubbling in his mind, clamouring to be said, but the habit of years was too strong for him. He met the unwinking stare of his wife's slightly protuberant blue eyes for a moment and then wavered, the game was up. 'Very well, my dear,' he said, and resumed his toast and marmalade. Mrs Radcliffe relaxed and smiled indulgently, poor old Stanley! She, who was so used to triumph, could afford to be magnanimous. She leant across the table and patted his hand affectionately then, generously wiping the episode from her mind, she embarked on the fourth page of Mrs Riddle's letter about the Holy Land.

Mr Radcliffe, a half-an-hour later, sat in the corner of a third-class smoking compartment on the train to London puzzling out in his mind the most tactful way in which he could repay some of the Boulders' hospitality. He could, of course, invite them to dine at a restaurant and perhaps get seats for a play afterwards, but even so he was terribly afraid that the absence of Adela and the fact that they had never been asked to the house might hurt their feelings. People were extremely touchy about things like that. The last time he had visited them Mrs Boulder had dropped a few hints. Suddenly, with a rush of blood to his face, he remembered that that same evening, just after dinner, he had, in a moment of expansion, definitely invited them. He remembered his very words, 'You must come and dine one night soon and we'll have some Bridge – my wife is so anxious to get to know you better.'

When the train arrived at Cannon Street he went straight to the telegraph office, walking slowly as if he were tired. He wrote out the telegram carefully. 'Boulder, "The Nook", Bromley. Very disappointed unable accept your kind invitation for this afternoon regards Radcliffe.'

3

Mrs Radcliffe rose from her desk in the morning-room with a sigh and patted her hair in front of a mirror on the wall. She had been absent-mindedly disarranging it while writing that difficult letter to Cousin Laura. She looked at her reflection for a moment and then, smiling, shook her head sorrowfully at herself. 'You must really break yourself of that bad habit,' she said with mock firmness, and then looked hurriedly to see if Mildred had happened to come in without her noticing. It would be too ridiculous to be caught by a servant talking to oneself. All was well, however. Mildred had not come in. As a matter of fact Mildred was at that moment in her bedroom at the top of the house crying her eyes out.

That letter to Laura had certainly been difficult, but Mrs Radcliffe felt a sense of great relief at having at last written it. It had been hanging over her for days. Laura was her Aunt Marion's daughter and they had been at school together. Laura's whole life, in Mrs Radcliffe's opinion, had been untidy, inefficient and annoying. To begin with she had married a drunkard with no money who had finally deserted her and died in Rio de Janeiro. After that for several years and with two young children on her hands she had contrived to run a tea-shop at Hove and carry on a scandalous affair with a married man at the same time. In the year 1912 she had married again, a handsome but vague young man also with no money to speak of, who had later been killed in the retreat from Mons. In the intervening years between the Armistice and 1930 she had fortunately been abroad running a pension in some dead-and-alive seaside town in Northern Italy. Meanwhile the children of her first marriage had grown up. The boy, Frank, had married and gone off to plant rubber in Burma and was seldom heard from, while the girl, Estelle, had also married and, with an inefficiency obviously inherited from her mother, had died in child-birth, having misjudged her time and been caught in labour on a Channel Island steamer in the middle of a storm. Laura, now a woman of over sixty, had been living ever since in a small house in Folkestone only just managing to pay the rent every quarter by taking in paying guests. Almost the most irritating thing about her was her unregenerate cheerfulness. Even in the begging letter Mrs Radcliffe had received from her a few days back there had been an irrepressible note of flippancy. Mrs Radcliffe picked it up from the desk and re-read it for the third time. – 'My dear Adela,' she read, 'I am in the soup this time and no mistake. Please forgive me for worrying you with my troubles, but I really don't know where to turn. Mr Roland, one of my extra quality streamlined P.G.s, upped and left me on Saturday without paying his month's board and lodging and I was counting on it to pay off the last instalment on my dining-room set. I owe eighteen pounds on it and unless I pay it by Friday they'll come and take every stick away and poor Mr Clarence Sims and Mr Brackett, my other two gents, will have to sit on the bare floor. I do feel dreadful asking you to lend me ten pounds temporarily. I can raise eight all right on mother's silver, but if you possibly can spare it do please help me as I am in a flat spin and worried to death. I promise to pay it back within the next three months. Your distracted but affectionate cousin, Laura.' Mrs Radcliffe replaced Laura's letter in its envelope and read once more her own firm and admirable answer to it.

My dear Laura, your letter was a great surprise to me, not having heard from you for so long. Believe me, I sympathise with you more than I can say in all your worries. If you will remember I always have (underlined). *How very disgraceful of your lodger to leave without paying you. Wasn't it a little unwise to take in that sort of man in the first place? However, it's no use crying over spilt milk, is it? With regard to your request for ten pounds, I am afraid that is quite out of the question at the moment. As you know I have many calls upon my purse in these trying times especially now that the Orphanage, of which I am vice-president, is becoming so overcrowded that we find ourselves forced to build a new dormitory for the little ones to which we all, that is the committee and myself, have had to subscribe a great deal more than we can afford. You see we all have our little troubles! However, as we are such old friends, let alone actual blood relations – I always think that sounds so unpleasant, don't you? – I cannot bear to think of you in such dire straits, so I am enclosing a cheque for three guineas. This is most emphatically not a loan as I cannot bear the thought of money transactions between friends. Please, dear Laura, accept it in the spirit in which it is offered. Stanley joins me in the warmest greetings. I remain, your affectionate cousin, Adela Radcliffe.'*

Mrs Radcliffe sat down at the desk again and wrote out the cheque, then, having placed it with the letter in an already addressed envelope, she licked it down and stuck a stamp on it with an authoritative thump of her fist. This done she sat back in her chair and relaxed for a moment. What a pleasant thing it is, she reflected, to be in the fortunate position of being able to help those who, owing to defects in character and general fecklessness, are so pitifully unable to help themselves. In this mood of justifiable satisfaction, and humming a little tune, she went down into the kitchen to interview the Cook.

4

Mrs Brodie had cooked for Mrs Radcliffe for nearly three years and had, on the whole, proved satisfactory. Mrs Radcliffe's tastes were simple. She disapproved of high seasoning, rich sauces, and the complicated flubdubbery of the French school. She designated any dish that was not strictly in accordance with the wholesome English culinary tradition as 'Messy', and nobody who knew Mrs Radcliffe even casually could visualise her for a moment sitting down to anything messy. Mrs Brodie filled the bill perfectly. True, there were times when she displayed a certain tendency to flightiness. There had been one or two slip-ups. The Malayan curry, for instance (Mrs Brodie's brother was a sailor), and the dreadful time the Piggots came to dinner and had been offered soufflé en surprise, the cold middle part of which had so surprised Mrs Piggot's wisdom tooth that she had had to lie down on Mrs Radcliffe's bed and have her gum painted with oil of cloves. All that, however, was in the past, although an occasional reminder of it came in handy as a curb whenever Mrs Brodie showed signs of rebellion.

This morning there was no spirit in Mrs Brodie at all, she had her own private troubles, as indeed who has not, and today they had come to a head. In the first place her widowed sister had been whisked off to the hospital to be operated on for gall-stones, thereby leaving no one to look after Mrs Brodie's husband who had had two strokes in the last nine months and was due for another one at any moment. This had necessitated some quick thinking and the sending of a telegram first thing to a niece in Southampton, together with a money order for fare and expenses. Mrs Brodie devoutly hoped that at this moment the niece was already in the train. In the meantime she had telephoned to Mrs Marsh, her next-door neighbour, asking her to pop in from time to time during the day and see that Mr Brodie was all right. She planned to slip over herself during the afternoon to see that the niece was safely installed, and call at the hospital for news of her sister. This obviously meant asking Mrs Radcliffe's permission, as Mrs Brodie's home was in Maidstone, twenty miles away by bus, and in order for her to get there and back dinner would have to be later than usual and a scratch meal at that. At Mrs Radcliffe's first words her heart sank. 'Good morning, Cook. I want a particularly nice dinner tonight. The Vicar and Mrs Duke are coming, also Miss Layton and Mr Baker. Have you any suggestions?' Mrs Radcliffe spoke kindly, in the special smooth voice she reserved for the Lower Orders. The lower orders, she knew, appreciated differences in class as keenly as anybody, that was one of the fundamental virtues of the English social structure and the reason that no nonsensical experiments such as Bolshevism or Communism or anything like that could ever take root in the British Isles. Class was class and there was no getting away from it, you only had to look at the ineffectiveness of those little men who shouted from sugar-boxes in Hyde Park to realise how secure England was from disintegration. Everybody knew that they were paid by the Russians anyhow.

Mrs Brodie looked at her mistress's gentle, pale face and pleasant smile and, for one wild instant, contemplated telling her about her sister's gall-stones and Mr Brodie's imminent and probably final stroke and imploring her to cancel her dinner-party for tonight. The impulse died as soon as it was born and she found herself trembling at her temerity in even having thought of such a thing.

'Very good, 'um,' she said. 'We might start with cream of tomato' – Mrs Radcliffe nodded – 'then fillets of plaice?' Mrs Radcliffe pursed her lips thoughtfully and then shook her head. 'Lemon sole,' she said. Mrs Brodie wrote 'lemon sole' down on a slate; the slate pencil squeaked causing Mrs

Radcliffe to draw in her breath sharply and close her eyes. Mrs Brodie went on——

'Rack of lamb, mint jelly, new potatoes, beans or peas?'

'Peas,' said Mrs Radcliffe laconically.

Here Mrs Brodie, having gallantly consigned her personal sorrows to the back of her mind and feeling oppressed by the uncompromising ordinariness of the menu, ventured a daring suggestion——

'I read a lovely new receipt for a sweet in *Woman and Home* the other day,' she said eagerly, doubtless feeling sub-consciously that the thrill of a new experiment might drug her mind into forgetfulness of her troubles '– it's called "Mousse Napoleon" and——'

Mrs Radcliffe cut her short. 'I would rather we took no risks tonight, Cook,' she said firmly. 'We will have Apple Charlotte and a baked custard for Mrs Duke who, as you know, has only recently recovered from influenza'; then, detecting in Mrs Brodie's eye a fleeting but unmistakable expression of defiance, she thought it advisable to show the whip, not use it, just show it. She laughed indulgently and with the suspicion of an edge in her voice said, 'We don't want any repetition of that unfortunate experience we had with the soufflé for Mr and Mrs Piggot, do we?'

Mrs Brodie lowered her head. 'No, 'um,' she murmured.

'Then that will be all,' said Mrs Radcliffe lightly. 'I shall be out to lunch.'

Mrs Brodie watched the door close behind her and sat down at the kitchen table. She felt low, dispirited, as though the hand of God were against her. It wasn't only Alice's gall-stones and Mr Brodie and the nuisance of Eileen having to be sent for and boarded and fed. Those were the sort of things in life that had to be faced. It was less than that and yet somehow more. Suddenly her whole being was shaken by a blind, vindictive hatred for Mrs Piggot. 'Silly old bitch!' she said out loud. 'Wisdom tooth indeed! I'd like to yank the whole lot out with the pliers!' In a moment her rage subsided and she felt ashamed. She sat there idly for a moment wondering whether or not it would do her good to give way and have a nice cry. She was a great believer in a nice cry from time to time when things got on her nerves, it sort of loosened you up; however, the fact that Mildred had been crying steadily for two hours dissuaded her. 'It would never do for all of us to be mooching about the house with red eyes,' she reflected. 'Whatever would happen if someone came to the front door! A nice thing that would be!' The clock on the dresser struck half-past ten, at the same moment Mildred came into the kitchen, pink and swollen, but calm.

'Cheer up, Mildred,' said Mrs Brodie comfortingly. 'There's just as good fish in the sea as ever come out of it. Let's make ourselves a nice hot cup of tea.'

5

After her successful interview with Mrs Brodie, Mrs Radcliffe went upstairs to put on her hat. She debated in her mind whether she should catch the eleven o'clock train to London which would get her to Charing Cross at twelve-five, thus giving her a whole hour to fill in before she was due to lunch with Marjorie and Cecil, or wait for the twelve o'clock which would get her to Victoria at twelve-fifty. She could certainly utilise that extra hour in town by doing Swan and Edgar's before lunch instead of afterwards, but on the other hand as she had arranged to spend the entire afternoon shopping with Marion anyhow, perhaps an hour in the morning as well might be too much of a good thing. Also, if she took the twelve o'clock she would have time to call in at the Orphanage on the way to the station and have a little chat with Matron. She made one of her characteristically quick decisions. The twelve o'clock.

Mrs Radcliffe's little chats with Matron took place on an average of about once a fortnight. They were unofficial and the other members of the executive committee, who met on the first Tuesday of every month, were unaware that they took place at all. If they had they might conceivably have been a trifle annoyed, people were like that, reluctant to take a practical personal interest themselves over and above their official capacities and yet oddly resentful of anyone who did. This regrettable human weakness was clearly recognised by both Matron and Mrs Radcliffe, and, without saying so in so many words, they had tacitly agreed upon a policy of discreet silence. As Matron boldly remarked one day, 'What the eye doesn't see the heart doesn't grieve over.' These clandestine meetings were very useful to Mrs Radcliffe. The various tit-bits of information and gossip concerning members of the staff, the oddities of the children, etc. – some of them not always pleasant – all combined to give her a knowledge of the inner workings of the institution that came in handy at meetings. Had it not been for Matron she would never have been able to unmask that most distressing business last year of Hermione Blake and Mr Forrage, a hirsute young man who tended the garden and did any other odd manual jobs that were required of him. She remembered how, fortified by her private information, she had swayed the whole committee. Mr Forrage, due to her eloquence, had been summarily dismissed, while Hermione Blake, a sullen girl obviously devoid of moral principles, had, after a long cross-examination and ultimate confession, been justly robbed of her status as a prefect and forbidden, on threat of being sent to a Reformatory, to speak to anybody whatsoever for three months. This punishment had not worked out quite as effectively as had been hoped, for apparently, according to Matron, the girl, after moping and crying for a week or so, had decided to treat it as a sort of game and invented a series of extravagant gestures and signs that caused so much laughter in the dormitory that Matron had been forced to send her to sleep in one of the attics by herself.

A plump, spotty girl, Ivy Frost by name, ushered Mrs Radcliffe into Matron's private sanctum. It was a small room congested with personal effects. There were a great number of photographs of Matron's friends and relatives; a varied selection of ornaments, notably a small china mandarin whose head wobbled if you trod on the loose board by the table on which he sat, and a procession of seven ivory elephants on the mantelpiece, graded in size, and being led by the largest one towards a forbidding photograph of Matron's mother sitting under a lamp.

'Well, Ivy,' said Mrs Radcliffe benevolently as she ensconced herself in a creaking cane armchair by the fireplace and loosened her furs, 'and how are you?'

'Very well, thank you, mum.'

'That's right.' Mrs Radcliffe put her head a little to one side and scrutinised her through half-closed eyes as though measuring the perspective in a water-colour with which she was not completely satisfied.

'Your spots seem to be worse than ever,' she said.

Ivy blushed and looked down. Her spots were the curse of her existence. Nothing she did for them seemed to do any good. A whole pot of cuticura ointment in three weeks, to say nothing of hot compresses and boracic powder, had achieved no signs of improvement; on the contrary, two new ones had appeared within the last few days, one small, on her chin, and the other large, on the side of her nose. She had been teased about them a good deal by the other girls, Mabel Worsley in particular, who, on one occasion, had persuaded all her dormitory mates to shrink away from her shielding their faces with their hands for fear of contamination. This joke had lasted a long while and provided much merriment. Mrs Radcliffe went on, kindly, but with a note of reproof, 'You're at an age now when you should take an interest in your appearance. I expect you eat too many sweets and don't take enough exercise – isn't that so?'

'Yes, mum,' muttered Ivy, her eyes still fixed on the carpet.

'Well there you are then,' said Mrs Radcliffe with finality.

Ivy shifted her feet unhappily. It was not true that she had been eating too many sweets. No sweet had crossed her lips for months. Nor was it true that she didn't take enough exercise. She took as much exercise as the other girls and, being a member of the hockey team, more than a great many of them. But she had learned from bitter experience that it was never any use denying anything to those in authority. Authority was always in the right and you were always in the wrong. Much better keep quiet and say as little as possible.

Mrs Radcliffe, feeling that further discussion would be unproductive, spoke the longed-for words of dismissal:

'Run along now, child, and tell Matron I'm here.'

Ivy darted to the door with alacrity and vanished through it, but not quickly enough to escape Mrs Radcliffe's parting shot – 'And the next time I come I expect to see a nice, clean, healthy skin!'

Ivy, safely in the passage with the door closed behind her, contorted her face into the most hideous grimace she could manage and then, with a deep sigh, went off in search of Matron.

The Matron was a small, faded woman of fifty. Her sight was poor, which necessitated her wearing glasses with very strong lenses. These gave her a sinister expression which sometimes had a scarifying effect on the smaller children. However, she was a kind enough creature on the whole, that is to say as kind as it is possible to be without imagination. This deficiency occasionally caused her to be crueller in the discharging of her duties than she really intended to be. A few of her charges liked her, the majority tolerated her, while only a very small number actually detested her.

She was in the middle of her weekly locker inspection when Ivy Frost burst in and told her that Mrs Radcliffe had arrived, and notwithstanding the fact that she had just found a lipstick together with a packet of 'papier poudré' in Beryl Carter's locker, cunningly concealed in the leg of a pair of combinations, and had already sent for Beryl in order to confront her with her guilt, she immediately decided that, shocking and urgent though the matter undoubtedly was, it would have to be dealt with later. Mrs Radcliffe, not only in her capacity as vice-president, but by virtue of her social position in the town, was not the sort of person to be kept waiting for a moment. Also her visits were a great pleasure to Matron. It was, indeed, flattering to be on terms of almost conspiratorial intimacy with anyone so aristocratic and imposing. She hurried along the passages and down the stairs with the eagerness of a romantic girl on the way to meet her lover. By the time she arrived she was quite breathless. Mrs Radcliffe shook hands cordially, but without rising, Matron pulled the chair away from her writing-desk and sat down on it, quite close to her visitor as though to emphasise the confidential character of the interview.

'Well, well, well,' she said, flushing with pleasure. 'This *is* a nice surprise!'

'I am on my way up to town,' said Mrs Radcliffe, 'to lunch with my daughter and her husband and do a little shopping, and I thought, as I had a little time to spare, I would drop in and ask you if everything was running smoothly and satisfactorily.'

Matron smiled deprecatingly and replied in a tone of bright resignation:

'As well as can be expected.'

'You look a little tired, Matron. I hope you haven't been overdoing it?'

'Oh no, Mrs Radcliffe.' Matron shook her head. 'Of course, there *is* a lot to be done and with such a small staff we all get a bit fagged sometimes, but still it's no use complaining, is it? After all, that's what we're here for.'

Mrs Radcliffe smiled understandingly and there was silence for a moment. These preliminaries had by now become almost a ritual, the actual phrasing might vary with different visits, but the essence remained the same. Mrs Radcliffe was always on her way to somewhere else and just happened to drop in casually, and Matron was always overcome with flattered surprise. Mrs Radcliffe unfailingly commented upon Matron's tiredness, and Matron invariably denied it with an air of gallant stoicism. This over, they wasted no time in getting down to brass tacks.

'How is Elsie Judd?' said Mrs Radcliffe, lowering her voice and leaning forward in her chair, which gave an ominous crack as though anticipating the worst. The adolescent processes of Elsie Judd, an over-developed girl of fourteen, had been causing some anxiety.

'Better,' replied Matron, also lowering her voice. 'I thought it advisable to call in Doctor Willis. He examined her most thoroughly and told me afterwards that if we kept her quiet and watched her carefully for a few months it would all blow over.'

Mrs Radcliffe nodded approvingly. 'Is the new gardener satisfactory?'

Matron gave a little shrug. 'In a way he is,' she said. 'I mean, he keeps everything quite tidy, but he's very slow over odd jobs and, of course, he can't drive the Ford like Mr Forrage could.'

The truth of the matter was that Matron secretly regretted Mr Forrage. She often reproached herself for having divulged the Hermione Blake business to Mrs Radcliffe. There might not have been very much in it really, although everybody seemed to think there was, and if she had only kept her mouth shut, and perhaps spoken to Mr Forrage privately, a great deal of fuss and trouble might have been avoided. The new man, viewed as a possible menace to the chastity of the older girls, was, of course, as safe as houses! In addition to having a wall eye, he was seventy-three and suffered from rheumatism. This, together with his age, not unnaturally restricted the field of his activities somewhat. Running errands, chopping wood, and the various odd jobs of domestic plumbing and carpentry at which his predecessor had been so invaluable, were obviously out of the question. Apart from this, he was disagreeable, which Mr Forrage had never been. Yes, Matron definitely regretted Mr Forrage, and although nothing would have persuaded her to admit it to Mrs Radcliffe, whose moral indignation had been the cause of his dismissal, she made an inward vow to be a little more wary of her disclosures in the future. However, no major upheaval could possibly result from her discussing with Mrs Radcliffe the perfidy of Beryl Carter. On the contrary, Mrs Radcliffe's advice, which was always sensible and the epitome of kindly justice, might prove very useful in helping her to deal with the situation.

'I am very worried,' she said, lowering her voice still further, 'about Beryl Carter!'

Mrs Radcliffe rustled expectantly. 'Beryl Carter? Isn't that the rather fast-looking girl we had trouble with at the theatricals?'

'It is,' said Matron. 'And she's been a nuisance ever since. I don't know what's to be done with her, really I don't. Only just now I found a lipstick and one of those Papier Poudré things in her locker – wrapped up in her combinations,' she added, as though that made the whole affair more shameful than ever. Mrs Radcliffe assumed a judicial expression.

'How old is the girl?'

'Getting on for sixteen.'

'Hum——' Mrs Radcliffe thought for a moment. 'What was her mother?'

Matron had her answer ready to this, clear and accurate. She had looked up Beryl's dossier in the files only the other day. 'A prostitute,' she said. 'She died when Beryl was three. The child was looked after by a charwoman, some sort of relative I think, until she was eight, then she was sent here.'

'There's no doubt about it,' said Mrs Radcliffe sagely, 'heredity accounts for a great deal. You'd better send for the girl and let me talk to her.'

This was rather more than Matron had bargained for. A little wise advice was one thing, but a cross-examination in her presence might conceivably undermine her own personal authority, and in defence of her personal authority Matron was prepared to fight like a tigress.

'I don't think that would be altogether advisable,' she said, and observing Mrs Radcliffe stiffen slightly, added hurriedly, 'She's rather an unruly girl, I'm afraid, and she might be rude. I should hate there to be any unpleasantness.'

'You needn't be afraid of that,' said Mrs Radcliffe in a voice that brooked no argument. 'I flatter myself that I am capable of dealing with a child of fifteen, however unruly. Kindly send for her at once, Matron. We can decide what is to be done with her after I have talked to her.'

It may have been the unexpected peremptoriness of Mrs Radcliffe's tone, or it may have been that Matron, having passed a sleepless night owing to neuralgia, was inclined to be more irritable than usual that morning. It may have been the weather or it may even have been some obscure cosmic disturbance. Whatever it was; whatever the cause; what took place was shocking to a degree. Matron lost her temper. To do her justice, she felt it happening and made a tremendous effort to control it; but alas! to no purpose. She felt herself go scarlet and then white again. She was aware of a strange singing in her ears, of great forces at work, rumbling through the room, pushing her over the precipice. She looked Mrs Radcliffe fair and square in the eye and said, 'No!' Not even, 'No, Mrs Radcliffe.' Not even, 'I'm very sorry, Mrs Radcliffe, but what you ask is quite impossible.' Just a plain unequivocal, 'No,' spoken more loudly than she intended and without adornment. There ensued a silence so profound that even the infinitesimal creaking of Mrs Radcliffe's stays as she breathed, could plainly be heard. So charged with tension was the atmosphere that Matron felt numbed, robbed of all sensation, as though she had been electrocuted. She continued to stare at Mrs Radcliffe's face, because there didn't seem to be anywhere else to look, also she couldn't have moved a muscle if you had paid her. She watched a small nerve in the region of Mrs Radcliffe's right eyebrow twitch spasmodically and her expression of blank astonishment slowly give place to one of glacial anger. Still the silence persisted. From the world beyond those four walls, the ordinary, unheeding outside world, a few familiar sounds penetrated: the grinding gears of a car; a dog barking in the distance; a tram clanking around the corner of Cedar Avenue into the High Street; but Matron heard them vaguely, remotely, as though they belonged to another existence. She experienced the strange sensations of one who is coming to from an anæsthetic. That unutterable fatigue. That reluctance to take up the threads of life again. That deadly, detached lassitude. At last Mrs Radcliffe spoke. 'I beg your pardon?' she said, with such terrifying emphasis on the 'beg' that Matron jumped as though someone had fired off a revolver in her ear. Again, to her own amazement, anger seized her. How dare Mrs Radcliffe speak to her in that tone as though she were a menial? What right had she to come here and demand to interview Beryl Carter, or anybody else for that matter? It was nothing more nor less than an unwarrantable liberty, that's what it was. 'I'm very sorry, I'm sure,' she said, 'but I'm afraid I cannot allow you to interview any of the girls without the authority of the committee.' This was shrewd of Matron, although not an entirely true statement of fact. Mrs Radcliffe, as vice-president, was perfectly within her rights in asking to see any of the girls, and Matron knew it as well as she did, but Matron also knew, owing to Mrs Radcliffe's expansiveness on one or two occasions, that the committee would be far from pleased if it discovered that she was in the habit of making surreptitious visits to the Orphanage behind its back. Mrs Poindexter in particular who was also a vice-president and who, in addition, was well-known to be on far from cordial terms with Mrs Radcliffe, would undoubtedly take full advantage of such an excellent opportunity of attacking her in front of everyone. Mrs Poindexter had a sharp tongue as Matron knew to her cost. If anyone could floor Mrs Radcliffe she could. All this and more had already passed through Mrs Radcliffe's mind and, angry as she was, she fully realised that an open quarrel with Matron would be impolitic to a degree. There were other ways, she reflected, of dealing with a woman of that type. Matron, after all, was not indispensable. She was efficient within her limits, but she was certainly getting on in years, the committee might well be persuaded in the course of the next few months to replace her with somebody younger and more in tune with modern ideas of hygiene. Obviously, poor thing, she had been denied the benefits of breeding and education over and above the regulation course of hospital training, but still an ignorant woman, in such a very responsible position, was perhaps just a trifle dangerous? She was convinced that the Hermione Blake affair could never have occurred had there been a younger, more authoritative Matron in charge. Observing the palpable vulnerability of her adversary as she sat there opposite her, strained and tense on the edge of her chair, her eyes staring through her spectacles immovably, as though they had been stuck into them from the back, she almost felt it in her heart to be sorry for her. In fact, she definitely was sorry for her; poor stupid woman, having the impertinence to say 'No' to her in that shrill hysterical voice, the temerity of referring to the authority of the committee! Authority of the committee, indeed! Mrs Radcliffe almost snorted, but restrained herself. She rose from her chair slowly and grandly, complete mistress of the situation, captain of her soul. 'Matron,' she said, and Matron, also rising, quivered at the sound of her voice as a small fish will quiver when transfixed by a spear. 'I must admit I am very surprised, very surprised indeed.' She spoke evenly and pleasantly without heat. 'Not that you should consider it inadvisable to send for this girl when I asked you to, in that you are perfectly justified; after all, you are in charge here and I am sure we are all only too willing to accede you the fullest authority that your position entitles you to – but——' Here she paused for a moment and adjusted her silver fox – 'that you should adopt an attitude that I'm afraid can only be described as downright rude is quite frankly beyond me——'

'Mrs Radcliffe,' began Matron cravenly. The grand manner had triumphed, all anger had evaporated, all passion spent, she felt abject and ashamed – Mrs Radcliffe overruled her by holding up her hand and smiling, a smile in which there was worldly understanding with just a soupçon of grief——

'Please let me go on,' she said gently. 'The whole thing has been the most absurd misunderstanding. It was exceedingly tactless and foolish of me to suggest sending for Beryl Carter. I am sure you are perfectly capable of dealing with the matter as it should be dealt with. I was only that I allowed myself to be carried away by my very real interest in this Orphanage and all the young lives for which we are responsible. I only wish sometimes that some of my fellow-members of the committee felt as personally about it as I do, but doubtless they are too occupied with their own worries. But one thing I must say, Matron, before I leave, and I must go in a moment, otherwise I shall miss my train, and you really won't take offence at this will you? – you are a little touchy you know, sometimes——' She laughed lightly – Matron quivered again and braced herself. Mrs Radcliffe went on. 'It's this – I really hardly know how to put it – but for some time, and this I assure you has nothing to do with this morning whatever, for some time I have been rather concerned about you, in fact only the other day I mentioned it to Mrs Weecock and Doctor Price at the end of the meeting. You see,' here Mrs Radcliffe paused again as though really at a loss to know how to handle a situation of such appalling delicacy, 'you see, you really are a little old to be doing work which demands such an immense amount of physical energy. I am often amazed that you manage as well as you do – and I have noticed, especially just lately, that you have been looking very, very seedy——'

'I assure you, Mrs Radcliffe——' began Matron again, but once more Mrs Radcliffe silenced her – 'We were wondering whether it wouldn't be a good idea for you to have a little change,' she said. 'Of course, I haven't mentioned this in full committee yet, I felt that I should like to discuss it with you first – what do you think?'

Here it was, retribution, the axe! Matron saw it there above her head suspended by a hair. A series of sickening pictures flashed across her mind – a letter from the committee containing her dismissal with, at best, a minute pension. The dismantling of her room, the packing of her things. The confused squalor of her married sister's house at Whitby, she wouldn't be able to afford to live anywhere else. All very well for Mrs Radcliffe to talk about 'a little change,' she knew what that meant all right; the thin end of the wedge. She made a gallant effort to speak calmly, to prove by her perfect poise that she was in the best of health and fit to manage a dozen orphanages for at least another twenty years, but her nerves, which for a considerable time had been stretched beyond endurance, betrayed her. Her humiliation was complete. She burst into floods of tears. Mrs Radcliffe regarded her pityingly for a moment and then put her arm round her. Matron, her glasses misted with tears and knocked half off her nose by Mrs Radcliffe's bosom, was unable to see and could only hear and smell. She could hear Mrs Radcliffe's heart beating and her even, comfortable breathing, and smell a sharp tang of eau-de-Cologne and the rather animal, fusty scent of her fur. Presently she withdrew herself and dabbed blindly at her eyes with her handkerchief. She heard, as though from a long way off, Mrs Radcliffe's voice saying with a trace of impatience, 'Come, come, Matron, there's nothing to cry about. The whole episode is forgiven and forgotten.' Then she heard the shutting of the door and a brisk retreating step in the passage and realised that she was alone. Still sobbing, she sank down on to her knees on the floor, groping for her glasses which had finally fallen off entirely. The small china mandarin nodded at her.

6

Mrs Radcliffe walked to the station with a springy tread. It was a radiant morning. The air was balmy; the sun was shining and a procession of large white clouds was advancing across the sky. They looked beautiful, she thought, so majestic, so removed from the pettiness, the insignificant sorrows and joys of human existence. Mrs Radcliffe often derived great pleasure from the changing sky. Times out of number she had sat at her window just gazing up into that vast infinity and allowing her thoughts to wander whither they would, occasionally chiding herself humorously for the extravagant fancies that took shape in her mind. How fortunate to be blessed with imagination, to possess that inestimable gift of being able to distinguish beauty in the ordinary. Many of her acquaintances, she knew for a fact, hardly glanced at the sky from one year's end to the other unless to see if it was going to rain. She remembered once saying to Cecil, Marjorie's husband, who after all was supposed to be a painter, when they were standing in the garden one summer evening before dinner, that sunset and sunrise were

God's loveliest gifts to mortals if only they were not too blind to be able to appreciate them. Cecil had laughed, that irritating, cynical laugh of his, and replied that many thousands of people would appreciate them more if they were edible. She recalled how annoyed she had been, she could have bitten her tongue out for betraying a fragment of her own private self to someone who was obviously incapable of understanding it. On looking back, she realised that that was the first moment that she really knew that she disliked Cecil. Of course, she had never let Marjorie suspect it for an instant, and never would. What was done was done, but still it was no use pretending. 'Know thyself,' was one of the corner-stones of her philosophy. Poor Marjorie. Poor wilful, disillusioned Marjorie. That Marjorie was thoroughly disillusioned by now, Mrs Radcliffe hadn't the faintest doubt. Nobody could be married for seven years to a man like Cecil with his so-called artistic temperament, his casualness about money, her money, and his complete inability to earn any for himself, without being disillusioned. Mrs Radcliffe sighed as she turned into Station Road. What a tragedy!

Marjorie Radcliffe had met Cecil Garfield at a fancy-dress ball at the Albert Hall in 1930. She was up in town for a few days visiting a married school friend, Laura Courtney. There had been a buffet dinner before the ball, in Laura's house in St John's Wood, and Marjorie, dressed as Cleopatra, a very effective costume that she had designed and made herself, was escorted to the Albert Hall by Roger Wood, a cousin of Laura's who was in the Air Force. Roger was not dressed as anything in particular. He was a hearty young man and baulked at the idea of tidying himself up; the most he had conceded to the carnival spirit of the occasion was a false moustache and a dark blue cape lined with scarlet which he wore over his ordinary evening clothes. Marjorie had been rather bored with him and was much relieved when, upon arrival at the ball, they had been accosted in the foyer by a group of hilarious young people none of whom she knew, but all of whom seemed to know Roger. They were whirled off to the bar immediately, to have a drink before even attempting to find Laura and the rest of their party. Among the group was Cecil Garfield, and Cecil was dressed as Mark Antony. This coincidence provided an excuse for a great deal of playful comment from everybody. It would be useless to deny that Cecil looked very attractive as Mark Antony. His physique, much of which was apparent, was magnificent. He had a quick wit and a charming smile and Marjorie danced several dances with him.

At about three in the morning everybody, Laura and her husband included, adjourned to Cecil's studio in Glebe Place to cook eggs and bacon. It was there that Marjorie first realised that he was an artist. Now the word 'Artist', to Marjorie, held an imperishable glamour. She had long ago decided that a life such as her mother would have wished her to lead with a conventional husband, a cook and a baby, was out of the question. Marjorie wholeheartedly detested her suburban existence and, if the truth were known, was none too fond of her mother. Of this unnatural state of affairs Mrs Radcliffe was mercifully unaware, and if Mr Radcliffe occasionally had an inkling of it, he was wise enough to keep his suspicions to himself. Marjorie's predilection for the artistic life had originally started when she was in her 'teens. Miss Lucas, her drawing mistress at school, had, perhaps unsuitably, lent her *The Life of Van Gogh*. Profoundly impressed by this, Marjorie had gone from bad to worse. *My Days with the French Romantics*, *The Beardsley Period*, *Isadora Duncan's Autobiography*, and *The Moon and Sixpence*, had followed each other in quick succession. By the time she was twenty, she had assimilated a view of life so diametrically opposed to her mother's that existence at home became almost insupportable. She was an intelligent girl, however, wise beyond her years and practised in deceit. A certain proficiency in this direction being essential with a mother like Mrs Radcliffe, and with a secretiveness that could only be described as downright sly, she kept her own counsel.

When Marjorie first met Cecil she had just turned twenty-one. She was a tall girl with a pale, almost sallow skin, dark hair, and keen, well-set blue eyes. Her figure was good although, as Mrs Radcliffe frequently remarked, her movements were inclined to be a little coltish; however, she would doubtless soon grow out of that. With common sense unusual in one so young, she had faced the fact that, though she longed for it above all things, she had no creative ability whatsoever. This does not mean that she had not explored every possibility. She had written poems and begun novels – she had taken a course of line drawing at the Slade School, this only after a series of endless arguments with her mother, who had finally given way on condition that she travelled back and forth to London in company with Phyllis Weecock who was taking a stenography course at the Polytechnic. She had sat at the piano for hours trying to string chords together into a tune but alas, with no success, as she invariably forgot the ones she had started with and was incapable of remembering any of it at all the next day. She had, of course, made a bid for the stage, but on this Mrs Radcliffe had put her foot down firmly. Poor Marjorie. None of it was any good. Her musical ear was non-existent, her drawing commonplace, and her writing devoid of the faintest originality. However, undaunted by all this, she flatly refused two offers of marriage, one from Kenneth Eldridge, the son of one of the partners in her father's firm, and, worse still, Norman Freemantle, whose aunt, Lady Walrond, was not only the widow of a baronet, but owned an enormous mansion near Dorking and was as rich as Crœsus.

Mrs Radcliffe had risen above Kenneth Eldridge, but the rejection of Norman Freemantle went through her like a knife.

Cecil and Marjorie had sat in a corner together that night after the ball and talked. A few days later they met by the Peter Pan statue in Kensington Gardens and talked a lot more. They talked of literature, music, religion and morals and agreed on all points. Of painting they talked more than anything. Cecil's gods were Cézanne, Van Gogh, Matisse and Manet. He considered Picasso an intrinsically fine painter, but misguided. Cecil, when he talked of painting, betrayed his heart. Marjorie watched him fascinated. She noted the way his body became tense, the swift, expressive movements of his hands, how, when he was describing some picture that meant much to him, he would screw up his eyes and look through her, beyond her, beyond the trees of the park and the red buses trundling along on the other side of the railings, beyond the autumn sunshine and the people and the houses, beyond the present into the future. It was himself he was staring at through those half-closed eyes, himself having painted a successful picture, several successful pictures. Not successful from other people's point of view, perhaps, but from his own. It was when she first saw him like that, unselfconscious, almost arrogant, demanding so much of life and of himself and of anybody who had anything to do with him, that she knew she loved him. More than this, she knew that she could help him and comfort him and look after him. At last she had found someone in whom she could sublimate her passionate, unresolved yearning for creativeness. Five months later she had crept out of the house early on a bleak wet morning in February, travelled to London by the seven-forty-five train, met him under the clock at Victoria station and married him at nine-thirty at a Register Office in Fulham.

Needless to relate, this insane headstrong gesture left a wake of sorrow and suffering in the Radcliffe household only comparable to the darkest moments of Greek tragedy. However, after bitter letters had been exchanged and after over a year had passed, during which time Marjorie and Cecil

had endured a penurious hand-to-mouth existence in a small
flat in Yeoman's Row, a fortunate miscarriage of Marjorie's,
if such an inefficient catastrophe could ever be called fortunate, and her subsequent illness, had at last effected a reunion.
Mrs Radcliffe had come to London. Still grieving, still
shocked by filial ingratitude, still licking the wounds in her
mother's heart, nevertheless she came. About a month later it
was arranged that Mr Radcliffe should resume the small
allowance that he had given to his daughter before her
disastrous marriage. This generosity undoubtedly owed
something to a remark of Mrs Poindexter's at a bridge party,
when she was heard to say loudly to Mrs Newcombe that the
manners and cruelty of the Radcliffes in permitting their only
child to live in abject poverty was nothing short of medieval.

All this had taken place six years ago. Since then the
allowance had been raised, on the stubborn insistence of Mr
Radcliffe, to almost double. Consequently, the Garfields were
enabled to live in comparative comfort in a small house
behind Sloane Square with a studio at the back converted, at
certain expense, from a conservatory.

The fact that Cecil only very rarely managed to sell a picture
was a source of great irritation to Mrs Radcliffe. Having at
last, soothed by the passage of time, consented to bury the
hatchet and accept her artistic son-in-law, it was extremely
frustrating not to be able to refer to his work with any conviction. To say 'My son-in-law is quite a well-known painter,
you know,' was one thing, but it was quite another to say,
'My son-in-law is a painter,' and upon being asked what kind
of a painter, to be unable to explain. If only he would do
portraits that had some resemblance to the sitter, or land-
scapes which gave some indication, however faint, of what
they were supposed to be. It was all very fine to argue that a
painter painted through his own eyes and nobody else's, and
that what was green to one person might very possibly be
bright pink to another. All that sort of talk smacked of

affectation and highbrowism. What was good enough for Landseer and Alma-Tadema was good enough for Mrs Radcliffe, and, she would have thought, good enough for anybody who had their heads screwed on the right way.

With these reflections she settled herself into the corner seat of a first-class compartment and opened a copy of *Vogue* that she had bought at the bookstall. Just at the instant of the train's starting three people clambered into the carriage. Now it is an odd frailty in the human character that however benevolent and kindly you may be by nature, the influx of strangers into an empty compartment that you have already made your own by getting there first, is very annoying. Mrs Radcliffe was no exception to this rule. She looked up testily and was shocked to observe that the interlopers, apart from the initial tiresomeness of their interloping, were quite obviously of the lower classes. Now one of the reasons that Mrs Radcliffe, who was naturally thrifty, always paid without regret the extra money for a first-class ticket instead of a third, was in order to avoid contact with the lower classes. Not that she had anything against the lower classes, she hadn't. She defied anyone to be more democratic-spirited, to have a warmer, more genuine sympathy and understanding for those who happened to be in less fortunate circumstances than herself. But when she bought a first-class ticket she demanded the first-class privileges that the ticket entitled her to. Therefore she was perfectly justified in regarding these three most unprepossessing-looking people with marked disapproval. The man, who wore a cloth cap and a dirty handkerchief round his neck, was smoking a cigarette. The woman, probably his wife, was pasty and dressed in a shabby grey coat and skirt, a pink blouse, a mustard-coloured beret and black button boots. The third interloper was a boy of about eleven. He had no hat, unbrushed hair, a sore on his lip and a long mackintosh with one of the pockets hanging out.

Mrs Radcliffe gathered herself together. 'I think you

have made a mistake,' she said. 'This is a first-class carriage.'

The man and woman looked guilty. The little boy didn't look anything at all, he just stared at her. The woman spoke in a husky, whining voice.

'The third class is full,' she said. 'If we 'adn't of 'opped in 'ere double-quick we'd 'ave missed the train.'

'In that case,' said Mrs Radcliffe, 'you will be able to get out at the next station and change.'

'I don't see 'ow it's any of your business any'ow,' muttered the man sullenly.

Mrs Radcliffe ignored him and looked out of the window. There was silence for a moment which was broken by the little boy saying loudly, ' 'Oo does she think she is ?'

The woman giggled.

'Never you mind,' she said. 'The Queen of Roumania as like as not!'

'Shut up!' said the man. There was another pause and then the woman spoke again. 'I will say it's a treat to be able to take yer weight off yer feet for a minute,' she murmured. 'I'm worn out and that's a fact.'

'Shut up grumbling,' said the man.

'I wasn't grumbling,' she replied with spirit. 'Just talking to pass the time.' The man shot a baleful glance at Mrs Radcliffe. 'Well, pass the time some other way,' he said, 'you might upset 'er ladyship.'

Mrs Radcliffe peered out of the window as though she had suddenly recognised a horse that was grazing in a field.

'That would never do,' said the woman with another giggle. 'She might 'ave us sent to jail, I shouldn't wonder. Be quiet, Ernie, and stop fiddling with that mac, you'll 'ave the button off in a minute.'

Presently the train drew into a station. Mrs Radcliffe withdrew her gaze from the window and looked the man straight in the eye. He held his ground for a moment and then quailed. Nobody moved. The train stopped.

'I don't wish to have to complain to the guard,' said Mrs Radcliffe.

A thunderous look passed over the man's face, he spat out his cigarette violently so that it fell at Mrs Radcliffe's feet, then he jumped up.

'Come on, Lil,' he said. 'Look lively.' He opened the door and they all three clattered out on to the platform. He slammed the door and then pushed his face in at the window causing Mrs Radcliffe to shrink back.

'I'll tell you what your sort need,' he snarled. 'And that's a nice swift kick up the What's-it!'

The woman giggled shrilly again and they were gone. Mrs Radcliffe fanned herself with *Vogue*. What a very unpleasant experience.

7

When Mrs Radcliffe arrived, Marjorie opened the door to her herself. They had a maid but she was in the kitchen preparing the lunch. Cecil was still working in the studio and so Marjorie and her mother sat in the drawing-room to wait for him. The drawing-room was on the ground floor and the dining-room opened out of it. The house was small and rather dark and smelt of cooking. Marjorie had tried to mitigate it by burning some scent in a heated iron spoon, but she had done this a little too early, and by now the scent had mostly evaporated whereas the cooking had not. Mrs Radcliffe glanced around the room with a scarcely perceptible sigh of regret. It was simply furnished and neat enough, and there was a profusion of flowers, Marjorie's one extravagance was flowers, but it was far, far removed from the setting her maternal imagination had originally painted for her only daughter. Mrs Radcliffe looked at her only daughter curled up in the corner of the sofa, so unlike her in every respect, with her dark cropped hair, her large horn-rimmed glasses and her serviceable oatmeal-coloured frock over which she wore a flamboyant bolero jacket of bright scarlet, and marvelled that from her loins should ever have sprung such a baffling disappointment. Marjorie at the same time was observing her mother with equal wonderment. It was always like this. They always met as strangers, and it usually took quite a while to establish a point of contact. Mrs Radcliffe's visits were fortunately rare. Marjorie wholeheartedly dreaded them, and it is possible that her mother did too, but immutable forces insisted on them taking place. It is doubtful whether Marjorie would have shed a tear had she been told that she was never going to set eyes on her mother again. It is also doubtful whether Mrs Radcliffe would have minded much either. She would shed a tear certainly, many tears. She would be, for a time, inconsolable, but genuine grief, the desolate heart, would be lacking.

'How's father?' asked Marjorie.

'Very well indeed. He had one of his liver attacks last week but it didn't last long. He made a great fuss about it, you know what father is.'

Marjorie nodded understandingly, the ice thawed slightly in the warmth of their both knowing what father was. Marjorie jumped up from the sofa and went over to a table by the window.

'Let's have some sherry,' she said. 'Cecil will be here in a minute.' She poured out two glasses and brought them over carefully. 'I'm afraid I've filled them rather too full.'

Mrs Radcliffe took hers and held it away from her for the first sip in case a drop should fall on her knees.

'How is Cecil?'

'Bright as a button. He's been working like a dog for the last two weeks.'

'Really?' The vision of Cecil working like a dog did not impress Mrs Radcliffe. In the first place she didn't believe it.

She didn't consider that painting away in that studio constituted work at all. It was just dabbing about. Cecil, as far as she could see, spent his whole life dabbing about. She naturally didn't say this to Marjorie. Marjorie was inclined to be over-vehement in defence of her husband's activities.

'Has he managed to sell any more pictures lately?' she enquired. The 'any more' was purely courtesy. As far as she could remember Cecil had only sold one picture in the last eighteen months and for that he had received only twenty pounds.

An expression of irritation passed over Marjorie's face, but she answered amiably enough. 'He's planning to have an exhibition in June. Lady Bethel is lending him her house for it.'

This caused Mrs Radcliffe to sit up as Marjorie had intended that it should.

'Is that the Lady Bethel who organised that charity pageant just before Christmas?'

'Yes,' said Marjorie. 'She's a darling, there was a lovely picture of her in the *Tatler* last week: going to a Court ball,' she added wickedly.

Mrs Radcliffe was clearly puzzled. Lady Bethel was certainly an important figure. If she was willing to lend her house for an exhibition of Cecil's paintings it might mean – here her reflections were disturbed by Cecil himself coming into the room. He had washed and tidied himself for lunch, but for all that he looked ill-groomed. His hair was too long, he wore no tie and there were paint-stains on his very old grey flannel trousers. He bent down and kissed Mrs Radcliffe on the cheek and then poured himself out some sherry.

'How are you, Marm?' he said breezily. He always addressed her as 'Marm' and there was a suggestion in his tone of mock reverence which never failed to annoy her. 'You look shining and beautiful.'

Mrs Radcliffe deplored extravagance of phrase. She answered rather tartly, 'Very well indeed, thank you, Cecil.'

Cecil came over and leant against the mantelpiece, looking down at her. She was forced to admit to herself that he was handsome in a loose, slovenly sort of way, but she could never be reconciled to that hair, never, if she lived to be a thousand.

'I've been telling mother about Lady Bethel promising to lend her house for your exhibition,' said Marjorie a trifle loudly.

Was it Mrs Radcliffe's fancy or did Cecil give a slight start of surprise?

'Yes,' he said with marked nonchalance. 'It's sweet of the old girl, isn't it?'

Something in Mrs Radcliffe revolted at Lady Bethel, *The* Lady Bethel, being referred to as an old girl, but she didn't betray it.

'It certainly is very nice of her,' she said. 'But she has a great reputation, hasn't she, for giving a helping hand to struggling artists.'

Cecil, disconcertingly, burst out laughing. 'Touché, Marm,' he said. 'Come along and let's have some lunch.' He helped her out of her chair with elaborate solicitude and led the way into the dining-room.

Lunch passed off without incident. The conversation, although it could not be said to sparkle, was at least more or less continuous. Cecil was in the best of spirits. He was extremely attentive to Mrs Radcliffe, always it is true with that slight overture of mockery, that subtle implication in his voice and his gestures that she was a great deal older than she was, and had to be humoured at all costs. He insisted, with playful firmness, that she drank some Chianti which she didn't really want, as wine in the middle of the day was apt to make her headachy in the afternoon. He displayed the most flattering interest when she described her visit to the Orphanage and the tact and kindliness she had had to exert in dealing with Matron, and when she told of her unpleasant adventure in the train, he was shocked beyond measure and said that that sort of thing was outrageous and that something ought to be done about it. During this recital Mrs Radcliffe observed that Marjorie was bending very low over her plate, and wondered whether her near-sightedness was getting worse. Although fully aware that her long experience and inherent social sense were responsible for the success of the lunch party, Mrs Radcliffe was not too occupied to notice that the soup was tepid, the fillet of steak much too underdone and that there was garlic in the salad. All of this saddened her. It was indeed depressing to reflect that Marjorie, with the lifelong example of her mother's efficiency before her, was still unable to turn out a simple, well-cooked meal. However, with her usual good-humoured philosophy she rose above it. It took all sorts to make a world and if, by some caprice of Fate, her own daughter had turned out to be one of the less competent sorts, so much the worse.

After lunch was over and they had had their coffee (luke-warm), in the drawing-room, Mrs Radcliffe expressed a desire to see Cecil's pictures. This request was made merely in the spirit of conventional politeness. She had no real wish to see his pictures, as she knew from experience that there was little or no chance of her admiring them. Cecil and Marjorie were also perfectly aware of this, but nevertheless, after a little humming and hawing Cecil led the way into the studio. Marjorie walked behind with rather a lagging tread. The untidiness of Cecil's studio always struck Mrs Radcliffe with a fresh shock of distaste. It was inconceivable that anyone, however artistic, could live and breathe amid so much dirt and squalor. The table alone, which stood under the high window, was a sight to make the gorge rise. On it were ashtrays overflowing with days-old cigarette-ends, two or three used and unwashed tea-cups, a bottle of gin, a noisome conglomeration of paint-tubes of all shapes and sizes, many of them cracked and broken so that their contents were oozing out and all of them smeared with a brownish substance that looked like glue, a pile of books and magazines, countless pencils and crayons and pieces of charcoal and, most disgusting of all, a half-full glass of milk, round the rim of which a fly was walking delicately. The rest of the room was equally repulsive. There was a model throne draped with some dusty material, a gas-fire with a bowl of water in front of it, in which floated several more cigarette-ends, two easels, several canvases stacked against the wall, a large divan covered in red casement cloth and banked with paint-stained cushions and a pedestal supporting a sculpture in bronze of a woman's breast. It was only by the greatest effort of self-control that Mrs Radcliffe repressed a cry of horror.

The picture on which Cecil was working stood on the bigger of the two easels in the middle of the room. It represented a man, or what passed for a man, sitting in a crooked rocking-chair without any clothes on. His legs, which were fortunately crossed, were enormously thick. Upon a slanting table at the right-hand side of the picture was what appeared to be a guitar together with a vase of flowers, a bottle and a fish. The paint on the canvas looked as though it had been flung at it from the other side of the room. There was not a trace of what Mrs Radcliffe had been brought up to recognise as 'fine brush work.' In fact there didn't appear to be any brush work at all. She regarded in silence for a moment and then shook her head. 'It's no use,' she said, trying to keep the irritation out of her voice. 'I don't understand it.'

'Never mind, Marm,' said Cecil cheerfully. 'It's not really finished yet, anyhow.'

'But what does it mean?'

'It's called "Music",' said Marjorie as though that explained everything.

'I still don't understand what it *means*,' said Mrs Radcliffe.

Cecil exchanged a quick look with Marjorie, who shrugged her shoulders. This annoyed Mrs Radcliffe. 'I'm sure you think I'm very ignorant and old-fashioned,' this time making no attempt to control her irritation, 'but I don't approve of this modern futuristic art and I never shall. To my mind a picture should express beauty of some sort. Heaven knows, there is enough ugliness in the world without having to paint it——'

'But we don't think that picture is ugly, mother,' said Marjorie with an edge on her voice. Cecil looked at her warningly. Mrs Radcliffe sniffed.

'You may not think it's ugly and your highbrow friends may not think so either, but I do,' she said.

'Our friends are not particularly highbrow, Marm,' he said gently. 'And as a matter of fact, nobody has seen this picture yet at all. You're the first, you should feel very honoured,' he added with a disarming smile. Unfortunately, however, the smile was not quite quick enough and failed to disarm. Mrs Radcliffe was by now thoroughly angry. The Chianti at lunch had upset her digestion as she had known it would and, having endured that inferior, badly cooked food and done her level best to be pleasant and entertaining into the bargain, to be stood in front of a daub like this and expected to admire it was really too much. In addition to this, both Cecil and Marjorie had a note of patronage in their voices which she found insufferable. All very fine for them to be patronising when they were living entirely on her money, or rather Mr Radcliffe's, which was the same thing. All very fine for a strong, healthy young man of Cecil's age to fritter his time away painting these nonsensical pictures when he ought to be in some steady job shouldering his responsibilities and supporting his wife in the luxury to which she had been accustomed. All very fine to allude to Lady Bethel as an 'old girl' and a 'darling' in that casual intimate manner and boast that she was going to lend her house for an exhibition of

Cecil's paintings. If Lady Bethel considered that that sort of nonsense was worthy of being exhibited she must be nothing short of an imbecile. In any case, she strongly doubted that Lady Bethel had promised any such thing. She recalled the swift look that had passed between Cecil and Marjorie before lunch, and the rather overdone nonchalance of Cecil's tone. The whole thing was nothing but a lie in order to impress her. The suspicion of this, which had lain dormant at the back of her mind throughout the whole of lunch, suddenly became a conviction. Of course that was what it was. A deliberate lie calculated to put her in the wrong, to make her feel that her criticisms of Cecil's painting in the past had been unjust, and to try to deceive her into the belief that he was appreciated and understood by people who really knew, whereas all the time he was nothing more nor less than the complete and utter failure he always had been and always would be. Mrs Radcliffe decided to speak her mind.

'Cecil,' she said in an ominous voice, 'I have something to say to you that I have been wishing to say for some time past.'

The smile faded from Cecil's face, and Marjorie walked across purposefully and slipped her arm through his.

'Fire away, Marm,' he said with a certain bravado, but she saw him stiffen slightly.

'I want to suggest,' went on Mrs Radcliffe, 'that you give up this absurd painting business once and for all and find some sort of job that will bring you in a steady income——'

'Give up his painting, mother, you must be mad!' said Marjorie angrily.

Cecil patted her arm. 'Shut up, darling,' he said.

Mrs Radcliffe ignored the interruption and continued, 'I have talked the matter over with my husband.' This was untrue, but she felt that it solidified her position. 'And we are both in complete agreement that it is nothing short of degrading that a young man of your age should be content to live indefinitely on his wife's money.'

There was dead silence for a moment. Mrs Radcliffe's face was flushed and the corners of Cecil's mouth twitched.

'I'm sure father said no such thing,' said Marjorie.

'Kindly let me speak, Marjorie.' Mrs Radcliffe looked at her daughter coldly.

'I think, Marm,' interposed Cecil, 'that anything more you said might be redundant.'

'Nevertheless,' went on Mrs Radcliffe, 'I would like to say this——'

Marjorie broke away from Cecil and came close to her mother. Her face was white with anger. 'You will not say another word,' she said. 'You will go away now out of this house and you will never set foot in it again!'

Mrs Radcliffe fell back a step, genuinely horrified at the passionate fury in her daughter's face. 'Marjorie!'

'I mean it,' Marjorie was clenching and unclenching her hands. Cecil stepped forward and put his arm round her, but she shook him off.

'No, Cecil, this is between mother and me. She says that for a long time she's been wishing to say those cruel, insulting things to you. Well, I've been waiting a longer time to say a few things to her. I've been waiting all my life and now I'm going to——'

'Darling!' Cecil put his arm round her again and this time held her. He spoke gently, but with an unaccustomed note of sternness. 'For God's sake don't. It won't do any good, really it won't, and you'll only regret it afterwards. Whatever you said she'd never understand, never in a thousand years.'

Marjorie looked up at his face and he gave a little smile, her lip trembled. 'All right,' she said in a low voice. 'You needn't hang on to me, I won't do anything awful——'

He let her go and she went quickly over to the window and stood with her back turned looking out on to the narrow stretch of garden that separated their house from the house next door. For a moment, while he had been talking something had pierced Mrs Radcliffe. She was shocked, outraged, angry; all that her affronted pride demanded her to be, but in addition to this, for a brief instant, the flash of a second, she had been aware of a sharp, overwhelming sense of loneliness. It passed as swiftly as it had come and she was secure again, secure in righteous indignation, wounded as only a mother can be wounded by her daughter's base ingratitude. She closed her lips in a tight line and surveyed Cecil and Marjorie and the studio and everything in it with an expression of withering contempt. Cecil put his hand under her elbow and piloted her to the door. 'I think it's time we put an end to this distressing scene,' he said. 'Come along, Marm, I'll see you to the front door.'

They walked through the yard and in through the french windows of the dining-room without a word. She collected her bag and fur from the sofa in the drawing-room.

'Shall I telephone for a taxi?' he asked.

'Thank you, no,' she replied with frigid politeness. 'I prefer to walk.'

He held the front door open for her and she descended into the street. A child bowling an iron hoop nearly cannoned into her. She drew aside as an Empress might draw aside from some unmentionable offal in her path and, with a barely perceptible nod to Cecil, walked away.

When Cecil got back into the studio Marjorie was smoking a cigarette. She looked swiftly at him as he came in at the door and noted, with a little tug at her heart-strings, that his face was white and drawn.

'Sorry, darling,' she said as lightly as she could.

He looked at his unfinished picture for a moment and then flung himself on to the divan. 'Well!' He spoke in a taut, strained voice. 'That was highly instructive, I must say.'

'Mother's a very stupid woman,' Marjorie said perfectly evenly, there was no anger in her any more. 'She doesn't know anything about anything. The fact that we're happy together infuriates her.'

'Are we!' said Cecil.

'Oh, Cecil!' Marjorie's eyes filled with tears and she turned away. 'How can you be such a bloody fool!'

'There's a certain element of truth in what she says,' went on Cecil, intent on masochism. 'After all, I do live on your money, don't I?'

'And why in the name of God shouldn't you?' Marjorie flared. 'What's money got to do with it? We love each other and trust each other, isn't that enough?'

'It would be nicer though,' he said with fine sarcasm, 'if *somebody* apart from you and Bobbie Schulter thought I was a good painter! It would be nicer, really a great deal nicer, if I could sell just one God-damned picture occasionally.'

'Oh, darling!' Marjorie came over and sat by him on the divan. 'Please, please don't go on like that. It's absolutely idiotic and you know it as well as I do. It hurts me terribly when you lash out and say bitter, foolish things that I know in my heart that you don't really mean. Look at me – please look at me and snap out of it.'

Cecil looked at her and made a gallant effort to smile. It wasn't entirely successful, but it was the best he could do. Marjorie flung both her arms round him and drew his head down on to her shoulder. She stroked his hair gently and he wouldn't have known she was crying if a tear hadn't happened to drop on to his neck.

8

Mrs Radcliffe's blood was boiling and continued to boil through several quiet squares and streets until she turned into Brompton Road. Here she stopped for a moment and consulted her watch which hung from a little gold chain on her

bosom. The watch said twenty minutes past two. Marion was
meeting her in the piano department at Harrods at half-past,
not that either she or Marion intended to buy a piano, but it
was as good a place to meet as anywhere else and less crowded.
It would never do for Marion to suspect that her blood was
boiling, because she would inevitably ask why, and Mrs
Radcliffe would have either to tell her or invent a convincing
lie, neither of which she felt inclined to do. She sauntered very
slowly towards Harrods in order to give herself time to deal
efficiently with her unruly emotions. It was no use pretending
one way or the other, she reflected. Marjorie was no daughter
of hers. This, of course, was rhetorical rather than accurate,
her memories of the pain and indignity of Marjorie's arrival,
even after thirty years, were still clear, but still the fact of dis-
owning Marjorie in her mind, of denying her very existence in
relation to herself, somehow reassured her. Mrs Radcliffe
searched in vain through the past to find one occasion on
which Marjorie had proved to be anything but a disappointment. Even as a child she had been unresponsive and sometimes actually belligerent. She recalled, still with a blush of
shame, the dreadful tea-party when Marjorie, aged four, had
spat a whole mouthful of Madeira cake at poor kind old Mrs
Woodwell, who had bent down to kiss her. She recalled how a
few years later she had, quite unnecessarily, been sick over the
edge of the dress circle during a matinée of *Peter Pan*. She
remembered the countless times during adolescence that she
had been rebellious, sly, untruthful and sulky. Heaven knew
it had been explained to her often enough and with the
utmost patience and kindness that an only daughter's primary
duty was to be a comfort and support to her mother, and a fat
lot of good it had done. Marjorie had never been even
remotely a comfort to her mother. On the contrary she had
been a constant source of grief and pain to her ever since she
was born. Then, of course, the secretiveness and cruelty of
running off and marrying Cecil without a word of warning,

turning her back on her parents and her home and all the love and affection of years without a regret, without a shred of gratitude. No, Marjorie was certainly no daughter of hers. Much better to face the truth fair and square. The reconciliation a year after the marriage had been a great mistake, she realised that now; in any case, the miscarriage and illness and everything had probably been greatly exaggerated in order to play upon her sympathy and get the allowance renewed. There was no love in Marjorie, no gentleness, no affection. That was what was so heartbreaking. If she had been merely self-willed and obstinate. If she had done all she had done and yet betrayed at moments just a scrap of sweetness and understanding, an indication that there was just a little soft womanliness in her character somewhere, then Mrs Radcliffe would have forgiven her and stood by her and done everything she could to mitigate the disastrous mess she had made of her life, but no, there was no love in Marjorie, not a speck of softness, she was as hard as nails. Better to cut the knot once and for all rather than compromise, rather than humiliate her spirit by making any further bids for a love and affection that, she knew now, had never existed and never could exist, and proceed in pride and loneliness to the grave. Mrs Radcliffe stopped by a confectioner's at the corner of Ovington Street and wiped away a tear, then she blew her nose and proceeded in pride and loneliness to Harrods.

Marion was dutifully waiting in the cathedral quiet of the piano department. She was the type of woman who is always a little too early for everything, not from any pronounced sense of punctuality so much as an innate determination not to miss a moment. Life to Marion was a glorious adventure. Her zest for enjoyment even after fifty-seven years of strict virginity was unimpaired. She had a small income bequeathed by her father, who had been a colonel in the Indian Army, the top part of a house in Onslow Gardens, a collection of theatre programmes dating back to eighteen ninety-eight, and a parrot called Rajah, upon which she lavished a great deal of brusque affection. She smoked incessantly and belonged to a small ladies' club in Dover Street which was rather dull, but useful to pop into from time to time and write letters. Her friendship with Mrs Radcliffe went back to their school-days and was based on romance. Adela Radcliffe, Adela Wyecroft as she had been then, had captained the lacrosse team and had been revered and adored by most of the school and by Marion Kershaw most of all. She still possessed a snapshot of Adela taken when she was sixteen, standing against a background of fierce waves, wearing a small boater, a white dress with high, puffed sleeves and holding an anchor. It was a striking photograph and although the dust of ages lay over the tears that Marion had once shed over it, she cherished it with a certain merry nostalgia.

Adela's attitude to Marion had been then, and was still, one of affectionate tolerance, not entirely free from patronage. In her opinion, Marion was a good sort, but rather a fool and definitely unstable emotionally. She could have married quite well if she had only concentrated a little more. Mrs Radcliffe could remember several occasions when a little common sense and proper management could have achieved the altar; that young Critchley boy for instance, he had been quite keen on her, and even Admiral Mortimer's son, although on the whole it was just as well she hadn't married him as he had had to be sent out of the Navy for something or other when he was twenty-four. But Marion was hopeless. She was always getting these wild enthusiasms for people and then dropping them like hot cakes. Look at that Sylvia Bale! A tiresome whining creature if ever there was one. Marion had gone on about how wonderful she was in the most ridiculous way and even went so far as to share a flat with her but not for long. Mrs Radcliffe remembered how she had chuckled inwardly when Marion, trembling with rage, had recounted to her the beastly behaviour of Sylvia Bale. Mrs Radcliffe had refrained from saying 'I told you so,' she was not one to rub it in, but she certainly had known all along and warned her into the bargain.

Today, Marion was at her most exuberant. She was wearing a tailor-made, none too well cut, a white blouse with rather an arty-looking coloured scarf tied in a knot in front and one of those new-fangled hats perched much too far forward. She was smoking, needless to say. Mrs Radcliffe was aware of the strong smell of tobacco as she kissed her. Marion, who had nearly finished her cigarette, couldn't find anywhere to crush it out and so before anything could be discussed at all they had to wander about among the Steinways in search of an ash-tray. This was typical of Marion. Finally, of course, she had to stamp it out on the carpet and one of the assistants gave her a most disagreeable look.

Marion was full of conversation. She hadn't seen Adela for ages, but not for *ages*! and there was really so much to tell her that she couldn't think where to begin. Mrs Radcliffe was really rather grateful for this volubility, for although by now she had regained complete command of herself and had contrived, at God alone knew what cost to her nerves, to present an outward mien as unruffled and tranquil as usual, the fact remained, she was still upset. However strong in character you may be, however bitterly you may have learned through sad experience to discipline yourself to withstand the cruel bludgeonings of Chance, you are after all but human. And Mrs Radcliffe felt, in justice to herself, that in view of all she had recently gone through, to say nothing of the courage with which she had faced to the full the whole agonising tragedy of the situation, she might be forgiven a little inward weakness, a little drooping of the spirit. There were not many mothers, she reflected, who were capable of cutting their only child out of their hearts at one blow and go out shopping with Marion as though nothing had happened.

Marion, unaware of the abyss of suffering so close to her,

continued to chatter like a magpie. 'You'd never believe it,' she said. 'But I did the most idiotic thing the other night. I'd been to the Old Vic with Deirdre Waters, you remember Deirdre Waters, she married Harry Waters and then he left her and now they're divorced and she's living with Nora Vines and they're doing those designs for textiles, some of them are damned good, too, I can tell you. Well, Deirdre arrived to call for me and kept the taxi waiting, fortunately I was ready, but she rushed me out of the house so quickly that I forgot to take my latchkey out of my other bag. Well, my dear, of course I didn't think a thing about it, it never even crossed my mind, how I could have been such a fool I can't think and, of course, when I got home there I was! Can you imagine? Thank Heaven it wasn't raining but it was bitterly cold and I was in evening dress with only that Chinese coat between me and the elements.' She laughed hilariously and went on. 'Well, I really was in the most awful state, I couldn't think *what* to do. I knew it wouldn't be any use banging on Mrs Bainbridge's window, she has the downstairs part you know, for even if I could have climbed across the area railings and reached it she'd never have heard, she's deaf as a post and sleeps at the back anyway. I was absolutely flummoxed. I looked up and down the street and there wasn't a soul in sight and then I walked to the corner to see if I could see a policeman. Of course I couldn't, you can never find one when you want one. I was in despair. I could have gone to the Club of course, but it would have meant waking up the night porter and I hadn't any night-things or anything and anyhow there probably wouldn't have been a room, it's awfully small you know. Then I thought of Deirdre and Nora, but you can't swing a cat in their flat and the vision of spending the night on their sofa didn't appeal to me very much I can tell you.'

She paused for breath as they turned into the scent department. 'Well – just as I was about to just sit down on the pavement and cry I saw a man, quite a youngish-looking man in a silk hat! I rushed up to him and I must say he looked horrified, but *horrified*! I daren't imagine what he must have thought but I explained and he was absolutely charming. He walked back with me to the house and my dear, would you believe it? He noticed something that I hadn't noticed at all. Mrs Bainbridge's window was open a little bit at the top! Well, what did he do but take off his coat and hat and put them on the top step and then climb over the railings and break into the house. I was terrified of course that old Mother Bainbridge would think it was a burglar and have a stroke or something but I couldn't help laughing. In a minute or two – I was shivering by this time as you can imagine – I saw the light go up in the hall and he opened the front door and let me in. Of course I asked him to come up and have a whisky-and-soda but he refused; then I helped him on with his coat and hat and off he went! There now. Wasn't that fantastic? I mean the luck of him just coming along at that moment. I couldn't get over it honestly I couldn't. All the time I was undressing and going to bed I kept on saying to myself, "Well, really!" ' The recital might have continued even longer if Mrs Radcliffe had not interrupted it by demanding of an assistant the price of a bottle of Elizabeth Arden vanishing cream. She had paid scant attention to what Marion had been saying, her thoughts being elsewhere. Even if Marion had known this it is doubtful whether she would have minded much. Talking, with Marion, was an automatic process like breathing. She didn't talk to inform, or to entertain, or to be answered. She just talked.

They visited several departments and made several minor purchases, Mrs Radcliffe leading the way, dignified and decisive, with Marion in full spate, yapping at her heels. When finally they emerged into the warm spring sunshine Mrs Radcliffe was feeling distinctly better. The business of pricing things and buying things had occupied her mind and soothed her. Marion of course was still talking – 'And when he walked up to the cage,' she was saying, 'Rajah put his head on one side and gave him a look and, my dear, if looks could kill that one would have! Needless to say I was *terrified*! You see he's always perfectly all right with women and of course he adores me but he hates *men*. Parrots are like that, you know, always much more affectionate with the opposite sex to what they are themselves; it is extraordinary, isn't it? I mean how sex instincts come out even in birds. Not of course that I ever look on Rajah as a bird, he's a person and a very definite person at that I can tell you. Well, my dear poor Mr Townsend said "Poll, Pretty Poll," or something and put his finger between the bars of the cage if you please. I gave a little scream. "Oh, do be careful, Mr Townsend," I said. "He takes a lot of knowing, he does really." "I'm used to parrots," said Mr Townsend, "we had one at Epsom for years." The Townsends live at Epsom you know, and my dear as he said it, before the words were out of his mouth Rajah bit his finger through to the bone! Now can you imagine?' Marion paused dramatically, this time evidently demanding some sort of response. Mrs Radcliffe looked at her absently and with an effort wrenched her mind from wondering whether it would be better to do Swan and Edgar's now or leave it until another day.

'How dreadful,' she said.

'I didn't know what to do——' Marion was off again having used Mrs Radcliffe's perfunctory comment as a sort of spring-board. Mrs Radcliffe, still undecided, led the way up Knightsbridge towards Hyde Park Corner. Perhaps on the whole it would be wiser to leave Swan and Edgar's until next week. She felt she really couldn't face the exertion of getting into a crowded bus and going all that way. The most sensible thing to do would be to have a cup of tea somewhere. Just as they were crossing Sloane Street Marion broke off in the middle of a description of Mr Townsend's obstinate refusal to allow her to telephone for a doctor. 'Adela,' she cried, 'I'd nearly forgotten. I'd promised to go to Maud Fearnley's shop just for a minute, it's only a few doors down and she'd so love it if you came too. She's the one I told you about you know, whose husband was killed in that motor accident, not that she cared for him very much, but he left her without a penny and so she started this hat shop. I do think people are awfully plucky, don't you? I mean it takes a lot of grit to do a thing like that. Anyway she calls herself "Yolande et Cie" and gets a lot of the newest models from Paris, at least, between you and me, I believe what she really does is to pop over there from time to time and just copy the models but for heaven's sake don't say I said so. She's a very old friend of mine and she really is having a terribly uphill struggle. Do come, she'd be so thrilled!'

Mrs Radcliffe hesitated for a moment and then, swayed by the thought of the obvious pleasure she would be bestowing upon Yolande et Cie by visiting her shop and also by the reflection that if Yolande et Cie was having such an uphill struggle as all that she wasn't likely to be very expensive and it might be possible to find a smart new hat at a lower price than elsewhere, she consented benevolently and they turned down Sloane Street.

Maud Fearnley was a vague, faded woman in the early forties. Marion's enthusiastic allusion to her pluck and spirit and her picture of her as a shrewd, capable business woman dashing back and forth between Paris and London, gallantly fighting step by step to conquer misfortune, was unhappily a trifle inaccurate. True she had been left penniless by the death of her husband and, bolstered up by the energy and financial support of a few strong-minded friends, she certainly had taken over the lease and 'good will' of Yolande et Cie, but for all that Maud Fearnley was not the stuff of which conquerors are made. She was a drifter. She had drifted into marriage, drifted into widowhood, and now she had drifted into a milliner's shop in Sloane Street. On the one occasion when she had happened to drift over to Paris, the results, commercially speaking, had been so far from successful that her friends had implored her never to do it again.

She rose from a small desk when Mrs Radcliffe and Marion entered the shop and advanced towards them with the incredulous smile of a lonely traveller who unexpectedly happens upon two old school friends in a jungle clearing. She embraced Marion gratefully and was introduced to Mrs Radcliffe. Mrs Radcliffe sized her up at a glance. Her quick eye noted the dejected beige dress, the blue knitted wool jacket slung round the shoulders with the sleeves hanging, the mouse-coloured hair and the amiable, rather silly expression. The woman's a fool, she decided immediately, probably another of Marion's ridiculous enthusiasms, likely as not they had both planned this casual visit to the shop in order to get her to spend some money. Mrs Radcliffe, in common with a great many other women of her social position, cherished a firm belief that there existed a sort of tacit conspiracy, among those not as comfortably situated as herself, to get at her money. This was not meanness on her part, she knew herself to be generous to a fault, it was merely a resigned acceptance of the frailties of human nature. No one could accuse her of being disillusioned. She was an idealist first and last but in her wide and varied experience of life she had been forced to admit that if you allowed people to suspect that you had an assured income it was often liable to bring out the worst in them. One of her complaints against Marion had always been that she never, if she could possibly help it, made the slightest gesture towards paying for anything. Not that she would have permitted her to for a moment, she was perfectly aware of her financial situation and anyhow to be paid for by Marion would have been somehow incongruous, as well imagine a bird of paradise being entertained by a woodpecker. No, it wasn't that she wished Marion to pay for a thing but if she just occasionally made the effort she would have respected her a good deal more. Now in this dim little shop, its whole atmosphere charged with genteel failure, Mrs Radcliffe scented danger. Mrs Fearnley's greeting of Marion had been a little too surprised, a tiny bit overdone. The whole thing had probably been arranged over the telephone that morning. To do Marion and Mrs Fearnley justice it is only fair to say that Mrs Radcliffe's suspicions on this occasion were unfounded. Mrs Fearnley had been quite genuinely surprised to see them come into the shop; in fact, poor thing, she was always surprised if anyone came in, and one of her fundamental weaknesses as a saleswoman was her inability to control it. She betrayed too desperate an eagerness, too flagrant an anxiety to please her infrequent customers. She wooed them and fawned upon them to such an extent that they sometimes left the shop in extreme embarrassment without buying a thing. Today, confronted by the majesty of Mrs Radcliffe she could hardly contain herself. She gave a series of little gasps and cries of pleasure and one of pain when she happened to pinch her finger in the sliding glass door of one of the show-cases. She showed Mrs Radcliffe several hats, offering them to her with the despairing subservience of a beggar displaying the stump of an amputated arm and imploring charity. Marion kept up a running fire of comment on each model as it appeared – 'There,' she said, 'isn't that sweet?' – 'Ah, now that one I really *do* like.' 'Look, Adela, at the way that's turned up at the back! Isn't that the smartest thing you've ever seen?' Mrs Radcliffe looked at them all but without enthusiasm. She even agreed to try two or three on after a lot of coaxing from both Mrs Fearnley and Marion. They both fluttered about behind her as she stood in front of the glass, heading this way and that and regarding her ecstatically from all angles. Finally she discovered one that really wasn't so bad. It was perfectly plain, which was more than could be said for most of the others, made of black straw with just one greenish-blue quill in it. It really was quite stylish. Mrs Radcliffe tried it on twice and then returned to it and tried it on once more. She revolved slowly before the mirror holding a hand-glass and scrutinising it from the back and from both sides. It certainly suited her, there was no doubt about that. The excitement of Mrs Fearnley and Marion rose to fever pitch. At last she turned to Mrs Fearnley.

'How much is it?' she asked.

Mrs Fearnley was foolish enough to shoot a triumphant look at Marion.

'Four guineas,' she said self-consciously.

'Four guineas!' Mrs Radcliffe stared at her as though she had gone out of her mind. 'Four guineas – for this!'

'It's my very latest model,' said Mrs Fearnley. 'It came over from Paris only last week by aeroplane.'

Mrs Radcliffe took it off with a gesture that implied that it could circumnavigate the globe by aeroplane for all she cared and still not be worth four guineas.

'I'm afraid that's far beyond my poor resources!' she said with a cold smile.

'Oh, Adela!' wailed Marion. 'It suits you down to the ground.'

'I would be willing to make a slight reduction,' ventured Mrs Fearnley.

'I fear that it would have to be a great deal more than a *slight* reduction to satisfy me,' said Mrs Radcliffe with an acid note in her voice. She had not failed to note Mrs Fearnley's exultant look at Marion before she had quoted the price and it had annoyed her profoundly. It was just as she suspected, nothing more nor less than a put-up job, she wouldn't be at all surprised if this Mrs Fearnley hadn't agreed to pay Marion a commission. A nice state of affairs when you couldn't even trust your oldest friends. It really was too disheartening the way people behaved, always on the make; it was degrading. But they would find to their cost that it was not so easy to swindle her as they thought. She looked Mrs Fearnley steadily in the eye. 'To ask four guineas for that hat, Mrs

Fearnley,' she said, 'is nothing short of outrageous. You know as well as I do that it isn't worth a penny more than a guinea if that!'

Mrs Fearnley, quailing before this onslaught, was about to speak when Marion forestalled her. Marion's face was quite pink and she looked furious.

'Really, Adela,' she said, 'I don't think there's any necessity to talk to Mrs Fearnley like that.'

'I resent being swindled,' said Mrs Radcliffe picking up her own hat and putting it on carefully in front of the glass.

'Oh, Mrs Radcliffe,' Mrs Fearnley burst out in horror, 'how *can* you say such a thing. I'm sure I never——'

'Well, really,' exclaimed Marion, 'I never heard of such a thing, honestly I didn't, never in all my life. Adela, you should be ashamed of yourself, honestly you should. I mean – you can't behave like that, really you can't——'

Mrs Radcliffe looked at her crushingly. 'Don't talk to me like that, Marion,' she said. 'And don't imagine that I can't read you like an open book because I can. I know perfectly well why you're in such a state. I'm not quite such a fool as you and your friend seem to think I am. I should be interested to know how much commission you expected to receive if I had been stupid enough to pay four guineas for this, this monstrosity.' There now, it was out, she had said it and a good job too. She looked coolly at Marion in the shocked silence that ensued and was gratified to observe that her eyes were filling with tears. Serve her right, that would teach her not to take advantage of a generous life-long friendship.

Marion, making a tremendous effort not to cry, spoke with dignity. 'If it was your intention to hurt me,' she said, 'you have succeeded beyond your wildest dreams. I am very sorry you said what you did, Adela, more sorry than I can say . . .'

'I must say,' interposed Mrs Fearnley, gaining a sort of bleak courage from Marion's obvious distress, 'I have never been so insulted in my life, never,' she said bridling. 'If it were not for the fact that you are a friend of dear Marion's, I should be forced to ask you to leave my shop.'

'I have no wish to stay,' said Mrs Radcliffe with hauteur, 'and I shall certainly never set foot in it again, nor, I assure you, will any of my friends.' She glanced at Marion. 'I mean naturally my real friends,' she added. 'Good afternoon.'

Mrs Fearnley and Marion watched the door swing shut behind her and her stately figure pace along by the window and disappear from view; then Marion gave up to the tears she had been so gallantly trying to restrain and sank down on to a small gilt chair with her face buried in her hands.

'Oh dear,' she wept. 'Oh dear, oh dear – how dreadful – how absolutely dreadful.'

Mrs Fearnley placed her arms round her for a moment and patted her sympathetically and then, with commendable tact, left her to have her cry out while she put the offending hat back into the show-case.

9

Those who knew Mrs Radcliffe only slightly would have been surprised, whereas those who knew her well would have been downright amazed had they chanced to be strolling through Hyde Park between the hours of four o'clock and six o'clock and observed her sitting on a seat, not even a two-penny green chair, but a seat, alone! Their amazement would have been justifiable because with all her failings, and after all Mrs Radcliffe was not perfect, she was no loiterer. One could imagine other people, Mrs Weecock for instance or even, on occasion, the redoubtable Mrs Poindexter, idling away an hour or so, but Mrs Radcliffe, never. Hers was far too energetic and decisive a character for it to be conceivable that, in the admirable organisation of her days, she should have an hour to spare. But there she was, sitting alone, leaning a trifle against the back of the seat, with her hands folded on her lap. She had taken off her glasses for a moment and on each side of the bridge of her nose there was a little pink line. Before her, in the mellow afternoon light, the unending pageant of London life passed by. Nurses with perambulators and straggling children; dim-looking gentlemen in bowler hats; a few soldiers arrogant in their uniforms; neatly dressed young women of uncertain profession; various representatives of the lower orders, their children making a great deal more noise than those of higher birth; occasionally somebody's paid companion walking along meekly with a dog, all parading before her weary eyes. In Knightsbridge the constant procession of taxis, private cars, lorries, bicycles and buses provided a soothing orchestration to the scene while every now and then a common London sparrow flew down from the trees and chirruped shrilly quite close to her.

Mrs Radcliffe however was aware of all this only subconsciously, her conscious mind being occupied, to the exclusion of everything else, with the cruelty and ingratitude of human behaviour. What a day! What a disillusioning day she had had, beset on all sides by ignorance, stupidity, defiance, deceit, rudeness and, in the case of Marion and Mrs Fearnley, sheer treachery. Why? she wondered without anger, she was no longer angry. Why should all this be visited on her? What had she done to deserve it? She put on her glasses and looked up at the sky, beyond which her indestructible faith envisaged a kindly God, in the vague hope that she might receive some miraculous sign, some indication of where she had erred to merit such harsh treatment. Perhaps, it was just within the bounds of possibility, she had unwittingly committed some trifling sin, some thoughtless act of omission which had brought down this avalanche of suffering upon her. She scanned the heavens humbly, supplicatingly, but no sign was forthcoming. True there was

an aeroplane flying very high over in the direction of West-
minster Abbey, and for a moment the light of the sun caught
it so that it shone like burnished silver before disappearing
behind a cloud, but that could hardly be construed as a sort of
reassuring wink from the Almighty. She lowered her eyes
again. It was, she reflected without bitterness, inevitable that
a woman of her temperament should feel things more keenly,
with more poignance than ordinary people. It was one of the
penalties of being highly strung. After all, that awareness of
beauty, that unique sensitiveness to the finer things of life,
had to be paid for. Everything had to be paid for. Your
capacity for joy was inexorably balanced by your capacity for
sorrow. It was all a question of capacity. Other people, such as
Stanley for instance, just existed. Stanley really couldn't be
said to live, really live, for a moment. Sometimes, she gave a
wry smile, she almost envied him. No ups and downs for
Stanley. No ecstasies, no despairs. Just an even, colourless
monotony from the cradle to the grave. How extraordinary
to be like that and in some ways how fortunate. Here she gave
herself a little shake, she was becoming morbid. It was surely
better to live life to the full and to pay the price, however high
it might be, than to be a drone without punishment and
without reward.

At this rather more comforting stage of her reflections her
attention was diverted by a handsome, well-dressed woman
in the middle forties and a distinguished grey-haired man in a
silk hat and frock coat, who sat down on a seat almost immediately opposite her. They were unmistakably of high
breeding, possibly even titled. They were talking with
animation and every now and then, obviously in response to
something amusing he had said, she gave a pleasant laugh.
Mrs Radcliffe looked at them with great interest. They had
probably been to some grand social function, a reception
perhaps or a wedding, although it was a little late for it to have
been a wedding. The woman's face seemed familiar to her

somehow, she racked her brains for a minute and then suddenly remembered, of course, it was Lady Elizabeth Vale, *The* Lady Elizabeth Vale, she was almost certain it was. Mrs Radcliffe made no effort to repress a feeling of rising excitement. Lady Elizabeth Vale was one of the most famous women in London society, or in fact any society. An intimate friend of royalty and the wife of one of the most brilliant of the younger Cabinet Ministers, she was well known to combine impeccable breeding with considerable wealth. She was much photographed and she travelled extensively. Her moral reputation was as untarnished as could be expected with such a glare of limelight beating upon her. Her most ordinary activities received the closest attention in the gossip columns but so far no definite hint of scandal had stained her name. It was possible that even if it had Mrs Radcliffe would have forgiven it. People of the social position of Lady Elizabeth Vale could demand from Mrs Radcliffe, should they so wish, an inexhaustible meed of Tolerance and Christian Charity. As she sat there watching the couple out of the corner of her eye, she indulged in a few fleeting fancies. That capacity for reverie so soothing to the bruised ego was strongly developed in Mrs Radcliffe. She often admonished herself with a lenient smile. 'There you go,' she'd say, 'dreaming again!'

Today, possibly owing to the disillusionment she had suffered, her imagination was especially vivid. The real world was too pitiless, too sharply cruel. Was it not natural enough that she should seek refuge for a while in the rich gardens of her mind? She gave fantasy full rein. How pleasant it would be for instance if Fate, in the guise of some minor accident such as a child falling down and having to be picked up, should enable her to establish a friendship with Lady Elizabeth Vale. It would of course begin quite casually. 'There dear, don't cry.' 'Poor little thing, I wonder where its mother is.' Something quite simple and ordinary like that. Then, the child disposed of somehow or other, a little desultory conversation during which Lady Elizabeth would swiftly recognise what a charming, delightful creature Mrs Radcliffe was and, with one of those graceful impulses that were so typical, invite her to tea! Mrs Radcliffe saw herself clearly ensconced in a luxurious drawing-room in Belgrave Square; discreet footmen hovering about with delicacies; the light from the fire gleaming on priceless old family silver; the conversation cosy and intimate——

'Dear Mrs Radcliffe, I know you'll think it fearfully unconventional of me on the strength of such a short acquaintance, but I would so like it if you would call me Elizabeth, Lady Elizabeth sounds so stuffy somehow between friends and I'm sure we're going to be real friends, I felt it at once, the moment I saw you——' Here Mrs Radcliffe paused for a moment in her flight to ponder the likelihood of it being 'Elizabeth' or 'Betty'. 'My dear Elizabeth'. 'My dear Betty'. Betty won. 'My dear Betty, of course I should be charmed, and you must call me Adela.' Her mind jumped to a Bridge party at Mrs Poindexter's which she had accepted for next Wednesday. 'I'm so sorry, I can't start another rubber, really I can't. I must fly home and dress, I'm dining with Betty Vale and going to the Opera——'

At this point her attention was dragged back to reality by the consciousness that a figure was standing close to her. She looked up and saw the most dreadful old woman. Mrs Radcliffe positively jumped. The old woman was wearing a threadbare jacket, a skirt literally in rags, gaping boots and a man's old straw hat from under which straggled wisps of greasy white hair. Her face was grey and her eyes red-rimmed and watery. 'Please, lady,' she murmured hoarsely, 'spare us a copper, I 'aven't 'ad a bite to eat all day, honest I 'aven't.' Mrs Radcliffe's first instinct naturally was to tell her to go away at once. These beggars were everywhere nowadays, it was really disgraceful. She glanced round to see if there were a policeman in sight and in doing so observed Lady Elizabeth Vale looking full at her. Automatically, without thinking, like the reflex action of a motorist who suddenly swerves to avoid a dog that has run out into the road, she plunged her hand into her bag and gave the woman a half-a-crown. The woman looked at it incredulously and then burst into a wail of gratitude. 'God bless yer, lady,' she cried. 'God bless yer kind 'eart'; she wandered away clutching the coin and still mumbling her blessings. Mrs Radcliffe, with a smile of mingled pity and good-natured tolerance, looked across at Lady Elizabeth Vale for her reward. They would exchange a glance of mutual understanding, a glance expressing a subtle acknowledgment of what had passed, of the bonds of class and distinction that bound them together. That reciprocal glance would imply so much, administer such balm to Mrs Radcliffe's battered spirit. Unfortunately, however, Lady Elizabeth didn't look at her again, she was immersed in conversation. After a little while she got up, her escort helped her to arrange her sable cape more comfortably round her shoulders and, still talking, they walked away. Mrs Radcliffe only distinguished a few words as they passed her seat. The man, placing his hand protectively under Lady Elizabeth's elbow said, in an intimate tone of mock exasperation – 'My *dear* Elizabeth——'

10

At a quarter to eleven that evening Mrs Radcliffe went upstairs to bed. The dinner had been a success on the whole, marred only by the clumsiness of Mildred who had banged against Mrs Duke's chair while proffering her the baked custard and caused the spoon, with a certain amount of custard in it, to fall on to her dress. Stanley had, as usual, not contributed very much, but the Vicar had been splendid, he had kept everyone highly amused with his imitation of Miss

Lawrence trying not to sneeze while she was playing the organ at choir practice, and, after dinner, he had sung 'Now Sleeps the Crimson Petal', by Roger Quilter, with great charm and feeling. Miss Layton of course had been rather silly, but then she always was, making sheep's eyes at Mr Baker all the evening and laughing in that affected way, as though he'd ever look twice at a dried-up frump like her. That dress! Mrs Radcliffe, as she was taking the pins out of her hair, paused for a moment to smile at the memory of Miss Layton's dress. It really was too absurd, a woman of her age, she must be fifty if she was a day, dolling herself up with all those frills and fol-de-rols. She'd have been much better advised to wear a plain black frock. Mrs Radcliffe remembered having whispered this naughtily to Mr Baker who had been on her left, and smiled again.

Presently Stanley came upstairs, she heard him go into his room on the other side of the landing. Stanley really was a very peculiar man. Fancy asking Miss Layton to play like that the moment the Vicar had sat down, indeed, before Mrs Duke had even left the piano stool. How unobservant men were. Couldn't he have noticed that the one thing she had been trying to avoid was the possibility of Miss Layton playing. To begin with she had a very heavy touch and no style whatsoever, also she always insisted upon the piano being opened fully which was a great nuisance as it meant taking off the shawl, the vase and the photographs. In any case it was quite obvious that she only wanted to play at all in order to make an impression on Mr Baker; however, she certainly hadn't succeeded. Mr Baker had paid very little attention, even when she had embarked upon 'The Gollywogs' Cake-Walk' by Debussy with all that banging in the bass, he had only nodded politely and raised his voice a trifle.

Presently Stanley came in to say 'Good-night'. She came out of the bathroom and there he was, fiddling about with the things on her dressing-table. Poor Stanley, he was undoubtedly beginning to show his age, she wished he'd learn to stand up a little straighter, stooping like that made him look much older than he really was. If only he had a little more grit, more strength of character. If only he were the sort of man upon whom she could lean occasionally when she felt weary and sick at heart, the sort of man who would put his arms round her and comfort her and bid her be of good cheer. But No; no use expecting any sympathy or demonstrativeness from Stanley. He was utterly wrapped up in himself and always had been. She had contemplated for a moment, while she was dressing for dinner, telling him about Marjorie's behaviour, but she had quickly put the thought out of her mind. Stanley always stood up for Marjorie, he would be sure to have twisted the whole thing round into being her fault and then said something sarcastic. He had one of those blind, uncritical adorations for Marjorie that so many elderly fathers have for their only daughters. It was sometimes quite ridiculous the way he went on about her. He even liked Cecil, and said that in his opinion he was a damned intelligent, straightforward young fellow. Straightforward, if you please! Mrs Radcliffe knew better.

Hearing his wife enter, Mr Radcliffe stopped fiddling with the things on the dressing-table and looked at her. She was in her nightdress and pink quilted silk dressing-gown; on her feet were her ostrich feather bedroom slippers, looking a trifle draggled; on her large pale face was a layer of Elizabeth Arden cold cream which made it even paler. Her grey hair was tortured into several large curling pins.

'Stanley,' she said. 'What a fright you gave me.' This was untrue. He hadn't given her a fright at all, she had known perfectly well he was there as she had heard him come in when she was in the bathroom, but still it was something to say.

'Sorry, dear,' he replied. 'I just came in to say "good-night".'

Mrs Radcliffe kissed him absently. 'Good-night, Stanley.'

This being said, she turned away expecting him to have gone by the time she turned round again, but when she did he was still there, kicking at the edge of the rug with the toe of his shoe. He looked at her again, his forehead was wrinkled, he obviously had something on his mind.

'What's the matter, Stanley?' she asked, a little impatiently.

'I think you were a bit hard on poor Miss Layton tonight,' he suddenly blurted out. 'Talking to Mr Baker like that all the time she was playing. She noticed, you know, and it upset her very much. I walked to the corner with her and she was nearly crying.'

'Really, Stanley,' said Mrs Radcliffe with extreme ex-asperation, 'you are too idiotic.'

'Idiotic I may be,' retorted her husband with unwonted spirit, 'but you were unkind and that's worse!'

Mrs Radcliffe opened her mouth to reply, to give full vent to the annoyance he had caused her, not only at this moment, but the whole evening long, but before she could utter a word he had gone out of the room and shut the door, almost slammed it, in her face. She stood quite still for an instant with her eyes closed and her hands tightly clenched at her sides. This was too much. At the end of a dreadful day like she'd had, for Stanley, her own husband, to fly at her and accuse her of being unkind. After a little she moved over to her bed, quivering at the injustice of it all. She knelt down automatically to say her prayers, but it was quite a while before she was able to will herself into a suitable frame of mind. Suddenly, like a ray of light in the dark cavern of her unhappiness, the incident of the beggar woman in the park flashed into her memory, and with that all disquiet left her. It was like a miracle. When she had finished her prayers and got into bed she was smiling. Unkind indeed!

Nature Study

THE heartiness of Major Cartwright had grown beyond being an acquired attribute of mind and become organic. He exuded it chemically as a horse exudes horsiness; as a matter of fact he exuded a certain amount of horsiness as well. He was large and blond and his skin was brickish in colour, the end of his fleshy nose shaded imperceptibly to mauve but not offensively; it blended in with the small purple veins round his eyes which were pale blue and amiable. His best point really was the even gleaming whiteness of his teeth, these he showed a good deal when he laughed, a loud, non-infectious, but frequent laugh.

The barman treated him with deference and he was popular on board owing to his genial efficiency at deck games. In the early morning and later afternoon he played Deck Tennis in saggy khaki shorts, below which he wore neatly rolled stockings and gym shoes and above a rather old blue silk polo shirt opened generously at the neck exposing a few curling fronds of dust-coloured hair.

He was at his best in the smoking-room after dinner, expanding into 'outpost of Empire' reminiscence and calling for 'stengahs', a bore really but somehow touching in his fidelity to type. It wasn't until after Marseilles, where most of the cronies had disembarked to go home overland, that he turned his attention to me. We sat together in the little winter garden place aft of the promenade deck and had a drink before dinner. The lights of Marseilles were shimmering on the horizon and there was a feeling of emptiness in the ship as though the party were over and there were only a few stragglers left. The stragglers consisted of about a dozen planters and their families and three or four yellowish young men from the Shell company in Iraq, who had joined the ship at Port Said and were going home on leave.

He talked a lot but slowly and with great emphasis, principally, of course, about himself and his regiment. On the few occasions when he forsook the personal for the general it was merely to let fly a cliché such as 'That's women all over', or 'A man who has a light hand with a horse has a light hand with anything'. I gently interposed 'Except with pastry', but he didn't hear. He suggested that he should move over from his now deserted table in the saloon and join me at mine for the rest of the voyage. I was about to spring to my usual defence in such circumstances, which is that I always have to eat alone as I am concentrated on making mental notes for a book or play, but something in his eyes prevented me, they were almost pleading, so I said with as much sincerity as I could muster that nothing would please me more, and that was that.

Our tête-à-têtes for the next few days were, on the whole, not as bad as I feared – he was perfectly content to talk away without demanding too many answers. By the time we reached Gibraltar I knew a great deal about him. He had a wife, but the tropics didn't agree with her so she was at home living with her married sister just outside Newbury, a nice little place they had although the married sister's husband was a bit of a fool, a lawyer of some sort with apparently no initiative.

The Major had no doubt that his wife would be damned glad to see him again. He was proposing to take a furnished flat in Town for part of his leave and do a few shows, after that Scotland and some shooting. A friend of his, for some unexplained reason called 'Old Bags', had quite a decent little shoot near a place the name of which the Major had as much difficulty in pronouncing as I had in understanding.

I listened to this conversation attentively because I was anxious to discover what, if anything, he had learned from the strange places he had been to, the strange people he had met, the various and varied differences in climate, circumstances, motives and human life that he had encountered. There he sat, sloughed back in a big armchair in the smoking-room, his large legs stretched out in front of him and a brandy glass in his hand – talking – wandering here and there among his yesterdays without any particular aim and without, alas, the gift of expressing in the least what he really wanted to say and, worse still, without even the consciousness that he wasn't doing so. His limited vocabulary was shamefully over-worked – most of his words did the duty of six, like a small orchestra of provincial musicians thinly attempting to play a complicated score by doubling and trebling up on their instruments. I wondered what he knew, actually knew of the facts of life, not complex psychological adjustments and abstractions, they were obviously beyond his ken and also unnecessary to his existence. But any truths, basic truths within his own circumscribed experience. Had he fathomed them or not? Was there any fundamental certainty of any-thing whatever in that untidy, meagre, amiable mind? Were the badly-dressed phrases that he paraded so grandiloquently aware of their shabbiness, their pretentious gentility? Did they know themselves to be ill-groomed and obscure, or were they upheld by their own conceit like dowdy British Matrons sniffing contemptuously at a Mannequin Parade?

I tried to visualise him in certain specified situations, crises, earthquakes, or shipwrecks, or sudden native uprisings. He would behave well undoubtedly, but why? Could he ever possibly know why? The reason he stood aside to allow the women and children to go first; the exact motive that prompted him to rush out into the compound amid a hail of arrows, brandishing a Service revolver? The impulses that caused his actions, the instincts that pulled him hither and thither, had he any awareness of them, any curiosity about them at all? Was it possible that an adult man in the late forties with a pattern of strange journeys behind him, twenty years at least of potentially rich experience, could have lived through those hours and days and nights, through all those satisfactions, distastes, despondencies and exhilarations without even a trace of introspection or scepticism? Just a bland unthinking acceptance without one query? I looked at him wonderingly, he was describing a duck shoot in Albania at the moment, and decided that not only was it possible but very probable indeed.

After dinner on the night before we arrived at Plymouth he asked me into his cabin to see some of his snapshot albums. 'They might interest you,' he said in a deprecatory tone which was quite false, as I knew perfectly well that the thought that they might bore me to extinction would never cross his mind. 'There's a damn good one of that sail-fish I told you about,' he went on. 'And that little Siamese girl I ran across in K.L. after that Guest Night.'

I sat on his bunk and was handed album after album in chronological order, fortunately I was also handed a whisky-and-soda. They were all much the same: groups, picnic parties, bathing parties, shoots, fishing parties, all neatly pasted in with names and initials written underneath. 'Hong-Kong, March 1927. Mrs H. Cufly, Captain H., Miss Fried-lands, Stella, Morgan, W.C.' He always indicated his own presence in the group by his initials. I need hardly say that W.C. figured largely in all the albums. He had the traditional passion of his kind for the destruction of life, there was hardly a page that was not adorned with the grinning, morose head of some dismembered animal or fish.

Suddenly, amid all those groups of people I didn't know and was never likely to know, my eyes lighted on a face that I recognised. A thin, rather sheep-like face with sparse hair brushed straight back and small eyes that looked as if it were only the narrow high-bridged nose that prevented them from rushing together and merging for ever.

'That,' I said, 'is Ellsworth Ponsonby.'

The Major's face lit up. 'Do you know old Ponsonby?'

I replied that I had known him on and off for several years. The Major seemed, quite agreeably, stricken by the coincidence.

'Fancy that now!' he said. 'Fancy you knowing old Ponsonby.' He sat down next to me on the bed and stared over my shoulder at the photograph as though by looking at it from the same angle he could find some explanation of the extraordinary coincidence of my knowing old Ponsonby. Old Ponsonby in the snapshot was sitting in the stern sheets of a small motor-boat. Behind him was the rich, mountainous coastline of the Island of Java, on either side of him were two good-looking young men, one fair and one dark and both obviously bronzed by the sun. Ellsworth Ponsonby himself, even in those tropical surroundings, contrived to look as pale as usual. The word 'Old' as applied to him was merely affectionate. He was, I reflected, about forty-three. He was narrow-chested and wearing, in addition to his pince-nez, a striped fisherman's jersey which was several sizes too big for him. The young men were wearing, apparently, nothing at all. I asked who they were, to which the Major replied that they were just a couple of pals of old Ponsonby's, quite decent chaps on the whole. They were making a tour of the Islands in Ponsonby's yacht, the noble proportions of which could just be discerned in the right-hand corner of the photograph.

'Never seen such a thing in my life,' said the Major. 'Talk about every modern convenience, that yacht was a floating palace; marble bathrooms to every cabin, a grand piano, a cocktail bar, a French chef – those rich Americans certainly know how to do themselves well. I ran across him first in Batavia – I was taking a couple of months' sick leave – had a touch of Dengue, you know, and thought I'd pay a call on an old pal of mine, Topper Watson – wonder if you know him? – used to be in the Sixth – anyway, he'd been invalided out of the army and had this place in Java, plantation of some sort, quite good shooting and some decent horses, unfortunately married a Javanese girl – quite a nice little woman, but that sort of thing gives one the shudders a bit – not that it was any of my affair, after all a man's life's his own to do what he likes with, still it seemed a pity to see a chap like old Topper on the way to going native.'

'Ellsworth,' I said wearily. 'Ellsworth Ponsonby.'

'Oh yes, old Ponsonby.' The Major gave one of his strong laughs – 'Ran up against him in the bar of the Hotel des Indes – got to yarning – you know how one does, and finally he asked me on board this damned yacht of his. By God, I hadn't eaten such a dinner for years, and the brandy he gave us afterwards!' Here the Major smacked his lips and blew a lumbering kiss into the air. 'We sat on deck into the small hours talking.'

I wondered if the Major had really permitted Ponsonby to do any of the talking. Apparently he had for he heaved a sigh and said, 'Damned sad life old Ponsonby's, he had a raw deal.'

As that did not entirely fit in with what I knew of Ellsworth I asked in what way he had had such a sad life and such a raw deal.

'Wife left him,' replied the Major laconically, pursing up his large lips and ejecting a smoke-ring with considerable force. 'God, but women can be bitches sometimes! Did you ever know her?'

'Yes,' I said. 'I knew her.'

'Ran off with his own chauffeur – can you imagine a decently bred woman doing such a thing? Old Ponsonby didn't say much but you could see it had broken him up completely – woman like that ought to be bloody well horse-whipped. He showed me a photograph of her, pretty in rather a flash sort of way, you know, the modern type, flat-chested, no figure at all, not my idea of beauty, but each man to his own taste. After we'd looked at the photograph we went up on deck again – you could see old Ponsonby was in a state, he was trembling and hardly said a word for about ten minutes and then damn it if he didn't start blubbing! I must say I felt sorry for the poor devil, but there was nothing I could say so I poured him out some more brandy and after a bit he pulled himself together. That was when he told me about her running off with the chauffeur – after all he'd given her everything, you know – she was a nobody before she married him. He met her first in Italy, I believe, just after the War, and they were married in Rome – then he took her over to America to meet his people – Boston, I think it was. Then they had a house in London for a couple of seasons and another one in Paris, I believe. Then this awful thing happened.' The Major wiped his forehead with his handkerchief, it was getting rather stuffy in the cabin. 'My God,' he said pensively, 'I don't know what I'd do if a woman did a thing like that to me – Poor old Ponsonby——' He broke off and was silent for a moment or two, then he turned to me. 'But you knew her, didn't you?'

'Yes,' I said. 'I knew her.'

2

Jennifer Hyde was nineteen when she first met Ellsworth Ponsonby in Alassio just after the War. She was staying at the Pension Floriana with her Aunt and a couple of girl cousins. Ellsworth was at the Grand Hotel with his mother. Old Mrs Ponsonby was remarkable more as a monument than a human being. Her white hair was so permanently waved and arranged that it looked like concrete. Her face was a mask of white powder and her eyes were cold and hard. Beneath her chin, which was beginning to sag, she wore a tight black velvet ribbon by day, and at night a dog-collar of seed pearls and diamonds. She sat on the terrace of the hotel every morning from eleven until one, lunched, rather resentfully, at a window table in the dining-room, retired to her bed regularly from two until four and then took a short drive through the surrounding country. She over-dressed for dinner and played bridge afterwards, wearing an expression of thinly disguised exasperation whether she won or lost. Ellsworth sometimes ate with her, drove with her, and played bridge with her. Whenever he did, the look in her eyes softened a trifle and her face relaxed. She watched him greedily, every gesture that he made, when he was shuffling the cards, when he was taking a cigarette from his elaborate Cartier cigarette-case and lighting it, whatever he did her eyes were on him sharp and terribly loving. When he was not with her he was usually with Father Robert. They would walk up and down the beach sometimes in the moonlight after dinner, their dark shadows bumping along behind them over the dry sand. Father Robert was plump with fine eyes, a thick, sensual mouth and wide soft hands which moved gently when he talked, not in any way to illustrate what he was saying, but as though they were living a different, detached life of their own. Jennifer and her girl cousins used to allude to him as 'The Black Beetle'.

Ellsworth had been converted to the Catholic Faith when he was nineteen. Oddly enough his mother had put forward no objections; in some strange intuitive way she probably felt that it would keep Ellsworth close to her, and in this she was right. He had always been emotional as a boy and this Catholic business seemed somehow to calm him, also it was an outlet that he could discuss with her without outraging any proprieties. She had hoped, in her secret heart, that once away from the strong guiding influence of Father Ryan in Boston, he might, amid the interests and excitements of travel, become a little less ardent; this hope, however, was doomed to disappointment, for on arrival in London they had been met by Father Hill; in Paris by Father Jules; in Lausanne by Father MacMichael; in Rome by Father Philipo; and here, in Alassio, by Father Robert. She had not really minded the other Fathers, in fact Father MacMichael had been quite amusing, but she quite unequivocally detested Father Robert. This was in no way apparent, as her Bostonian upbringing had taught her to control any but her more superficial feelings; however, the hate was there, lying in her heart, vital, alert, and waiting.

Ellsworth, even if he suspected it, showed no sign and continued to enjoy Father Robert's company as much as he could, which was a great deal.

Mrs Ponsonby first noticed Jennifer in the lounge of the Hotel, sitting with a young man in flannels and two non-descript girls. Jennifer looked far from nondescript. She radiated a clear, gay, animal vitality. She was wearing a neat white tennis dress and the ends of her dark hair were damp and curly from bathing. Mrs Ponsonby watched her for a little, covertly, from behind a novel; quick movements, good teeth and skin, obviously a lady, she smiled a lot and talked eagerly in a pleasant, rather husky voice. When she got up to go on to the terrace with the two girls and the young man, still talking animatedly, Mrs Ponsonby rose too and went up to her room.

From that moment onwards Mrs Ponsonby proceeded upon a course of stately espionage. Her sources of information were various. Mrs Wortley, who was a friend of Jennifer's Aunt; the English padre Mr Selton; Giulio, the barman in the hotel, even the floor waiter was questioned discreetly as his wife was a laundress in the town and dealt with the washing from the Pension Floriana.

In a few days she had found out quite a lot. Jennifer was nineteen, the daughter of a doctor in Cornwall, her name was Hyde. She was evidently not well-off as she had travelled out from England second-class, but she apparently had some wealthy relatives in London, had been out for a season and been presented. Mrs Wortley was quite enthusiastic about her. 'A thoroughly nice girl,' she said. 'Modern in one way and yet old-fashioned at the same time, if you know what I mean. I do think, of course, that it's a pity she puts quite so much red on her lips, but after all I suppose that's the thing nowadays, and one is only young once. I remember myself when I was a girl my one idea was to be smart. I remember getting into the most dreadful hot water for turning one of my afternoon dresses into an evening frock by snipping off the sleeves and altering the front of the bodice——' Here Mrs Wortley laughed indulgently, but Mrs Ponsonby had lost interest.

A couple of evenings later on the terrace Mrs Ponsonby dropped her book just as Jennifer was passing. Jennifer picked it up and returned it to her with a polite smile and, upon being pressed, agreed to sit down and have a glass of lemonade. She talked without shyness but also, Mrs Ponsonby was pleased to observe, without too much self-possession. Before she left to join her friends who were standing about giggling slightly in the doorway, Mrs Ponsonby had extracted a promise from her to come to lunch on the following day.

The lunch party was quite a success. At first Mrs Ponsonby had been rather disconcerted to discover that Ellsworth had invited Father Robert, but it was not very long before she decided in her mind that it had been a good thing. To begin with, the presence of Jennifer made Father Robert ill-at-ease. Mrs Ponsonby watched with immense satisfaction the corners of his mouth nervously twitching. She also noted that he didn't talk as much as usual. Ellsworth, on the other hand, talked nineteen to the dozen; he was obviously, she observed happily, showing off. The general narrowness of Ellsworth was not so apparent in those days, he was only twenty-six and had a certain soft personal charm when he liked to exert it. On this occasion he was only too keen to exert it. He discussed books and plays wittily with Jennifer, and whenever she laughed at anything he said, he shot rather a smug look at Father Robert. Altogether everything was going very well and Mrs Ponsonby's spirit purred with pleasure as she watched, with cold eyes, Father Robert's left hand irritably crumbling his bread.

About a week later, during which time Jennifer and Ellsworth had struck up a platonic, pleasant friendship, Mrs Ponsonby made her supreme gesture by dying suddenly in the lounge after dinner.

3

Jennifer Ponsonby was, to put it mildly, a reckless gambler, but her gaiety at the tables whether winning or losing was remarkable. She had a series of little superstitions, such as placing one card symmetrically on top of the other and giving the shoe two sharp peremptory little whacks before drawing – if she drew a nine she chuckled delightedly, if she made herself Baccarat she chuckled equally delightedly. Her luck, on the whole, was good, but she won gracefully, shrugging her shoulders and giving a little deprecatory smile when anyone failed to win a Banco against her.

It was the summer of 1933, and I had stopped off in Monte Carlo on my way home from Tunis. Everybody was there, of course, it was the height of the summer season. The Beach Hotel was full and I was staying at the Hotel de Paris which, actually, I preferred. Jennifer was staying with old Lily Graziani on Cap Ferrat, but she escaped whenever she could and came over to Monte Carlo to dine and gamble. I played at the same table with her for an hour or two, and then when I had lost all that I intended to lose, I asked her to come and have a drink in the bar while the shoe was being made up.

We perched ourselves on high stools and ordered 'Fine à l'eaus' and talked casually enough. She asked me where I'd been and whether or not I'd seen so-and-so lately, and I asked her what she'd been up to and what had become of so-and-so. Presently a chasseur appeared and said that her table was starting again. She slipped down from her stool and said, almost defiantly, 'You haven't asked after Ellsworth, but you'll be delighted to hear that he's very well indeed,' then she gave a sharp little laugh, more high-pitched than usual, and disappeared into the baccarat room.

I felt a trifle embarrassed and also vaguely irritated. I hadn't mentioned Ellsworth on purpose. (A), because it might have been tactless as I hadn't the remotest idea whether they were still together or not; and (b), because I didn't care for him much anyhow, and never had. I ordered another drink and, when I had drunk it, strolled upstairs to watch the cabaret. There was an inferno of noise going on as I came in, the band was playing full out while two American negroes were dancing a complicated routine in white evening suits and apparently enjoying it. I sat down at a corner table and watched the rest of the show. It was reasonably good. The usual paraphernalia of elaborately undressed beauties parading in and out. The usual low comedy acrobatic act. The usual mournful young woman crooning through the microphone. I glanced round the room occasionally. All the same faces were there. They had been here last year and the year before, and would be here next year and the year after. They changed round a bit, of course. Baby Leyland was with Georgie this year, and Bobbie had a new blonde. The Gruman-Lewis party looked tired and disgruntled, but then they always did. I felt oppressed and bored and far too hot. I watched Jennifer come in with Tiny Matlock. They were hailed by Freda and Gordon Blake and sat down at their table. It was one of the noisier tables. I think Alaistair who was sitting at the end, must have been doing some of his dirtier imitations, because they were all laughing extravagantly, rather too loudly, I thought, considering the hundreds of times they must have heard them before.

Jennifer laughed with the rest, meanwhile refurbishing her make-up, holding the mirror from her vanity-case at one angle in order to catch the light. Her movements were swift and nervous, she stabbed at her mouth with the lipstick and then, holding the glass at arm's length, looked at it through narrowed eyes and made a slight grimace. Suddenly, in that moment, I can't think why, I knew quite definitely that she was wretched. My memory ran back over the years that I had known her, never intimately, never beyond the easy casualness of Christian names, but always, I reflected, with pleasure. She had always been gay company, charming to dance with, fun to discover unexpectedly in a house-party. I remembered the first time I had met her in London, it must have been 1920 or 1921, the pretty young wife of a rich American. That was a long time ago, nearly thirteen years, and those years had certainly changed her. I watched her across the room. She was talking now, obviously describing something, gesticulating a little with her right hand. There was a moment's lull in the general noise, and I caught for a second the sound of her husky laugh, quite a different timbre from that which she had given as she left the bar. 'You haven't asked after Ellsworth, but you'll be delighted to hear that he's very well indeed.'

I decided to walk back to my hotel, rather than take a taxi, the night was cool and quiet after the cigarette smoke and noise of the Casino. I had nearly reached the top of the first hill when I heard a car coming up behind me. It seemed to be coming a great deal too fast, so I stepped warily against the parapet to let it go by. It came whirling round the corner with a screech of brakes, a small open Fiat two-seater. It stopped noisily about a yard away from me and I saw that Jennifer was driving it. 'I saw you leaving the Casino and chased you,' she said rather breathlessly, 'because I wanted to say I was sorry.'

I stepped forward. 'What on earth for?'

'If you didn't notice so much the better, but I've had a horrid feeling about it ever since I left you in the bar. I tossed my curls at you and spoke harshly, it's no use pretending I didn't because I did, I know I did.'

'What nonsense!' I said.

'Get in, there's a darling, and I'll drive you wherever you want to go – where do you want to go? I've got to get to Cap Ferrat.'

'Not as far as that anyhow, just the Hotel de Paris.'

I got in and sat down beside her. She let in the clutch and we drove on up into the town. The streets were deserted as it was getting on for three in the morning. Suddenly she stopped the car by the kerb in front of a sports shop; the window was filled with tennis racquets, golf clubs and sweaters.

'I'm now going to do something unforgivable,' she said in a strained voice. 'I've been trying not to for hours, but it's no use.' She sat back in the driving seat and looked at me. 'I'm going to cry. I hate women who cry, but I can't help it, everything's absolutely bloody, and I know it's none of your business and that this is an imposition, but we've been friends on and off for years and——' Here she broke off and buried her face in her hands. I put my arm round her. 'I don't think you'd better be too sympathetic,' she muttered into my shoulder. 'It'll probably make me worse.' Then she started to sob, not hysterically, not even very noisily, but they were painful sobs as though she were fighting them too strongly——

'For God's sake let go!' I said sharply. 'If you don't you'll probably burst!'

She gave me a little pat and relaxed a bit. Two or three cars passed, but she kept her head buried against my shoulder. I sat quite still and looked gloomily at the tennis racquets. I felt rather bewildered and quite definitely uncomfortable. Not that I wasn't touched, that out of all the people she knew she should surprisingly have selected me to break down with. My discomfort was caused by a strange feeling of oppression, a similar sensation to that which one experiences sometimes on entering a sad house, a house wherein unhappy, cruel things have taken place. I almost shuddered, but controlled it. Some intuition must have made her feel this, for she sat up and reached her hand behind her for her vanity case. 'I am so dreadfully sorry,' she said. I smiled as reassuringly as I could and lit a cigarette for her. She wiped her eyes, powdered her nose, took it and sat silently for a little – I noticed her lip tremble occasionally, but she didn't cry any more. Suddenly she seemed to come to some sort of decision and leant forward and re-started the engine. 'I'll drop you home now,' she said in a stifled voice which struck me as infinitely pathetic; there was an almost childish gallantry in the way she said it, like a very small boy who has fallen down and broken his knee and is determined to be brave over it.

'You'll do nothing of the sort,' I said quickly: 'You'll drive me up on to the Middle Corniche and there we'll sit and smoke ourselves silly and watch the sun come up.'

She protested, 'Honestly, I'm all right now – I swear I am.'

'Do what you're told,' I said.

She gave the ghost of a smile and off we went.

We stopped just the other side of Eze, left the car parked close in to the side of the wood, having taken the cushions out of it, and arranged ourselves facing the view, with our backs against a low stone wall. Jennifer hardly spoke, and we sat there for quite a long while in silence. Far below us on the right, Cap Ferrat stretched out into the sea like a quiet sleeping animal. Occasionally a train, looking like an elaborate mechanical toy, emerged from a tunnel, ran along by the edge of the sea for a little way and then disappeared again, the lights from its carriage windows striping the trees and rocks and houses as it passed. The rumbling sound of it came to us late when it was no longer in sight. Every now and then, but not very often, a car whirred along the road behind us and we could see its headlights diminishing in the distance, carving the darkness into fantastic shapes and shadows as it went. The path of the moon glittered across the sea to the horizon and there were no ships passing.

'I suppose it would be too obvious if I said, "Now then"?'

Jennifer sighed. ' "Now then," is a bit discouraging,' she said. 'Too arbitrary – couldn't we lead into it a little less abruptly?'

'How is Ellsworth?' I said airily. 'Or rather, where is Ellsworth?'

'Very well indeed, and in Taormina.'

'Why Taormina?'

She fidgeted a little. 'He likes Taormina.'

There was a long silence while we both looked at Ellsworth in Taormina. I can't vouch for Jennifer's view, but mine was clear. I saw him going down to bathe, wearing sandals, a discreetly coloured jumper and flannel trousers with a faint stripe. I saw him at lunch in the cool monastic hotel dining-room, talking earnestly with a couple of Catholic Fathers. I saw him in the evening, after dinner, sitting in a café with a few of the young locals round him, standing them drinks and speaking in precise, rather sibilant Italian with a strong Bostonian accent.

'He can't get sunburnt, you know,' said Jennifer irrelevantly. 'And he does try so hard. Isn't it sad?'

'Not even pink?'

'Only very occasionally, and that fades almost immediately.'

'Freckles?'

'A few, but in the wrong places.'

'How much does he mind?'

'Desperately, I think.' Jennifer sighed again, deeply. 'It's become a sort of complex with him. He has quite a lot of complexes really. The Catholic Church, Italian Gothic, Walt Whitman and not over-tipping. He's a beauty-lover, I'm afraid.'

'You should never have married a beauty-lover.'

She nodded. 'Beauty-lovers certainly are Hell.'

'Why did you?'

'Why did I what?'

'Marry him.'

'Hold on to your hats, boys, here we go!' She laughed faintly and said, 'I think I'd better have another cigarette, I'm told it gives one social poise. I'm afraid my social poise has been rather over-strained during these last few years.'

I gave her a cigarette. 'Why not begin at the beginning?' I suggested. 'You know it's all coming out eventually, you might just as well go the whole hog.'

'I wonder where that expression originated?' she said. 'It doesn't really make sense – you can't go a hog, whole or otherwise.'

'Never mind about that.'

'I don't really.'

'Why did you marry him?'

'I was an innocent girl,' she replied. 'When I say innocent girl, I naturally mean a bloody fool. I was ignorant of even the most superficial facts of life. Circumstances conspired against me – doesn't that sound lovely? – but it's honestly true, they did. I was in Italy, staying with Aunt Dora in a pension, and Ellsworth and his mother were at the Grand Hotel. They had a suite, of course, and as far as the hotel was concerned they were the star turn on account of being American and very rich. The old girl took a fancy to me, why I shall never know, and asked me to lunch, and there was Ellsworth. He really was quite sweet in those days and funny; he said funny things and knew a lot and was nice to be with. There was a priest there, too, Father Robert, who I suspect had his eye on the

Ponsonby fortune – some priests on behalf of their Church have a strong commercial sense – anyhow, he took a hatred to me on sight which I rather enjoyed. Then came the moment when circumstances conspired against me. Old Mrs Ponsonby upped and died of a heart attack in the lounge of the hotel just as we were all having our after-dinner coffee. It really was very horrid, and I was desperately sorry for poor Ellsworth. That was where the trouble started. Pity may be a Christian virtue, but it's dangerous to muck about with, and can play the devil with common sense. Well, to continue, as they say, from that moment onwards Ellsworth clung to me; you see, I had unwittingly and most unfortunately ousted Father Robert from his affections. He cried a good deal, which was natural enough, as he'd never been away from his mother all his life. I went with him to the funeral, which was pretty grim, and did my best to comfort him as well as I could. Then, the night after the funeral he suddenly appeared at our pension and said he wanted to talk to me. My Aunt Dora was in a fine flutter, being one of those nice-minded British matrons who can only see any rich young man as a prospective bed-mate for their younger unattached female relatives. I think she probably regretted that Ellsworth didn't want to talk to Grace or Vera, who were her own daughters – and God knows she couldn't have regretted it half as much as I did later – but still, I was an unmarried niece, and half a loaf is better than whatever it is, and so out I went into the sweet-scented Italian night with Ellsworth and her blessing. We walked for a long way, first of all through the town and then along the beach. Ellsworth didn't say much until we sat down with our backs to a wall, rather like we're sitting here, only without the view, just the sea lapping away and a lot of stars. Then he started. Oh dear!' Jennifer shifted herself into a more comfortable position. 'He told me all about himself from the word go, not in any exhibitionistic way, but as though he just had to get it out of his system in spite of caution and decency

and traditionally bred reticence – again like I'm doing now.'
She laughed rather sharply. 'I wonder why people do it? I
wonder if it's ever any use?'

'It's all right,' I said, 'when there are no strings attached.
'Don't get discouraged, it will do you a power of good.'

'You're very sweet,' she said. 'I do hope I'm not going to
cry again.'

There was silence for a few moments and then she went on,
speaking more quickly.

'I can't possibly tell you all he said, because it wouldn't be
fair. I couldn't ever tell anybody, but the main thing was that
he was frightened, frightened to death of himself. That was
why he had become a Roman Catholic, that fear. He wasn't
very articulate about it really, and he jumped from one thing
to another so that on the whole I was pretty bewildered, but I
did feel dreadfully touched and sad for him, and foolishly,
wholeheartedly anxious to help him. He said, among other
things, that he'd always been terrified of women until he met
me and that the thought of marriage sort of revolted him. Of
course, he hadn't had to worry about it much as long as his
mother was alive, but now he was utterly lost, he couldn't
face the loneliness of having no one. Father Robert had tried
to persuade him to join the Church in some capacity or
other, I don't exactly know what, but he fought shy of this,
because he didn't feel that he had a genuine vocation or
enough faith or something. He went on and on rambling here
and there. One minute he'd be talking about Father Robert
and how wonderful the Church was, because it knew everything about everyone, and could solve all problems if only one
believed enough. Then he'd jump back, a long way back, into
his childhood and talk about a friend he had at the prep school
called Homer – aren't Americans awful giving their children
names like that? – Homer was apparently very important, he
kept on cropping up. You've no idea how strange it was
sitting there on the sand with all that emotion and fright and

unhappiness whirling round my head. I was only nineteen and didn't understand half of what he was talking about, but I do remember feeling pent-up and strained and rather wanting to scream. Presently he calmed down a bit and said something about how terrible it was to live in a world where no one understood you, and that Society was made for the normal, ordinary people, and there wasn't any place for the misfits. Then, then he asked me to marry him. To do him justice he was as honest as he could be. He said I was the only person he could trust and that we could travel and see the world and entertain and have fun. He didn't talk about the money side of it, but he implied a great deal. I knew perfectly well he was rich, anyhow——' She paused for a moment, and fumbled in her bag for her handkerchief. 'But that wasn't why I married him, honestly it wasn't. Of course it had something to do with it, I suppose. You see, I'd been poor all my life, Father's practice wasn't up to much and the idea of having all the clothes and things that I wanted, and being able to travel, which I'd always longed to do, probably helped a bit, but it wasn't the whole reason or anything like it, I swear it wasn't. The real reason was much stranger and more complicated and difficult to explain. On looking back on it, I think I can see it clearly, but even now I'm not altogether sure. I was very emotional and romantic and really very nice inside when I was young, far nicer than I am now. There ought to be a law against bringing children up to have nice instincts and ideals, it makes some of the things that happen afterwards so much more cruelly surprising than they need be. I can see now, that I quite seriously married Ellsworth from a sense of duty – doing my good deed for the day. Girl Guides for ever. I knew perfectly well that I didn't love him, at least my brain knew it and told me so, but I didn't listen and allowed my emotions, my confused, adolescent, sentimental emotions, to drag me in the other direction. I remember forcing myself to imagine what it would be like, the actual sex part, I mean, and thinking, quite blithely, that it would be lovely and thrilling to lie in Ellsworth's arms and be a comfort to him and look after him and stand between him and his loneliness. Of course, my imagination over all this wasn't very clear, as my sex experience to date had consisted of little more than an unavowed and beautiful passion for Miss Hilton-Smith, our games mistress at St Mary's, Plymouth, and a few daring kisses from a young man at a hunt ball in Bodmin. Obviously, I hadn't the remotest idea what I was letting myself in for, so I said "Yes", and two days later, still in a haze of romantic and emotional confusion, we went off to Nice, without letting anyone suspect a thing, and were married in some sort of office by a man with a goitre.'

Jennifer held out her hand for another cigarette. I lit one for her and without saying a word, waited for her to go on.

'Then the trouble started.' She gave a slight shudder. 'I'm not going to tell you all the details, but it was all very frightening and horrid and humiliating, I think humiliating more than anything else. After a few weeks, during which time Father had appeared and Aunt Dora and a very pompous uncle of Ellsworth's, and there had been a series of scenes and discussions and a great deal of strain, Ellsworth and I went to Rome and stayed there for months. In due course I was received into the Church. I didn't have much feeling about that one way or another and Ellsworth was very insistent, so there it was. We were finally married properly with a great deal of music and rejoicing and a lot of American-born Italian Marchesas giving parties for us. As a matter of fact, old Lily Graziani was one of them, the nicest one, I'm staying with her now.' She indicated Cap Ferrat with a vague gesture. 'Then we went away, practically right round the world, starting with Boston and all Ellsworth's relations. Oh, dear!' she gave a little laugh. 'That was very tricky, but some of them were all right. After that, we went to Honolulu and Japan and China, then to India and Egypt and back to

England. That was when we first met, wasn't it, at the house in Great Cumberland Place? By that time, of course, I'd become a bit hardened. I was no longer romantic and innocent and nice. I'd learned a lot of things, I'd joined the Navy and seen the world. All those lovely places, all those chances for happiness, just out of reach, thrown away. Don't misunderstand me, it wasn't the sex business that was upsetting me, at least I don't think it was. I'd faced the failure of that ages before. Oh no, it was Ellsworth himself. I should have been perfectly happy, well, if not happy, at least content, if Ellsworth had played up and been kind and ordinary and a gay companion, but he didn't and he wasn't. I suppose people can't help being beastly, can they? It's something to do with glandular secretions and environment and things that happened to you when you were a child. I can only think that the most peculiar things certainly happened to Ellsworth when he was a child and his glandular secretions must have been something fierce. At any rate, I hadn't been with him long before I knew, beyond a shadow of doubt, that he was a thoroughly unpleasant character. Not in any way bad in the full sense of the word. Not violent or sadistic, or going off on dreadful drunks and coming back and beating me up. Nothing like that, nothing nearly so direct. He was far too refined and carefully cultured, you said it just now, a beauty-lover, that's what he was, a hundred per cent rip-snorting beauty lover. Oh dear, how can one reconcile being a beauty lover with being mean, prurient, sulky and pettishly tyrannical almost to a point of mania? The answer is that one can, because there are several sorts of beauty lovers. There are those who like kindness and good manners and wide seas and dignity, and others who like Bellini Madonnas and Giottos and mysticism and incense and being able to recognise, as publicly as possible, a genuine old this or old that. I don't believe it's enough——' Jennifer's voice rose a little. 'I don't believe it's enough, all that preoccupation with the dead and done with, when there's living life all round you and sudden, lovely unexpected moments to be aware of. Sudden loving gestures from other people, without motives, nothing to do with being rich or poor or talented or cultured, just our old friend human nature at its best! That's the sort of beauty worth searching for; it may sound pompous, but I know what I mean. That's the sort of beauty-lover that counts. I am right, aren't I? It's taken me so many miserable hours trying to puzzle things out.' She stopped abruptly, almost breathless, and looked at me appealingly.

'Yes,' I said, 'I think you're right.'

'The trouble with Ellsworth,' she went on more calmly, 'was that he had no love in his heart for any living soul except himself. Even his mother, who I suppose meant more to him than anyone else, faded quickly out of his memory. After the first few weeks he hardly ever referred to her, and if he did it was lightly, remotely, as though she had been someone of little importance whom he had once met and passed a summer with. If he had been honest with me or even honest with himself, it would have been all right, but he was neither. He dealt in lies, small, insignificant lies; this was at first, later the lies became bigger and more important. He made a lot of friends as we pursued our rather dreary social existence, some of them appeared to be genuinely fond of him, at any rate in the beginning; others quite blatantly fawned on him for what they could get out of him. I watched, rather anxiously sometimes, and occasionally tried to warn him. I still felt there was a chance, you know, not of reforming him, I wasn't as smug as that, but of reaching a plane of mutual companionship on which we could both live our own lives and discuss things and have a certain amount of fun together without conflict and irritation and getting on each other's nerves. But it wasn't any use. He distrusted me, principally I think because I was a woman. There wasn't anything to be done. It was hopeless. Then, after we'd been married for several years, a situation occurred. It was in New York, we were staying at the Waldorf, and it was all very unpleasant and nearly developed into a front-page scandal. I'm a bit vague as to what actually happened myself, there were so many conflicting stories, but anyhow, Ellsworth was blackmailed, and I had to interview strange people and tell a lot of lies, and a lot of money was handed out and we sailed, very hurriedly, for Europe. After that, things were beastlier than ever. He was sulky and irritable and took to making sarcastic remarks at me in front of strangers. All the resentment of a weak nature, that had been badly frightened, came to the top. Finally, I could bear it no longer and asked him to divorce me. That was the only time I have ever seen him really furious. He went scarlet in the face with rage. He was a Catholic and I was a Catholic. That was that. There could be no question of such a thing. Then I lost my head, and told him what I really thought of him, and that I was perfectly sure that the Catholic business was not really the reason for his refusal at all. He was really worried about what people would say; terrified of being left without the nice social buttress of a wife who could preside at his table, arrive with him at pompous receptions and fashionable first nights and in fact, visually at least, cover his tracks. We had a blistering row, and I left the house, that was the house in Paris, you remember it, in the Avenue d'Iéna, and went to London to stay with Marjorie Bridges. He followed me in about a week, and a series of dreary scenes took place. He actually cried during one of them, and said that he was really devoted to me deep down and that he would never again do anything to humiliate me in any way. I think he was honestly dreadfully frightened of me leaving him. Frightened of himself, I mean, that old fear that he had told me about, sitting on the beach, when he first asked me to marry him. I gave in in the end. There wasn't anything else to do really. And that's how we are now. He goes off on his own every now and then and does what he likes, but never for very long. He hasn't the courage for real adventure. Then we join up again, and open the house in Paris, and give parties, and do everything that everyone else does. Sometimes we go for a yachting cruise through the Greek Islands, or up the Dalmatian coast or round about here. Actually, I'm waiting now for him to come back, and I suppose we'll collect a dozen people that we don't care for, and who don't care for us, and off we shall go to Corsica or Majorca or Tangier. It's a lovely life.'

She sat silently for a moment, looking out over the sea, then she rose to her feet and began to kick a stone with the toe of her evening shoe. 'That's about all,' she said.

I got up, too, and we clambered over the wall and walked slowly over to the car.

'Not quite all,' I said mildly, putting the cushions into the car. 'You haven't yet told me why you were crying.'

'Isn't that enough?'

'Not quite.'

She got into the car and started fiddling with the engine. She spoke without looking at me. 'I have never been unfaithful to Ellsworth,' she said in a dry, flat voice. 'I know I could have easily, but it always seemed to me that it might make the situation even more squalid than it is already. Anyhow, I have never found anyone among the people we meet whom I could love enough to make it worth it. Perhaps something will happen some day – I wouldn't like to die an old maid.'

She started the car and drove me back to Monte Carlo. It was getting quite light and the whole landscape looked as though it had been newly washed. She dropped me at the Hotel de Paris; then, just as she was about to drive away, she leant over the side of the car and kissed me lightly on the cheek. She said, 'Thank you, darling, I'll be grateful always to you for having been so really lovingly kind.'

I watched the car until it had turned the corner and was out of sight.

4

' – But a chap's own chauffeur,' the Major was saying. 'I mean that really is going too far——'

'Where are they now?' I interrupted. 'She and the chauffeur – did he tell you?'

'Out in Canada, I believe; the man's a Canadian. They run a garage or a petrol station or something – funnily enough, she wouldn't take any of old Ponsonby's money, he offered it, of course, he's that sort of chap, you know; "quixotic", is that the word?'

'Yes,' I said, 'that's the word.'

The Major collected the photograph albums and packed them in his suitcase, as he did so he hummed a tune rather breathily. My mind went back to that early, newly washed morning four years ago – driving down through the dawn to Monte Carlo. I remembered the emptiness in Jennifer's voice when she said, 'Anyhow I have never found anyone among the people we meet whom I could love enough to make it worth it – perhaps something will happen some day – I wouldn't like to die an old maid.'

The Major straightened himself. 'What about a nightcap?' he said.

We went up on deck. The air was clear and cold, and there was hardly any wind. Far away on the port bow a lighthouse on the French coast flashed intermittently.

In the smoking-room the Major flung himself, with a certain breezy abandon, into a leather armchair which growled under the strain.

'Fancy you knowing old Ponsonby,' he said. 'The world certainly is a very small place. You know there's a lot of truth in those old chestnuts.' I nodded absently and lit a cigarette. He snapped his fingers loudly to attract the steward's attention. 'I shall never forget that night as long as I live, seeing that poor chap crying like a kid, absolutely broken up. It's a pretty bad show when a man's whole life is wrecked by some damned woman. What I can't get over——' he leant forward and lowered his voice; there was an expression of genuine, horrified bewilderment in his, by now, slightly bloodshot eyes – 'is that she should have gone off with his own chauffeur!'

'I suspect,' I said gently, 'that was why he was crying.'

'Steward! Two stengahs!' said the Major.

A Richer Dust

"—There shall be
In that rich earth a richer dust concealed;
A dust whom England bore, shaped, made aware,
Gave, once, her flowers to love, her ways to roam,
A body of England's, breathing English air,
Washed by the rivers, blest by suns of home.
RUPERT BROOKE

CHAPTER I

SIDNEY'S letter arrived on 12 May 1941, and Joe brought it down to the pool. Lenore was at the bar mixing two tomato-juice cocktails with an extra dash of Worcester sauce, as they both felt a bit liverish after Shirley's party and had made a mutual pact not to touch any hard liquor before sundown. Joe came shuffling down the white steps and Morgan felt irritated before he even saw the letter; the scraping of Joe's shoes set his teeth on edge; he snatched the letter from Joe's hand, recognised the handwriting and felt more irritable than ever. Joe went off again up the steps, still shuffling his feet. Morgan dried his hands on the corner of the towel and opened the letter, and when Lenore came out with the cocktails he had read it and was gazing out over the Beverly Hills to the sea with an expression of set exasperation. Lenore noted the expression and placed the tomato-juice gently beside him, then she sat down herself on the edge of the diving-board and rummaged in her bathing bag for her sunglasses. She was aware that she probably felt a bit better than he did because she had quite shamelessly cheated while mixing the tomato-juice and given herself a shot of rye; her

stomach felt smoother and the sensation of nausea and
dizziness which had been plaguing her all the morning had
passed away.

Morgan continued to gaze out into the blue distance in
silence. Lenore contemplated for an instant making a little
joke such as – 'Cut – the scene stinks anyway!' or 'Is there
anything wrong with the sound?' but thought better of it and
kept quiet. She rubbed her sun-glasses with her handkerchief
and put them on. The world immediately became cooler and
less harsh; the sky took on a pinky glow and the light on the
hills softened. Morgan's body looked even more tanned than
it actually was; he never went very dark, just an even golden
brown. It was certainly a fine body, long legs, strongly-
developed chest tapering to a perfect waistline, hardly any
hips and no bottom to speak of. She gave a little sigh and
wistfully regretted that they had had a tumble that morning
on waking – those 'over-in-a-flash' hangover tumbles were
never really satisfactory, it would have been much more
sensible to have saved it for later, now, for instance, in the hot
sun. Obeying an overwhelming impulse she slid her hand
along his thigh. Even as she did it she knew it was a mistake;
he jumped violently, and said in a tone of bored petulance,
'Lay off me for one minute, can't you.' Discouraged, she withdrew her hand as requested, muttered, 'Pardon me for living,'
and took a swig of tomato juice which brought tears to her
eyes owing to the sharpness of the Worcester sauce. Morgan,
his mood of retrospection shattered, gave a disagreeable
grunt and went off into the change room to have a shower.
Lenore picked up the letter. The handwriting was neat and
clear, and the address at the top was H.M.S. *Tagus*, c/o G.P.O.
London. It started 'Dear Les' – she smiled at this, he hated
being called Les and very few people in Hollywood knew
that it was his name. She turned the page over and saw that it
was signed – 'Your affectionate brother, Sid'. Then, still
smiling, she read it through.

DEAR LES,

I expect you'll be surprised to hear from me after so long, but I've been at sea now for several months. You'll see where I am by the postmark and we're moving along in your direction in a few days time all being well. So expect me when you see me and hang out the holly and get the old calf fatted up because I shall probably get forty-eight hours leave. Mum and Dad and Sheila were all well when last heard from. One of my mates wants to meet some film lovelies in the following order – Betty Grable, Loretta Young, Paulette Goddard and Marlene Dietrich, failing these he doesn't mind settling for Shirley Temple at a pinch as he likes them young. I just want to see you and a nice big steak, done medium, with chips.

Your affectionate brother,
SID.

In the change room Morgan had a shower and dried himself with grim efficiency; he then emptied some toilet water, tactfully labelled 'For Men Only', into the palms of his hands and rubbed it over his chest and under his arms. The long mirror reflected his expression which was still set in exasperation; he stared at himself, for once almost without enthusiasm, and lit a cigarette; his mouth felt tacky and unpleasant and the cigarette did nothing to improve it. 'Dear Les' – 'Your affectionate brother, Sid'. 'Les and Sid' – he shuddered and slowly pulled on a pair of dark red linen trousers and a sweater. The awful thing was that 'Your affectionate brother, Sid' was true. Ever since they were tiny kids trudging home from school across Southsea Common Sid had been affectionate, much more so than Sheila really, although it was generally supposed to be sisters who lavished adoration and hero-worship on their elder brothers. Sheila, however, had never been the hero-worshipping type; plain and practical, she had always, even when very young, refused to be impressed. Sid, on the other hand, had been a push-over from the word go; whatever Morgan, or rather 'Les', said or did was perfection. There were so many occasions that Morgan could remember when Sid had taken the rap for him. During the roof-climbing phase for instance, when seventeen slates had been broken and gone crashing down into Mrs Morpeth's back garden – Sid had taken all the blame for that and, what's more, been punished for it. Then there was the ringing door-bells and running away episode when Morgan, who had instigated the whole affair, had managed to hop over somebody's garden wall and lie panting in a shrubbery while Sid was captured and led off to the police station. Sid, with admirable *Boy's Own Paper* gallantry, had resolutely refused to divulge the name of his accomplice. The policeman had finally brought him home where, after a big family scene during which Morgan remained ignobly silent, Sid was whacked by Dad and sent to bed supperless. There were many other like instances, through childhood and adolescence and right on until they were grown men. Sid certainly had the right to sign himself 'Your affectionate brother', and the strange thing was that through all the years this steady, un-demanding affection had merely served to annoy the recipient of it, sometimes quite intolerably. Perhaps deep down beneath the armoured shell of Morgan's self-esteem there were remnants of a conscience which had not quite atrophied, perhaps, who knows, there were moments every now and then when in his secret private heart he was ashamed? Whether this was so or not, the presence or even the thought of Sid invariably made him ill at ease and irritable. Now Sid was going to appear in his life again; six years had passed since they had seen each other. Six eventful years for the world and even more eventful for Morgan, for in course of time he had climbed from being a small-part English actor to being one of the biggest film stars in Hollywood.

CHAPTER 2

IN 1933, aged nineteen, Leslie Booker was a floor-walker in the novelty department of Hadley's. This position was procured for him through the civic influence of his Uncle Edward, who, owing to certain connections on various Boards and Committees, knew Fred Cartwright, one of the Directors of Hadley's. Uncle Edward privately thought no great shakes of his nephew but being strong in family conscience and devoted to his sister Nell, who was Leslie's mother, he decided to do what he could for the boy. His misgivings about Leslie were based more on intuition than actual knowledge of his character. This intuition told him that Leslie was idle, over good-looking, excessively pleased with himself and flash, and that his younger brother Sid was worth twenty of him any day of the week; however, he was Nell's eldest and he couldn't ride about the countryside indefinitely on a second-hand motor-cycle with a series of tartish young ladies in flannel slacks riding pillion behind him with their arms clasped tightly round his stomach, so something had to be done. Mr Cartwright was invited to the 'Queen's', given an excellent lunch and, when sufficiently mellowed by Hock and two double Martell Three Star brandies, was finally persuaded to give Leslie a three months' trial in the shop.

The three months passed swiftly and proved little beyond the fact that Leslie was idle, over good-looking, excessively pleased with himself and flash. However, he did more or less what was required of him, which was mostly to smile and look amiable and tactfully coax the customers to buy things that they didn't really want and so he was re-engaged for a further six months with a vague promise of a raise in salary if he did well. It was during these six months further probation that Adele Innes arrived in Portsmouth to play a week's try-out of a new farce which was due to open in the West End. Adele was a conscientious young actress with good legs and little talent. In the farce she played the heroine's best friend who made a lot of pseudo-sophisticated wisecracks and was incapable of sitting down without crossing her legs ostentatiously and loosening her furs. On the Monday of the try-out week, after a tiring dress-rehearsal, she popped into Hadley's on her way home to the digs to buy a few roguish little first-night gifts for her friends in the Company. Leslie Booker helped her assiduously to choose a china Pierrot scent-burner, two green elephant book-ends, a cunning replica of an apple made of china which could be used, Leslie assured her, either as a paper-weight or a door stop, and a small scarlet leather book-shelf containing four minute dictionaries which were virtually illegible owing to the smallness of print. Having made these purchases she lingered a little, chatting nonchalantly with the affable young salesman. She was a democratic girl quite uninhibited by any sense of class distinction, so uninhibited indeed that she deliberately allowed her hand to rest against his while he was totting up the bill. During the ensuing week they had morning coffee twice at the Cadena, went to Gosport and back three times on the ferry in between the matinée and evening performances on the Wednesday, which was early closing day; and went to bed together once in her digs between the matinée and evening performances on the Saturday which, although not early closing day, was perfectly convenient as the shop shut at six and she didn't have to be in the theatre again until eight. A few weeks later, after some impassioned correspondence, Leslie abandoned Hadley's novelty department for ever and arrived in London with seventeen pounds ten shillings; nine pounds of which were savings and the rest borrowed from brother Sid. According to pre-arranged plan he went directly to Adele's flat just off the Fulham Road which she shared with a girl friend who was at present away on tour. Thus comfortably established with bed and board and convivial company he managed, through Adele's influence, to get into the chorus of the current revue at the Caravel Theatre which, as he was without theatrical experience and could neither sing nor dance, said a great deal for Adele's influence.

By 1934 the revue at the Caravel had closed and he was sharing the flat of a husky-voiced singer called Diana Grant in St John's Wood. Diana was large, possessive, generous, exceedingly bad-tempered and had a rooted objection to going to bed before five a.m. and rising before noon. Leslie's brief but tempestuous association with her depleted his natural vitality to such a degree that when he was offered, through a friend of a friend of hers, a general understudy and small part job in a repertory company in Dundee, he accepted it from sheer self-preservation.

By 1936 he had played several insignificant parts in several insignificant productions both in the Provinces and in London and was playing a young dope fiend in a thriller called *Blood on the Stairs*. In this piece he had one of those sure-fire scenes in Act Three in which he had to break down under relentless cross-examination and confess to a murder. The breakdown entailed all the routine gurglings and throat clutchings which never fail to impress the dramatic critics, and so consequently he received glowing tributes from the *Daily Mirror*, the *Daily Express* and the *Star*, an honourable mention in the *Daily Telegraph* and an admonition against over-acting in *Time and Tide* which he immediately ascribed to personal jealousy and wrote a dignified letter of protest to the Editor. *Blood on the Stairs* was a fatuous, badly-written little melodrama which, having received enthusiastic notices, closed after a run of seven and a half weeks, but as far as Leslie Booker was concerned it achieved some purpose, for during its brief run he was sent for and interviewed by a visiting American manager at the Savoy Hotel who was on the look-out for a clean English type to play a young dope fiend in a mystery murder play he was presenting in New York in the fall. The visiting American manager's name was Sol Katsenberg and he prided himself, generally inaccurately, upon his unique flair for discovering new talent. He was noisy and friendly and gave Leslie two double whiskies and sodas which he described as highballs and which contained too much ice, too much whisky and too little soda. He also gave him a graphic description of the super-efficiency of the American Theatre as opposed to the English. He said 'Christ Almighty' a great many times but without religious implication and by the end of the interview Leslie, slightly dizzy, had signed a contract for three hundred dollars a week and had agreed to change his name, for, as Sol explained, Leslie Booker sounded too Christ Almighty dull. The name agreed upon after a great deal of discussion was Morgan Kent, a name, had they but known it, that was destined to flash over all the movie screens of the world.

The Sol Katsenberg production of *Blood Will Tell* opened in Long Branch on 17 September 1936, and closed, after three changes of cast and two changes of author, on 29 October in Pittsburgh. The name Morgan Kent rang no urgent tocsin in the stony hearts of the American out-of-town critics which was odd because, in the last act of the play, he had a scene in which, crazed by dope, he had to break down under relentless cross-examination and confess to a murder. He gurgled and clutched his throat with even more abandon than he had exhibited in *Blood on the Stairs* but to no avail. Nobody cared, not even *Variety* which merely listed him among the minor players and spelled his name Kant instead of Kent. Reeling under this blow to his pride, Leslie, or rather Morgan, was driven to sharing a small apartment in West 31st Street, New York City with Myra Masters, a statuesque red-haired ex-show girl who had played a vampire in the deceased *Blood Will Tell*. Myra was a cheerful, open-hearted girl with what is known as 'contacts'. These contacts were mostly square-looking business men from Detroit and points Middle West who cherished tender memories of her in George White's *Scandals* and Earl Carroll's *Vanities*. One of them, fortunately for Morgan, was in Advertising, and before Christmas had cast its pall of goodwill over Manhattan, magazine readers were being daily tantalised by photographs of Morgan Kent (nameless) discussing with another young man (also nameless) the merits of 'Snugfit' men's underwear. Both young men in the photograph were depicted practically nude in the change room of a country club where presumably they had been swimming or playing polo or doing something equally virile; but whereas one was wearing what appeared to be rather baggy old-fashioned underpants, the other, Morgan, was pointing proudly to his groin which was adorned with none other than the new 'Snugfit'. The dialogue beneath the photograph, although uninspired, proved its point.

1st Y.M.: 'Gee, Buddy – don't you find that those little old pants you're wearing spoil your game?'

2nd Y.M.: 'Well, Chuck, as a matter of fact they do.'

1st Y.M. (*triumphantly*): 'Well, you old son of a gun, why not follow my example and try SNUGFIT!'

The result of this well-paid but unromantic publicity was as inevitable as the March of Time. Morgan was traced through Myra Masters, sent for and interviewed brusquely by a film agent in an ornate office in Rockefeller Plaza. The film agent, Al Tierney, had astute eyes jockeying for position over a long ponderous nose, a gentle rather high voice and a sapphire and platinum ring. He explained to Morgan that his fortune was in his face and figure and that if he would sign a contract authorising him, Al Tierney, to deal exclusively with his affairs within the year he would be on the up and up and saving thousands of dollars a week.

In due course Morgan bade farewell to Myra and set out for Hollywood.

CHAPTER 3

THE first months in Hollywood were conventionally difficult. Morgan virtually starved, waited in queues outside casting offices, wandered up and down the boulevards homesick and weary; lived on inadequate sandwiches in snack bars; made innumerable tests; made a few casual friends on the same plane of frustration and failure as himself and lived in celibate squalor in a pseudo-Mexican apartment-house in a side street off Willshire Boulevard in which he had one room with shower and could, when desperate and his financial circumstances permitted, have a blue plate dinner in a teeming restaurant on the ground floor for seventy-five cents, service included.

Al Tierney, his exclusive agent, remained exclusively in New York; occasionally his Hollywood representative Wally Newman granted Morgan an interview, in course of which he outlined in glowing colours the lucky breaks and golden opportunities there were waiting just round the corner; in addition to these optimistic flights of fancy he contrived now and then to get him a few days crowd work which was of more practical value although less heartening. In these dreary months Morgan deteriorated in looks owing to malnutrition but gained perceptibly in moral stature, it being a well-known fact that just as travel broadens the mind, so a little near-starvation frequently broadens the spirits. Leslie Booker alias Morgan Kent, the assured, charming, flash young salesman from Southsea, the complacent, attractive, promising young actor from London, had suddenly time, far too much time, to reflect; to look at himself, into himself and around himself, to discover bitterly that a handsome face, wide shoulders and small hips were not enough in this much-publicised land of opportunity. Day after day he waited about in casting offices with dozens of handsome young men with as wide if not wider shoulders and as small if not smaller hips. Women, who had hitherto been his solace both physically and financially in times of stress, were, in Hollywood, either too tough, too blasé or too pre-occupied with their own ambitions to devote their time and energy to a, by now, only comparatively good-looking young film extra. Morgan was forced to face the unpalatable truth that masculine good looks in the outer fringes of the movie industry were as monotonously prevalent as the eternal sunshine, the painted mountains and the cellophane-wrapped sandwiches. Had this dismal state of affairs continued much longer; had his self-esteem received just a few more kicks in the teeth; had his shrinking ego shuddered under just a few more bludgeonings of Fate, who knows what might have happened? He might conceivably have given up the struggle, begged, borrowed, earned or stolen enough money to get himself back to New York or London and started again playing small parts and learning to become a good actor. He might have given up all idea of either stage or screen and worked his way home on a freighter or even as a steward on a liner in which capacity he would have done very well. There are a thousand things he might have done had not Fate suddenly relented and whisked him from penury and frustration into such flamboyant notoriety that he was dazzled, bewildered and lost for ever.

It all came about, as usual, through hazard, chance, an accident, somebody else's misfortune. The somebody else was a young man called Freddie Branch and the accident occurred on number seven stage in the M.G.M. lot when they were in course of shooting a big ballroom scene which purported to be taking place in one of the stately homes of England. The set was impressive. There was a Tudor staircase at the top of which stood the stand-in for the hostess wearing white satin and a tiara and elbow-length gloves. At the foot of the stairs stretched the vast ballroom flanked by footmen in powdered wigs; there were also heraldic shields, suits of armour, Gothic windows and two immense Norman fire-places, one on each side, in which gargantuan logs were waiting to flicker realistically. The floor, rather erratically, was made of composition black marble and upon it were grouped hundreds of extras cunningly disguised as members of the effete British Aristocracy. The accident which was negligible happened to poor Freddie Branch after he had been standing quite still clasping his hostess's hand for three hours and four minutes. The whistles blew for a rehearsal, bejewelled ladies and eccentrically be-uniformed and be-tailed gentlemen stiffened to attention and proceeded, as previously rehearsed, to revolve like automatons. Freddie Branch retreated to the foot of the stairs and proceeded, as previously rehearsed, to walk up them again. Upon gaining the top step he suddenly felt an overwhelming desire to be sick, grabbed frenziedly at his collar, murmured 'Jesus' in audible tones and fainted dead away. Morgan, whose proud task it was to follow him, jumped nimbly aside and watched his inert body roll and sprawl to the bottom of the stairs. There was an immediate uproar; more whistles blew, the unconscious Freddie was carried off the set and Morgan was detailed to take over his business.

That was Fate's gesture to Morgan Kent – the striking down of the wretched Freddie Branch, who had barely had time to come to from his faint before Morgan was ascending those shining stairs in his place. He continued to ascend them at intervals for the rest of the morning. Miss Carola Blake, the star, finally emerged from her dressing-room and took over from her stand-in and the scene was taken. It was taken at 2 o'clock, at 2.20, at 2.45, at 3.10, at 3.40, at 4.15 and, owing to hitch in the sound, at 8, 8.30 and 9 onwards during the following morning. By the following evening, Miss Carola Blake had shaken Morgan's hand – plus rehearsals – forty-seven times and become aware in the process that he had fine eyelashes, an excellent physique, although a little on the thin side, and a deep and attractive speaking voice. (Having spent the thirty years of her life in Illinois and California her ear was naturally oblivious to any subtle Cockney intonations and, to do Morgan justice, these were becoming increasingly rare.) When the ballroom scene had been packed away in the can, Morgan together with the other extras was paid off. Only a few days later he received a peremptory call to report at the casting office. To his surprise he was greeted with a welcoming smile from the outer secretary, arch friendliness by the inner secretary and downright effusiveness by the casting director himself. It appeared, after some casual conversation and the offer and refusal of a cigar, that the sharp-eyed observers on the set had noted his charm, poise and talent and that he was to be tested for a scene in a speed-boat – Miss Carola Blake, the casting director added with an oblique look, had actually consented to do the test with him herself. Later on the same day Morgan, wearing abbreviated swimming trunks, spent three and a half hours with Miss Carole Blake, also scantily clad, sitting in the built-up bows of a speed boat with, behind them, a back projection screen upon which were monotonously depicted the swirling waters of the Caribbean.

Five weeks later he moved unostentatiously into Carola Blake's elaborate house in Beverly Hills.

A little later still they were married.

CHAPTER 4

BY the autumn of 1938, while the English Prime Minister was shuttling back and forth between England and Germany, two things of considerable importance had happened to Morgan Kent. The first was his sensational success in a picture called *Loving Rover* in which he played an eighteenth-century pirate who, after many nautical and amorous vicissitudes, finally evaded death by a hair's breadth and found true love in the arms of a beautiful New England girl with a pronounced Middle Western accent. The second was his divorce from Carola Blake on the grounds of mental cruelty. The publicity of the latter almost surpassed that of the former with the result that his fan mail reached unheard of proportions and he signed a new seven years' starring contract, the terms of which were published inaccurately in every newspaper in the United States. Throughout 1939 and the beginning of 1940 he made no less than seven successful pictures, one of which was quite good. He bought a delightful house in the hills behind Hollywood which commanded a spectacular view of the town especially at night, when the myriad lights blazed from Sunset Boulevard to the sea. Here he enjoyed a carefree bachelor existence with, in order of their appearance and disappearance, Jane Fleming, Beejie Lemaire, Dandy Lovat, Glory Benson and Brenda Covelin.

In the spring of 1940, at the time of the evacuation of the British Expeditionary Force from the beaches of Dunkirk, he had just completed a grim but exciting war picture entitled *Altitude*, in which he portrayed to perfection a taciturn but gallant fighter pilot whose ultimate death for the sake of his fiancée and his best friend created on the screen a dramatic climax hitherto unparalleled in the art of film-making. While making *Altitude* he met for the first time Lenore Fingal who was cast as his fiancée. Their meeting was described by all observers as an absolute and concrete example of love at first sight and before the picture was half finished they had flown together over the border into Mexico on a Saturday, been married on the Sunday and flown back again in time for work on Monday. A little later he gave up his bachelor establishment and they moved into a larger and more convenient house in Beverly Hills.

CHAPTER 5

LENORE FINGAL, at the time of her marriage to Morgan Kent, was twenty-five years old. She was small and dark, with a good figure, an attractive husky voice and very lovely grey-blue eyes. These eyes were undoubtedly her best feature but they were deceptive. There was an appealing expression in them, a tender naïveté, a trusting friendly generosity which, although effective in 'close-ups', was actually at variance with her character. Lenore was neither tender, naïve, trusting, nor particularly generous. The exigencies of her life in the treacherous shallows of the motion picture industry had not allowed her much time for the development of these qualities. She was hard, calculating, and although occasionally senti-mental, never emotional. In course of her journey from the slums of Los Angeles to the heights of Beverly Hills she had, once or twice, permitted herself the luxury of a love affair, that is to say she had consciously directed her will into an emotional channel in order, presumably, to discover what it was all about, but, as her heart had never seriously been involved, she had discovered very little. She had played a few stormy scenes, shed a few tears, and emerged unscathed and tougher than ever. It is doubtful that she even imagined herself in love with Morgan. He was physically attractive to her and, in the dazzling light of his rise to stardom, an excellent matrimonial proposition. Now, in the spring of 1941, they had been married for a year, a professionally successful year for them both. He had made three pictures and was in process of making a fourth. She had made two apart from him and one with him in which she had portrayed a gallant British Red Cross nurse who rescued her lover (Morgan) from the beaches of Dunkirk by rowing out from Dover in a dinghy. The picture when shown in New York and London had had a disappointing reception from the critics and so it had been decided, for the time being anyhow, that it would be wiser to cast Lenore and Morgan separately, and wiser still to keep Lenore away from the perils of English pronunciation and allow her to exhibit her undoubted talent securely enclosed in her own idiom. Domestically their first year of marriage had also been fairly successful. They had quarrelled a good deal, naturally enough, and had once come to blows, but the blows given and received had not been violent and the original cause of the row swiftly lost for ever in a haze of alcohol.

The arrival of the letter from brother Sid, coming as it did on the morning of a hangover, had both irritated and depressed Morgan considerably, and the arrival of brother Sid himself a few days later irritated and depressed him still more. They were all sitting round the pool drinking 'Old-Fashioneds' before going over to dinner at Beejie's: Morgan, Lenore, Coral Leroy, Sammy Feisner, Charlie Bragg and Doll Hartley. Sammy was just reaching the point of a long story about a scene between Hester Norbury and Louis B. Mayer when there was a loud 'Hallo there' from the upper terrace and Sid came bounding down the steps, followed by another sailor who was red-haired and covered with freckles. Sammy stopped abruptly on the verge of his story's denouement; Morgan rose from a canvas chair, leaving on it the dark imprint of his damp swimming trunks, and, with a valiant smile masking his annoyance, advanced to meet his brother.

Sid, in appearance, temperament and character, was everything Morgan was not. Whereas Morgan was tall, lithe and dark, Sid was short, square and fair. Whereas Morgan's temperament was naturally solemn, Sid's was ebullient and permanently cheerful. Sid was trusting, kind and uninhibited; Morgan was suspicious, egocentric and, since his early Hollywood struggles, frequently a prey to misgivings. Sid had none. It would never have occurred to him that he wasn't immediately welcome wherever he went. He flung his arms affectionately round Morgan and banged him heartily on the back. 'My God, Les,' he said, 'I've been looking forward to this for months!' The word 'Les' went through Morgan's heart like a poisoned spear and he shuddered. Lenore, who had also got up to greet the new arrivals, noticed it and giggled. Morgan, with an excellent display of brotherly affection, introduced Sid to everyone. Sid introduced his friend, Pete Kirkwall, who shyly shook hands all round; Charlie Bragg got up to mix fresh drinks; there was a lot of shifting of chairs and finally Sid found himself ensconced between Morgan and Lenore on a striped swing seat which creaked plaintively whenever any of them moved. Morgan realised with a sinking heart that Sid and his friend would not only have to be offered the best guest-room but would have to be taken with the others to dinner at Beejie's. They would also without doubt expect a personally-conducted tour of the studios the next day and a glamorous lunch in the commissariat. It was not that he was ashamed of Sid. There was nothing to be ashamed of in a reasonably nice-looking sailor brother, but there was, as there always is in such circumstances, a wide gulf to be bridged. None of his friends either at the studio or at Beejie's would have much in common with Sid and Pete. In envisaging the social strain involved, the effort he would have to make not to shudder when called 'Les', nor to flush at Sid's over-British naval repartee and, above all, not to betray to anybody the fact that he devoutly wished that his brother had never been born, almost overwhelmed him. He knew that Lenore was watching, waiting for a chance to sneer, to get in a crack at him. He also knew that she would extract from Sid as much information as possible about his early years and fling it in his face the next time an opportunity offered. Sid on the other hand, sublimely unaware of the conflict raging in his brother's heart, was perfectly happy and at ease. He kept a weather eye open to see that Pete was doing all right and was relieved to see that he was thawing out a bit and exchanging 'Player's' cigarettes for 'Lucky Strikes' with a blonde woman, whose breasts seemed about to burst exuberantly from a tightly-stretched bandana handkerchief. He had already taken a fancy to Lenore whom he considered to be on the skinny side but friendly and attractive. Charlie Bragg handed him an Old-Fashioned, and called him 'Pal', Les – good old Les – asked him how long his leave was, and said that of course he and Pete must stay in the house and that he'd take them round some studios the next day. Everything in fact had turned out as well as, if not better than, he had hoped. After a few more drinks and a swim in the pool, during which he churned up and down doing a rather clumsy 'crawl' and treating the water as though it were a personal enemy, he squeezed himself back into his 'Tiddley' suit which, being his best, was moulded tightly to his stocky figure, and, with bell-bottomed trousers flapping and vitality unimpaired, climbed into a blue Packard with Lenore, Sammy Feisner and Coral Leroy. Pete was with Morgan and the others in a beige Chrysler convertible.

Beejie's house was in another canyon which entailed a sharp and tortuous descent from Morgan's house and a sharper and more tortuous ascent on the other side of the valley. Sid, who was sitting next to Lenore in the front seat, was both fascinated and alarmed at the firm assurance with which her small brown hands gripped the wheel. During the drive she gave him a few hints as to what he was to expect from the evening.

'It isn't that Beejie isn't all right,' she explained. 'Beejie's as right as rain, but don't go outside with her after she's had more than three drinks.'

'If you take my advice,' interposed Coral from the back seat, 'you won't go outside with her at all, drink or no drink. She's the biggest rip-snorting Nympho between here and Palm Springs!'

'Maybe the sailor would like to have a few passes made at him,' said Sammy. 'After all he's only got forty-eight hours.'

'He's my brother-in-law——' Here Lenore swerved sharply round a curve. 'My baby brother-in-law – and so help me God I'm going to protect him from evil if it kills me!'

Sid laughed loudly at this and was rewarded by an affectionate pat on the thigh. He gathered in course of the drive that his imminent hostess had been married four times; had made a smash hit some years before in a picture called *Honey Face*, but had never really had a success since; that her present husband was a surgeon whose speciality was the quasi-miraculous removal of gall-bladders, and that in 1939 she had had a brief but tempestuous affair with Morgan. This neither shocked nor surprised him. He had always viewed Les's sexual promiscuities with tolerant good-humour not entirely devoid of admiration. Good old Les had always been a quick worker even way back in the old days in Southsea. He recounted with brotherly pride an episode in Morgan's adolescence which concerned a chemist's daughter called Dodo Platt and her official fiancé who was in the Wool business. As a story it wasn't perhaps extravagantly amusing but Coral, Sammy and Lenore laughed satisfactorily and Lenore made a mental note of Dodo Platt. Encouraged by this and the general atmosphere of warm conviviality, Sid obliged with a few more light-hearted anecdotes about Morgan's early youth, all of which were rapturously received. At last, with a screeching of brakes, the car swirled through a pink plaster archway and drew up before what looked like a Spanish Sanatorium.

The phrase 'Hollywood Party' has become synonymous in the public mind with drink, debauch, frequent violence and occasional murder. This is both unjust and inaccurate, but the reason for it is not far to seek and lies, obviously enough, in the publicity value of the hosts, or the guests, or both. The movie colony lives, breathes and functions in a blaze of publicity. Many members of it make a point of leading quiet lives and evading the limelight as much as possible, and in the old days, when the various social strata were more clearly defined, it was easier for certain groups of the upper hierarchy to move about unobtrusively among themselves, to give little dinners and to visit each other's houses without the world at large being informed of it. But during the last few years this has become increasingly difficult owing to the misguided encouragement of a new form of social parasite, the gossip columnist. This curious phenomenon has insinuated itself into the life-stream not only of Hollywood but of the whole of America, and what began as a minor form of local social and professional scandal-mongering has now developed into a major espionage system, the power of which, aided and abetted by the radio, has reached fabulous proportions. It would not, I think, be incorrect to say that today the minds of millions of citizens of the United States are affected by it. A column of inconsequential gossip is written daily by Mr So-and-So or Miss Such-and-Such. This column, in addition to being printed in the newspaper for which it is written, is syndicated throughout the country. Mr So-and-So and Miss Such-and-Such also – as a rule – have a weekly, or sometimes daily, half an hour on the radio, during which they recapitulate what they have already written and give pointers as to what they are going to write. The effect of this widespread assault upon the credulity of an entire nation must inevitably be confusing. It would not be so were the information given checked and counter-checked and based on solid truth, but unfortunately it seldom is, therefore anybody who has the faintest claims to celebrity is likely to have his character, motives and private and public actions cheerfully misrepresented to an entire continent. This is not done, except on rare occasions, with any particularly malicious intent, but merely to gratify one of the least admirable qualities of human nature: vulgar curiosity. The accuracy of what is written, stated, listened to and believed is immaterial. The monster must be fed, and the professionally employed feeder of it is highly paid and acquires a position of power in the land which would be ridiculous were it not so ominous. In Hollywood, where this epidemic first began to sap the nation's mental vitality, no large, and very few small, social gatherings can take place without one or several potential spies being present. An exchange of views between two directors; a light argument between two leading ladies; a sharp word, spoken perhaps only jokingly, by a young husband to his young wife, will, by the next day, have been misquoted, distorted, magnified, read and believed by several million people. This reprehensible state of affairs concerns our story vitally because at Beejie Lemaire's party, in the regretted absence of Miss Louella Parsons and Miss Hedda Hopper, there was present an up-and-coming young lady journalist called Ruthie Binner, who ran a column in a locally-read magazine, *Hollywood Highlights*. The column was headed 'Nest Eggs' and consisted of a series of staccato mis-statements purporting to have been whispered to Ruthie by a little bird. The inventive capacities of Ruthie's little bird could have found no parallel in the annals of ornithology.

To describe Beejie's party as 'informal' would be an understatement. It began hilariously with one of her ex-husbands, Peppo Ragale, falling down three steps in the bar with a plate of cheese appetisers and breaking his ankle. Her present husband, Grant Lawrence, who, apart from his deft manipulation of gall-bladders, could also reset bones and apply compresses, dealt with the matter with gay efficiency and the party went on from there. Morgan drank steadily throughout the evening and became more and more depressed. Lenore drank too, but not to excess as she was anxious not to miss anything that was going on. Sid and Pete were received enthusiastically by Beejie and everyone present. Soon after the buffet dinner Pete retired into the garden with Doll Hartley and was not retrieved until it was time to go home. Sid enjoyed every moment. He had seven Old-Fashioneds before dinner and a number of Scotch highballs after dinner. He answered questions about the war, the British Navy, 'dear old London', and, volubly, about his brother. He had an unproductive but enjoyable interlude with Beejie on a chintz-covered divan in what she laughingly described as 'The Library'. He helped Beejie's husband to scramble eggs in the kitchen at 2 a.m. At 2.20 a.m. he was beckoned alluringly to a seat at the edge of the swimming pool by a vivacious dark girl who said her name was Ruthie. He found her outspoken, amusing and sincerely concerned about the progress of the war. He was also touched and charmed by her evident devotion to 'Les' and his career. They talked cosily for a long while and finally returned to the house to find Lenore rounding up her party to go home.

On the following morning Morgan, who was not working, stayed in bed and turned Sid and Pete over to Lenore who took them on to several of the M.G.M. stages and showed them Joan Crawford, Jeanette Macdonald and Myrna Loy in the distance and Mickey Rooney, Spencer Tracy, Judy Garland and Nelson Eddy close to. They lunched in the cafeteria and consumed vast glasses of milk and cartwheel slices of tomato on acres of hygienic lettuce. They were then shown some convulsive rough-cuts of incomplete movies in a projection room, where they sprawled in gargantuan arm-chairs flanked by ash-trays and cuspidors so that they could sleep and smoke and spit whenever they so desired. In the evening, after a merry cocktail gathering down by the pool, they were taken by Morgan and Lenore to a much grander dinner party than Beejie's. This was given by Arch Bowdler, one of the most prominent Hollywood executives, in a resplendent house that had been furnished with the utmost care. Attired as they were in the usual 'Square-Rig' of British Ordinary Seamen, they caused a mild sensation except among the English actors present, who of course recognised it immediately.

After a suitable sojourn in a cocktail bar laboriously decorated to represent an open-air café in the Place Pigalle, they were ushered into a long, pale-green room where they were placed at little tables for dinner. Sid found himself opposite a dim English actor who asked him a few lachrymose questions about New Malden, where apparently he had been born, and then lapsed into a gloomy silence, and between two ladies of outstanding glamour. One was Mae Leitzig, who had been whisked by the host from under the iron heel of the Nazis in Vienna and was about to star in a picture about Charlotte Corday, and the other, Zenda Hicks, a tough little blonde, who had recently won an award for the best minor performance of February 1941. She explained to Sid during the meal that it was just 'one of those crazy things' and that no one had been more surprised than she was. On the whole he got along better with her than with Mae Leitzig, who was rather sombre and seemed to be worried about something. Zenda obviously was not worried about anything. She told him all about her first marriage and divorce and also about her present husband who was Mexican and terribly jealous. She told him the entire story of the picture she was working in at the moment and gave her free and unprejudiced opinion of her director, who had a knowledge of life and humanity in general which was nothing short of 'dreamy'. He also, it appeared, thought very highly of her own talents and was in the habit of sitting up to all hours in the morning with her asking her advice about his unhappy marriage, discussing world affairs and occasionally breaking into uncontrollable sobs at the sheer hopelessness of everything. These nocturnal but strictly platonic interludes had been the cause of many bitter quarrels between her and Juano, but as Juano was apparently nothing but a big baby anyway, everyone was as friendly as could be and there was no harm done. She was just about to describe her early life in Omaha, Nebraska, when there was a sharp call for silence and the host rose to his feet. He was a round man with very small hands and black hair. He made a long speech bidding everyone welcome to his house and board, and then, to Sid's slight embarrassment, launched forth into an impassioned eulogy of England and the British war effort. He sat down at last amid loud applause having called upon Robert Bailey, one of the leading British actors present, to respond. Robert Bailey spoke well and slowly with an underlying throb of patriotism in his voice. He paused once or twice to find a word and it was obvious to all that he was making a brave effort to restrain his emotion. He was followed by an English character actress of high repute who waved her arms a good deal and talked about the women of England and how staunchly they had behaved during the blitzes. She concluded by reading a letter from her married sister in St John's Wood upon which it appeared bombs had been raining incessantly for months. By this time Sid was getting restless, bored and a little sleepy. He roused himself however when Morgan was called upon to speak. Morgan rose shyly to his feet and stood in silence for a moment, twisting the stem of his champagne glass. His speech was mercifully brief, but in every word of it pulsated a love of his native land which was intensely moving. Sid was genuinely surprised having no idea that 'Les' thought of the Old Country in those terms. He was still more surprised and utterly shattered when 'Les' finished up by asking everyone to join with him in drinking the health of – 'My sailor brother and The British Navy'. There were resounding cheers at this and everyone rose solemnly and clinked glasses. Sid, sweating with embarrassment, was forced to stand up and make a brief response. He cleared his throat, wishing devoutly that he was safely in his ship and at the other side of the world and said:

'On behalf of my friend and I – thanks a lot for making us so welcome here tonight and for giving us such a good time.

When we tell our shipmates about all the wonderful people we've seen they'll be green with envy and that's no lie.' Here he paused for a moment and cleared his throat again. 'As you are all aware . . .' Realising that he was speaking rather loudly he lowered his voice. 'As you are all aware, the Navy is known as "The Silent Service", so you will not expect from an ordinary seaman such as I myself am – anything high-falutin in the way of a speech, speech-making not being much in my line as you might say. – But I would like to say, on behalf of the Old Country which I proudly belong to and the fleet in which I serve – thanks a lot for all the kind things that have been said here tonight and, as far as the war goes, Down with old Hitler and Musso and God Save the King.' He sat down abruptly amid tumultuous applause; someone shouted 'Good old England' and an Irish actress who had been playing 'bit' parts for thirteen years burst into loud sobs.

After this everyone was shepherded into an enormous blue room, the walls of which were lined with sets of the classics bound in different colours. Here trays of highballs were handed round, a movie screen rose noiselessly from the floor, and the party settled down to a preview of Clyde Oliver in *The Eagle Has Wings*. The screen titles, which were printed in glittering white against a background of moving planes and clouds, proclaimed that the story was a simple human document concerning a New York Playboy who found his true self in the crucible of war, and that the producer was Arch Bowdler, the associate producers, Josh Spiegal and Chuck Mosenthal; the director, Bud Capelli, and the cameraman, Vernon Chang. The titles further stated that the story was by Norma and Perce Fennimore adapted from the novel by Cynthia Stein; that the screen play was by Max Macgowan and Eloise Hunt with additional dialogue by Olaf Hansen and Benny Zeist, and that the music had been specially composed by Gregor Borowitz with orchestrations and vocal arrangements by Otto von Stollmeyer. Then came a long list of lesser people who had operated the sound; supervised the make-up; designed the hair styles; organised the publicity, and supplied extra effects. As an afterthought it was explained that the whole thing was a 'Bowdler-L.N.G.-Peerless Production'.

It took one hour and fifty-five minutes for the hero to find his true self in the crucible of war because before doing so he was constrained to find a great many other things as well. These included a tough friend with a hairy chest who cried on the least provocation; a drunk Canadian sergeant-pilot with a heart of gold who crashed in flames half-way through the picture; a lovable but brusque British peeress who lived in some Tudor tea-rooms on the Yorkshire moors; and last, but unfortunately not least, an adorable American girl of great courage and vivacity who was continually hiding herself in the cockpits of Eagle Squadron bombers. Finally, after a moving scene in a hospital run by some over made-up nuns, all mis-understandings were straightened out and the picture ended with the hero and heroine walking up a steep hill to the deafening accompaniment of a celestial choir.

When the lights went up several members of the party were discovered to be in tears. Pete was fast asleep with his head resting on the bare breast of his dinner partner. Morgan and Lenore were bickering in a corner and Sid was utterly exhausted and wished to go home.

The next day, Sunday, was passed peacefully. A few people came over for drinks before lunch and stayed until three. After lunch everyone slept, either in the house or by the pool, and at seven o'clock, fortified by some Old-Fashioneds and peanut butter appetisers, Sid and Pete were dispatched to their ship in Morgan's car. When they had gone Morgan and Lenore continued the squabble they had begun the night before and went on with it intermittently for the rest of the evening. The gist of it was, of course, Sid. Actually Lenore had found him rather boring but she spoke of him constantly with enthusiastic admiration in order to irritate Morgan. In this she succeeded easily. He rose to the bait every time. Finally, towards the end of dinner, he got up from the table violently and retired to the pool where he remained for an hour by himself, leaving Lenore in lonely triumph with the strawberry shortcake.

The visit of the two sailors had undoubtedly been a great success. Neither of them had behaved badly nor said anything shaming. Sid, of the two, had been the more popular because of his natural ease, lack of shyness and vitality, but they had both made a good impression on everyone they had met and had been pressed on all sides to return for further hospitality should their ship ever again be in the vicinity.

Morgan was not much given to introspection, nor was he particularly adept at analysing his own feelings. In his early years when his ego was more easily satisfied and assuaged by sexual promiscuity, and his ambition was goading him to succeed, he had had little time to sift, weigh and evaluate his motives. Perhaps if he had, the impact of his sudden fame might have steadied him instead of confusing him. As it was he was in a muddle, and somewhere, deep in his subconscious, he knew it. He was aware, dimly, that he had changed; that his reactions were less gay, less volatile than they used to be; that his capacity for enjoyment seemed to have dwindled and that with the increasing burden of his stardom he was considerably less happy than he had been before. He was also aware, not dimly but very clearly, that he was much to be envied. He was young, successful, immensely publicised and sought after. Big executives argued and fought for the loan of his services; his financial position was assured and his contract with C.R.P.I. (Cinesound Radiant Pictures Incorporated) was watertight with automatic raises of salary for the next four years. True he was sick of Lenore, but she was still physically satisfactory and, when not determined to be bitchy, fairly good company.

The arrival of Sid had disturbed him by bringing into his mind something that for years he had been striving to shut out: memory of the past, concern for his family, perhaps – who knows – even a little concern for his country. During the last years he had written home occasionally; dutifully remembered his mother's and Sheila's birthdays and sent them presents at Christmas. Sid he had ignored. Sid had always been a thorn in his flesh. He knew that there was no reason for this. Sid was devoted to him; was loyal, affectionate and true, whereas he, Morgan, was none of these things and wasn't even sure that he wanted to be. Sid was the trouble all right. Sid was the weight on his conscience. Ordinary Seaman Sidney Booker, brother of Morgan Kent – sailor brother of Morgan Kent. What the hell had Sid wanted to join the Navy for in the first place, and having joined it why the hell couldn't he have stayed with the Home Fleet and not come dashing romantically out to the Pacific in a destroyer? Sitting gloomily by the pool while Lenore amused herself up in the house with the radio, Morgan was compelled to face one fact honestly and without compromise, and that was that he wished his good-humoured, loyal, affectionate sailor brother dead and at the bottom of the sea. He crushed down this unedifying reflection as soon as it seared across his mind but it remained there dormant until the next morning when it re-emerged with even greater force. Lenore wandered into his bedroom wearing peach-coloured pyjamas. She had a glint in her eye and *Hollywood Highlights,* which was published with dreadful regularity every Monday, in her hand.

'Well, "Les",' she said cheerfully, 'our Ruthie's little bird certainly worked overtime at Beejie's the other night. Just cast those dway big violet eyes over this.' She threw the magazine lightly on to his chest and lit a cigarette.

Morgan, with dry mouth and a sinking heart, read Ruthie's column, flung the magazine on to the floor, stamped into the bathroom and slammed the door. Lenore languidly picked it up and read it again with a quizzical smile. 'A very cute little bird talked to Ruthie the other evening – the cutest little bird you've ever seen, with curly fair hair, blue eyes and bell-bottomed pants – now don't try to guess, girls, because you never will. It was our Morgan Kent's sailor brother and was our Morg's face red when S.B. called him "Les", because, girls, "Les" is what his name really is. Les Booker from Southsea, England. There had been a lot of bombs falling on Southsea lately, so it's nice to think that at least one of the Booker boys is out trying to stop them.'

CHAPTER 6

IN the December following Sid's visit to Hollywood the Japanese, to the astonishment of a great many people, dropped a number of bombs on Pearl Harbour, an American Naval Base on the island of Oahu. The reverberations of those bombs echoed across the Western World, and that lesser world bounded by Los Angeles in the East and Santa Monica in the West was shaken to its foundations. Enemy invasion was expected hourly; vital and momentous decisions were made; the course of many a contract was drastically changed and several important projects abandoned. One of these was a Technicolor Musical with a Japanese setting entitled provisionally, *Get Yourself a Geisha*, which was to have been a starring vehicle for Linda Lakai, a new Hungarian soprano with tiny eyes and an enormous range. A quarter of the picture had already been shot and so its sudden abandonment caused acute financial anxiety, until fortunately one of the script writers conceived the brilliant idea of altering the locale from Japan to China, a gallant country with which everyone was in sympathy. This change was immediately put into effect and, with only minor alterations to the costumes, the picture ultimately emerged as *Pekin Parade* starring

Laurine Murphy. There were of course other equally momentous but more personal upheavals in the movie colony, among them the sudden discovery, by careful X-ray, of an ulcer in Morgan Kent's duodenum. This unforeseen disaster, although not directly attributable to Oriental treachery, must certainly have been aggravated by it and it entailed immediate and radical changes in Morgan's professional and private life as well as in his diet. His alcohol consumption was grimly rationed to two Scotch highballs a day and no Old-Fashioneds at all. He was obliged to withdraw from a 'Period' picture he had only just begun called *Hail Hannibal* and retire sadly to a rented bungalow in Palm Springs for a prolonged rest. Here Lenore visited him occasionally for week-ends, bringing with her the gossip of the town and a few friends to cheer his loneliness. The gossip of the town at that time was rich in surmise and agitation. Nation-wide conscription was inevitable; Robert Bailey had flown to Canada to enlist but had been invalided out after three weeks training on account of an undescended testicle, an embarrassment which hitherto had been unsuspected by his friends. Ross Cheeseman, Sonny Blake and Jimmy Clunes were on the verge of being drafted, and Joan Ziegler, obsessed by the fear of Japanese invasion, had had a nervous collapse, left poor Charlie, and fled to her mother's home in Iowa with the three children. Dear old Paul Newcombe had been absolutely splendid and was organising vast projects for British War Relief, and Lulu Frazer had volunteered to make a tour of personal appearances for the Red Cross and had designed for herself two uniforms, one for day work and one for night work, and both in sharkskin. There were many other titbits of news to relieve the tedium of Morgan's enforced seclusion, but happily, after three months, Doc Mowbray – who was a personal friend as well as a physician and had originally diagnosed the ulcer and arranged the X-ray – announced that the patient had so much improved in his general condition that, provided that he took things easily and remained true to his diet, he could come back and start work on a new picture.

The next year was a successful one for Morgan. He happened to be given two good scripts one after the other and both of them were completed pictures within seven months. In November he was loaned to the 'Arch Bowdler-L.N.G. Studios' to play the much-coveted rôle of Jumbo in *Jumbo R.A.F.*, a story based on the sensationally successful novel of the same name and which, as everyone in the industry had already prophesied, would certainly be the Picture of the Year and had as good as won the critics' award before the first reel was in the can. This, being an 'Epic' production, took a long while to make and it wasn't until June 1943 that it was finished, sneak-previewed and finally given its world première at Grauman's Chinese Theatre. Of all premières given in that great theatre since war had cast its shadow over American life, none had approached within a thousand miles of the brilliance and distinction of this one. To begin with, the picture had been discussed and publicised over a long period. There had also been trouble with the Hays Office over certain scenes which were considered to be too realistic and out-spoken, notably one in which a tough but good-hearted squadron leader said to the hero, 'By God, Jumbo, in spite of your crazy flying, you're a lovable bastard!' This phrase had of course been viewed with slight scepticism at the pre-liminary script conferences, but, as it was the climax of one of the most memorable scenes in the original book, it had been left, in the hope that it would get by. The Hays Office how-ever, its ears protectively attuned to the fragile sensibilities of the American movie-going public, was inexorable and the line had to be changed to: 'By Gosh, Jumbo, in spite of your crazy flying, you're a fine kid.' This, together with some other similar assaults upon national decency, necessitated retakes which put several weeks extra time on to the production schedule. Also, as the whole Hays episode had been widely discussed in the press, public anticipation had been worked up to fever pitch.

The première itself was attended by everyone of note in the motion picture industry and by a great many who weren't. Special cordons of police were employed to beat back the eager crowds; arc lamps bathed the occasion in shrill blue light; the immaculately shod feet of certain stars were pressed into wet cement and the imprints duly autographed and every celebrity upon arrival was led to a microphone in the lobby where, amid the whirring and clicking of cameras, he or she gave his or her message of goodwill to an expectant radio public of several millions.

The auditorium of the theatre had been draped with R.A.F. flags and on the stage was grouped the Los Angeles Civic Choir in its entirety appropriately dressed in R.A.F. uniforms. When finally the audience was seated and the choir had rendered 'Oh for the Wings of a Dove' and 'There'll Always be an England', a British Ministry of Information 'Documentary' was shown which, although a little slow in tempo, proved conclusively that London really had been bombed. This was followed by an inaudible speech from the British Consul and a 'Donald Duck' cartoon. Then at last – at long last – came the picture itself, which, on the whole, was very good. There were of course a few minor anachronisms here and there; a Brittany fisher-girl who spoke French with a pronounced Hessian accent; a scene in a blossom-laden English orchard in June at the end of which the hero's humble mother, wearing a tea-gown, presented her son's fiancée with a large bunch of chrysanthemums; and an amusing but unconvincing episode between the hero and a cockney greengrocer who, late at night in the spring of 1942, happened to be wheeling a barrow down Piccadilly piled with Sunkist oranges. Apart from these insignificant errors which only a carping mind would have noted, the story moved along

to its climax with gathering emotional strength and commendable speed. Some of the air battle sequences were
magnificent and the escape of the hero from a Nazi prison
camp was breath-taking. Morgan Kent as 'Jumbo' gave unquestionably the finest performance of his career. He played
his love scenes with sincerity and beautifully restrained
passion, and his portrayal of grim determination mixed with
terror when he was forced to bale out of a blazing plane
brought forth a spontaneous burst of applause. When it was
all over there was prolonged cheering from the audience, and
Morgan was almost torn to pieces by the crowd outside who
unhappily had not been able to see the picture at all.

There was a party afterwards at the Arc de Triomphe night
club which had been taken over for the occasion by Arch
Bowdler, and it wasn't until 3.30 a.m. that Morgan and
Lenore, tired but exalted, let themselves into their house and
found, propped up on the bar, a telegram. Lenore opened it
while Morgan was fixing a 'night-cap' – she said, 'My God!'
under her breath, and handed it to him. He read it and slowly
put the bottle of Bourbon he was holding back on the shelf. It
said, 'Sid reported missing presumably killed. Mother terribly
upset. Please cable. Love. Sheila.'

CHAPTER 7

In the months following, Morgan, on the advice of the
Studio Publicity Department, went out very little and wore a
black armband. People were wonderfully kind and sympathetic and he received many letters of condolence. Arch
Bowdler indeed was so profoundly moved when he heard the
news that he suggested organising a memorial service for
Morgan's sailor brother in the Sweetlawn Baptist Temple on
Sunset Boulevard. Upon reflection, however, the idea was
abandoned, but he did give a small dinner for twenty-eight

people in Morgan's honour, at which Sid's memory was toasted reverently before the party adjourned to the Blue Room to see the new L.N.G. Musical, starring Glenda Crane and Bozo Browning.

Morgan, who had cabled his mother immediately upon receiving the telegram and flogged himself into writing a long letter of commiseration, accepted the attitude of his friends and acquaintances with dignity and restraint and it was evident to all that he was bearing his loss with the utmost fortitude. Another effect of his bereavement was the strange lessening of friction in his home life. Lenore, softened perhaps by the passing wings of the Angel of Death, became kinder in her everyday manner, drank a little less and made fewer sarcastic wisecracks. Life went on much as usual except that in the autumn of 1943 both of them, Morgan and Lenore, together with a group of other stars, went on a flying tour through the United States and Canada in order to make personal appeals for a great War Bond drive. This was publicly a great success and privately not without its rewards. They had a special plane to take them from place to place; they were entertained lavishly and photographed and interviewed ad nauseam; they had to sign thousands of autograph books which was of course dreadfully tiring, but they took it in their stride upheld by the reflection that they were working for a magnificent cause and doing something really worth while.

Morgan actually enjoyed the Canadian part of the tour a little less. His well rehearsed and beautifully delivered patriotic appeal was received politely but without quite the same vibrant acclaim that it had been in the States. In fact on one occasion, in an enormous cinema in Toronto, someone at the back shouted something apparently uncomplimentary. No one ever found out exactly what it was, but the tension of the moment was snapped and he found it difficult to recapture the audience's attention. The War Bond tour came to an end in Washington where they were all entertained at the White

House and photographed still more; inside and outside and in the garden. Later on they were photographed again; outside the Capitol; outside the headquarters of the F.B.I.; and posed reverentially in front of the Lincoln Memorial. *Life* Magazine published a six-page photographic survey of the whole expedition and *Time* devoted an entire page to a eulogistic article under the heading 'Stars Calling'.

CHAPTER 8

In November 1943 Morgan celebrated his thirtieth birthday by giving a party. This had to take place on a Saturday night because he was in the middle of a French Resistance picture called *Hidden Flames* and had to get up at six o'clock every morning excepting Sundays. The party was a great success up to a certain point. A large number of people came, most of them bearing gifts; there was an entertaining quarrel between Hester Roach and Lois Levine, two exquisitely proportioned young starlets who had unfortunately both fallen in love with the same agent; Tonio Lopez brought his guitar and sang Mexican folk songs for an hour and a half by the pool; the buffet supper was delicious; Gloria Marlow choked over a fishbone in the kedgeree and had to be taken to the bathroom to be sick; everyone drank a great deal and enjoyed themselves immensely. Morgan himself was at the top of his form and, in addition to being a perfect host and seeing that all his guests were looked after, contrived to have a brief but satisfactory affair with Opal Myers in the bath-house. He emerged with admirable suavity from this episode, leaving Opal to reappear a little later. Tonio was still singing his songs; the moon was shining and although it was cold by the pool, there were enough mink coats to go round and everyone seemed to be happy. From the house above, where Lenore was dispensing drinks in the bar, came a cheerful buzz of chatter and laughter. Morgan picked his way through the group of muffled figures lying about on the canvas furniture, their cigarettes glowing like red fireflies in the moonlight, and went up the steps. He was aware of contentment. Life was good and God was in his heaven. It was at this moment, this instant of rare and perfect fulfilment, that Destiny elected to kick him violently in the stomach. There was a honking of a klaxon in the drive and, coinciding with Morgan's arrival on the porch, a taxi drew up. Morgan, still serene, still swathed in physical satisfaction and mental ease, went forward hospitably to welcome the late-comers. There was however only one late-comer. The taxi stopped with a screech of brakes, there was a hearty roar of 'Les' from inside it, and Sid leapt out of it, bounded up the porch steps and clasped Morgan in his arms. It was a moment of extraordinary poignancy. Lenore, hearing the noise, came out of the bar with several others and gave a loud shriek. The distant murmur of Tonio's baritone down by the pool came to an abrupt stop; there was a babel of voices; Sid was hugged and kissed and slapped on the back and swept into the bar. With him was swept into bitter oblivion Morgan's peace of mind. His sudden, transient awareness of the joy of living turned brown at the edges, curled up and died. The moon went behind a cloud; the wind from the Pacific Palisades blew chill and his heart writhed with dreadful, unacknowledged dismay. From then on the party, for him, became a nightmare. The gay, excited clamour of his guests rasped his nerves; the very recent memory of Opal Myers' surrender lay stately on his senses, and Lenore's fatuous, incredulous, welcoming screams irritated him to such an extent that he longed to bash her perfectly-capped teeth down her throat. To do him justice, however, his outward behaviour was beyond reproach. He installed Sid in a comfortable chair, plied him with drink and food and gave over the whole evening to him without stint and without betrayal. It must frankly be admitted that Sid accepted it wholeheartedly. He was looking ill and emaciated and was wearing creased khaki slacks and a stained tropical tunic, but his good spirits were in no way impaired. Before the party was over he had told the story of his escape four times, each time leavening its drama with impeccable British understatement. It was a thrilling, almost incredible story and was received by the assembled company with gasps and groans of excitement. To begin with, his ship had been sunk off the coast of Borneo in the summer of 1942. He had clung to a raft in shark-infested waters for eleven hours before being picked up by an armed Japanese trawler. He had escaped from a pestilential prison camp in Malaya with two comrades, both American, in July 1943. One of them was a big, husky fellow from Texas and the other a Jewish boy from Brooklyn who possessed qualities of courage and endurance which were nothing short of fantastic. The three of them, after terrible vicissitudes, managed to get to Ceylon in an open boat. From there, after weeks in hospital, they were sent in a transport plane to Honolulu via Australia, New Zealand, New Caledonia and Fiji. In Honolulu they parted company. Tex and Lew, the Brooklyn boy, remained in Schofield barracks awaiting leave while Sid, through the goodwill of an American Naval Intelligence officer, was given space in a bomber which was flying to San Francisco. In San Francisco he reported to the British Consul who had notified the Naval attaché in Washington, who in turn notified the Admiralty in London. After three days, during which he had lived in a small hotel on money supplied by the Consul who had been extremely decent to him, the order came through from London that he was to take a week's leave and report to H.M.S. *Taragon* which was refitting in Norfolk, Virginia. He had cabled his mother and Sheila, but had purposely not let Morgan know that he was alive and safe because he wanted it to be a surprise. Well, here he was and it was certainly a surprise. He was finally led to bed, happily drunk, and the party broke up.

The next three days, the duration of Sid's visit, were a perpetual embarrassment to Morgan. Of course he told himself repeatedly how delighted he was that Sid, instead of being missing and presumed killed, was alive and kicking and exuberantly cheerful, but the strain was considerable.

The Sunday following upon Sid's dramatic arrival was hectic beyond all bearing. The house was besieged by reporters and cameramen. Sid was photographed interminably; inside the house, outside the house, by the pool, on the porch, with Morgan, without Morgan, with Lenore, without Lenore, with Fred, the coloured butler, and alone, in the shower. The telephone rang incessantly; sheaves of telegrams arrived; Arch Bowdler called personally and insisted on giving a dinner for Sid that very night. It was enormous, noisy and successful. Everybody, as usual, made speeches and for once no movie was shown, the emergence of Morgan's sailor brother from the jaws of death being a far greater attraction than any preview.

On the Monday, Ruthie's column in *Hollywood Highlights* was one long scream of hero-worship. All the other papers also were plastered with photographs of Sid, articles on Sid, anecdotes about Sid and interviews with Sid. Louella Parsons flung her arms round him in The Brown Derby and burst into tears and Hedda Hopper, looking extremely chic, appeared at a cocktail party wearing a new toque made entirely of palm fronds and white ensigns. To do Sid justice all this embarrassed him almost as much as it embarrassed Morgan, but for different reasons. Morgan's reactions, entangled as they were with family conscience, subconscious jealousy and an agitated inferiority complex, were difficult to define accurately. Sid's were quite simple. He was glad to be alive; delighted to see 'Old Les' again; pleased up to a point with all the fuss that was being made of him but aware in his heart that it was perhaps a bit overdone, and impatient, above all else, to get home – via Norfolk, Virginia– as soon as possible.

Fortunately on the second day of his visit, Gareth Gibbons, a new and handsome L.N.G. 'Heart-throb' was arrested for driving a car while under the influence of alcohol, and attempting to rape a sixteen-year-old waitress in a milk bar in Brentwood Heights. This happily deflected the full blaze of publicity away from Sid, and his departure, on the Wednesday, was achieved, much to his relief, almost without comment.

The repercussions of his visit however were apparent for a long while. Morgan's behaviour had been exemplary throughout and most people had taken his carefully adjusted acceptance of Sid's reflected glory at its face value. Hollywood, however, is a strange place. It is filled with charming and talented people who work hard and do much to alleviate the miseries and troubles of the world. It is climatically amiable and steady; scenically it has much to offer; beautiful mountains surround it, efficient clear-cut architecture adorns it and blue skies, as a rule, smile down upon it. In spite of these advantages and a great many more besides, there is, as in all highly sensitive communities, an inevitable streak of cruelty and personal envy lying just below the radiant surface. There are, the fact must be frankly admitted, a few hard-boiled, over-sophisticated, unkind characters abroad whose pleasure it is to strike down the successful, undermine the contented and distort, whenever possible, the pure motives of human behaviour. These minds, it must also be frankly admitted, are frequently employed by the newspapers, for is it not from the newspapers that we first receive intimations that all is not well with our friends? In Morgan's case it was Ruthie's little bird that first started the trouble. The ungenerous innuendo made by that feathered scavenger two years before had been quickly forgotten, but now, reinforced by Sid's second and far more spectacular arrival in the colony, it chirped again and again with increasingly malicious effect. Presently, in the columns of larger, more revered periodicals than *Hollywood Highlights* unpleasant paragraphs about Morgan began to appear. Several of his magnanimous gestures towards the war effort were deprecated and questioned. His successful War Bond tour of the preceding year was alleged to have been mere publicity-hunting; his duodenal ulcer, which had been troubling him acutely since Sid's visit, was mocked at and above all the fact that he had large-heartedly given his entire salary for *High Adventure* to the British War Relief was smeared with the suggestion that, as this picture was one over his schedule for the year, he evaded a great deal of super-tax by doing so. All this of course was unmannerly and reprehensible, but alas, in public life it is often necessary to take the rough with the smooth, and occasionally with the rough. This Morgan was temperamentally incapable of doing. His spirits were not particularly resilient and his morale crumbled easily. As the insidious attacks upon his integrity increased and spread he became more and more nervy, irritable and morose. Lenore, to her eternal credit, stood by him loyally. On one occasion she even went so far as to slap Mona Melody's face in The Beachcomber when that lady unequivocally stated that Morgan's moving-picture career was shot to hell. But in spite of his wife's steadfastness and the devotion of his friends, things went from bad to worse.

High Adventure opened simultaneously in New York, Chicago and Hollywood, and was unanimously voted by the critics to be the worst picture to come out of Hollywood since the war. Morgan's personal notices were insulting and occasionally downright vituperative. He was torn to pieces with all the gleeful savagery that only well-established, perennially successful stars can ever inspire. Al Tierney, his agent, flew especially to the coast from New York and grave consultations ensued between him, the Studio Publicity Department, Lenore and Morgan himself. It was finally decided that he must publicly renounce his next two contracted pictures and go immediately on a tour of the war areas under the aegis of U.S.O. Morgan protested against this decision at first on the reasonable grounds that, being unable either to sing or dance, there was little that he could contribute to the entertainment of troops. He ultimately gave in, however, on the assurance that his rôle would be that of Master of Ceremonies and that all that would be required of him would be to talk nonchalantly into a microphone, tell a few funny stories, and introduce the more musical artists supporting him.

In March 1944 the party set forth across the Atlantic in a transport plane. They all wore khaki uniforms with U.S.O. 'flashes' on their shoulders and had a farewell party given for them at the Stork Club in New York on the eve of their departure.

The tour was strenuous but triumphant. They played Gibraltar, Oran, Algiers, Tunis, Tripoli, Malta and Cairo. Then, after a few days rest, they went on to Sicily, Naples and Rome. The show, being speedy, efficient and abundantly noisy, was received enthusiastically almost everywhere. Morgan had been paralysed with nerves at the first few performances but he gradually became more relaxed and began to enjoy himself. He discovered that the less effort he made, the more the troops liked him. He had been supplied with a few good stories before leaving and these he interspersed with impromptu comments of his own, some of which brought forth gratifying roars of laughter. The company consisted of Zaza Carryl, a slumbrous 'Blues' singer, who moaned lugubriously into the microphone and was invariably cheered to the echo; Ella Rosing, a very small starlet with a piercing coloratura, who went on first and sang 'Je Suis Titania' and 'The Bells of St Mary's'; Gus Gruber, who did card tricks interlarded with rather suggestive patter and finished up by playing a ukelele and singing and dancing at the same time; and Okie Wood and Buzzie Beckman, a vaudeville act who had the star position at the end of the programme and monotonously tore the place up. Lenore had been left behind in Beverly Hills, and Morgan, after a few half-hearted approaches to Ella Rosing, who was not really his type, finally settled on Zaza Carryl as the partner of his private pleasures. She was an amiable, uncomplicated creature and they got on very well.

Upon arrival in Rome towards the end of July, orders came through that when their week there was over they were to proceed to England. This caused a lot of discussion in the troupe and a great many jokes were made about food rationing, Doodlebugs and Rocket Bombs. Morgan, naturally enough, was tremendously excited at the thought of returning to his homeland after so many years absence and in such circumstances. He realised, without cynicism but with sheer common sense, that, from the publicity angle alone, it would be an excellent thing to do. Imagine therefore his bitter disappointment when, three days before they were due to leave he collapsed in agóny half-way through a performance they were giving at an air base in the Campagña. He was hurried immediately into hospital, examined by several doctors, and X-rayed. Nothing definite appeared in the X-ray, but as his pains, although sporadic, were intense and he was also in a bad state of nervous exhaustion, it was deemed wiser to fly him directly back to the States rather than let him risk continuing the tour.

His plane was met at Los Angeles by Lenore, Arch Bowdler, the deputy head of the Studio Publicity Department, Doc Mowbray, and an ambulance in which he was whisked off to a clinic where he stayed for three weeks undergoing various tests and gradually regaining his strength. The publicity accruing from his misfortune was, on the whole, innocuous. Even Ruthie's little bird, although a trifle sceptical, was forced to admit that Morgan's tour of the battle areas had been an unqualified success and that he had done a fine job and been popular with the 'Boys'.

CHAPTER 9

IN the autumn of 1945 Morgan's dream of returning home to
England at last came true. During the defeat of the Nazis in
Europe and the dropping of the Atomic Bomb on Hiroshima
he had made two immensely successful pictures. His position
now was more unassailable than it had ever been even in the
year of his first meteoric rise to stardom. Only one thing
marred the joy and gratification of his spectacular 'come-
back' into public favour, and that was Lenore's unexpected
and crude announcement that she was sick to death of him,
was passionately in love with Tonio Lopez, and wished for a
divorce as soon as it conveniently could be arranged. There
were some violent scenes and much bitter recrimination
during which the names of Opal Myers and Zaza Carryl were
hurled at his head with, it must be admitted, certain justification. Finally, with the assistance of two lawyers and the
Studio Publicity Department and a lot of bickering, it was
arranged that Lenore should divorce him on the grounds of
mental cruelty and acute incompatibility of temperament.
Soon after this Lenore unostentatiously left the house and
retired, for discretion's sake, to her married sister's home in
Salt Lake City. Morgan meanwhile, oppressed by a sense of
matrimonial failure, was dispatched, in a blaze of publicity, to
attend a Royal Command Performance of his latest picture
The Boy from the Hills at the Empire Theatre, Leicester Square,
London.

His reception in England surpassed not only his own but
the Studio Publicity Department's wildest dreams. From the
moment he stepped ashore from the *Queen Elizabeth* at
Southampton he was mobbed by wildly cheering crowds.
Sid, wearing inconspicuous civilian clothes, met him at the
dock. His mother and Sheila remained at home on the advice

of the English representative of the Studio Publicity Department who had organised for Morgan a triumphant return to
Southsea on the coming Saturday and wished the long-
awaited reunion of mother and son to be handled in the
proper manner at the proper time.

At Waterloo Station Morgan was nearly trampled underfoot
by his English fans and the expectant crowd outside Claridge's
was so vast that special mounted police had to be deployed to
keep it in order and deflect the traffic. The première at the
Empire the next evening was, to Morgan, the accolade of his
whole career. He received an ovation upon entering the
theatre; was presented, with others, to the King and the
Queen, and cheered with heartwarming enthusiasm at the end
when he stepped on to the stage to make his personal appearance.

His return to his home-town of Southsea on the Saturday
was even more tumultuous and, although not graced by the
presence of Royalty, almost equally moving. The streets were
hung with banners and flags; his mother and Sheila and the
Mayor greeted him on the steps of the Town Hall, and it
wasn't until after a reception at the Queen's Hotel, at which he
was called upon to make one speech for the news-reels and
another for the B.B.C., that he was allowed to relax in the
bosom of his family. Even then the street remained thronged
with adolescent enthusiasts for quite a while. His first impression on entering the familiar sitting-room was that it was
much smaller than he remembered it to be. Sheila, married
now and with two children, was as brusque and downright
as ever. His mother had aged a good deal but her eyes were
glistening with excitement and she was inclined to be tearful.
After tea conversation flagged a bit. All family news had been
exhausted. Father's death and funeral in 1943 had been
described in detail, also Sheila's wedding, the birth of both her
children and Sid's intended marriage to a Miss Doris Solway
in a few months' time. Strangely enough the devastation of

the town in the early years of the war was hardly mentioned. Even the fact that Hadley's, where Morgan had once worked as a salesman, was now nothing but a mound of grass-covered rubble was only once lightly commented upon by Sheila.

Morgan found himself glancing furtively at his watch and hoping that the studio car would soon arrive to drive him back to London. It is sad to reflect how many family reunions are spoiled by anti-climax. The excitement and anticipation have been so strong; the moment so often and so gloriously pre-envisaged that the human heart seems unable to sustain the joy of actuality. Morgan's homecoming was naturally poignant and touching and happy. Not only this but it was publicly spectacular into the bargain. And yet, inevitably, when the first greetings were over, the occasion wilted and became soggy; little nervous jokes were made and there were unexplained silences. Presently the car arrived and Morgan got up to go. He kissed Sheila, wrung Sheila's husband's hand and banged Sid on the back. There was suddenly a renewed burst of conversation as though everything was perfectly normal. Morgan's mother, after a swift, appealing glance at Sheila, went out with him into the hall. He took her in his arms and was aware of a genuine surge of emotion. She felt frail and old and somehow pathetic. She stood away from him and gave her hair a little pat. 'Come back soon, Les,' she said, and then with a tremor in her voice, 'We didn't know anything about the ulcer, dear, it must have been dreadful.'

Morgan squeezed her arm affectionately. 'That's all over now, Mum, don't worry.'

'It isn't that . . .' she seemed to be speaking with an effort – 'But if anyone mentions your tubercular lung – do remember that we *had* to say something.'

Mr and Mrs Edgehill

(1)

MRS EDGEHILL had walked along to the 'Split' and sat down with her back against Roper's Folly. Roper's Folly was the remains of a wooden look-out house which Mr Roper, since deceased, had begun to build many years ago and discarded. It was a pleasant place to sit and she came there often in the evenings when she had washed up the tea things. It was silly of poor Mr Roper ever to have thought of building a house on that particular spot; for one thing it was too exposed and lay right in the path of the Trade Winds. Also, if he had ever completed it, it would have necessitated making a path all the way from the landing stage. There would have been no peace in the house either, stuck right out there on the edge of the surf, and in really bad weather it might quite conceivably have been washed away, indeed bits of it already had been. Last March year when the cyclone had passed quite close to the island waves had broken clean over it.

Mrs Edgehill sat there idly with her hands in her lap. She could, of course, have brought her knitting or a book but it was nicer just to do nothing at all. On her right the vivid water swirled through the 'Split' into the lagoon; when it had escaped the foam and turbulence of the surf it flowed swiftly and looked solid like blue-green glass. Directly in front of her was nothing but sea and sky. The sky, as usual at this time of year, was pale and without a cloud; the line of the horizon was sharp and the enormous rollers advanced monotonously, as though they had been strictly disciplined, to break on the outer rocks of the reef. Occasionally in the troubled water she would see the sinister dorsal fin of a shark slip by, or a school of porpoises flinging themselves through the waves just before they broke. She had a soft corner in her heart for the porpoises, they were so gay and abandoned and seemed to enjoy life. At her feet, among the shells and seaweed and myriad pieces of broken coral, hermit crabs scuttled about; some of them were enormous and had almost outgrown their borrowed shells. She always longed to catch one in the act of changing into a larger shell but she'd never been lucky. Her back was to the island – it wasn't really an island in the proper sense of the word, merely a coral reef some hundred feet wide enclosing a large lagoon – but when the sun went down she would of course turn round. This was a ritual. Eustace pulled the flag down at sunset and he liked her to stand up wherever she happened to be just for those few solemn moments. She loved him for insisting on this even if there was no one to see – even when they had been alone on the island for months she had always stood rigidly and watched the flag slowly fluttering down the mast and Eustace in his faded khaki shorts hauling away at the ropes.

There was still a half an hour or so to go before sunset so she could afford to relax and let her thoughts wander about. She was rather given to doing this; Eustace had said years and years and years ago when they were first married that her mind was like a rag-bag. She remembered having been vaguely hurt by this at the time but later she had had to admit that there was a certain justification for what he said. Her mind was rather like a rag-bag – she viewed it quite literally as being a hotch-potch of odds and ends and bits of coloured stuff and thimbles and needles and whatnot – the trouble was that she could never get it really tidied up and she was by nature a tidy woman. Here, of course, sitting by herself looking at the sea, it didn't matter how casually her mind behaved; it could jump backwards and forwards through time and space as much as it liked. She could even talk out loud to herself if she wanted to, there was nobody to hear her except the hermit crabs. She sometimes tried to string together piece by piece the last twenty years, all the adventures and excitements and joys and despairs, but she nearly always got side-tracked; some particular memory would hold the stage for too long and, in reliving it, the story would become unstuck and muddled. It was quite a story too when you came to think of it. If you could write it for a magazine; put it down clearly without having to worry about spelling or keep on stopping to think of the right words. Up until she had first met Eustace of course there hadn't been any story at all, that is, nothing out of the ordinary. Just a girl with a mother and father and three sisters and one brother living in a country town. She closed her eyes for a moment against the bright, alien sea and walked along Hythe High Street; she turned to the left just after passing the Red Lion and walked across the bridge over the dyke, past Mrs Vernon's, and along for a bit until she got on to the Front – the tide was out, only just out because the sands still looked wet. Away to the right were the Romney Marshes and the sea-wall with the Martello towers sticking up against the evening sky – there was Eustace coming towards her arm-in-arm with that awful Elsie Mallet, there was her Fate walking into her life with a slight sailor's roll and his cap too much on the back of his head and a tuft of tow-like hair jutting out over his forehead. She had often, in later years, felt slight conscience pangs about Elsie Mallet. After all, he was her second cousin and had come down from Chatham on week-end leave. Mrs Edgehill opened her eyes again and permitted herself a complacent smile. Poor Elsie. No need to pity her really, they hadn't been actually engaged, but still . . . That had been the beginning – the very beginning – twenty-five years ago. She turned her head and looked back towards the hotel and the landing-stage. Eustace was still fiddling with the canoe; he looked very small and thin in the distance, like a sunburned little boy. She did wish he could put on a little more weight, but still he was the thin type and although he was over fifty he'd always look young for his age. Her mind ran lightly back to the honeymoon at Blackpool. That was nineteen-nineteen – she never liked thinking about it very much because she hadn't enjoyed it. It wasn't Eustace's fault – it wasn't anybody's fault really – but she hadn't known it was going to be quite like that. Later on she had to admit that she'd been a bit silly over the whole thing; but Blackpool of all places, so common and noisy and all those thousands of people and that awful bedroom in the Marine Hotel and the picture of the soldier saying good-bye to the dead horse. Waking up to that every morning was no picnic, it almost made her cry to think of it. And being sick on the scenic railway and Eustace getting drunk on the Saturday night and then having that dreadful quarrel on the pier. . . . Then came London and the flat in Acacia Mansions and Eustace leaving the Navy and getting the job at Bartlett's. Whoever it was that said the first year of married life is the most difficult was dead right and no mistake. It was funny to look back on bitterness and utter misery and not mind about it any more. Perhaps if it hadn't been for the operation and the baby dying and her being so ill for all those months nothing would ever have come right. Eustace might have gone on at Bartlett's; they might have had other children and gone on living in that flat and quarrelling and not understanding about each other or anything. Eustace might have left her eventually – run off with somebody else – her heart contracted painfully at the very thought of it. None of the rest might ever have happened, none of the adventures and troubles, none of the true love . . . . she sighed and then smiled – she wouldn't change places, not with anyone in the world, she wouldn't go back five minutes but she wouldn't change. She looked back again. Eustace had at last left the canoe and was walking back to the house. He saw her and waved his hand. She watched him go in by the back door followed faithfully by Sandy; Sandy probably thought that there was a bit of fish going.

The sun was getting lower and the sea colour was changing; a spider crab suddenly popped out of a hole in the sand and went dancing down to the water's edge on its high, spindly legs as though it were being blown by the wind. Mrs Edgehill settled herself comfortably again, there was no hurry.

(2)

COWRIE ISLAND is a small coral ring in the South-West Pacific. Officially it is designated as belonging to the outer Samolan Group, but this is merely for the purpose of identification as it is entirely isolated. Actually it is nearer to Fiji than to Samolo but it comes under the jurisdiction of the Samolan Governor. It was first charted in the year 1786 by the redoubtable Captain Evangelus Cobb who was driven by a gale on to its reefs. Forunately the damage to his ship was comparatively slight for there was no water on the island and had he been forced to stay there he would, with his crew, have died of thirst. As it was, however, he was only stranded for a few days and was able to report with lyric enthusiasm in his log book that it was . . . 'a reef of personable size o'er which fluttered small white birds of exquisite beauty . . . so tame were these gentle, fragile creatures that they were willing, nay eager, to accept biscuit crumbs from the naked hand!'

In the nineteenth century when the Samolan group was taken over by the British, Cowrie Island was, rather casually, included in the deal. Since then it had remained uninhabited until the early nineteen-twenties when the then Governor of Samolo, Sir Vivian Cragshore, had, with extraordinary foresight for a Colonial Governor, realised its possible potentialities as a future seaplane base. He had, with commendable

promptitude and in the face of considerable opposition from
the Colonial Office, equipped an expedition consisting of ten
people: three Samolans, four half-castes, all of whom had
passed with honours through an engineering course at
Pendarla University, and three Englishmen, or rather two
Englishmen and a Scotsman called Ian Strachan. Ian Strachan
was in charge of the party and they swiftly and efficiently set
to work to build rain tanks, several huts – most of which were
demolished by the weather in later years – and a flagstaff
which, although it blew down every now and then, survives
to this day. After a few months of extremely primitive living
the expedition departed leaving only Strachan and the hardy
Samolans. These exiles were supplied with necessities by a
ship which called twice a year. Strachan lived there in
solitude, with the exception of the Samolans who fished
incessantly, until nineteen thirty-five, when he died of blood
poisoning, having had his heel torn off by a barracuda while
swimming in the lagoon. At this time the Airways were
already casting covetous eyes on the Island with a view to
using it as a convenient overnight stop for their intended
Trans-Pacific Clipper service. Representations were made
from Washington to the British Government for either a lease
or sale of the Island; meanwhile Sir Humphrey Logan, who
had succeeded Sir Vivian Cragshore in Samolo, dispatched
Eustace Edgehill, who had been for two years trying not very
successfully to run a pineapple plantation on the sea coast near
Naruchi, and bade him build a house and install himself as
British Resident, pending the results of the Anglo-American
discussions.

In May 1936 Eustace Edgehill arrived at Cowrie Island.
He brought with him adequate but not extravagant supplies
and six Samolan boys of excellent physique but dubious
reputation, dubious that is to say from the standpoint of the
Church of England Mission School in Naruchi. To begin
with they were beach boys, and beach boys, in the view of the

God-fearing, were definitely lesser breeds without the law. They had spent most of their extreme youth and adolescence diving for pennies for the edification of visiting tourists. For the further edification of the tourists they were known to be obliging in many other ways. They were cheerful, amoral and they could all play the 'akula' (a local form of 'ukelele') with impeccable rhythm. They could also sing charmingly, although some of their native, hybrid songs were not entirely guiltless of sensual implication. They were expert fishermen and were tough, willing and without malice. It was for these latter qualifications that Eustace Edgehill chose them to accompany him. There was a certain amount of fuss in Church circles in Naruchi, in fact a question was asked in the House of Assembly in Pendarla, but Eustace, who took a bleak view of missionaries and was none too enthusiastic about the Church of England anyhow, finally got his way and, amid scenes of local jubilation, they set sail.

For Eustace the whole thing was a tremendous adventure. In the first place the title 'British Resident' filled him with pride; secondly, the thought of going off into the unknown, starting as it were from scratch, building himself a house and installing himself as Lord of all he surveyed fluttered his heart with excitement and gratification. All his life he had been like that, not only willing but eager to cast away the substance for the shadow. Not that the pineapple plantation could in truth be called substance; it had been unsatisfactory and unremunerative from the word go, also for him, with his irrepressible spirit of adventure, far too sedentary. For Dorrie, his wife, this new challenge to Fate was full of menace. After all they were neither of them as young as they were and he might be bitten by a barracuda like poor Mr Strachan or get sunstroke all by himself on an exposed coral reef. She hadn't enjoyed the pineapple experiment any more than he had, but at least, with all its disappointments and difficulties, they had been together. Now he was leaving her behind, by order of the Governor, until the house was built and he could send for her. He swore that it would only be a question of a few months at the outside, but she remained sceptical, heavy-hearted and full of dark forebodings. When he had finally sailed she went dismally back to the house, looked with distaste at the crop of undersized pineapples, and had a good cry.

(3)

THE arrival at Cowrie Island was, on the whole, discouraging. There was a heavy sea running, a seventy mile an hour gale and driving rain. Three days of this had to be endured before they could come close enough in to land a boat and negotiate the 'Split'. After several hazardous journeys, during one of which the boat nearly capsized, they finally managed to get themselves and their supplies ashore. Eustace, wearing a pair of shorts, gumboots, a raincoat and a topee, looked around him and sighed. The sight that met his eyes was not entirely up to what his imagination had pictured. The driving rain did little to enhance the cheerfulness of the scene. The island was about twenty-eight miles in circumference and, where he stood by the rickety landing-stage, about three to four hundred yards wide; beyond the 'Split' on the right and also about a quarter of a mile away on the left it narrowed until at certain places there was less than a hundred yards between the pounding surf and the lagoon. There were no trees or shrubs of any sort except one large rather sullen-looking bush that looked like a vast green hedgehog. The huts that the Strachan expedition had built were still standing but were in a bad state of disintegration. Over by the 'Split' stood a strange stone edifice which had obviously never been finished at all. This had been started in a moment of enthusiasm by Mr Roper who had been Ian Strachan's second in command. The

Captain of the ship was standing with Eustace on the landing-stage. He waved his hand contemptuously in the direction of Mr Roper's unfulfilled dream; 'Bloody silly,' he said, 'any fool would have known better than to try to build a house right on the point like that.' Eustace smiled desolately and agreed with him.

The largest of the Strachan huts still had enough roof over half of it to keep out the rain, and so, pending further explorations, Eustace directed the boys to dump the supplies and themselves in there until the weather abated a little. The Captain, who was obviously concerned about getting his boat through the 'Split' and back to the ship, wrung Eustace's hand with ill-disguised sympathy, slapped him a thought too heartily on the back and departed with many shouted promises to see him again in about three months' time. Eustace walked over to the sea side of the reef and watched the boat battling through the surf. When it had safely navigated it and was rapidly becoming a small black speck in the distance, he turned and walked back to the hut. The boys were still staggering up from the landing-stage with packing-cases. Ippaga, the eldest of them, was sucking at a sodden cigarette and shouting orders. He smiled broadly at Eustace, exposing two rows of perfect teeth, and shrugged his shoulders as much as to say, 'Well – here we are – it's bloody awful but all we can do is to make the best of it!' Eustace smiled back at him and suddenly felt more cheerful.

A few hours later, a little before sundown, a miracle happened. The rain stopped abruptly, the skies cleared and the whole island was bathed in soft, luminous yellow light; the lagoon was transformed from a waste of choppy grey waves into a sheet of vivid emerald and blue with multi-coloured coral heads pushing up above the surface of the water. The boys who had been profitably employed in rigging up a tarpaulin over the unroofed part of the principal hut gave loud whoops of joy and, tearing off whatever odd garments they happened to have on, ran down to the landing-stage from which they dived, clean as arrows and with hardly any splash at all. Eustace watched them indulgently and, lighting a cigarette, sat down on one of the rotting wooden rails of the veranda. While he was sitting there a very small delicate white bird circled twice round the hut and then, quite unafraid, settled on his hand. The sky suddenly became a pageant; the vanished storm had left wisps of cloud that took fire from the last rays of the sun; every colour imaginable flamed across the heavens. Eustace nodded his head contentedly. 'Dorrie will like this,' he said to himself.

(4)

Doris Edgehill was a woman of fortitude. She was also what has been described in a popular song as a 'One Man Girl'. She had met and fallen in love with Eustace in nineteen-seventeen and in spite of the disappointments, crudities and, in her case, actual tragedies of early married life she had remained in love with him and would continue to love him until the end of her days. It is indeed fortunate for the sanctity of marriage vows that women of her type still exist. Not that she ever gave much thought to sanctity of any sort. Once Eustace had whisked her away from her home and family and the ambiguous religious ministrations of the local vicar she was perfectly content to accept his views on God and man and the universe without argument and without question. She seldom troubled her mind with conjectures on the life hereafter, being far too occupied with the continued effort of adapting herself to the occasionally alarming circumstances of life as it was. Eustace's incorrigible adventurousness and sudden inexplicable enthusiasms led her convulsively, but on the whole happily, through the years. It is true that she sometimes reflected on the strange unorthodoxy of her married life as compared with the romantic visions of it that she had originally cherished. These visions of course had been the natural outcome of her home environment which was nothing if not conventional. A hard-working husband, a house or flat, several children and a tranquil old age. This perhaps was what she had hoped for, but it was so long ago that she couldn't really accurately remember. At all events it certainly couldn't have panned out more differently. If, during those far-off early days, any prophetic instinct had so much as hinted at the shape of the years to come she would have been aghast. Here she was, rising forty-five, with greying hair and a skin toughened by tropic suns and varied weathers, sitting, grass-widowed, on a failing pineapple plantation on one of the remoter British Colonial possessions. It really was laughable. If it wasn't for being worried about Eustace and separated from him by hundreds of miles of ocean, she could have laughed with more wholehearted enjoyment. Even as it was she couldn't help seeing the funny side. This perverse but undaunted sense of humour had come to her aid in far worse situations than the one in which she now found herself. There was that time when they had first come out to the South Seas and landed themselves in Suva with that dreadful copra business. Then there was the collapsible aeroplane which Eustace had had sent out in crates from England with a view to revolutionising the inter-island communications. That had been the worst really on account of its being so dangerous, let alone all their savings being invested in the damn thing. She could never remember without a shudder the black day when Eustace and Joe Mortimer and the native boys had at last managed to put the machine together and were preparing for the trial flight. Joe Mortimer had been in the Royal Flying Corps in the last war and so he was the pilot. Eustace, poor old Eustace was, apart from being the promoter of the whole enterprise, the observer! She could see it now, that long stretch of sandy beach with the aeroplane surrounded by giggling natives and Eustace in a cap and goggles that made him look like a beetle. Then the propeller being 'revved' up; going round faster and faster, then a lot of shouting and the natives scattering in all directions and the machine, slowly but with gathering speed, starting off along the beach. It was all over in less than five minutes but it had seemed to her like five years. On it went, growing smaller and smaller in the distance until it almost reached the bluff of coco palms jutting out into the sea, then it took off – she remembered distinctly giving a loud scream – and flew out over the lagoon cumbersomely and jerkily as though it were being pulled by a string. Then, horror of horrors, wallop it went into the sea, just the other side of the reef where there was heavy surf. She stood transfixed with misery and waited, all her life it seemed that she waited, watching the plane like a large wounded bird bobbing about in the waves. A big roller took it as lightly as though it were a paper boat and, turning it upside down, dashed it against the reef. It was then that she started to shout loudly. Kumani the fisherman had the canoe ready and was just pushing it off when she, sobbing and breathless, jumped into it. Eustace and Joe were both on the reef when they got there. Joe looked all right but Eustace was lying twisted up and deathly still. When they finally managed to get him into the canoe he had regained consciousness and was groaning. He had three broken ribs, a fractured thigh and a lump on his head the size of a cricket ball, and that was that. Joe's nose was bleeding pretty badly but apart from that he was unhurt. The aeroplane, having been repeatedly dashed against the rocks, finally disappeared from view. With it disappeared their joint savings of several years.

After that there were no other adventures for quite a long time. Eustace was in the hospital at Suva for eleven months and in a plaster cast for six of them. During this time Dorrie had managed to get a job as teacher in the mission school. She taught only the very smallest native children and hated every

minute of it but it sufficed to keep a roof over her head. A little
later on, just before Eustace was well enough to leave the
hospital, Providence, which always favours the feckless,
obligingly arranged for Uncle Ernest to die in Cumberland,
and Uncle Ernest, whom she hadn't clapped eyes on since she
was fourteen, had, by some oversight, left her five hundred
pounds in his will. On receipt of the solicitors' letter from
London explaining this incredible bit of good fortune, she
had gone immediately to Eustace in the hospital and they had
made plans for the future. There had been a lot of argument
and, on her part, some tears, but Eustace was quite determined. They had had enough of Fiji. They must go away
somewhere quite different and make a fresh start. Dorrie
fought this gallantly but without much conviction, she never
had much conviction when Eustace was really set on something, and finally it was decided that the moment he was well
enough they would set sail for the Samolan Islands. Eustace
was wildly enthusiastic about this because a man who had
been in the next bed to him when he first came into hospital
had been Samolan-born and swore that it was a veritable
paradise and full of the most fantastic opportunities for
anyone who had the faintest grit and initiative. Dorrie
ultimately gave up the struggle and so to Samolo they
went.

That was all ten years ago. Samolo hadn't turned out to be
quite the heaven on earth that Eustace's bedmate had
depicted but on the whole, up until the pineapples, they
hadn't done so badly. During the ten years Eustace had been
respectively a barman in a new luxury hotel in Pendarla which
failed; a warder in the prison, which unenviable job he
relinquished voluntarily because he said it depressed his
spirit; an assistant office manager in the Royal Hawaiian and
Samolan Shipping Company – this lasted over three years and
might have gone on indefinitely if Eustace hadn't had a
bloody row with one of the Directors. Finally came the pine-

apple scheme which she was now concerned with liquidating as soon as possible. Eustace's appointment as Resident on Cowrie Island had come as a staggering surprise to them both. Dorrie privately considered it to be a wild eccentricity on the part of the Governor who had met Eustace at a Rotary luncheon and taken a fancy to him. Her innate loyalty to Eustace prevented her from ever implying either by word or deed that, in her humble opinion, he was not of the stuff of which successful Residents are made. Residents that is to say according to the conventional conception of what a Resident, a representative of His Majesty's Government, should really be. Eustace was small and undistinguished physically by either height or girth; his attitude towards religion was undoubtedly tinged with mockery; he was utterly lacking in pomposity; he had a slight but quite unmistakable Cockney accent. True his loyalty to his country and its traditions was strong and at moments downright truculent; he had an undistinguished passion for four-letter words and bawdy songs and very little tolerance of any kind. But still if the Governor thought he was suitable for the job she would obviously be the last person to say anything against it. Once the immediate depression of his departure was over she set to work diligently to get rid of the pineapple plantation as soon as possible. She actually had some good luck over this and finally managed to dispose of three-quarters of the land to a new real-estate company who wished to turn the East Naruchi beach into a bathing resort. The other quarter, which was to the West and slightly elevated above sea level, she held on to, reflecting logically that land was land whichever way you looked at it and that if the Naruchi beach scheme ever amounted to anything it would probably treble its value in a few years' time. Having achieved all this she stored all their furniture and personal belongings against the happy day when the house on Cowrie Island should be ready for her, and rented a small furnished flat in Pendarla.

Pendarla was the main town on the Island and the seat of Government. It was situated on the North Coast and boasted a wide and lovely harbour. A range of mountains swept straight up from the sea, and over the foothills sprawled the town itself. Dorrie's flat was in a new building at the far end of the Mallaliea road. This meant that she was within an easy tram ride from the centre of the town with the additional advantage of being more or less in the country. Her flat was on the seventh storey, one floor from the top, and she had a small balcony which commanded a view over the harbour to the right, and to the left over Imano Point to the open sea. She spent many hours sitting there with her sewing and gazing, a trifle forlornly, out over the curling breakers to where she imagined Cowrie Island lay. As a matter of fact it really lay about three hundred miles directly behind her, but maps and distances and geography had never been her strong point and it didn't really matter anyway.

After she had been there a few weeks she was astonished, and considerably shattered, to receive an invitation to lunch at Government House. It hadn't yet occurred to her that as the wife of the new Resident of Cowrie Island she would automatically be received into the higher Samolan social circles. This unexpected contingency really upset her very much. She knew herself to be completely lacking in social graces, she had no gloves and only one passable afternoon dress which she knew to be several years out of date. She was also oppressed with the fear that either by talking too much or too little or losing her head and doing something stupid she might let Eustace down. It was therefore in a state of miserable panic that she finally drove up in a taxi and turned into the impressive drive of Government House. An immense Samolan in a white tunic and a scarlet fez opened the door of the cab and she was received by a cherubic young Naval officer with an unmistakable twinkle in his eye. He led her through a large hall and along a shady patio into the drawing-room. She was painfully aware that her shoes were squeaking loudly on the parquet. There was a small group of people clustered round a sort of trolley table on which were decanters and jugs and glasses – she was too nervous to notice who anybody was. Lady Logan came forward to meet her followed by Sir Humphrey. Lady Logan was tall, immeasurably distinguished, with rather untidy white hair and an easy, friendly smile. Sir Humphrey was large and shaggy and exuded an air of benign frowziness; his white silk tropic suit hung on his enormous frame with the utmost casualness. He placed a vast hand under her elbow and piloted her towards the other guests. There was a smartly-dressed, drained-looking woman, Lady Something-or-other, who was on a visit from England and staying in the house, an Admiral with gentle blue eyes and aggressive eyebrows; a Captain of Marines, very handsome with curly hair, a curly mouth and a most curly moustache. Vivienne and Sylvia, the two Logan daughters came forward and greeted her warmly. She of course knew them by sight but had never spoken to them before. They were pretty, fresh-looking girls in cool linen frocks. Last of all she was introduced to a Professor Carmichael who, the Governor explained, was making a tour of the islands at the head of an entomological mission. Dorrie hadn't the faintest idea what that meant, but she nodded knowingly as she shook his withered little hand. The Naval A.D.C. offered her the choice of either a dry martini, tomato-juice or sherry. She chose the dry martini and then wished she'd plumped for the tomato-juice. Lady Logan motioned her to a place beside her on the sofa and asked her if she had had any news of Eustace and whether or not she was looking forward to her exile on Cowrie Island. Dorrie replied in a prim, constricted voice that she was certainly looking forward to going to the Island but that she was afraid that it would be a long time before she got there.

Lady Whatever-it-was chimed in here and said that the

whole thing sounded too entrancing for words and that she envied her with every fibre of her being.

Vivienne, the elder Logan girl, said, 'Really, Aunt Cynthia, you know perfectly well you'd hate it.'

Lady Logan laughed. 'I'm afraid it wouldn't be quite your affair, darling,' she said. 'You've always been a great one for your comforts and on Cowrie Island there is apparently nothing but coral, coral and more coral.'

'But I adore coral,' protested Lady Cynthia, handing her empty cocktail glass to the A.D.C. 'I don't mean those dismal little pink necklaces that German governesses wear, they're absolutely bloody of course, but coral qua coral is sheer heaven!'

Dorrie, who had jumped slightly at the surprising use of the word 'bloody' in such high circles, was trying to decide in her mind whether Lady Cynthia really was idiotic or merely, for some obscure reason, pretending to be, when luncheon was announced and they all went into the dining-room. Lady Cynthia sat on the Governor's left and Dorrie on his right. As the meal progressed Dorrie began to lose a little of her shyness. Lady Cynthia continued to talk and behave like somebody out of a back number of the *Tatler*, but Dorrie had to admit to herself that she was now and then quite amusing and apparently without guile. H.E. talked incessantly on a variety of topics. The two girls chattered gaily in high, shrill, very English voices, and flirted mildly with the Captain of Marines. Lady Logan, at the other end of the table, grappled gallantly with the Professor who was obviously rather heavy in the hand. The Admiral uttered a short bark at intervals.

When lunch was over they all sat out on the patio and had coffee. The afternoon sun blazed down on the smooth, perfectly-kept lawn, but under cover, in the shade of the pink plaster arches, it was pleasantly cool. Dorrie relaxed and allowed the gentle, effortless atmosphere to smooth away her agitations. It was stupid, she reflected, to be shy of people and get into a state. After all, as long as you were yourself and didn't pretend or try to show off, nothing much could happen to you. Lady Cynthia, who had been upstairs to powder her nose, came back and sat down next to her on a swing seat; she rocked it languidly backwards and forwards with her foot and offered Dorrie a cigarette. 'I must say,' she said pensively, 'I really do think you're bloody brave!'

'Why?' said Dorrie in surprise.

'Well . . .,' Lady Cynthia held up her hand and scrutinised her nails with some distaste, 'going off into the blue like that and settling down on a little dump and not clapping eyes on anybody from one year's end to another.'

'It won't be so bad as all that,' said Dorrie. She suddenly felt confident and almost superior. Perhaps she really was a good deal more dashing than she had ever thought she was. 'After all I shall be with my husband.' This sounded rather flat and she immediately wished that she hadn't said it. Lady Cynthia gave a little laugh and then suddenly her face looked sad and much older.

'What's he like?' she said.

Dorrie stiffened as though to ward off an attack and then, realising that there was really no offensive intent in Lady Cynthia's question, merely a frank curiosity, she relaxed and give a little laugh. 'He's not much to look at really,' she said, 'that is he isn't what you'd call exactly handsome. But still it's a nice face, if you know what I mean, and he's full of go and always keen on getting things done.'

'What sort of things?' said Lady Cynthia inexorably.

'All sorts . . .' There was pride in Dorrie's voice. 'He can turn his hand to anything, the trouble is . . .' she paused, 'he sometimes gets a bit carried away.'

'I shouldn't imagine that he'd have many opportunities of getting carried away on Cowrie Island.'

'Well you never know,' said Dorrie simply. 'He's building a

house at the moment and I must say I wish I was there to keep an eye on it.'

'How long have you been married?'

'Eighteen years next August.'

'Good God!' Lady Cynthia looked genuinely astonished. 'And you still love him all that much?'

Dorrie tightened up again and Lady Cynthia, immediately realising it, suddenly patted her hand and smiled; a charming smile which completely banished the habitual look of weary boredom from her face. 'Please forgive me,' she said gently. 'You mustn't think I'm being bloody. I'm always far too inquisitive about people, particularly if I happen to take a fancy to them.'

The unmistakable sincerity of Lady Cynthia's tone utterly flabbergasted Dorrie. The idea of being taken a fancy to by anyone so ineffably poised and remote from her own way of life as Lady Cynthia, seemed quite fantastic. How surprised Eustace would be when she told him about it. She felt herself blushing with pleasure and embarrassment. When she spoke her voice was very low and there was a slight catch in it. 'How did you know I loved him so much?' she said.

'It's pretty obvious really,' Lady Cynthia smiled again but this time a trifle wryly. 'I envy you. I've run through three husbands in twenty-eight years, perhaps I'm not as lucky as you, or as sensible – or even as nice,' she added.

This was plainly Dorrie's cue and she took it unstintingly. 'I'm quite sure you couldn't be nicer,' she said boldly, and then was glad she'd done so because Lady Cynthia looked so obviously pleased.

'It's always pleasant, isn't it?' she said, 'to meet new friends. I shall be here for another two weeks, do ring me up and we might have lunch and gossip or go to a movie or something.'

Dorrie, quite overcome, murmured that she'd certainly love to. Then Lady Logan made a slight but perceptible movement indicating that it really was time that the party broke up. There was a brief flurry of general conversation. The Naval A.D.C. said that he was driving into the town and would give Dorrie a lift and, after the various good-byes had been accomplished, she followed him out through the vast, echoing hall into the hot sunshine.

(5)

ON Christmas Eve 1936 Eustace sat down on an upturned canoe a few hundred yards away from the landing-stage and lit a pipe. In order to do this he had to crouch down and bend himself almost double because there was quite a strong South-Wester blowing. Having lit it successfully he sighed luxuriously, wriggled his right sandal to shake a pebble out of it, and looked with pride on his achievements of the last seven months.

First and foremost there was the house. It stood about twenty yards back from the narrow beach. The last coat of bright blue paint was still drying on the doors and window-frames. It was, to him, a beautiful house. It was his; he had built it, and he loved it with all his heart. It consisted of two large rooms separated by a partition that reached not quite up to the roof so that whatever cool breeze there might be could blow through it. The kitchen, scullery and larder were built out on one side. This, although unsymmetrical from the more æsthetic architectural point of view, was undeniably convenient as it ensured that the smell of cooking would only invade the main rooms when the wind was blowing from the north, which it very, very seldom did. The lower part of the house up to the level of the window-sills was constructed of thick coral rocks, hewn roughly but efficiently by the boys. Above this was ordinary teak clapboarding stained brown and varnished in order the better to withstand the elements. The roof was pink corrugated tin and fitted snugly. He had been held up for weeks waiting for that damned roofing to arrive in the supply ship. However, there it was complete in every detail except for the crazy-paving path which he intended to start work on on Boxing Day. At the moment of course there was no furniture beyond a camp-bed, a couple of wooden tables and chairs and a Frigidaire. This worked on an oil burner and was surprisingly successful. Dorrie was due to arrive any time within the next week with the rest of their belongings. His heart fairly jumped in his breast when he thought of showing it all to her. To the left of the house, slightly nearer to the lagoon, was the Radio Station (nearly complete as far as equipment went) and the flagstaff with the Union Jack fluttering bravely in the evening sunshine. Two of the disintegrating Strachan huts had been pulled down and the materials used for bolstering up the remaining three. In one of these the boys lived in haphazard chaos ruled authoritatively by Ippaga. The other two were used for stores. The landing-stage had been reinforced and repainted and neat paths had been made so that it was possible to walk in comfort from hut to hut without crunching along through loose coral.

At the moment, work being over for the day, the boys were whooping and splashing down by the landing-stage. Eustace looked at them affectionately. They were good boys and had worked well and were to have tomorrow off entirely in addition to an extra ration of beer and cigarettes. They were also, he reflected dispassionately, extremely beautiful. He watched Ayialo, who had won the native swimming championship three years running at Naruchi, do a double back somersault into the lagoon. Still puffing at his pipe he sauntered down to the landing-stage to join them. The water at the end of the landing-stage was about twenty feet deep and crystal clear. Shoals of vividly coloured coral fish glittered just below the surface like precious stones. He slipped off his shorts and dived in. The water was still a bit too warm for his liking. It would cool off a bit after the sun had gone down.

He swam out a couple of hundred yards to a coral head; his swimming was of the sedentary, Margate breast-stroke variety. Three of the boys accompanied him, streaking through the water like seals, their arms and legs acting apparently independently of each other but with perfect rhythm and grace; their heads seemed to be almost continually submerged as though they were able to breathe as comfortably below the surface as above it. Eustace rather envied them this easy familiarity with an element that he had always regarded with slight suspicion. They had often attempted to teach him how to 'crawl' and do other aquatic contortions but it was never any good. He invariably choked and spluttered and got too much water up his nose and finally decided that he was too old a dog to learn such exhausting and complicated tricks. He clambered up on to the coral head, wriggled his bottom into a comparatively comfortable position and sat looking back at the shore. Ayialo and Ippaga sprang out of the water and sat down next to him. He glanced at their sleek, glistening bodies and wondered, rather perplexedly, whether or not he ought to insist on them wearing bathing-trunks when Dorrie arrived. Not of course that Dorrie would give a hoot but perhaps from the point of view of Christian decency . . . he suddenly laughed out loud. Ippaga looked at him questioningly. Eustace, whose Samolan was still, after several years, far from fluent, felt that the effort of explaining what he was laughing at would be too complicated and so he waved his hand vaguely and said 'Mo Imana' which meant 'I am very happy'. Ippaga nodded understandingly and, looking towards the house, clapped his hands violently as though to applaud their combined handiwork. Then he and Ayialo, almost in one combined movement, shot into the sea. He watched them swimming strongly down and down through the clear water, their bodies becoming increasingly paler in the blue depths; their breath control was really fantastic and it seemed to be several minutes before their heads bobbed up above the surface again. They decided to race each other to the shore. Ippaga gave a loud cry and off they went at an astonishing rate. Eustace sighed a trifle enviously and remembered, when he was their age, the nightmare swimming lessons he had had to endure in St Michael's baths; the damp, dank smell; the hairy-chested, implacable swimming instructor shouting at him from the side, and the clammy nastiness of the water wings rubbing against his shoulders. This was certainly a far cry from Sydenham all right.

A few days after Christmas, Eustace was awakened from his afternoon snooze by a great commotion outside. He jumped up from the camp-bed and looked out of the window. Ippaga was jumping up and down in a frenzy of excitement and all the other boys were yelling and pointing out to sea. His heart gave a leap and he dashed out, hurriedly doing up the top two buttons of his shorts which he always undid before relaxing after lunch to give his stomach freedom to expand and help the digestion. It had often been a false alarm before but this time it wasn't. There was the ship, a smudge on the horizon with a thin wisp of black smoke curling up from its funnel into the pale sky. He stood stockstill for a moment or two and was suddenly aware that his eyes were stinging with tears. He ran back into the house again and began to find a clean shirt, then he sat down on the bed and started to laugh. There was an hour at least to go before the ship came in close enough to send off a boat and here he was carrying on as though the house were on fire. He had ample time to have a salt-water shower and a shave and get the cups out for tea. He laughed again, this time with less hysteria and more whole-hearted glee and went out to the hut where the shower was. He caught himself doing a little dance step as he went, then he stopped because he didn't want to betray too much emotion in front of the boys.

An hour and a half later he was standing in clean white shorts and shirt and stockings and shoes on the edge of the

'Split' by Roper's Folly, watching the ship's boat slowly, maddeningly slowly, making its way towards the surf. He had been there for three-quarters of an hour. Horrible macabre thoughts rushed through his mind. The boat might capsize; Dorrie would be flung into the sea among the sharks – there were always hundreds of them just out there beyond where the waves broke – he would see her disappearing and be powerless to do anything – perhaps he would even hear her scream – her last dying despairing shriek. . . . He began to jump up and down in an agony of agitation. The boat came nearer and nearer. Just before it reached the surf he saw Dorrie. She was sitting in the stern and she waved a white handkerchief. He waved back frantically and shouted but she couldn't possibly have heard because of the wind and the sea. The boat got through the surf without any trouble at all and slid into the smooth water of the 'Split' and suddenly there she was, just a couple of yards away from him, looking very cool and calm in pink cotton dress and a white sun-helmet. He called out 'Welcome, darling,' in a strangled voice and was quite unaware that the tears were streaming down his cheeks. He started to run, breathlessly, to the landing-stage.

Late that evening they were sitting in deck-chairs side by side just outside the house. The moon was up and made a glittering path of light across the lagoon. The furniture had been dumped, some of it in the house and the rest down by the landing-stage; the Captain and the First Officer had gone back to the ship. The boys had all gone to bed for the night. Dorrie and Eustace had each a whisky-and-soda and a cigarette, but they had to keep putting one or other of them down in order to hold hands. Dorrie had told him all about the pineapple plantation sale and Lady Cynthia and Government House and the various incidents and discomforts of her journey. Eustace had told her all about the building of the house and the set-backs and the four days' gale in November and the giant sting-ray that had got right into the lagoon through the 'Split'. Lots of other bits and pieces of news would come to light later, there was infinite time, all the time in the world. At the moment there seemed to be nothing more to say. There they were, together again, the stars were blazing down on them; they could hear the gentle lap of the small wavelets of the lagoon against the supports of the landing-stage and the steady, soothing roar of the surf behind them. Eustace flipped his cigarette away, placed his whisky glass carefully down on a bit of rock and, kneeling by the side of Dorrie's deck-chair, put his arms tightly round her and buried his face in her breast.

'Careful!' she said automatically, putting down her glass too.

'Do you like it?' he asked huskily, 'the house, I mean, and the island and the whole place?'

Dorrie smiled in the darkness and stroked his hair. 'I will say this for it,' she said, 'it's one up on Blackpool.'

(6)

By the end of the year 1937 Washington and London had finally come to an agreement about Cowrie Island. For months and months negotiations had been under way. Thousands of Civil Servants in thousands of offices had typed memoranda and filed and unfiled letters, telegrams, reports, cyphers and suggestions in duplicate, triplicate and often quadruplicate. There had been meetings, conferences and discussions, official, semi-official and private. Clerks and secretaries and shorthand-typists and stenographers had gone wearily home evening after evening on buses in England and trolley cars in Washington sick and tired and bored with the very name of Cowrie Island. Finally, at long, long last, the decision was arrived at that America and Britain should share the island fifty-fifty. It was, in fact, to be known henceforward as a Condominium. In many high official quarters it was confidently asserted that this arrangement would have a beneficial and lasting effect on Anglo-American relations. The President of the United States was jubilant; the President of Pan-American Airways positively ecstatic, and the Colonial Minister in London relieved, resigned, and, on the whole, indifferent. A few Middle-Western Senators asked some irrelevant questions; one of them, a slightly obtuse gentleman who had been inaccurately briefed on the situation, made a rambling speech in Des Moines, Iowa, filled with withering references to 'Perfidious Albion', while Sir Humphrey Logan, His Majesty's representative in Samolo who had been opposed to the whole business from the start, bowed his head to the inevitable. The only people who knew nothing about the transaction whatever were the British Resident and his wife on the Island itself. For them, the months slipped by in peace and contentment. The crazy-paving was laid down and completed. Ayialo and Ippaga were chased by a nine-foot shark in the very middle of the lagoon but managed to clamber to safety on a coral head. (The shark was later caught by the combined efforts of all the boys together and a chunk of bleeding raw meat from the Resident's Frigidaire.) Dorrie found a wounded love tern, one of the Island's little white birds, and nursed it devotedly back to health and strength, since when it refused to leave her and Eustace built a little dovecot for it behind the house. Sandy, the little ginger cat which had been presented to the Edgehills by the Captain of the supply ship, in defiance of all apparent biological laws, suddenly produced a litter of five kittens in the middle of Roper's Folly. This, to all intents and purposes, immaculate conception caused a profound sensation on the Island.

As far as Dorrie was concerned it was the happiest year she had ever spent in her life. She learnt to float on her back without moving at all, an accomplishment that she had always

envied in others. She went off with Eustace on excursions to
the far side of the lagoon in a little boat that the boys had built
and for which Eustace had rigged up a sail. She became a
passionate collector of shells and sometimes one or other of
the boys would dive down deep enough to procure for her
some lettuce coral which, when bleached by the sun, made
the loveliest house decorations imaginable. Every morning at
dawn and every evening at sunset Eustace performed, with
correct solemnity, the ritual of the Flag. For this all the boys,
in brightly-coloured sarongs, the only moments in the day or
night that they ever wore anything, stood respectfully to
attention. Dorrie stood to attention too and, once in a while,
permitted herself the luxury of a nostalgic tear or two.
Thoughts of home dropped into her mind. The soft, wet
green of the Romney Marches; the brightly-coloured traffic
in Piccadilly on a spring morning, the crowded pavements of
Oxford Street; the bargain basement at Selfridge's, and the
Changing of the Guard. She occasionally received letters from
home, from her sisters and her brother and one or two faithful
friends. She devoured these eagerly enough but they never
moved her so much as watching Eustace hauling away at that
little flag. She had been away for so many years that she
realised that if she did go back everyone she had ever known
would be changed beyond all recognition. Only the aspects of
England that were unchangeable would still be familiar. This
thought saddened her a little sometimes but not for long. She
had Eustace and the house and the sun and the sea and the sky
and her world was at peace.

(7)

IN March 1941 Lady Cynthia Marchmont was sitting in the
American-bound Trans-Pacific Clipper reading a rather
highly-coloured romantic novel about the American Civil

War. Her mind, however, was only partially concentrated on what she was reading. She was dressed in the uniform of the Mechanised Transport Corps. It was a smart uniform and it suited her. She took a small 'compact' containing powder, lipstick and mirror out of her pocket and scrutinised her face with detached interest. She decided that she looked a bit tired and that the lines were deepening under her eyes and round her mouth. This, oddly enough, depressed her far less than it might have done a few years ago. There was every reason for her to be looking tired as she had just completed a lecture tour of Australia and New Zealand and the whole business had been fairly exhausting. She was perfectly aware that she was not a particularly experienced nor inspired public speaker but the lecture tour had, on the whole, been a success. Her subject had been the women of Britain in wartime and the efficiency of their contribution to the war effort. She herself since September 1939 had been working unremittingly. In the beginning she had plunged immediately into the organisation of canteens and rest rooms for the troops. Later, being an excellent driver, she had enlisted in the M.T.C. as an ordinary private and worked her way up to her present rank of Commandant. She was conscious, sometimes almost shame-facedly so, that for the first time for many years she was no longer bored. It was strange to reflect that all the dis-tractions and small happinesses she had so assiduously sought during the Twenties and the Thirties were no longer attractive or even valid. On the surface they had been gay, those years, monotonously gay. On looking back, her mind refreshed and renovated by so much violent change, she was surprised to realise that her memories even lacked poignancy. There they lay, strewn behind her, all the love affairs and parties and yachting trips and summers in the South of France and the Lido; all the trivial strains and stresses and febrile emotions that had woven the pattern of her life and the lives of her friends. She remembered a phrase that she had read years ago in a book of historical memoirs, a phrase spoken by a dying French actress of the eighteenth century who had achieved triumph and fame and been reduced to penury. '*Ah les beaux, les beaux jours, j'étais si malheureuse!*' She smiled to herself and wondered how miserable she had really been? Certainly a great deal more than she had realised at the time. Not the obvious, genuine unhappiness, like Clare dying in that frowsy little hospital in Paris, and Henry being killed in the motor smash, and poor Philip getting muddled up with that bloody woman and finally committing suicide. Those tragedies and sufferings had been real and would have been real in any circumstances, whatever sort of a life she'd led; but the general tone of all those years, the perpetual, un-recognised, hectic boredom. She had lived through so much of all that pretending to herself and to everyone else that she was enjoying it. She smiled again, and then sighed and put her 'compact' back into her pocket. It really had been too idiotic.

She looked out of the window of the plane. They were flying at about eight thousand feet and the evening sky was clear except for a bank of fantastic cloud formations far away on the horizon. She glanced at her wrist-watch. According to schedule they should have arrived at Cowrie Island an hour ago, but there had been a headwind nearly all day since they had left Noumea in the grey hours of the morning. The light faded from the sky and the empty, outside world disappeared. About an hour and a half later there was a light commotion in the forward end of the plane and the steward came bustling through with a tray of cocktails in little cardboard cups. 'It's all right,' he said, 'we've sighted the Island.' There was a ring of restrained excitement in his voice and Lady Cynthia wondered idly whether or not the pilot and observer had perhaps been getting a little agitated. She looked out of the window and there, far far below them in the darkness, was a little cluster of twinkling lights. One of them seemed to be moving and was changing alternately, red and green and white. That would be the pilot launch. Lady Cynthia began to collect her things and the lighted notice flashed on – 'Please fasten your belts.' The Clipper, sweeping lower and lower over the lagoon, finally, with an almost imperceptible bump, touched down on the water; spray obscured the windows; everyone unfastened their belts and began to move about, collecting their books and overnight bags. The engines stopped; there was a confused noise of shouting outside and after a considerable time the giant machine was towed gently alongside the landing-stage. The pilot went out first, then two of the officers. Lady Cynthia waited, sitting quite still in her seat; she always hated hurrying for no particular reason and much preferred the other passengers to disembark before her. When they all had gone she rose, a little wearily, and stepped on to the landing-stage. The hot night air seemed to strike her in the face. She walked along the wooden pier, brightly illuminated by two enormous arc lamps, and up a short rock path to the hotel. It was all on one storey and on entering the main lounge she was immediately impressed by the incongruity of so much expensive luxurious-ness flourishing on a small coral reef in the middle of the Pacific Ocean. She registered at the reception desk and the manageress, Mrs Handly, a smartly-dressed little American woman with a strong Middle-Western accent, insisted on showing her to her room herself. The room was pleasantly furnished with its own private showers and toilets. Mrs Handly was both amiable and voluble and said that dinner would be ready in about half an hour and would Lady March-mont, when she had washed and freshened up, care to come along to her private suite and meet her husband, Robb, and have a cocktail? Lady Cynthia accepted gracefully, although inwardly she would much rather have been left alone, and Mrs Handly departed saying that she would send one of the boys for her in ten minutes.

The Handlys were an oddly-assorted couple. It would be

impossible, reflected Lady Cynthia, to imagine two people more thoroughly opposite from each other in every respect. Mrs Handly, Irma, had shrewd, sharp eyes and was impeccably soignée, her simple linen frock was perfectly cut and pressed and her hair looked as if it had been done by an expert Fifth Avenue hairdresser that very afternoon. Robb, her husband, was entirely casual both in appearance and manner. He was nice-looking and had a certain loose-limbed charm. His eyes were a trifle too pale and his fair hair was untidy.

Captain Elliot, the pilot of the Clipper, a large friendly beefy man, was also present together with the airport manager, a tall austere young man whose surname Lady Cynthia didn't catch but who was referred to by everybody as 'Brod'.

Robb Handly mixed an excellent dry martini with the efficiency of an expert. Lady Cynthia was very grateful for it. She felt tired and the drumming of the plane was still in her ears. Conversation was general and consisted mainly of 'shop'. The new hospital for the ground staff was nearly finished; the west-bound Clipper had been held up in Honolulu and would be a couple of days late at least; there was a cyclone about a hundred miles off which would probably mean that the supply ship would be late too, which was irritating because they were beginning to run out of cereals and cigarettes. Lady Cynthia allowed the talk to flow around her and, sipping her cocktail, idly took in the details of the room. It was pleasantly done, in excellent taste. There were no flowers except for one vase of zinnias on a side table. The whole atmosphere was typical of a well-run hotel or country club anywhere in the United States. The windows were shuttered; the air-conditioning plant made an occasional clicking sound and, apart from the distant noise of the surf pounding on the reef, it was impossible to imagine that you were anywhere but in the midst of civilisation. Suddenly a name in the conversation galvanised her into attention –

'Edgehill' – it struck a forgotten chord in her mind. 'Brod' was talking. . . . 'That guy makes me tired, he's always beefing about something or other.'

Mrs Handly laughed. 'Well . . .', there was a slightly amused drawl in her voice . . . 'he hasn't got much else to do, has he?'

'But it isn't as if we didn't do all we could to be co-operative.' 'Brod' turned earnestly to Captain Elliot. 'We never have a film showing without inviting them to it – Robb and Irma are constantly sending them over supplies whenever they run short. . . .'

'I like her,' said Irma. 'I think she's just darling, but I must admit he gives me a bit of a headache now and then.'

'Who are the Edgehills?' interjected Lady Cynthia.

Robb refilled her cocktail glass. 'He's the British Resident, Ma'am.'

Lady Cynthia, flinching slightly at suddenly being addressed as royalty, remembered in a flash – Mrs Edgehill! The nice little woman at Government House, Pendarla, when she was staying with Humphrey and Eloise. 'Is she here now?' she asked.

'All of two hundred yards away,' said Robb. 'In the Residency.' Everybody laughed at this, it was obviously a standard joke. Lady Cynthia felt quite definitely irritated. She rose and said with a sweet smile, 'They're very old friends of mine. I must call on them at once.'

At this there was a general outcry. Mrs Handly protested that dinner would be ready in a very few minutes and that wouldn't it be better to go over afterwards. Lady Cynthia was quite inflexible. 'I had no idea they were still here,' she said. 'I really must go. I really don't want any dinner, I ate far too much in the plane.' She smiled at the Captain. 'The food was delicious. I wonder if anyone would be kind enough to show me the way to . . .' she paused, 'to the Residency?'

Robb escorted her out of the side door of the hotel. It was a very dark night and he had brought a large electric torch with him. Hermit crabs scuttled away from the coral path as the beam of light struck them. The air was soft and a little cooler; a wind had sprung up and the noise of the surf was like thunder. In a minute or two they arrived at Edgehill's house; there was a glow of lamplight showing through the window. Robb shouted 'Huroo' loudly and then knocked on the front door. After a moment a man opened. Lady Cynthia couldn't see what he looked like as he was silhouetted against the light inside.

'Here's a friend to see you,' said Robb with great breeziness.

Eustace peered into the darkness and said, 'Oh – who is it?' rather dimly.

Lady Cynthia, remembering that five minutes ago she had asserted that they were her oldest friends, rested her hand lightly on Robb's arm and whispered, 'I want it to be a surprise – thank you so much for showing me the way . . .'; she gave him a little push but, obtusely, he wouldn't move. 'What about you getting back?' he asked.

'I can get back perfectly all right,' she said firmly.

'Okay, Ma'am,' he said and, to her immense relief, called out 'Good-night, Mr Edgehill,' and went off into the night. Eustace Edgehill was still standing at the door; behind him appeared Mrs Edgehill. Lady Cynthia really felt a little foolish; she had obeyed a sudden impulse and now it looked as though it might all be a great failure. After all she'd only met Mrs Edgehill once and she probably wouldn't know who she was from Adam. She spoke quickly and was surprised to note that there was definitely a note of nervousness in her voice.

'I'm Lady Cynthia Marchmont,' she said. 'I had the pleasure of meeting your wife at Government House in Pendarla years ago. I'm just here for the night and am leaving again in the Clipper at crack of dawn. I do hope I'm not disturbing you by coming so late but I should hate to leave without seeing her again.'

Mrs Edgehill gave a little cry. . . . 'Well!' she gasped. 'Isn't that extraordinary, just fancy you remembering me.' She gave Eustace a little shove. 'Get out of the way dear.' She seized both Lady Cynthia's hands in hers. 'Please come in – this is the nicest surprise I've ever had in my life.' She drew her inside. 'This is my husband,' her voice sounded quite breathless. 'You never met him, did you, but I remember we talked about him.' Eustace shook hands. He was a wizened little man, deeply tanned by the sun and wearing nothing but shorts and sandshoes. Lady Cynthia noticed that in spite of the fact that his hair was thinning a little, he still retained a slightly boyish air, as though he had never quite grown up. He shut the door carefully and led her politely to a rickety-looking but comfortable chair. 'If only I'd *known*,' cried Mrs Edgehill, 'I'd have put on a dress instead of receiving you in shorts and a blouse like this.' As a matter of fact she did look rather peculiar. Her shorts had obviously originally belonged to her husband and her blouse was of startlingly flowered printed silk. It would have been an excellent design for chintz chair-covers but was a trifle overpowering as it was.

'Get out the whisky, Eustace,' she said and then, a thought striking her, 'have you had dinner?'

Lady Cynthia's eye quickly took in the cups and plates and dishes on the table. It was obvious that they had just eaten. She nodded. 'Yes,' she said, 'I dined the moment I got off the plane, but I should love a soft drink of some sort.'

'You must have some Johnny Walker, you really must,' said Mrs Edgehill. 'This is an occasion.' Lady Cynthia was touched to see that her whole face was quivering with pleasure. She called out to her husband who had disappeared into what was probably the kitchen. 'The soda's in the Frigidaire.' She produced a packet of Gold Flake cigarettes. 'I'm afraid these are all we have to offer you until the next supply ship comes, unless you'd rather have an American one. Eustace can pop over to the hotel in a minute.'

Lady Cynthia shook her head. 'I much prefer these.'

Mrs Edgehill lit her cigarette and then lit one for herself and drew up a chair. 'I wish I'd known, really I do. I'd have had the house tidy for you. It does look like a pigsty, doesn't it?'

At this moment Eustace came back bearing a bottle of whisky, two bottles of soda and an opener. Lady Cynthia looked round the room. It certainly was the strangest mix-up she had ever seen. There was an old sofa with a faded chintz cover; rather a good Spanish-looking sideboard; a gramophone, one of the old-fashioned kind with a livid green horn; two or three deck-chairs; a portable radio; and a table covered with shells of different shapes and colours and some gleaming white, graceful branches of bleached coral. On the stained wooden walls there were two or three dim watercolours; a whole row of six perfectly charming old prints of London and, in the place of honour, on the wall of the partition facing the stove, a framed photograph of the King and Queen. The frame, obviously home-made, was of varnished wood and the photograph was quite dreadful. It had apparently been cut out of one of the illustrated papers and some kind of disaster had happened to it. Mrs Edgehill caught her looking at it and smiled sadly. 'Isn't it dreadful?' she said. 'We had a terrible storm about six months ago and the rain came in and trickled all down the inside of the frame and ruined it. It makes me feel ashamed every time I look at it, but we can't take it down because it's the only one we have.'

'Surely,' said Lady Cynthia, 'as official British Resident you should have an official portrait of the King and Queen?'

'We've asked for one over and over again,' said Eustace, prising open one of the bottles of soda, 'but there's a new Governor in Samolo now and nobody's ever paid any attention.'

'As a matter of fact we really do feel it a bit,' said Mrs

Edgehill with an over-bright little smile. 'You see we are the only two British people here and it's been a little difficult to keep our end up since the Americans came.'

(8)

IT was long after midnight when Lady Cynthia finally tore herself away. Eustace accompanied her back to the hotel, took her in through the side door and showed her the way to her room. When she said good-night to him he gripped her hand and held it for quite a while. 'It was awfully nice of you to drop in,' he said; his voice sounded rather hoarse. 'It'll set Dorrie up no end – she has so often talked about you. She always wanted to ring up, you know, when you asked her to that time at Government House, but she never dared. You've no idea how much this evening has meant to her, really you haven't.' He let go her hand and then added shyly, 'You won't forget about that photograph, will you? It isn't really for us, ourselves, we're little people and we don't matter very much, but I would like these Americans to know that we had it. You see they don't quite understand how difficult it is sometimes for us to be the only British people here with the war going on and everything and being such a long way away from home. . . .' He broke off abruptly and, with a muttered 'good-night', turned and walked away along the passage.

Lady Cynthia went into her room and, closing the door quietly behind her, sat down at her dressing-table and observed, without surprise, that her eyes were filled with tears. 'I'm getting old,' she reflected, 'old and possibly rather maudlin, but all the same I'm learning a good deal more than I ever learned before.' She undressed slowly and lay on the bed without switching out the light, knowing that sleep was miles away from her. She glanced at her travelling clock, ten past one; she was to be called at three-thirty because they were taking off just before dawn. It really wasn't any use attempting to sleep, she could sleep all day tomorrow in the plane anyway. She lit a cigarette and let her mind wander back over the evening.

She wasn't at all sure why it was that she had felt so highly strung and emotional all the time; perhaps because she hadn't had any dinner, or maybe it was that she was overtired and had had two strongish whiskies-and-sodas on top of the Handlys' dry martinis. There was nothing in the least sad about the Edgehills, they were obviously a devoted couple and serenely happy in each other's company from morning till night; whatever troubles had assailed them in their lives they had had each other and been able to share them. Perhaps this was what had given her that slight ache in her heart; the spectacle of two people who were secure in the knowledge that whatever might happen to them, provided it wasn't death or separation, they could never be lonely! Lady Cynthia sighed lightly and tried unsuccessfully to remember any one period of her life when she had felt that sense of security. There was Henry, of course, but then he had died too soon, before they had either of them had time to get through the first painful ecstasies and miseries of being married and in love. There had certainly been no security there, not even a semblance of tranquillity ever. She tried to imagine what would have happened if he had lived and their possessive, demanding passion for each other had simmered down with the passing of the years. What would have been left? Gentle domesticity, quiet acquiescence – understanding – tolerance? She suddenly laughed aloud and stubbed her cigarette out in the ash-tray on the table by the bed. What nonsense! They would never have had the remotest chance of it; all the cards would have been stacked against them; too much money and leisure and far too many shrill, predatory friends. The period had been against them too; those over-gay, strained nineteen-twenties. But still the Edgehills had lived through that period also – but there again that was different. They belonged to another world. They had had the inestimable advantage of having to work in order to live; every bit of pleasure or happiness they ever had they had earned, striven for and fully appreciated when they got it. That was where the difference lay, and it was a basic difference. She and Henry had had everything, everything but the essentials; an abundance of treacherous gifts poured into their laps. The Edgehills had had nothing, nothing but the essentials. Their security and gentleness and love for each other; their tranquil acceptance of life as it was; their immutable, inner convictions about themselves and each other hadn't been showered on them in coloured wrappings like so many wedding presents. Those things were never showered on anyone. But they were the lucky ones, luckier even than they knew.

She fixed the pillow behind her head and stared up at the ceiling. There was a small lizard in the corner using all its wiles to catch a fly. It stalked it very very slowly and then, suddenly, out shot its long tongue, there was no more fly, and the lizard relaxed. Lady Cynthia relaxed too. What an extraordinary evening. After the first half an hour, when they had had a drink and the initial shyness had evaporated, the whole atmosphere had changed, become intimate. Eustace Edgehill, who had hurriedly put on a clean shirt in her honour, took it off again and lay back in his deck-chair. Dorrie – Lady Cynthia smiled – Dorrie had put a large conch shell at her feet for cigarette ends and turned on the news on the portable radio. There they had sat, three English people, listening to an American voice, rich in dramatic overtones, describing a heavy air raid on London. Lady Cynthia remembered watching the expression on the Edgehills' faces, or rather the lack of expression. They had sat quite still staring straight in front of them. At one moment Dorrie had frowned and then closed her eyes wearily. After a while Eustace had got up and turned the radio off. 'No sense in sitting here and upsetting our-selves,' he said, and poured himself out another drink. Presently they had begun to talk about 'home' and ask questions. Did Lady Cynthia know Hythe and had it been knocked about much? Was London really as badly hit as the radio said it was? Eustace had a married sister living in Clapham who wrote to him occasionally. They hadn't heard from her lately but she never said much about the blitzes in her letters – perhaps they hadn't had it very badly in Clapham . . . ? Lady Cynthia told them all she could think of about London.

She described the first dreary, anticlimactic months of the war and then the tension when it really started; the miraculous, agonising days when the men came pouring back from Dunkirk. She had been at Dover, running a canteen on the station. Dorrie and Eustace drank in every word with passionate eagerness; Dorrie's right hand was tapping ceaselessly on the edge of her chair and her eyes were glisten-ing. She said that one of her cousins had been through Dunkirk but that she hadn't seen him since he was a little boy and didn't even know what he looked like now. Then they had sat silent for a little while; the refrigerator made a whirring sound every now and then and the noise of the sea seemed to get louder and louder. Later on in the evening they had told her about their lives on the Island from the very beginning when Eustace had come out with the boys and built the house. They spoke eagerly, interrupting each other and passing the story back and forth. It had been a bit of a shock when the Americans had first arrived but they had got used to it after a bit, although of course it wasn't half as quiet and peaceful as it had been before. They had had official instructions to do their level best to co-operate with them in every way possible. The Handlys were quite nice in their way. They had arrived just before the hotel was finished. They had been nothing if not friendly and civil from the word 'go' really but of course you couldn't get away from the fact that, being

Americans, they didn't really understand about the war. All they really seemed to be interested in was Pan-American Airways. Then Broderick Sarnton arrived, the new airport manager. He was all right really but the one that had been there before had been much nicer. Inevitably there had had to be several changes. The Americans had imported a whole lot of Chamorro boys from Guam and there had been quarrels between them and the Samolans until finally, after a lot of rows and arguments, Eustace had had to give in and send the Samolans home, all except Ippaga, who helped in the radio office. The Americans really weren't so bad. They were awfully kind about sending them over cartons of Lucky Strikes and Camels, but unfortunately they didn't like Lucky Strikes or Camels very much. They also asked them regularly every week to see the newest films which were brought by the Clippers, but they only accepted once in a while because they really didn't care to put themselves too much under obligation and they had no way of returning the hospitality.

There had been another rather unhappy incident. Lady St Merrion, the wife of the new Governor of Samolo, had arrived one night on the American-bound Clipper. There had been bad flying weather and the plane was unable to take off the next morning as usual. Dorrie, naturally expecting that Lady St Merrion would come to call as Eustace was the official British Resident, had worn her one and only afternoon frock all day long for three days, and Eustace had put on a shirt and tie and white flannel trousers, but she had never come. They had watched her every morning strolling by towards the 'Split' with the Captain of the Clipper and one or two of the other passengers. They used to fish for barracuda off the point by Roper's Folly. By the time Dorrie had finished retailing this unfortunate exposé of aristocratic bad manners, her face was quite red. 'You see,' she said to Lady Cynthia, 'it didn't matter about us really, but it was the flag. She never once even looked up at the flag!'

(9)

In October 1941 there was quite definitely a crisis on Cowrie Island. The crisis had no international complications and was entirely brought about by the weather. For three whole weeks a gale had been blowing. No Clipper had arrived either from Honolulu or Noumea and the supply ship was over a month late. There were no cigarettes left on the Island and very little food. The food situation of course wasn't really serious because fish could always be obtained easily from the further side of the lagoon. It was impossible to fish in the open sea because the waves were tumultuous and to attempt to get a boat out through the 'Split' was obviously out of the question. The lagoon fish, however, were reasonably edible although small and a trifle monotonous. Everyone's nerves became rather frayed. 'Brod' had a row with the Handlys. Some of the mechanics fell out with each other with the result that one of them had his head split open with a bottle and had to be put in the hospital. The hotel passed its days in echoing emptiness and acquired a greater air of incongruity than ever. Robb Handly, who had a secret store of Bourbon whisky, elected to get wildly drunk one night with the assistant airport manager and they both swam out to one of the further coral heads in the lagoon. Having reached it, they collapsed in complete exhaustion, and had to stay there until the following morning, when they were rescued by the launch and brought back to the landing-stage, stark-naked and shivering violently.

The Edgehills, as usual, kept to themselves. Eustace continued to perform the ritual of the flag every morning and evening. He was fully aware that this might appear foolish to the Americans, if not thoroughly irritating. On three occasions the flagstaff blew down, but he got it up again all right, assisted by Dorrie and Ippaga. They too were completely out of cigarettes, but Eustace had some pipe tobacco and so they shared a pipe amicably each evening. Dorrie almost grew to enjoy it. At last, on a dreadful day, when the rain was driving across the reef almost horizontally like staves of music, the supply ship was sighted. Everyone on the island was immediately galvanised into frenzied activity. 'Brod' rather lost his head and, against the advice of Eustace, the assistant airport manager and several others, insisted on sending the barge out through the 'Split'. Eustace and Dorrie, crouching in the lee of the rock walls of Roper's Folly, watched it anxiously as it edged out into the surf. Miraculously it managed to get through, or rather over, the gigantic rollers, and headed for the ship. In about two hours it returned, laden with packing-cases. This time disaster overtook it. It had just reached the entrance to the 'Split' when an extra large wave knocked it round broadside on to the reef. There was a panicstricken shout from the seven men on board, then an agonising pause until another wave capsized it completely. Dorrie gave a scream and sprang to her feet. Eustace left her side and started to run over the coral to the edge of the surf. She called after him to come back. In any event there was nothing that he could possibly do beyond just stand there in the driving wind and rain and watch the barge being battered to matchwood. Fortunately, the men managed to get themselves ashore. They were badly cut and bruised and three of them had to go to hospital. The worst aspect of the whole business was that all the packing-cases contained food supplies and cigarettes.

Four days later the weather abated sufficiently to enable the ship to send in a boat. It made three journeys during the day and managed to land the remaining supplies, among them a mail bag for the Edgehills. It was a very small mail bag containing two letters from Eustace's married sister; a long rambling letter from Ena Harris, a friend of Dorrie's in Pendarla; and an impressive-looking flat parcel. They opened the parcel last. Inside it was a typewritten letter and two thick pieces of cardboard sandwiching between them a signed photograph of Their Majesties The King and Queen. The letter was from a lady-in-waiting and started 'Dear Mr Edgehill. The Queen has commanded me to send you the enclosed photograph of Their Majesties. Her Majesty was most interested to hear from Lady Cynthia Marchmont. . . .' Dorrie said, 'Oh dear!' in a choking voice and, sinking down on the bed, burst into tears.

(10)

IN the spring of 1942 the American Authorities decided to evacuate Cowrie Island. The process took several weeks. Two destroyers appeared escorting a large freighter. The Clipper service had been cancelled ever since the month following Pearl Harbour. The Handlys had gone and the hotel had been closed for some months. The Edgehills, having received no instructions of any sort, were slightly at a loss and, as the weeks passed and the Island grew more and more denuded, they realised that they would have to make a decision. The Captain of one of the American destroyers had called politely on arrival and offered them passage on his ship which was bound for Honolulu, which offer they had felt bound to refuse pending instructions from Samolo. Now the evacuation was nearly completed, no instructions had come, and they were faced with having to decide whether to accept passage in the American ship and pack all their belongings on to the freighter, or to stay where they were and await events. The young American Captain, who was both helpful and sympathetic, strongly advised them to come with him. He explained that since the Japanese had declared war all radio communications in the Pacific had gone haywire, and that once they arrived in Honolulu the British Consul there would advise them what to do. Eustace, who felt that the dignity of his position demanded advice from rather higher authority than a mere Consul, was torn with indecision. Finally, after an anguished discussion with Dorrie which lasted nearly all night, he decided to go and they started to pack. The Americans were leaving on the following evening and the Captain was to call in the morning for their final decision. They had started to pack at about four-thirty a.m. listlessly and miserably. Any thought of sleep was out of the question. Just after dawn Dorrie went into the kitchen to cook some eggs and bacon. They were both worn out with arguing and utterly depressed and she thought that a little sustenance might cheer them up a bit. While she was putting the kettle on for the tea, she happened to glance out of the window. The kitchen window was at the back and looked out over the reef to the open sea. There was the freighter in the same place that it had been for the last few weeks. A little to the right and to the left of it lay the destroyers, but – she blinked her eyes and stared – there was a third ship, smaller than the American destroyers, but unmistakably warlike. She gave a loud cry. Eustace came running into the kitchen. She pointed with a quivering finger. 'Look at the flag,' she said breathlessly. 'Look at the flag!' From the third ship fluttered the White Ensign. Eustace gave a whoop of joy and flung his arms round her, the coffee-pot went flying off the stove and broke on the floor. Still with his arm tightly round her he rushed her out of the side door and they started to run towards the edge of the reef. Eustace was shouting, which was very foolish, as the ship was at least a mile off shore.

*   *   *   *

Just before sundown that evening they were sitting together in the stern of a boat being rowed out through the 'Split'. The boat's crew were sunburned British sailors. Dorrie was clasping her hand-bag and a large, flat package very carefully done up in sacking and string. She glanced at poor old Roper's Folly as they passed and felt a sudden catch in her throat. There were the hermit crabs and the little mound with the coloured shells on it where the love bird was buried. There was the house, their house that Eustace had built so lovingly; the lowering sun glinted on the windows making it look as though it were on fire. She almost wished that it was, it was hateful going away like this and leaving it empty and alone. The Union Jack still fluttered from the flagstaff; she wondered sadly how long it would stay there. Eustace, after a sidelong look at her face, leant close to her and put his hand on hers. 'Never mind, old girl,' he said softly, 'it was lovely while it lasted.' She returned the pressure of his hand and tried to smile, but it wasn't a great success so she turned her face towards the open sea and didn't look at the Island any more.

H.M.S. *Rapid*. May 1944.

Stop Me if You've Heard It

'PLEASE God,' she whispered to herself, 'don't let it be the one about the Englishman and the Scotsman and the American in the railway carriage, nor the one about the old lady and the parrot, nor the one about the couple arriving at the seaside hotel on their honeymoon night! – I'll settle for any of the others, but please, please be merciful, God, not one of those three – I can't bear it – if it's one of those three, particularly the Englishman and the Scotsman and the American in the railway carriage, I shall go mad – I shall do something awful – I'll shriek – I'll make a hideous scene – I'll bash his head in with a bottle——'

Her husband, sitting opposite to her at the table, cleared his throat. Her whole body became rigid at the sound. With a great effort she took a cigarette out of a little blue enamel pot in front of her and lit it. Some of the general conversation at the table died away into polite attentiveness. She was aware, wretchedly aware, of the quick, resigned glance that Louis Bennet exchanged with Susan Lake. She looked at her host, Carroll Davis, leaning forward politely, his good-looking face blank. Carroll was kind, Carroll understood, his manners were dictated by his heart – he wouldn't hurt Budge's feelings for the world, he would listen appreciatively and laugh at the right moments, saving his loudest, most convincing laugh for the point at the end, and Budge would never know, never remotely suspect for an instant that he hadn't been amused. The others would laugh too of course, but there would be an undertone of malice – their alert, cruel minds would be silently communicating with one another. 'Poor Budge,' they would be saying, 'the kiss of Death on every party – he never knows when to stop – in the old days he used to be funny on the stage but now he's even lost that – Why does Carroll ask him? Obviously for Marty's sake – she *must know* how awful he is – she must realise *deep down* that she's married to the most monumental cracking bore. Why doesn't she leave him? Why doesn't she at least come to parties without him? She knows we're all old friends – she knows we love her – Why the hell doesn't she leave that aggressive, over-eager little megalo-maniac at home?' Marty drew deeply at her cigarette.

Jane and Shirley and Bobby Peek were still talking and laughing at the other end of the table – they hadn't noticed – not yet – they were still unaware of doom. Budge shot them a quick, resentful look and cleared his throat again. They glanced up, and the light went out of their faces. Shirley stubbed out her cigarette, put her head back and closed her eyes.

Marty felt an insane desire to lean forward and slap her face violently – 'Listen, you languid, supercilious bitch – Budge Ripley's going to tell a story – sit up and listen and mind your manners. He was telling stories – amusing people – millions of people – making them laugh until they cried, making them forget their troubles – making them happy, before you were born. All right, all right – he may be a bore now – he may have lost his touch, but mind your manners – lean forward, look interested, whatever you feel – bitch – spoiled, supercilious bitch.'

'Stop me if you've heard it.' Budge's voice grated in the silence. He caught her eye, and painting an encouraging smile on her face she leaned forward. No more than a split second could have passed before he began, but in that split second the years of her life with him rolled out before her – jerkily and confused in memory like a panorama she had been taken to see at Earl's Court when she was a child. She had been getting on quite well twenty years ago when she had first met him – chorus and understudy and small parts here and there. She had never been pretty but there was something about her that people liked, a comic quality of personality. Carroll had always asked her to his grandest parties, regardless of the fact that she was really small fry in the theatre compared with his other guests – she had had wit always, a realistic unaffected Cockney humour, quick as a whip but without malice. It was at one of Carroll's parties – in this same house – that Budge had first noticed her. It was in this same house three years later after she'd slept with him hundreds of times that he had told her that his divorce was through and that they could get married. Seventeen years ago that was – they had moved into No. 18 – she had been so proud, so grateful, and he had been so sweet – No more stage work for her, no more prancing on and off for finales and opening choruses. She ran the house fairly well, went to all Budge's First Nights in a box or stalls – stood with him afterwards in the dressing-room while people came rushing in to say how marvellous he was – 'Funnier than ever.' 'I laughed until I was sick.' 'Nobody like you, Budge, the comic genius of the age – your inventiveness, your pathos too – only really great comedians have that particular quality, that subtle balance between grave and gay.' They gave parties at No. 18 – gay and amusing, lasting sometimes until dawn.

Several years of happiness passed – several years of excitement and success and occasional holidays in the South of France – then, insidiously the rot began to set in – very gradually at first, so gradually indeed that it was a long time before she even suspected it. A strange rot, composed of circumstances, small psychological maladjustments, mutual irritations, sudden outbursts of temper; the subtle cause of it all still obscure, still buried deep. It was about then that he began to be unfaithful to her – nothing serious – just an occasional roll in the hay with someone who took his fancy. Marty found out about this almost immediately and it hurt her immeasurably – she reasoned with herself of course – she exerted every ounce of common sense and self-control and succeeded bleakly in so far that she said nothing and did nothing, but from then on everything was different – there was no security any more and no peace of mind. It wasn't that she cared so desperately about his popping into bed every now and then with someone else – only a fool married happily for years to a famous star would make a fuss about that – it was something deeper – something that bewildered and gnawed at her, something more important that she knew to exist but somehow couldn't identify.

It was later – quite a long while later – that the truth suddenly became clear to her, that the answer to this riddle that had tortured her for so long suddenly flashed on to her consciousness with all the blatant clarity of a neon light – a neon light sign flashing on and off with hideous monotony one vulgar, piteous word 'Jealousy'. Budge was jealous of her. He was jealous of her wit, her gaiety, her friends. She could have slept with other men as much as she liked and he would have forgiven her; she could have drunk herself into a coma every night and he would have been loving and concerned and understanding, but because she was herself, because people of all kinds found her good company; because she could, without effort, embroider an ordinary anecdote with genuine humour and infectious gaiety and be loved and welcomed for it – this he could never forgive. This, she realised in that blinding flash of revelation, he would hate her for until the day he died.

'Stop me if you've heard it'. That idiotic insincere phrase – that false, unconvincing opening gambit – as though people ever had the courage to stop anyone however many times they'd heard it. Human beings could be brave – incredibly brave about many things. They could fly in jet-propelled planes – fling themselves from the sky in parachutes – hurl themselves fully clothed into turbulent seas to rescue drowning children – crawl on their mortal stomachs through bullet-spattered mud and take pins out of unexploded bombs or shells or whatever they were; but no one, no one in the whole twisting, agonised world was brave enough to say loudly and clearly – 'Yes, I have heard it – it is dull and un-funny; it bores the liver and lights out of me – I have heard it over and over again and if I have to hear it once more in any of the years that lie between me and the grave, I'll plunge a fork into your silly throat – I'll pull out your clacking tongue with my nails. . . .'

Marty suddenly caught sight of her hands. One was resting on the table, the other was holding her cigarette, both were trembling. She looked miserably round the table. They were all listening with exaggerated courtesy. Shirley was looking down; her long scarlet-tipped fingers were scratching about among the breadcrumbs by her plate, making them into little patterns, a circle with one larger one in the middle – then a triangle. Budge's voice grated on – The Englishman, the Scotsman and the American – 'I say, you know,' 'Och aye,' 'Gee'. Marty stared across the years at his face; there it was, aged a little but not much changed since she had loved it so, the same kindly, rather protuberant blue eyes, the straw-coloured hair, the fleshy nose, the wide comedian's mouth. His head was bent forward eagerly, he was talking a trifle too quickly because somewhere writhing deep inside him was a suspicion that his audience wasn't wholly with him, he hadn't quite got them. He finished the Scotsman's bit – Bobby Peek laughed – Marty could have flung her arms round his neck and hugged him for it. Budge's eyes shone with pleasure – 'Gee, Buddy——' There was quite a loud laugh at the end of the story. Carroll's kindness triumphed over his wisdom. 'That was wonderful, Budge,' he said. 'Nobody can tell a story like you.'

Marty's heart died in her – she made a swift instinctive movement to get up from the table. Budge looked at her and his eyes hardened; she sat still as death, chained to her chair. He cleared his throat again. 'Marty half-getting up like that reminded me of a good one,' he said. 'Do you know the one about the shy lady at the dinner party who wanted to go to the telephone?'

There was a polite murmur round the table. Shirley took her compact out of her bag and scrutinised her face in the little mirror. Louis Bennet coughed and exchanged another meaning glance with Susan. Budge pushed back his chair, recrossed his legs and started—— Marty stared down into her lap; there was some gold embroidery on her dress and it seemed to be expanding and changing into curious shapes because her eyes were filled with tears.

A hundred years later they were driving home – it was very late and the streets were almost empty. Budge was bunched up in his corner sulky and silent. Marty stared at the back of Gordon's neck. Gordon drove well but he was inclined to take risks. As a rule she was nervous and made him go slowly but tonight she didn't care, she wouldn't have minded if he had driven at sixty miles an hour, careering along Oxford Street, crashing all the lights. They arrived at No. 18 still in silence. Budge said good-night to Gordon and they went into the house. Rose had left the drink tray on the dining-room table and a plate of curly-looking sandwiches.

Budge poured himself out a whisky-and-soda – 'I'm going on up,' he said. 'I'm tired.'

Suddenly something seemed to crack inside Marty's head and she started to laugh – there was an ugly note in it which she recognised, but she had neither the strength nor the will to do anything about it. 'You must be,' she said. 'Oh my God, you certainly must be.'

Budge stopped at the door and turned and looked at her. 'And what exactly do you mean by that?' he said.

'Don't you really know? Haven't you got the faintest idea?'

Budge's already red face flushed and he advanced two steps towards her. 'What's the matter with you?'

Marty backed away from him still laughing miserably. 'This is a good one,' she said. 'Stop me if you've heard it –

stop me if you've heard it or not – because if you don't you'll never forgive me and I shall never forgive myself.'

Budge frowned. 'Are you drunk?'

Marty shook her head dumbly. She felt the tears starting and tried to wipe them away with the back of her hand. Budge came closer to her and looked carefully into her face. There was no more anger in his eyes, only bewilderment – she tried to look away, to escape from that puzzled anxious face, she backed further and, feeling the edge of a chair under her knees, sank down into it.

'What's the matter?' Budge persisted. 'You're not ill or anything, are you? Is it anything to do with me? What have I done?' He put his hand on her arm.

She felt the warmth of it passing through her sleeve. Suddenly her hysteria evaporated, she felt utterly exhausted but no longer wild, no longer shrill and nerve-strained and cruel. She put her hand up and pressed his more firmly on to her arm – then she gave a little giggle, not a very convincing one really but good enough. 'You may well ask what you've done,' she said. 'You may well ask if it's anything to do with you——' Her voice broke and bringing her face against his stomach she started crying thoroughly and satisfyingly.

Budge remained silent but his other hand smoothed her hair away from her forehead. After a moment or two she controlled herself a bit and pushed him gently away.

'You've given me a miserable evening,' she said huskily. 'You never took your eyes off Shirley Dale from the beginning of supper to the end – you then behave like a sulky little boy all the way home in the car and to round the whole thing off you help yourself to a drink without even asking if I want one and tell me you're tired! You're an inconsiderate, lecherous little pig and I can't imagine why I ever let you lead me to the Register Office.'

She rose to her feet and put her arms round him tightly – she felt his body relax. He gave a complacent chuckle. 'Of all the bloody fools,' he said, and the warmth was back in his voice, the crisis had passed and the truth was stamped down again deep into the ground. He led her over to the table and mixed her a drink. 'Shirley Dale indeed – you must be out of your mind!'

She stood there with one arm still round him, sipping her drink – nothing more was said until he'd switched off the lights and they had gone upstairs. They talked ordinarily while they undressed – the familiarity of the bedroom seemed over-eager to put their hearts at ease. Later on when he had attacked his teeth in the bathroom as though they were personal enemies, sprinkled himself with Floris 127 and put on his pyjamas, he came over and sat on the edge of her bed. She smiled and reached out and patted his hand. Then gently, almost timidly as though she were not quite sure of her ground she pulled him towards her. 'I've got something to tell you,' she said. 'Stop me if you've heard it.'

Ashes of Roses

LEONORA glanced idly through the pile of fan letters on her dressing-table; she had got in for the matinée earlier than usual and Alice hadn't arrived yet otherwise they would already have been opened and neatly arranged for her. Suddenly, among the genteelly coloured envelopes she came upon one that was white and quite plain, it looked business-like but was not typed: she turned it over in her hands and read an embossed address in an oval on the flap. 'Hogarth and Currie – Solicitors'. She looked at the writing again, it seemed vaguely familiar, the envelope was very tightly stuck down so she slit it open with her nail file.

MY DEAR LEONORA,

I expect you will be surprised to hear from me after so many years, perhaps you will have forgotten my very existence. In case you have I will remind you of *Lorelei* in 1924 and Hyde Park on a May afternoon. Those days seem very far away. I have spent most of the intervening years in Malaya but came home in 1939 just after the War broke out. Having been refused for the Army I have been up here ever since, working for the above firm. I have been married twice since the old days when we knew each other. Time does march on, doesn't it? – Judging by your photographs in the papers you have hardly changed at all! I am coming to the play tonight and wondered if you would be free to have supper with me afterwards at the Caledonian. It would be so nice to see you again and talk over old times. If by any lucky chance you are free could you leave a message for me with the stage-door man. I do hope you will be able to.

Yours sincerely,
FELIX MESEURIER.

Leonora slowly put the letter down and closed her eyes; she then opened them again and looked at herself in the glass with interest to see if the shock had done anything to her face; it hadn't. There she was looking exactly the same as she always looked when she was about to make up, the butter muslin was tied round her head as usual to prevent the powder getting into her hair, nothing erratic had happened to her features. She passed her hand wearily across her forehead, the gesture she always used in the last act in the 'Good-bye' scene with Henry – she looked lovely as she did it, lovely and hopeless and resigned; then she shook her head and smiled wanly and then suddenly, with neither loveliness, wanness nor resignation, she clapped her hand over her mouth and burst out laughing. Felix Meseurier! – Felix!! After nearly twenty years! It wasn't possible. She picked up the letter again and re-read it – 'Judging by your photographs in the papers you've hardly changed at all.' Like Hell she hadn't! She leaned forward and scrutinised her face in the mirror: 'hardly' was the operative word. She remembered herself distinctly, too distinctly, in *Lorelei* in 1924. That was the year she'd had the Foulsham and Banfield photographs taken at considerable personal expense, and had finally persuaded the 'Guv'nor' to allow a frame containing four of the best poses to be hung in the theatre foyer. She could see them clearly even now. One was a large head with the eyes looking upwards with a rather startled expression as if someone were going to throw something at her from a great height. In two of the others she was posed in an unrelaxed manner on a sort of music stool with spindly legs, and in the fourth she was looking archly round a screen with her hair down. She had been nineteen when those photographs were taken; now, looking at herself in the glass in the star dressing-room of the King's Theatre, Edinburgh, it was 1944 and she was forty. The face peering with such roguish assurance round that screen in Foulsham and Banfield's studio had been unlined and chubby; the face now looking back at her from the mirror was neither. It was a lovely face certainly, actually lovelier perhaps than it had been twenty years ago but youth had vanished from it for ever.

Alice came fussing in full of apologies: she had waited in a queue for twenty minutes for the tram and then, just as she'd reached the step, the conductress had shouted 'Full up' and given her a push into the bargain. Leonora began to make up. Helen, the assistant stage manageress, knocked on the door and said, 'Half an hour please, Miss Jarvis.' Alice bustled about the room getting her first act dress ready and running the tap into the basin so that the water would be warm and ready to wash in. Felix Meseurier! Leonora expertly massaged the Max Factor foundation into her skin and sighed; *Lorelei* – Hyde Park on a May afternoon!

A little while later when the first act had been called and she was getting into her dress she said with a casualness that was only a fraction overdone, 'Alice dear, leave a message at the stage door for a Mr Meseurier – you'd better spell it out MESEURIER – say that I shall be delighted to have supper with him tonight and will he come round after the show and pick me up.'

(2)

ONE of the greatest attractions of *Lorelei* at the Walgrave Theatre was undoubtedly the sextette which came in the middle of the third act. The girls who sang it were Maureen

Clayton, Josie Gay, Phyllis Greville, Leonora Jarvis, Etta Malvern and Violet Primrose. They all dressed together in No. 14 dressing-room on the third floor. They were a carefully picked little bunch of houris and all their twelve legs were impeccable although their voices were less uniformly perfect. Maureen, Etta and Phyllis carried the vocal ardours of the number while Josie, Leonora and Violet opened and shut their pretty mouths and emitted occasional thin, but not entirely unpleasant sounds. All six of them, however, had the charm of youth and the assurance of comparative inexperience. Maureen, aged twenty-six, was the eldest and had actually played two leads on tour. Josie Gay, twenty-five, was the veteran because she had been on the stage since she was nine. Etta, a pretty creature utterly devoid of ambition was the same age as Leonora, in fact they both celebrated their twentieth birthdays in the same week and there was a write-up about it in the *Daily Mirror*, with a photograph of them both cutting a large cake with candles on it and a few of the Principals standing around wearing strained, good-humoured smiles. Phyllis and Violet were the babies, being nineteen and eighteen respectively.

In the show the girls had comparatively little to do apart from the sextette. They had a concerted entrance in the first act when they all came chattering and laughing down a ship's gangway and, for a few minutes, provided a demure background for Martha Dorcas's first number. She was the leading comedienne and they were all supposed to be her daughters. After this they weren't on again until the finale of the second act, when, together with the entire Company, they had to stand about while Judy Clandon, the leading lady, sang a loud and reproachful aria to Clyde Markham, the leading man, at the end of which she flung a glass of champagne into his face and collapsed sobbing violently into the arms of Martha Dorcas. In the third act there was the sextette and the finale of the whole show. None of them had any lines to speak except

Maureen, who played a brief 'feed' scene with Budge Ripley, the comedian, in the opening of act three and in addition understudied Judy Clandon. No. 14 therefore was the real hub of their theatre lives. Here they argued, quarrelled, giggled, manicured their nails, tried new ways of doing their hair, made underclothes, gave tea parties on matinée days to other members of the Company (nobody outside the theatre was allowed back-stage during performances), and discussed sex in general and their own love affairs in particular. The dressing-room was presided over and kept in reasonable order by Mrs Leftwich, 'Leffie' their dresser. 'Leffie' was overworked, harassed, sharp-tongued and beloved by them all. She had been in the profession herself years ago and had, at one time, played quite good parts on tour. However, she had sacrificed her career at the age of twenty-nine and married an electrician in Bradford who had taken to the bottle. After some years of acute conjugal incompatibility he had been knocked down by a tram just outside the Kennington Oval tube station and had died in St Thomas's Hospital, leaving Leffie with the relief of his departure offset by the burden of having to bring up two children. Both of these were now adult. The son, Bob, had gone to Canada and married and settled down; the daughter, Nora, had also married, but far from settling down had run off with someone else only a month after the wedding. It was the general opinion of No. 14 that Nora had gone thoroughly to the bad because, however pressed, Leffie would seldom speak of her.

No. 14 came to life every evening at about 7.30 and on Wednesdays and Saturdays at 1.30. Leffie always arrived on the dot, took the key off the hook in the stage-door box and trudged up the three flights. She invariably unlocked the door and went in with a faint sinking of the heart just in case everything wasn't all right. There was really no reason why it shouldn't be as she herself was the last to leave at night having tidied up meticulously and placed neat chintz covers over each of the six dressing places, but this daily apprehensiveness was accounted for by the fact that years ago when she had been dressing May Gargon at the Vaudeville she had come in one night as usual to find that the room had been ransacked and all May Garson's clothes pinched, including her fur coat which, like a fool, she'd left hanging up in the cupboard. That had been a 'do' and no mistake – policemen and cross-questionings and one thing and another. The nightmare of it still lingered in her mind.

One evening towards the end of April 1924, when the show had been on for three months and had settled into an established success, Leffie was just about to take the key off the hook as usual when Frank, the doorman, jerked his head in the direction of a figure standing in the rather cramped space between the outer and inner doors. 'Someone wants to speak to you.' He gave a lewd wink and wiggled his tongue up and down in his cheek – 'I think he's after one of your young specials!'

Leffie went up to the stranger. He was a good-looking, well-dressed young man with a soft black hat pulled down over his eyes. This he raised politely. 'Are you Miss Jarvis's dresser?'

Leffie nodded. 'That's right,' she said.

The young man smiled, a charming smile exposing very white teeth. 'I wonder if you would be very kind and give her this note when she comes in?' He handed her an envelope and two half-crowns which she took rather dubiously.

'Do you know Miss Jarvis?'

He smiled again, 'Unfortunately not – that is not personally – I've seen her several times in the show.'

'I see.' Leffie put her head a little on one side and looked at him appraisingly.

'I know I could have left it in the rack in the ordinary way,' he went on. 'But I thought I'd rather give it you and be sure

she'd get it all right. My intentions,' he added, 'are quite
honourable.'

Leffie nodded laconically. 'All right,' she said, 'I'll see she
gets it.'

The young man raised his hat again. 'Thank you so much –
I'm very grateful.'

He went out into the alley – Leffie turned the note over in
her hands, put the five shillings into her pocket and went
thoughtfully upstairs. While she was whisking the covers off
the dressing places and setting the various wrappers over the
backs of the chairs all ready to be slipped on the moment their
owners arrived she hummed breathily a little tune to herself,
but behind the tune, somewhere in the back of her mind, she
was aware of a certain perplexity, a faint pang of questioning
conscience. It wasn't taking the note and the five shillings
exactly: there was nothing either wrong or unusual in that,
but there was something all the same, something that made
her feel uneasy. He was a nice-looking young man all right
and his clothes were good – she looked at the note which she
had propped up against Leonora's powder-box – quite
gentlemanly writing. Suddenly she sat down, still staring at
the note, and rubbed her chin pensively. Concentrated
thought processes were difficult for Leffie, she lived her life
almost entirely by instinct. What really was gnawing at her
conscience was a sense of responsibility. Not that there was
any logical reason for this. It was not part of her duties to
guard the moral behaviour of her charges; all she was paid for
was to dress them, keep them in order as much as possible and
see to it they went down when they were called and didn't
miss any entrances, but still, she was an elderly woman and
they were young and she wouldn't like any harm to come to a
hair of their heads.

A romanticist would, of course, be lyrically moved at the
thought of those six young creatures so full of life and
potentialities all starting their careers together with the

glamorous possibilities of stardom or wealthy marriages
beckoning them on into the future. A cynic would merely
have seen No. 14 dressing-room as a forcing house for egoism,
artificiality and female predatoriness. Mrs Leftwich was
neither a romanticist nor a cynic, she was a realist. To her,
Maureen, Josie, Phyllis, Leonora, Etta and Violet were six
girls whose job it was to make successes of their lives or their
careers, or both if possible. She had grown fond of them and
they of her; each of them tipped her regularly every Saturday
night, always the same sum which had obviously been agreed
on among themselves in secret conclave. They sometimes
borrowed money from her which was invariably paid back at
the end of the week. They always shared whatever they had
with her in the way of food or drink; above all, they trusted
her and frequently asked her advice. Occasionally the advice
was difficult to give. There was, for instance, that dreadful
Saturday not long after the show had opened when Phyllis
had lingered on in the dressing-room until all the others had
gone and then burst into floods of hysterical tears and con-
fessed that she was over two months gone and that something
would have to be done about it or she would kill herself. That
was a teaser and no mistake. Leffie had sent her home in a taxi
having promised to meet her next day outside the Piccadilly
Hotel at 2.30, and that same night had gone traipsing round to
the Palace to see old Mrs Greerson who knew a woman who
knew a doctor somewhere near Olympia. The next afternoon
they had met as arranged and had gone off to Addison Road.
Leffie would never forget that little jaunt to her dying day.
The doctor was an oily-looking man with spurts of iron-grey
hair growing out of his ears. Leffie had had to wait for two
hours in a sort of front parlour with nothing to look at but a
back number of *Woman and Home* without a cover and a large
picture over the mantelpiece of a dog with a rabbit in its
mouth. Fortunately it had all gone off all right and she had
taken Phyllis away in a taxi and deposited her at her cousins,

well briefed with a trumped-up story of having fainted at the pictures. It must here be noted that the ethics of stage life differ considerably from those of other, more conventional worlds.

Leffie, it is true, had been extremely shocked by this incident, not, however, on account of its moral aspects. Having been born and bred in the Theatre she had no inherent reverence for virginity: in her experience it was an over-rated commodity at the best of times and far too much fuss was made about it at that. What shocked her over this particular episode was not that Phyllis had had an affair with a gentleman un-named, but that she should have been silly and inefficient enough to let herself get into trouble through it and thereby jeopardise her professional career. In Leffie's opinion a strapping girl of nineteen ought to have more sense. The silliest part of it all of course was to let it drag on until she was well into her third month. However, all was well that ended well. What was worrying her now, about the young man and the note and the two half-crowns she was unable to explain to herself. Perhaps it was something to do with his teeth or his voice – a gentle, dangerous voice; at all events – she shrugged her shoulders – Leonora was a bright ambitious girl and well capable of looking after herself.

(3)

FELIX MESEURIER stood in the foyer of the Walgrave Theatre casually smoking a cigarette and occasionally glancing at his wrist-watch to give any of the attendants who might be observing him the impression that he was waiting for someone. From this particular point of vantage just to the left of the Box Office he commanded an excellent view of a large frame on the opposite wall containing four portrait studies of Leonora Jarvis. If being in love means a physical attraction of the first magnitude then Felix Meseurier was in love. He could hardly look at the photographs without trembling. There he stood, slim and handsome in his dinner-jacket listening to the orchestra tuning up for the overture and staring across the heads of the people passing by him. Every now and then he would look away but his eyes always returned avidly to that pert, lovely little face and those long exciting legs. He was rather a saturnine-looking young man, of this he was perfectly aware and secretly pleased about. His father had been French and had died years ago. His mother, a determined and thoroughly efficient woman, ran a small chemist's shop in Uxbridge. Her one weakness in life had been and still was Felix. He on his side was fond of her and reasonably filial in that he visited her dutifully once a week. He was a selfish creature but not more so than many other young men of his generation. Having been called up in 1916 he had been invalided out of the Army in 1917 with incipient T.B. This had necessitated his spending a year at a sanatorium near Woking from which he emerged completely cured a few weeks after the Armistice was signed. His sojourn in the Army had been undistinguished to the point of bathos, a dismal little record of influenzas, bad colds and finally pleurisy, the results of which obtained for him his ultimate discharge. With one part of his mind he regretted this; he liked to visualise himself as romantically valiant, as indeed who does not? His sense of realism, however, caused him to admit to himself in secret that he was relieved beyond words that he had never got nearer to the War than a bleak camp in Derbyshire.

In 1919, through his mother's resolute determination, he got a job as a clerk in a shipping office in the City and now, after four years, he had laboriously climbed to being a sort of secretary-cum-assistant to the manager of the branch. This dazzling eminence had been achieved less by hard work than by a romantic attachment to the manager's daughter, a plain but fiercely emotional girl two years his senior. It was an understood thing that ultimately when, in the words of the girl's father, 'he had proved himself' they were to be married. This whole situation might have been intolerable were it not for the fact that the manager, Herbert Renshaw, his wife and Sheila lived at Sevenoaks, just mercifully far enough away to make constant propinquity difficult. Felix lived on his salary with occasional assistance from his mother, in a bed-sitting-room in Ebury Street. Every now and then he went to Sevenoaks – as dutifully but even less enthusiastically than he went to Uxbridge. Sometimes, fortunately not very often, Sheila Renshaw came to London for the day. This involved much play-acting and nerve strain. First of all there would be the halting, boyish request to Mr Renshaw for an afternoon off; then lunch and a matinée followed by the inevitable, embarrassing taxi drive, hand in hand, to Victoria. Sometimes Mrs Renshaw would come up too and meet them archly for tea; this at least ameliorated the horror of the latter part of the afternoon. It was perfectly apparent that Sheila loved him intensely. She was a stocky girl with nice eyes and no neck to speak of. Felix alternated between tolerating her and actively loathing her. He hadn't yet really faced up to the ultimate show-down, but knew that sooner or later he would have to.

In the meantime life jogged along pleasantly and he had enough leisure to enjoy himself as much as he could. The fact must be faced that Felix's principal preoccupation was sex. Sex in any reasonable form whatever. This may or may not have been something to do with his T.B. tendencies, but whatever the cause it was his pre-eminent interest and had been for almost as long as he could remember. There was never a day in his life that he hadn't been ready and willing to respond to physical contact. So engrossed was he with the manifold physical pleasures that his body could provide that he had never given a desultory thought to other safety valves such as reading, debate, music or drink. What was most curious of all was the fact that he had never once experienced the emotion of being in love. He was highly predatory but completely unpossessive; sensual and passionate but incapable of jealousy. To go to bed with another fellow creature who attracted him seemed to him the most natural thing in the world and it was quite astonishing how far this amiable conviction carried him, but to feel himself in any way bound to them or in their debt would never have occurred to him. With all this it must not be imagined that he lacked subtlety when in pursuit of what he wanted; far from it, he was capable of infinite patience and also, alas, of infinite charm. This, then, was the affable young wolf who was standing in the foyer of the Walgrave Theatre gazing romantically at photographs of an attractive young woman of twenty.

(4)

LEONORA JARVIS had been on the stage for four years. Her father and mother had died when she was a baby and she had no memory of them; her earliest recollections were of Aunt May and Uncle Hubert and the house in Sandgate: it was a light, clean, chilly house overlooking the sea. At the age of eight she had been sent to a small day school nearby and, two years later, to a larger school in Folkestone in which she was a weekly boarder and could come home for week-ends every Saturday afternoon by catching a bus outside Timothy White's. Aunt May and Uncle Hubert were kind but undemonstrative and although her early years may have lacked the warmth of parental affection, they in no way lacked creature comforts. The house, during the summer months, accommodated boarders of aggressive gentility. Leonora naturally preferred the off seasons when there was no one left but old Mr Radlett, who was a permanent, because then she was permitted to move from the poky little room on the top floor at the back which she inhabited when the house was full, and spread herself in the second floor front. Here she could kneel on clear winter nights, with the window wide open and an eiderdown wrapped round her and look out over the dark sea. Sometimes, when it was very clear, she could see the rhythmic flash of the Gris Nez lighthouse below the horizon but reflected in the sky. Here, with the smell of the sea, the sound of the waves pounding the shingle and the sharp wind blowing the curtains out into the room, she could make plans for the future. She was not a particularly romantic child, but she had always been determined and since the second January of the War when she had been taken by a school friend and family to a Pantomime at the Pleasure Garden Theatre, she had formed one steadfast resolution and that was to be an actress. It took her three years to achieve even the beginnings of this ambition, but through Uncle Hubert dying, and Aunt May giving up the house and moving into a flat in Maida Vale, and various other helpful circumstances, achieve it she did.

In the year 1919 after a series of impassioned scenes with Aunt May and Miss Bridgeman, the rather fierce companion Aunt May had taken to live with her, Leonora was sent to Madame Alvani's Acting and Dancing Academy in Baker Street. In 1920 – aged sixteen – she played an animated water-lily in a Christmas production at the Villiers Theatre. For this she was paid three pounds a week, from which Madame Alvani deducted ten per cent commission. Her next engagement was on tour with an ancient but select farce. In this she played a small part and understudied the ingenue lead. Her salary was again three pounds a week but this time she hadn't to pay commission as she had got the job through Kay Larkin an associate water-lily a year older than herself, who knew the ropes and had taken her straight to the management. Aunt May's and Miss Bridgeman's fears for her chastity were allayed by the fact that she was sharing rooms with Kay and,

what was better still, Kay's mother. Had either of the good
ladies ever clapped eyes on Kay's mother they might have
been less tranquil. However, no moral harm came to Leonora
during the engagement and even if it had they would certainly
have been the last to hear about it.

By the end of November 1923, when Oscar Morley (the
Guv'nor) had engaged her for the sextette in the forthcoming
production of *Lorelei,* she had achieved quite a lot of experience if little fame. She had toured, been in the chorus of
two West End revues, done a whole season of repertory in
Nottingham and played a bright, gay prostitute with a heart of
gold in an ambitious problem play at the Everyman in
Hampstead which never came to the West End. Through all
these routine vicissitudes she had managed to remain,
through circumstance and a certain natural fastidiousness, a
virgin.

She had imagined herself to be in love on two occasions,
once with the leading man in Nottingham who was at least
fifteen years older than she was and heavily and happily
married, and then with a young man who had been invalided
out of the Navy and had appeared in her life when she was in
the chorus of the 1922 Revue at the Parthenon. This had been
quite serious and lasted all through the summer. He had taken
her out to supper at Rule's and occasionally the Savoy Grill.
He had driven her on warm, languorous Sunday evenings in a
small, spluttering two-seater to Maidenhead where they had
danced at Murray's and driven through the dawn, stopping at
the side of the road at frequent intervals to exchange ardent
but innocuous embraces. He was a nice, good-looking boy,
shy and with impeccable manners. On one of these romantic
jaunts he had stammeringly proposed marriage, but Leonora,
who by that time had been introduced to his mother and
sister at tea at the Carlton, knew with every instinct in her that
no good would come of it and that if she accepted him she
would somehow be betraying him as well as herself, so she

refused him firmly but with a sad heart, and a few weeks later he came tragically to say good-bye to her. His mother and sister had decided to go out to visit his other sister who was married and lived in New Zealand. He was to go with them on account of his health and being able to live an outdoor life and one thing and another. It all sounded rather garbled but Leonora thought she detected the underlying truth which was that he really did love her, more than was good for him, and his family, reasonably enough, were intent on getting him out of harm's way. They had a farewell supper at Rule's, sitting in an alcove staring miserably at each other over sausages and bacon and gins and tonics. The two-seater was outside and they drove down to Richmond and back although it was a raw October night. He dropped her off outside the flat in Fulham Road that she was sharing with Hester Lancaster. They stood sadly on the pavement hand in hand looking abstractedly at a street lamp swinging on the other side of the road, then he suddenly kissed her almost violently and said in a choked voice, 'I shall never forget you and some part of me will always love you.' With this he had jumped into the car and driven away. Leonora, blinded with tears had fumbled for her latch-key, let herself in, and flung herself sobbing on to Hester's bed, where finally, soothed by wise, sympathetic advice and hot Ovaltine, she fell into a deep sleep.

For quite a while after that she had been heavy-hearted, but gradually, assisted by Hester, and her own natural resilience, she forgot lost love in the every-day excitements of living. Hester was a laconic, dryly humorous woman in the late twenties. They had met, shared digs and become close friends during the tour of *Lady from Spain*. Hester's talent for acting was meagre; as far as a successful theatrical career was concerned she was doomed to disappointment and knew it; however, she had a swift, cultured mind, and was a wise restraining influence on Leonora. For over two years since the death of Aunt May they had been sharing the flat in Fulham Road.

Leonora came gaily into the dressing-room with Josie; Phyllis, Violet and Etta were already making up but Maureen was late as usual.

Leffie took her hat and bag and coat from her and hung them on a peg. 'There's a billy doo for you dear,' she said laconically. 'I propped it up against the tin.'

Leonora glanced at it casually as she slipped out of her dress. 'It's probably from the Prince of Wales,' she said. 'Badgering me to go to one of those dreary evenings at Buckingham Palace.'

'It might be from Alfie Stein,' said Josie. 'Badgering you for his ten per cent.'

'Not me.' Leonora sat down and pulled her wrapper round her. 'I've never had an agent in my life since Miriam Moss got me a tour that only lasted for three split weeks.' She opened the letter and read it through. Leffie, watching her in the glass saw her frown for a moment, then smile and then pass her hand rather abstractedly across her forehead.

'Well – come on, dear – don't keep us in suspense!' Josie banged on the dressing-table with the back of her brush.

Leonora folded the letter carefully and put it back in the envelope and sighed. 'Sorry to disappoint you all,' she said, slapping some grease on her face. 'It's only from my cousin Edward, he's eighteen, lives in Birmingham and has spots and he's coming to the Saturday matinée.' She turned to Leffie. 'Leffie darling, put that in my bag for me, will you, or I shall forget to answer it.'

Leffie, unsmiling, took it from her, put it in Leonora's handbag and snapped it to quite hard. Leonora gave her a swift look in the glass and then went on with her make-up.

(5)

FELIX stood in the alley outside the stage door. There was a group of girls near him, they were clutching autograph books and talking in whispers, occasionally one of them giggled. Felix, with elaborate nonchalance, took out his cigarette-case and lit a cigarette. His whole body was taut and tremulous with suppressed excitement. He had watched the show from the front row of the dress circle on the side: it was the seventh time he had seen it but he had never before been so near. During the second verse of the sextette Leonora had been actually only a few yards away from him; he had never taken his eyes off her for an instant, noting avidly every turn of her head; the little flounce she gave to her dress as she danced upstage; a secret smile she exchanged with one of the other girls when they were standing in a row right on the foot-lights for the last refrain; the demure, provocative swing of her hips as she went off, last but one, and the lissom grace of her curtsey when they all ran on to take the call. When the encore was over and they had finally gone he had discovered that his hands gripping on to the edge of the circle were moist with excitement and had left a damp mark on the plush.

One by one in groups, various members of the Company emerged from the stage door. Budge Ripley, the comedian came out in a hurry and went, almost at a run, up the steps at the end of the alley where a taxi was waiting for him. The autograph collectors argued among themselves as to whether it really had been him or not. One of the show girls came out in a chinchilla coat with a spray of gardenias fastened to the lapel with a jewelled clip. A uniformed chauffeur was waiting for her. He raised his cap respectfully and helped her carefully up the steps towards the car as though she were infinitely fragile and might break. Felix waited on. He recognised

Maureen Clayton and Etta Malvern walked by him engrossed in animated conversation. He nearly accosted them to ask if Leonora was on her way down but thought better of it and lit another cigarette. Judy Clandon came out followed by an elderly man in tails and a silk hat. The group of girls closed round her and she signed their books and said goodbye to them with a great display of unaffected charm. When she had gone they moved off. Felix was left alone except for a man in a mackintosh standing a little further down. He was smoking a pipe and reading an evening paper in the light of the hanging lamp over the Upper Circle exit. At last Leonora came out. His heart seemed to jump into his throat; she was alone. Raising his hat he stepped forward.

'Miss Jarvis.' His voice sounded as though it belonged to someone else.

She stopped and smiled. 'Are you Mr Mes – Meseurier?' She had a little trouble with the name.

'Yes.' He put out his hand which she accepted without embarrassment. 'I hope you didn't mind me writing that letter. I couldn't help it.'

She let her hand lie in his for a moment and then gently withdrew it. 'I thought it was a very nice letter.'

Suddenly, Felix's overstrung, nervous shyness vanished. Everything was going to be all right. He grinned with a mixture of boyish humility and slight roguishness. 'Is there any hope of your doing what I asked? Coming to have supper with me?'

Leonora shook her head. 'I'm afraid not,' she said. 'I have to get straight home.'

'Oh!' His voice was heavy with disappointment. They moved off together up the alley steps and into the street.

'You see,' said Leonora, 'I share a flat with a friend of mine and if I go out without letting her know, she gets rather worried.'

'Couldn't you telephone her? We needn't be late.'

Leonora shook her head. 'Not tonight – honestly I'd rather not tonight.'

'Where is your flat – is it far?'

'It's in the Fulham Road – I get the tube from Leicester Square.'

'Would you mind if I came with you?'

Leonora shot him a look out of the corner of her eye as they turned into Garrick Street.

'Wouldn't it be taking you out of your way?'

Felix smiled – rather a nice smile she thought. 'I wish you lived at Hendon!'

He slipped his hand under her elbow to guide her across the road and kept it there when they reached the other side, she could feel the warmth of it through the sleeve of her coat. She gave him another sidelong glance, his face was serious and, she had to admit, extremely attractive. He wore his soft dark hat with an air; she began to wonder if, after all, she hadn't been a little hasty in refusing to have supper with him; there really wouldn't be any harm in it and she was perfectly capable of looking after herself. The prospect of going straight home was rather dreary. Of course what she had said about Hester being worried about her wasn't strictly true. Hester probably wouldn't be home herself for an hour or more, she was playing a small part in a straight play at the Shaftesbury and it didn't ring down until half-past eleven and Hester always took her time anyway. She felt his hand tighten under her arm as they crossed St Martin's Lane. He must have sensed that her obduracy was cracking a little for he returned to the attack gently and very persuasively.

'I wouldn't like you to think that I made a habit of waiting outside stage doors and badgering girls to have supper with me.' There was a tone of urgent sincerity in his voice. 'As a matter of fact this is the first time in my life that I've ever done it and at that it's taken me weeks to summon up enough courage – you see——' He slowed down perceptibly – Leicester Square station was distressingly near.

'You see, I really meant what I said in the letter – it would mean so very much to me to get to know you a little. Don't you think you could probably change your mind – about supper, I mean? I'll drive you straight home in a taxi afterwards so you really wouldn't be so very much later than if you went in the tube.'

They came to a standstill in the entrance of the station. Leonora disengaged her arm from him and looked up at the clock. It was only five and twenty to twelve – there were a lot of people about and there was a long queue at the ticket window. The hot, familiar smell of the station assailed her nostrils unpleasantly. It would be far nicer to go home in a taxi and if they weren't more than an hour over supper she could be in bed by one o'clock at the latest. Felix watched her and was again aware of an inward trembling: her fawn-coloured coat was tight-fitting and most tantalisingly outlined the curves of her young body; she was wearing a perky red cloche hat from under which a wisp of chestnut hair escaped in a jaunty little curl; her eyes were grey-green, heavily lashed and set wide apart; her nose, which was short and retroussé, while it may have impaired the beauty of her face from the strictly classical point of view undoubtedly enhanced its vitality and charm; her mouth was enchanting, full-lipped and with a dimple in each corner; as Felix looked at it with longing it suddenly opened in a radiant smile and she said, 'Oh, all right!'

They had supper in a small restaurant in Soho. The atmosphere was oppressively Italian and there was a pervasive smell of garlic and cigar smoke, but the food was good, the chianti passable and the red-shaded lamp on the table seemed to isolate them from the rest of the room and enclose them in a glowing, shadowed, intimate world of their own. Felix ordered hors d'œuvres, ravioli, with powdered parmesan cheese to sprinkle over it and zabaglione in little shallow cups. He suggested liqueurs with the coffee but she refused, finally compromising by having a crême de methe frappée. Felix had brandy and bought himself a cigar. By this time all restraint and shyness had fled. Felix, with a masterly sensitivity that many an older roué would have envied, refrained from any suggestion of love-making, he talked gaily and naturally without a trace of flirtatiousness, his acute hunting instinct warned him to establish firmly a friendly basis before attempting anything further. Leonora, although not entirely deceived, thoroughly enjoyed herself, her instincts were also fairly acute and she had been about enough with ardent young men to be able to size up the situation without undue confusion. She found him attractive and nice-looking; she liked the way his eyes went up at the corners and the wave in his glossy dark hair. His eyes were brown and perhaps just a little too close together, he had a deep voice and his smile was infectious and charming, his teeth were perfect, even and gleaming white, no tooth-paste firm could wish for a better advertisement: his greatest attraction, how-ever, were his hands, they were muscular and slim with long tapering fingers; his wrists, she had to admit, were rather hairy but still you couldn't have everything.

They were almost the last to leave the restaurant; he took her coat from the cloak-room woman and helped her on with it himself. The Patron wished them an expansive good-night. Leonora noticed with satisfaction that Felix had tipped generously. When they got outside, the street was deserted and shone under the lights as though it had been raining. Their footsteps echoed in the silence as they walked down towards Shaftesbury Avenue.

Felix hailed a taxi just outside the Queen's Theatre and Leonora told the driver the address. When they had driven about half-way down Piccadilly Felix gently took her hand and held it. He said rather huskily, 'You don't mind, do you?'

She said, 'Of course not,' and inwardly commenting, 'Here we go,' she braced herself for the inevitable kiss. This, however, was not forthcoming, he seemed quite content to sit there silently holding her hand, every now and then he gave it a little friendly squeeze but that was all.

When the cab drew up outside her front door, Felix jumped out immediately and held her arm carefully as she stepped down on to the kerb. They stood there looking at each other for a moment. Leonora was aware of a faint but unmistakable disappointment that he hadn't kissed her.

'You were a darling,' he said, allowing a note of passionate intensity to creep into his voice, 'to come to supper after all. – You've no idea how much it meant to me!'

Leonora gave a slight giggle – she felt suddenly, unaccountably nervous – 'Don't be silly,' she said, aware that her voice sounded rather breathless. 'I had a lovely time.' She began fumbling in her bag for her latch-key; she found it and looked up at him. In the light from the street lamp she observed a little pulse beating in his temple – she held out her hand. 'Good-night and thanks a lot.' He shook hands with her silently and she turned and went up the little path to the front door. When she had, rather agitatedly, fitted the key into the lock she turned back and waved. He was still standing there staring after her. Her wave seemed to snap him out of his trance for he waved back, called 'Good-night,' quite ordinarily, gave an address to the driver and jumped into the cab. As she closed the door behind her she heard it drive away. She walked upstairs feeling a bit deflated. He hadn't kissed her, he hadn't even asked to see her again.

(6)

THERE is much to recommend Hyde Park on a sunny Sunday afternoon, particularly in spring when the grass is newly

green and there is a feeling of lightness in the air. Sub-
consciously affected by this, the most prosaic citizens frequently give way to a certain abandon. Fathers of families take
off their coats and waistcoats and lie on their backs chewing
bits of grass and gazing up at the sky; their wives sit near them
keeping an eye on the children and allowing the sun to burn
semi-circular areas of pink on to their necks. Younger people
lie unashamedly very close, sometimes asleep, sometimes
lazily awake, murmuring laconically to each other, sucking
sweets, smoking cigarettes, relaxed and content, soothed into
a sensual lassitude by the promise in the air and the gentle
weather. As a general rule decorum is observed although
occasionally passion flames suddenly between them and they
lie with arms and legs entwined, oblivious of passers-by, lost
in brief ecstasy. Police constables regulate these transient
excesses with admirable discretion, nothing is allowed to get
out of control, the decencies are upheld, the birds sing and the
cries of children, the barking of dogs and the far-off strains of
a military band together with the gentle, incessant rumble of
traffic in the distance provide a muted orchestration to this
unremarkable, but at the same time unique, London Pastoral.

On a Sunday afternoon in May 1924, Leonora and Felix,
having lunched at the 'Rendezvous' and strolled down
Piccadilly into the Park, lay in the shade of a tree near the
Round Pond. At least Leonora was in the shade because she
was afraid of getting freckles. Felix, intent on acquiring a tan,
had taken off his shirt and was stripped to the waist in the sun.

This was their third meeting since that evening two weeks
ago when they had had supper at the Italian restaurant and he
had driven her home in a taxi. He had called for her unexpectedly one Wednesday after the matinée and taken her to
tea at the Thistle tea rooms at the top of Haymarket. The day
after that he had sent a large bunch of flowers to her at the
theatre with a card on which was written, 'The words are old
and ever new – Forgive my heart for loving you.' This was a

quotation from Judy Clandon's number in Act Three of
Lorelei; under it were the initials F. M. The following Monday
night after the show he had called for her in the pouring rain
and they had supper together again, this time impressively at
the Savoy Grill: this time also he had kissed her on the way
home in the taxi, but not until they were past Brompton
Oratory and the drive was nearly over; the kiss however, well
timed and admirably executed, had lasted with mounting
intensity until the taxi drew up before her front door.

Today, from the moment they had met outside Piccadilly
Circus tube station until now, there had been no indication
either in his voice or in his manner that he had ever kissed her
at all or had the faintest intention of kissing her again.
Throughout lunch he had been gay and talkative. Never once
had his hand closed over hers, never once had she detected in
his cheerful brown eyes that look of sudden longing, of
suppressed desire. He had actually made fun of a couple
sitting in the far corner of the restaurant because they looked
so obviously, so overwhelmingly, in love.

Leonora's first reaction to this technique was one of acute
irritation. This was presently superseded by a strange unhappiness, a desolation of the heart, an inexplicable desire to
burst into tears. She rallied, however, with commendable
poise and chattered and laughed as gaily as he. This successful
effort at self-control had not only carried her triumphantly
through lunch and down Shaftesbury Avenue and the whole
length of Piccadilly, but had strung her nerves high; she had
worked herself into a mood of tingling, brittle defiance; she'd
show him all right the next time he started any of his nonsense,
that that kiss – the tremulous memory of which she hastily put
out of her mind – had meant as little to her as it obviously had
to him. Now, sitting under the tree with the warm spring
sunshine all around her, this mood suddenly and unaccountably evaporated leaving her shivering and vulnerable. Felix
was lying a yard or so away from her, his naked chest and arms

shone in the strong light, she felt a violent urge to fling herself on to him, to feel his mouth under hers and the warmth of his body pressed against her. Appalled by this sudden wave of passion which swept over her and receded leaving her trembling and exhausted, she leant her head back against the tree trunk and closed her eyes.

Felix, whose telepathic instincts seldom failed him, turned his head sharply and looked at her; swiftly and almost in one movement his arms were round her and his lips pressed into the hollow of her neck. She gave a little cry, he kissed her mouth lingeringly and then when her whole being seemed to be fused in an agony of surrender he rolled away from her and lay face downwards on the grass, still as death, with his face turned away from her. A little while later, his hand, familiar and comforting under her arm, guided her gently across Knightsbridge into the deserted Sabbath peace of Lowndes Square. She walked automatically in step with him, neither of them spoke but the feeling between them was tense, somewhere below her surface consciousness a conflict was raging – this was silly, cheap, immodest, dangerous – she would regret it until the end of her life. Walking through empty, echoing London Squares in the clear afternoon sunlight with her lover, a comparative stranger; being led inexorably to the squalor and glamour and ecstasy and defeat of a bed-sitting-room in Ebury Street. An empty taxi hoping for a fare drew up close to them as they crossed Eaton Square – she longed for the courage to shake off Felix's arm and jump into it – it ground its gears and drove off – they walked on in silence along Elizabeth Street and turned the corner.

Felix's bed-sitting-room was on the third floor at the back of a tall narrow house; the window looked out over a small yard, a grimy brick wall and the backs of the houses in Chester Square. The landlady lived in the basement and they had crept in and up the stairs unheard and unobserved. Leonora noticed a bottle of bright green hairwash on the dressing-table and a photograph of a squat, dark girl in an embossed leather frame. The bed was pretending to be a divan, it had neither head nor foot and was pushed against the wall, there were some coloured Liberty cushions on it arranged three-cornerwise and looking self-conscious; on the mantelpiece there were a few books leaning against a china dog, a tin of Gold Flake cigarettes, a large photograph of three young men in bathing-trunks, and a pair of dumb-bells. Leonora stood quite still in the middle of the room, staring uncertainly at the three young men and imagining vaguely that the one in the middle of the group was Felix himself; a beam of sunlight cut sharply through the net curtains and in the distance there was the noise of a train shunting. Felix turned the key in the door and then came over to her; he stood looking at her for a moment with a strange, furtive little smile, and then, with a sort of gentle violence he pulled her to him and as his mouth opened on hers she felt his left hand slip into the bosom of her dress.

(7)

On a Saturday evening a few weeks later, Leonora came into the theatre with Josie Gay. They were late and breathless having run all the way from Josie's family's flat in Covent Garden; the 'Half' had already been called and if Len Baxter, the stage manager, saw them they would be ticked off. The stage-door man handed Leonora a letter from the rack as she and Josie rushed through the folding-doors; she took it without looking at it.

Leffie glanced at them disapprovingly as they burst into the dressing-room. Leonora flung the letter face downwards on her dressing-table while she tore her clothes off and got into her wrapper. She felt gay and without a care in the world. Tomorrow was Sunday and she was meeting Felix as usual;

she had had a lovely time having dinner with Josie and the Prout family. Josie's father, Syd Prout, the well-known comedian, had died some years ago; he had left his wife with three daughters to bring up. Dawn (Dawn Lawrence), the eldest, had made quite a name for herself playing Cockney character parts. Josie came next and was doing reasonably well; she was a hard-boiled thoroughly experienced little 'Pro' and looked a great deal younger than twenty-five with her chubby face and fluffy blonde hair. The family's pride was Shirley, the youngest – the famous Shirley Dale who already at twenty-four was an established star. Leonora had met her for the first time this evening and had been duly thrilled and impressed. She had arrived unexpectedly and tempestuously just as they were sitting down to dinner, her clothes were perfect and her manner entirely natural and unaffected, the aura of stardom although unmistakable seemed in no way to have interfered with her alert, utterly theatrical sense of humour, a quality which most emphatically distinguished the whole family. Mrs Prout (at one time Rosie Claire) was obviously adored by the three girls, they laughed at her and teased her and told hilarious stories of her absentmindedness, her occasional predilection for having a 'couple over the odds', her swiftness of repartee and her frequent but always unsuccessful attempts to become what they described as 'County'. None of them ever called her 'Mother' or even 'Mum'. She was always 'Rosie' or sometimes 'Our Rosie'. There was certainly a warmth, a cosiness, an intrinsic down-to-earth reality about the Prout family. Leonora had been taken to their ramshackle, untidy house in Covent Garden several times; each time she had come away happy and stimulated and with a little envy in her heart, a regret that she had not had the luck to be born of a comedian and a Principal Boy and been brought up with the fun and jokes and glamour of the Theatre as her natural background.

It wasn't until she had put on the foundation of her make-up and was about to start on her eyelashes that she remembered the letter; she wiped her fingers on her face-towel, picked it up and turned it over in her hands. With a slight sinking of the heart she recognised Felix's handwriting; perhaps he was putting her off for tomorrow, perhaps he was ill or had to go and see his mother at Uxbridge or something. She opened it quickly and read it, then she sat quite still feeling sick, as though someone had hit her hard in the solar plexus. The chattering voices of the other girls seemed to recede into the remote distance. Like a sound from another world she dimly heard the call-boy's voice in the passage shouting 'Quarter of an hour please'. With an immense effort she read the letter through again.

DEAREST LEE,

I hate writing you this letter but I've got to do it, there is no other way out. I know you'll think me an awful cad for never having told you that I was engaged to be married but somehow I couldn't screw up the courage – I felt that it would spoil everything if you knew. I am utterly heartbroken and miserable – my fiancée's father has found out about you and me – I don't know how, but he tackled me with it and there's been the most awful row. He has forced me to promise never to see you again and he is sending me away to Holland for three months on the firm's business. By the time you receive this I shall already have left. Please try to forgive me. I daren't break my word to him because he is my Boss and my whole job depends on it. I feel so dreadfully unhappy – I can't write any more. Good-bye.

FELIX.

Leonora folded the letter and put it carefully back into the envelope and automatically began to do her eyelashes. Nobody must see that she was upset, nobody must notice anything wrong, she caught Leffie's eye in the mirror and forced herself to smile at her. Her hand was shaking and it caused her to smudge some eye-black on her cheek – she said 'Blast' loudly and heard to her surprise and relief that her voice sounded quite ordinary. She managed to get through the performance without betraying herself; only once, during the sextette, she nearly broke down – it was in the second chorus when she had her little solo bit to sing and just as she stepped forward out of the line a burning, agonising memory of Felix sprang at her from the darkness of the auditorium. Last Sunday afternoon – could it really only be last Sunday? – they had been lying together on the divan and he had suddenly jumped up and, wrapping a towel round his middle, minced across the room in an imitation of her singing these very words. She had laughed immoderately and he had silenced her by sliding on top of her and kissing her. . . . Now, with the other five girls humming 'bouches fermées' behind her, she suddenly felt her throat contract, she gave a painful little gulp and forced the rhymed couplet out the wrong way round. As they were dancing off at the end of the number Josie hissed out of the corner of her mouth, 'Drunk again, dear!' Leonora giggled as naturally as she could, 'I suddenly got the chokes!'

When the show was over she took longer than usual to get her make-up off. She was feeling exhausted and wretched and the strain of keeping up the pretence that nothing out of the way had happened to her was beginning to wear her down. When she had finally got her outdoor clothes on all the others had gone and she was fumbling in her bag to find Leffie's Saturday-night tip when her fingers encountered the shame-ful, heart-breaking letter; she had put it carefully in her bag before going down for the first act. Again a wave of sickness engulfed her, she caught Leffie's eye looking at her curiously, her legs seemed to give way under her and she sank down abruptly on a chair. In a moment Leffie's arms were round her.

'What's the matter dear? You've been looking peaky all the evening.'

Leonora tried gallantly to mutter that she was all right but the sympathy in Leffie's voice and the hopelessness and misery in her heart were too much for her, she buried her face against Leffie's shoulder and broke into violent, shaking sobs.

Leffie, with the tact born of long experience said nothing at all for quite a long while; she merely held her close and occasionally gave her a gentle, affectionate little pat. Presently, when the violence of her weeping had spent itself, Leffie went over to the cupboard over the washing basin and, taking out a medicine bottle with brandy in it, poured some into a glass and held it to Leonora's lips.

'Here, love,' she said, 'take a sip of this and I'll light you a nice cigarette.'

Leonora obeyed weakly; the brandy made her gasp a little. Leffie lit a cigarette and handed it to her, then sat down purposefully opposite her with her gnarled hands on her knees and said firmly, 'Now then – what's wrong? You'd better tell me and be quick about it, for if it's what I think it is there's no sense in fiddling about and wasting time!'

Leonora made a great effort. 'I don't think' – she gulped, 'I don't think it *is* what you think it is, Leffie – it's just that – that.' Here her eyes filled with tears again and she broke off.

'Is it that young man with the smarmy voice and the funny name?'

Leonora nodded.

'I knew it.' Leffie clicked her tongue against her teeth.

'Has he got you into trouble?'

Leonora shook her head wearily. 'No, not exactly – that is – not that sort of trouble.' Somewhere at the back of her misery she was aware of a flicker of amusement at Leffie's insistence on the obstetrical aspect of the situation.

'What *has* 'e done then?' – went on Leffie inexorably – 'led you up the garden path and then buggered off and left you?'

'That's right, Leffie.' This time Leonora really did manage a wan smile. 'That's exactly what he's done.' She reached for her bag, opened it, took out the letter and handed it to Leffie.

'Here – you'd better read it.'

Leffie took it, fixed her glasses on her nose and read it slowly through. Leonora watched her without emotion – she felt drained of all feeling and immeasurably tired.

Leffie finished the letter and put it back in its envelope. 'Well,' she said. 'That's a nice thing I must say. I knew that young gentleman was no good the first time 'e come here with that note for you and give me five bob.' She looked at Leonora sharply over her glasses.

'Have you been the 'ole 'og with him?'

Leonora nodded.

'Was it the first time you ever 'ad with anybody?'

'Yes.'

'Well then,' said Leffie with finality. 'The first thing you've got to do is to forget about him – he's a bad lot if ever I saw one – and the second thing is to keep a careful eye on yourself for the next few weeks – let's see now,' Leffie wrinkled her brow with the effort of calculation, 'you're not due again until the first week of July, are you?'

Leonora frowned slightly, Leffie's aggressive realism was a trifle distasteful. 'It's nothing to do with that, Leffie,' she said with a slight edge on her voice. 'That's not what's worrying me, really it isn't——'

Leffie's face softened suddenly. 'I know dear,' she said. 'You mustn't take any notice of me – I always look at the practical side of things first – I always 'ave done all my life, that is ever since I was old enough to learn a bit of horse sense and that's going back a bit I give you my word.' She leant forward and patted Leonora's hand. 'Now, look 'ere, dear——'

Leonora looked at her pale, kindly eyes and was surprised to see that there were tears in them.

'I know what's upsetting you all right – don't you make any mistake about that. You've let yourself fall in love with him and you thought that he was in love with you and now you suddenly find that all he was after was just one thing and that one thing you were fathead enough to let 'im have! Well – that's that, isn't it? What's done's done and you can't get away from it, but it isn't right to work yourself into a state and cry your 'eart out for a slimy young rotter who takes advantage of you and leaves you flat without as much as by your leave, is it now? He's not worth one minute of your time if you only knew it – mind you I'm not saying he isn't good-looking and nicely spoken and all that sort of thing – they always are – that type; but look at you now, you're young and pretty and getting on fine with your whole life before you – why should you worry just because some la-di-da young bastard 'asn't got the decency to treat you right! Why, if he had any sense he'd be jumping for joy at having the luck to take you out to tea let alone have an affair with you. Let him go, dear, and a bloody good riddance to him at that; don't cry any more and don't get upstage with me for speaking what's in my mind. You're the lucky one if you only knew it and a day will come and not so far off either when you'll laugh your 'ead off to think what a state you got yourself into over someone who wasn't fit to black your boots!' Leffie, exhausted by this peroration rose to her feet. 'If you'll wait two shakes of a duck's arse I'll tidy up and walk with you to the tube.'

Leonora got up too and straightened her hat in front of the glass, then she turned, her underlip trembling a little, and flung her arms round Leffie's angular, undernourished little body. 'Thank you, Leffie,' she said with a catch in her voice. 'Thank you a lot.'

(8)

LEONORA JARVIS was certainly a big draw in Edinburgh. As a matter of fact she was a big draw all over the country. Since 1940 she had, in common with most of the other West End stars, played in the Provinces more consistently than ever before in her life. Mr Gilmour, the house manager, stood by the Box Office at the end of the performance and watched the crowds passing through the foyer and on through the exit doors into the black-out. They all looked cheerful and animated as though they had had a good time. Leonora had made, as usual, a charming little curtain speech, Gilmour had stopped on the way down from his office to listen to it. With all his years of managerial experience it always amused him and pleased him to observe the technical grace and courtesy with which established stars handled their applause.

Leonora Jarvis was actually one of his favourites. She had played the theatre countless times and never been any trouble, always polite and charming to the staff, always controlled and assured and untemperamental even when things went wrong. He remembered the first time she had appeared there – a long while ago, 1927 or '28. She had played the second part in a Clarence Wellman comedy supporting Charles Lucas and poor old Jane Lorrimer. It had been the first week of the play's provincial try-out before going to the West End and on the opening night, after a disastrous dress rehearsal on the Sunday, Leonora had unquestionably walked away with the show. He remembered going round to her dressing-room to congratulate her – she had dressed upstairs in those days, not in the star room on the stage level where she was now; he remembered how flushed and happy and excited she had been and how proudly she had introduced him to her husband, a good-looking young naval lieutenant. Mr Gilmour sighed sentimentally; that completely happy marriage had been broken by Fate in 1933 when the husband had been killed in an air crash while on his way to rejoin his ship at Malta. The papers had been full of praise of Leonora's behaviour, all the usual journalistic tripe about her playing with a broken heart and never missing a performance. Lot of bloody nonsense, of course she hadn't missed a performance; being an old ex-actor himself he realised only too well how fortunate she had been to have a performance to give in a crisis like that. There's nothing like having responsibility and a job to do to get you through trouble. Tonight, watching her make her curtain speech, he had suddenly felt a surge of emotion. Nothing particularly personal, just professional emotion; the Theatre was the thing all right, a good artiste in a good play, gracefully acknowledging the enthusiasm of a packed house, you could never achieve a thrill like that in all the ornate, super-cinemas in the world! He nodded cheerfully to the doorman and, stubbing his cigar out in a brass ash-tray affixed to the wall outside one of the entrances to the stalls, he pushed the door open, walked down along the side of the empty auditorium and went through the pass door on to the stage.

A little while later when he was seated in Leonora's dressing-room having his usual chat with her while she put the finishing touches to her street make-up, there was a knock on the door.

Alice, Leonora's maid, disappeared discreetly into the passage for a moment then came back. 'It's that Mr – that gentleman who you are expecting,' she said.

Mr Gilmour saw a quick smile flit across Leonora's face.

'Tell him to give me just two minutes,' she said.

Gilmour immediately rose to his feet. 'I must be pushing off,' he said. 'Everything all right? – no complaints?'

'A million complaints.' Leonora patted his mottled red face affectionately. 'Those damned girls with their coffee trays rattling all through the beginning of the second act –

one of these nights I shall jump over the orchestra pit and bash their heads in!'

'All right, all right.' He held up his hand pacifically. 'It won't happen tomorrow night, I promise.'

'Does that go for tea as well? – tomorrow's a matinée day!'

'Tea-trays out before the curtain – cross my heart,' said Mr Gilmour. 'Good-night, my dear.'

'Good-night, Gillie.' Leonora kissed her hand to him as he went out of the door. She stood still for a moment in the middle of the room, surveying herself in the long glass. Her tailor-made was good, new silk stockings wonderful! God bless darling Bobbie Craig for coming back from Bermuda via Lisbon – her mink coat of course was the crowning glory – yes, she certainly looked well enough.

'It's all right, Alice,' she said with the faintest suspicion of a tremor in her voice. 'You can ask Mr Meseurier to come in now.'

Alice disappeared into the passage again and, after a moment or two, flung open the door. Leonora heard her say, 'This way, sir.'

Into the room walked briskly, if a trifle nervously, the first lover of her life, and at the sight of him her heart stopped dead in her breast and the charming welcoming smile was frozen on to her face.

'Leonora.' He took her hand. 'This is wonderful – wonderful – I can hardly believe it's really true!'

She felt her hand warmly enveloped in his and watched with awful fascination as with forced, self-conscious gallantry he bent down to kiss it. His head was practically bald except for a few strands of hair which were plastered across his scalp with infinite care like strips of damp patent leather. He straightened himself and gazed into her eyes with a whimsical expression tinged with stale amorousness, a macabre travesty of the way she remembered him looking at her in the past. His figure, that once lithe and graceful body, had assumed

with the years the shape of a pear-drop, sloping from the
shoulders and swelling into a paunch; his sagging skin was a
yellowish-grey and his eyes, the whites of which were slightly
bleared, seemed to have crept closer to the bridge of his nose
as though they were scared and anxious to get as near to one
another as possible. He was wearing a debonair pin-striped
brown suit which was a little tight for him and on the third
finger of his left hand was a large ruby ring. He had laid his
bowler hat and mackintosh on the couch when he came in.

With a supreme effort Leonora pulled herself together.
'Why, Felix!' The words seemed to stick in her throat. 'What
a lovely surprise! After all these years!' She was horribly
aware of the falseness in her voice but he seemed to be blandly
unconscious of it.

'You were splendid in the play tonight.' He gave a little nod
as though to emphasise his approval of her performance.
'What I said in my letter proved to be quite true, you've
hardly changed at all.'

'Neither have you – I should have known you anywhere.'
Mortified, she noted his serene acceptance of the glib,
conventional lie. Suddenly feeling that she couldn't bear to
look at him for another moment she hurriedly turned and
snatched up a cigarette-box from the dressing-table. 'Let's sit
down quietly and have a cigarette,' she said, 'before we go to
supper. Alice, ask the taxi man to be a dear and wait for five
minutes, will you? Then you can go.'

'All right, Miss Jarvis.' Alice took her hat and coat from
the peg behind the door. 'Good-night, miss – Good-night,
sir.' She went out and closed the door behind her.

Leonora and Felix were alone. With a quick, almost
subservient gesture, he whipped a lighter from his pocket and
lit her cigarette and then his own.

She murmured 'Thank you,' motioned him into the arm-
chair and inhaled the smoke deeply into her lungs. 'If only,'
she thought wildly, 'this one particular "Player's Mild" might

by magic contain some strong anæsthetic that would send
me off into complete unconsciousness!' She sat down at the
dressing-table and giving a nervous little dab at her hair she
tried frantically to think of something to say, but the leaden
silence crushed her down and numbed her brain. After an
eternity he broke it by leaning forward and saying, with
pregnant meaning, 'Well?'

She forced herself to turn and look at him. 'Well what?'
She gave a gay little laugh.

'Have you forgiven me?'

This was insufferable – how dare he, how could he be so
awful as to say that! She felt herself blushing with rage and
embarrassment. Still with a smile on her face she said
mechanically, 'There's nothing to forgive.'

Aware of the strain in the atmosphere but happily misunderstanding the cause, he allowed a distinctly roguish look
to come into his eyes and grinned, a slow, knowing, resolutely
seductive grin. That grin was the final horror, for in place of
the gleaming white teeth that in the past had so tremendously
enhanced his charm he was now exhibiting, with the utmost
complacency, a double set of shining dentures surmounted
by gums of gutta percha.

Leonora stared at them hypnotised and then the dreadful
thing happened; her control snapped and she started to laugh.
His grin persisted for a little but gradually faded; she saw his
expression change from such coquetry to bitter, tight-lipped
rage. He stood up. She tried incoherently to cover her
mounting hysteria by murmuring something about the
sudden shock and the excitement of seeing him again, but it
was no use, she was gone, sunk, lost irretrievably. The tears
rolled down her cheeks, she felt her face becoming suffused
and scarlet, some mascara ran into her eyes and the sharp,
stinging pain of it far from pulling her together merely sent
her off into further agonising paroxysms. She scrabbled
wildly in her bag for her handkerchief and, having found it,

dabbed ineffectually at her streaming eyes. She was aware also that she was making awful explosive noises, groans and gasps and grunts, her whole body was shaking uncontrollably and finally, beyond shame and far beyond all hope of restraint, she stretched her arms out on the dressing-table and, burying her face in them, lay there in utter abandon, sobbing helplessly, with her shoulders heaving.

When, after a considerable time, spent and exhausted, she raised her head the room was empty.

This Time Tomorrow

LOUISE came out of the Airways Terminal into the Spring sunlight and walked briskly along Buckingham Palace Road in the direction of Victoria Station. It was only a quarter to twelve and Sheila wasn't expecting her until one o'clock so there was lots of time. Realising that she was almost running, she slowed down and, waiting at the corner of Elizabeth Bridge for the traffic lights to change, crossed over to the other side. It would be sublimely idiotic to be knocked down by a bus now, at this particular moment of her life after all that money had been expended and the man with the pince-nez had been so nice and reassuring. Everything was in order: her passport, with a half a dozen extra photographs, her vaccination certificate, her ticket and a wad of B.O.A.C. brochures which explained in incomprehensible detail the flying hours and arrivals and departures of a myriad aircraft which now, at this very instant while her high heels were clicking along on the secure comforting pavement, were hurtling above the clouds of the world, taking off and landing, rocketing and bumping through electric storms, droning interminably along at immense altitudes over mountains and deserts and far-off seas, gliding down through velvety tropical darkness on to illuminated strips of asphalt, rising up through fogs and rains and snows into Arctic dawns, and scarifying infinity. It was absurd nowadays to be agitated at the thought of travelling by air, everybody did it, it was no longer spectacular or dashing or even romantic, ordinary people,

people like herself without any claims to heroism or gallantry, without even the impetus of urgency, clambered in and out of aeroplanes without a qualm; even poor Eileen, who had been so terrified of the blitzes that she had buried herself gloomily in Chiddingfold for the duration of the war, had flown to South Africa and back with her dreadful sister-in-law and never turned a hair! The man with the pince-nez really had been extremely considerate: he may have noticed that her hand was trembling when she wrote out the cheque, he may even have heard her heart pounding, but if so he had certainly given no sign; his attitude had been calm, businesslike and benignly unaware of the very possibility of anxiety. He had told her with gentle firmness that she must be at the terminal not one minute later than seven-fifteen and that on arrival at the airport her baggage would be weighed in and that if there were any excess she would be permitted to pay for it by cheque at the last minute. He had explained, patiently but unsuccessfully, the confusing differences in time that she would encounter in course of the journey and, when she had finally gathered up all the papers he had given her, he wished her 'Happy Landings' and turned the soothing balm of his personality to a mad-looking woman in a red beret who had been standing just behind Louise for quite a while and breathing stertorously.

This time tomorrow – she reflected as she turned into Eccleston Street – I shall be up very high indeed above the sea and the clouds and sitting in a pressurized cabin. Her heart missed a beat and, feeling that she might suddenly be sick or fall down, she stopped in front of an antique shop and pressed her forehead against the cool glass of the window. A woman inside, presumably the owner, wearing a mauve overall and a string of amber beads, looked at her suspiciously. Louise fixed her gaze intently on a pair of dusty red leather bellows and frowned as though she were trying to decide whether they were genuine or fake, then with an almost imperceptible smile of contempt she shrugged her shoulders and walked on. 'I must pull myself together,' she said to herself, 'I can't go staggering about the streets leaning against shop windows and making a craven, cracking fool of myself.' She glanced at her watch and seeing it was only five to twelve, she sighed irritably. Still more than an hour to go and only Cadogan Place to get to at the end of it which was not more than a few minutes walk. If only Sheila lived at Hampstead she could have got into a bus and sat down. She felt more than anything in the world a passionate longing to sit down. There were unfortunately no seats in Ebury Street and it was improbable that there would be any in Eaton Square. She strolled along aimlessly in the direction of Sloane Square where at least she could have a cup of coffee. Ebury Street was at last showing signs of rejuvenation after the drab deprivations of the war. There were still gaps between some of the houses and remains of rubble overgrown with grass and weeds but a few front doors had been newly painted and there was a general feeling of spring-cleaning in the air; a piece of newspaper blew out of the gutter and across the road and a small boy on roller skates charged at her with his head down and she had to step on to one of the door-steps to avoid his cannoning into her. If of course he had cannoned into her and knocked her down she might have broken her leg and been taken to hospital. She closed her eyes for a moment and stopped dead in her tracks at the blissful thought of lying in a clean, cool hospital bed, pain or no pain, relieved of awful fears, resigned and at peace. She wrote out in her mind the telegram to Henry, 'Darling – have had to cancel flight owing slight accident – nothing serious – don't worry – writing – love love love——'

She wondered, as she walked on again after her temporary sojourn in St George's Hospital, how and where, if such a telegram should be sent, Henry would receive it. She visualised him on a dim, green-shaded veranda sipping a long cool drink through a straw and wearing tropical shorts: not the baggy British-Raj kind that flapped around the knees and sometimes even below them, but the neat, abbreviated variety like those her cousin Derek had worn when he came back on leave from Cairo during the war. Henry would open the telegram casually, probably making a gay little joke over his shoulder to his friends as he did so, then he would read the words, 'Slight accident' – 'Nothing serious' – 'Flight cancelled' and stand quite quite still for a moment stunned with disappointment, while his left hand mechanically crumpled the telegram envelope into a ball. Perhaps on the other hand he wouldn't be stunned with disappointment at all but merely exasperated at the thought of all his plans and arrangements being upset, and stamp off with his cronies to the club where he would get drunk and curse the day that he had been stupid enough to tie himself up to a neurotic ass. 'That's what I am,' she told herself miserably as she turned into South Eaton Place, 'nothing more nor less than a neurotic ass!' She said the words 'neurotic ass' out loud in the hope that hearing them scathingly enunciated might shame her into a calmer attitude of mind and lay by the heels the foolish panic that had been tormenting her ever since Henry's letter had arrived ten days ago. A woman pushing a perambulator shot her a sharp, apprehensive glance as she passed and quickened her pace.

In the tea-shop she ordered a cup of coffee, fished for her cigarette-case in her bag, lit a cigarette, inhaled deeply and looked around her, pressing the familiarity, the ordinariness of the crowded café against her mind's eye, endeavouring by staring at it so closely, so clinically, to relegate its hordes of complacent shopping ladies, its clamorous children and anæmic waitresses to a limbo of commonplace, unadventurous servitude from which she, by means of the coloured papers in her bag, was about to escape for ever. Seen thus from the viewpoint of her imminent emancipation from all that they were and all that they represented, the very safety and security of their lives provided her with a bulwark against her fear and fortified her courage. A woman at the next table was wiping a smear of jam from her child's face. It was a fat child and its nose was running. A little further off two elderly ladies were squabbling politely with each other as to which of them should pay the bill. A highly made-up waitress flounced up to Louise's table and banged down a cup of coffee on it so sharply that some of it slopped over into the saucer. She gave a slight grunt of perfunctory apology and went away again. 'This time tomorrow——' Louise drew a deep breath and, with a concentrated effort of her will, stared firmly and unwinkingly at 'This time tomorrow'. There it was, so near in the future, waiting for her inexorably and it was no use trying to evade it or frighten it away or beat it out of her consciousness: it wouldn't give up and go home like one of those lazy sharks she had read about who scurry off in dismay when a local pearl fisher slaps the water with the flat of his hand: it would stay there smugly and inevitably until, after God knows how many more æons of terror-stricken imaginings, she would finally reach and pass it. 'Most of the time,' the man with pince-nez had said, 'you will be flying at approximately eighteen thousand feet.' He had said this without a suspicion of dramatic implication; pleasantly and informatively, just as he might have said 'You will pass a pillar-box on the right after which you turn sharp left and you will find the shop you require standing on the corner.' She wondered if the whole business was as normal and commonplace to him as he made it sound; if the routine monotony, day after day, of consigning his fellow creatures to excessive altitudes had atrophied his imagination; or if perhaps when he was a young man himself he had flown so much and so far that the perils of the air held no surprises and no fears for him and that now, in sedentary middle age, he could look back on electric storms, forced landings, blazing port engines and alien airfields blanketed in impenetrable fog, with nothing more than pleasurable nostalgia. She stirred the beige, unappetising coffee and stubbed out her cigarette. It really was too ridiculous that a woman of her age, thirty-two in May, five years married and in full possession of her faculties, should work herself into a state bordering on nervous collapse at the prospect of travelling in an aeroplane for the first time. It was degrading enough in any case to have to admit that it *was* the first time; everyone she knew flew as a matter of course; it just so happened that for one reason or another she never had and, during the last few years, owing to gruesome accounts of crashes in the newspapers and poor Ellen and Charlie being burnt to death on their honeymoon when their plane overshot the runway at Marseilles and nose-dived on to a hangar, she had become more and more firmly resolved that she never would. Now of course there was no help for it. Henry was in Jamaica and she was in England. Henry wanted her and she wanted him. Her timorous resolution had to go by the board; the die was cast and there was no turning back. Except of course for engine trouble! She repeated in her mind that sinister phrase 'Engine Trouble'. It was so ambiguous, so non-committal. It might mean so little, no more than an hour's delay, a temporary inconvenience set to rights with brisk efficiency by a few mechanics in blue dungarees with screwdrivers. On the other hand it might mean a great deal, the difference between life and death! One little nut or screw or bolt working itself loose balefully and secretly, unobserved by the pilot, undreamed of by the passengers, and then – suddenly – probably at eighteen thousand feet – Engine Trouble! She sipped her coffee and shivered. There were of course alternatives to flying to Jamaica. There were occasional cruise ships sailing from New York or from New Orleans; there were also fruit boats that sailed from Tilbury direct and took fourteen days, but these were very difficult to get on to because of limited space and limitless priorities, and travelling by them would almost inevitably entail sharing a small cabin with two, three or possibly four strangers. The thought of two long weeks of seasickness on the grey Atlantic mewed up in a confined space with dubious members of her own sex made Louise shudder again. Flaming death, although not exactly preferable, would at least be quicker and more final. In any event further surmise and havering was out of the question. Her ticket was bought and paid for, her light fibre suitcase was packed and ready, except for her toilet things which would be put in at the last minute, and she was leaving tomorrow morning at crack of dawn and no nonsense.

(2)

'I ENVY you,' said Sheila vivaciously – 'I envy you with all my heart and soul – just imagine——' she turned to Alice Layton who was seven months gone and poking indecisively at her salad – 'This time tomorrow, while I'm sitting gloomily under the dryer looking at *Picture Post* and you're lunching with your in-laws and poor Mona's flogging along the Great West Road in the Austin, Louise will be in mid-air!'

'At eighteen thousand feet,' said Louise mechanically.

'It's almost unbelievable,' Sheila rattled on, 'when you think that practically in our lifetime or at any rate only a minute or two before, those what-you-may-call-'em brothers were flying for the first time in a thing that looked like a kite made of string and three-ply and now here's Louise calmly hopping off across the Atlantic as if it were the most ordinary thing in the world!'

'Rather her than me,' said Mona with feeling. 'I loathe flying; I'm either sick as a dog, bored stiff, or terrified out of my wits.'

'Have you flown much?' Louise's determined effort to speak calmly made her voice sound supercilious.

'Constantly,' said Mona. 'Robert adores it. Every holiday

we've had since we've been married has been ruined for me by air travel – including our honeymoon.'

The thought of poor Ellen and Charlie rushed immediately back into Louise's mind and was resolutely dismissed.

'The thing I hate about it——' Sheila went on – 'is the hideous uncertainty – I don't mean crashes or coming down in the sea or anything dramatic like that, I mean the waiting about at airports and not being able to take off because of the weather and people keeping on coming to see you off and you never going. It took Laura Warren five days to get away from New York last winter, which really, what with the money restrictions and a whole week of farewell parties, was a bit much!'

'I'd rather go by sea and have done with it,' said Alice. 'At least you know you're going to get there.'

'During the war that was the last thing you knew——' Sheila signalled to the sullen parlourmaid to take away the plates. 'I came back in a convoy from Gibraltar in 1942 just before Simon was born and it was absolute Hell, nothing but emergency drills and life-belt inspections and everybody being strained and brave and making dreadful little jokes – I never took the damn safety jacket off night or day until we reached the mouth of the Mersey.'

'After all that was wartime,' said Alice plaintively. 'It isn't quite the same thing, is it?'

'There have been shipwrecks in peace-time, you know, dear – look at the *Titanic* and the *Empress of Whatever-it-was* that sank like a stone in the St Lawrence river.'

'That was before my day,' said Alice firmly.

Sheila laughed. 'It was before mine too – but it did happen, didn't it? I mean, whatever way of travelling you choose you've always got to take some sort of risk, haven't you?'

'At least in a shipwreck or a railway accident or a car smash you have a chance,' said Mona. 'But a plane crash is so horribly final.'

'Not necessarily,' Sheila spoke with authority. 'The thing to do at the first sign of trouble is to rush to that little lavatory at the back.'

'I do that automatically,' said Mona.

'But seriously——' Sheila went on – 'I was reading about it in Nevil Shute's book. You just wedge yourself in and when the front of the plane hits the ground, there you are up in the air and as right as rain!'

'What happens if the back of the plane hits the ground first?'

'I don't think it can,' Sheila frowned thoughtfully. 'Somebody told me why once but I've forgotten.'

'It's being burnt to death that I shouldn't like.' Alice helped herself to Creme Caramel.

'How curious,' said Louise tartly. 'Most of us love it.'

'I think we'd better change the subject.' Sheila patted Louise's hand. 'After all it isn't very tactful, is it, to go on nattering about flying accidents and horrors when Louise is on the verge of taking to the air for the first time?'

'The first time?' said Mona. 'Do you mean to say that you've never flown before?'

'I used to swing very high as a girl,' Louise replied lightly, and everybody laughed.

(3)

LOUISE'S great-aunt Esther lived in Connaught Square in a thin dark house crammed with Victorian and Edwardian knick-knacks. She was small and ivory-coloured and rising ninety; her faculties were unimpaired except for her hearing, which defect she sought to ameliorate by a series of patented appliances which invariably were 'miracles' at first and 'disgraceful swindles' when the initial enthusiasm had worn off. Her energy was boundless and her affection for Louise conscientious rather than effusive. Being her only living relative she felt in duty bound to admonish, criticise and disapprove whenever she considered it necessary and she usually seemed to consider it necessary for one reason or another whenever she saw her. Louise, having rung the bell and discreetly rat-tat-ed the brass knocker, braced herself against the inevitable. The door was opened as usual by Clara, a grey woman of sixty, who had tended Aunt Esther despotically for nineteen years. She showed Louise into the drawing-room on the first floor, announcing her name loudly and clearly but in a tone of resigned disapprobation as though she suspected her of some sinister purpose. Aunt Esther was sitting by the fire with an exquisite cashmere shawl round her shoulders reading the latest volume of Sir Osbert Sitwell's memoirs. 'The thing about this man,' she said, putting the book down as Louise kissed her, 'is that he's a gentleman.'

'He also writes well.' Louise sat down in a chair facing her.

'That's what I meant,' said Aunt Esther pushing forward a cigarette-box. 'You can smoke if you want to – I know you can't sit still for a minute without puffing away like a chimney so I told Clara to have all the paraphernalia ready for you – there's an ash-tray just by you.'

'Thank you, darling,' said Louise gratefully. 'You're sure it won't make you cough or anything?'

'I seldom cough,' replied Aunt Esther, 'unless I happen to have a cold or Bronchial Asthma and at the moment I have neither.'

'You're hearing very well,' said Louise ingratiatingly.

'Telex,' replied Aunt Esther. 'I put in a new battery because I knew you were coming so there's no need to shout.'

'I wasn't shouting.'

'I didn't say you were, I merely warned you that it wasn't necessary, it makes a horrible buzzing in my ears and I can't distinguish a word. Eva Collington came to see me last week and made such a din that I had to tell her to go.'

'How is she?' enquired Louise.

'In the depths as usual.' Aunt Esther complacently adjusted the shawl round her shoulders. 'She's years younger than I am but you'd think she was ninety the way she carries on, had to be helped up the stairs if you please, you should have seen Clara's face – it was killing!'

'But she did have an accident of some sort, didn't she? I remember you telling me about it last time I was here.'

'Accident!' Aunt Esther snorted contemptuously. 'She twisted her ankle getting out of a taxi in Pelham Crescent last December and we've never heard the last of it, such a hulla-baloo, you'd think she'd broken every bone in her body.'

There was silence for a moment broken only by the ticking of the clock on the mantelpiece and the distant yapping of a dog on the other side of the Square; the atmosphere of the room was close and oppressive. The furniture, the silver photograph frames, the accumulated bric-a-brac of years: snuff-boxes, miniatures, paper weights, porcelain cups and saucers and plates, all seemed to be immured in a sub-aqueous vacuum of old age. Life, eighty-eight vigorous years of it, had been reduced to this stuffy quiescence. Louise looked at her aunt curiously and repressed a wild impulse to ask her suddenly how it felt to be so immeasurably old with everything over and done with and nothing to look forward to; to find out once and for all if the fear of death was still alive in her or if the weight of her years had crushed it out of existence leaving her with nothing more than a vague, un-speculative resignation. At this moment Clara came in with the tea things which she placed on a low table beside Aunt Esther's chair. 'I brought it up earlier than usual,' she said loudly, 'because I thought Mrs Goodrich would be wanting to rush away.'

'Don't yell like that, Clara,' said Aunt Esther. 'You know perfectly well I've got a fresh battery in.'

'You can never be sure they'll work however fresh they

are.' Clara straightened herself. 'It's always hit or miss with those things as we know to our cost – one day we're up in the clouds and the next we're down in the dumps – there's no telling what's going to happen.' She turned to Louise. 'Talking about being up in the clouds I hear you're going off in an aeroplane tomorrow!'

'Yes,' said Louise with a bright smile. 'I've got my ticket in my bag and everything's packed and ready – I'm looking forward to it very much,' she added defiantly.

'Well, there's no account for tastes,' said Clara, 'but you wouldn't get me to set foot in one of those contraptions, not if you were to offer me a thousand pounds down.'

'That contingency is unlikely to arise,' snapped Aunt Esther.

'It's flirting with death if you ask me,' Clara went on. 'Fairly begging for it. Look at Mrs Morpeth and those two lovely little girls, the eldest couldn't have been more than five, setting off as gay as you please to join their Daddy in Egypt——'

'Never mind about Mrs Morpeth and her little girls now, Clara, that will be all for the moment.' She turned to Louise. 'Perhaps you'd like to pour out, dear? My hands are rather shaky.'

'Mine are none too steady,' said Louise.

'If God had intended us to fly he'd have given us wings, wouldn't he?' said Clara with finality and went out of the room.

'Clara's been getting more and more aggressive lately.' Aunt Esther sighed. 'She bites my head off at the least thing. – Just give me the tea, dear, I prefer to put in my own milk and sugar. – I'm afraid I shall have to talk to her seriously.'

Louise handed her her cup of tea and pushed the milk jug and sugar basin gently towards her. 'Poor Clara,' she said with a smile. 'I don't suppose she meant to be discouraging.'

'I wasn't thinking of that,' said Aunt Esther. 'I was thinking of the way she pounced at me about my new battery – really quite insufferable – she's becoming too big for her boots that's what's the matter with her – give that class an inch and they take an ell.'

'After all she has been with you for nearly twenty years!'

Aunt Esther was not to be placated. 'That's what she trades on. She thinks just because I'm chained to this house most of the time and more or less dependent on her that she can do and say whatever she likes. She was downright rude to poor Oliver Elliot when he came to luncheon the other day, just because he asked for some scraps for that dog of his that he always insists on dragging everywhere with him; he got quite hysterical when she'd gone out of the room – you know what an old woman he is.'

'I haven't seen him for ages,' said Louise.

'You haven't missed much,' Aunt Esther gave an evil little chuckle. 'He's sillier than ever and talks about nothing but his gall-bladder – I expect it will carry him off one of these days.' She paused and looked at Louise critically. 'Is that hat supposed to be the latest thing?'

Louise laughed. 'Not particularly, it's just a hat – as a matter of fact I've had it for some time – don't you like it?'

'Not very much,' said Aunt Esther. 'It makes your face look too big.'

'I'm afraid that's my face's fault more than the hat's.'

'Harriet Macclefield's girl came to see me the other day wearing one of the most idiotic hats I've ever seen – it looked as if it were going to fly off her head – she's managed to get herself engaged at last you know.'

'No,' said Louise, 'I didn't know.'

'Something in the Foreign Office I think she said he was, she showed me his photograph and I must say he looked half dotty; he can't be quite all there to want to marry her, she's grown into such a great fat lump, you'd never recognise her.'

'I don't suppose I should even if she hadn't,' said Louise. 'I've never seen her in my life.'

'Nonsense,' said Aunt Esther impatiently, 'she was one of your bridesmaids.'

'I didn't have any bridesmaids – Henry and I were married in a Register Office.'

'I remember now – it was Maureen's wedding I was thinking of – I knew she'd been somebody's bridesmaid.' Aunt Esther paused. 'How is he?' she asked abruptly.

'Henry? – Very well, I believe – I shall know for certain the day after tomorrow – it's incredible, isn't it,' she went on with a rush, 'to think one can get all the way to Jamaica – five thousand miles – in so little time?'

'I thought he was in Bermuda,' said Aunt Esther. 'But after all I suppose it's much the same thing.'

'No, darling.' Louise spoke firmly. 'It's quite, quite different. Jamaica is much more tropical.'

'A woman I met in that hotel at Bournemouth had lived in Bermuda for years,' said Aunt Esther. 'She swore by it.'

'I'm sure that Bermuda is charming,' said Louise, a slight note of exasperation creeping into her voice. 'But Henry happens to be in Jamaica which is why I'm going there.'

'Well, I must say I don't envy you,' said Aunt Esther, 'Henry or no Henry. All that rattling and banging and discomfort. I suppose they strap you in, don't they?'

'Only when the plane's taking off or landing I believe.'

'If you ask me, the whole world is going mad! All this scrambling about here, there and everywhere at breakneck speed. I can't see the point of it. No wonder everybody has nervous breakdowns.'

Louise, feeling that it would be useless to contest this statement, merely nodded reluctantly, as though she were really in complete agreement but was not prepared to commit herself.

'When I was a girl,' Aunt Esther went on, 'the actual

travelling to places was just as much fun as getting to them. I shall never forget, when I was very young, going all the way to Sicily with your Great-Aunt Mary and the whole family. My dear – the excitement of that journey – you can't imagine! We laughed and laughed and laughed! I shall remember it to my dying day.'

'I may laugh hysterically all the way to Jamaica.'

'You'll laugh on the wrong side of your face if the aeroplane falls into the sea,' said Aunt Esther grimly.

'There's always the remote chance that it won't fall into the sea.' Louise underlined the word 'remote' with deliberate sarcasm. 'After all, the percentage of air crashes is relatively small all things considered. Everybody flies nowadays. Look at Princess Elizabeth! I saw a newsreel of her getting into a plane at Malta only the other day.'

'More fool her,' said Aunt Esther.

'That,' said Louise reprovingly, 'is Lèse Majesté.'

Aunt Esther pushed a plate of scones towards her. 'You'd better have some of these, Clara made them especially for you.'

'How sweet of her.' Louise took one.

'You ought to feel very flattered. She doesn't put herself out as a rule. I don't know what's been the matter with her lately, she's for ever grumbling and getting lazier and lazier. I'm sick and tired of her. To hear the way she carries on sometimes you'd think I was a slave-driver. But that's typical of the lower classes. They get overbearing and spoilt before you can say Jack Robinson, and now of course with this unspeakable Government they're getting worse and worse.'

'There *have* been cases of the upper classes being overbearing and spoilt.'

Aunt Esther ignored this interruption and went on: 'Actually, apart from getting me up in the morning, giving me my meals, and getting me to bed at night, she has nothing to do but sit in the kitchen and twiddle her thumbs.'

Louise made no reply to this petulant outburst: such bare-faced, obtuse ingratitude, if genuine, was quite shocking and beyond comment. If, in the face of Clara's long years of un-remitting servitude, Aunt Esther could so glibly dispose of her as a human being; so arbitrarily relegate her to the status of a well paid automaton, an automaton, be it said, that might understandably by now be wearing out a little, growing rusty, creaking at the joints. If she could deceive herself into the sincere belief that the task of tending her efficiently morning noon and night, year in, year out, was such a sinecure that it allowed time and to spare for thumb twiddling! Then, Louise reflected, she was a wicked, graceless old megalomaniac. But of course it wasn't genuine, the words, however arrogant and bitter they might sound, had no depths and no validity, not even any particular impetus beyond a surface irritation, a sudden urge to show off, a determination to prove that, in spite of her great age and increasing infirmities, she was not yet done for, not yet subject to any dominance other than her own will.

'Well——' said Louise conciliatingly, 'however tiresome Clara may be, her scones are certainly a dream!'

'Fiddle!' cried Aunt Esther unexpectedly, hitting herself sharply on the chest. 'The battery's gone dead.' Clucking her tongue with irritation she proceeded to haul from the bosom of her dress a small, biscuit-coloured box which she opened expertly disclosing two little batteries. She scrutinized them angrily for a moment and then, with surprising energy, rose and pressed the bell by the fireplace. 'I suppose this will give Clara another opportunity to gloat over me,' she said, and observing that Louise was about to say something, made a quick, impatient gesture with her hand to silence her and sat down again. 'It's no use trying to say anything so you might just as well sit still until Clara comes. I've got another set upstairs.'

Louise obediently sat back in her chair and lit a cigarette.

Her recent resentment of Aunt Esther's crochety arrogance evaported and she felt a sudden rush of sentimental pity, an impulse to fling her arms protectively round those sharp, bony shoulders. There was something infinitely pathetic in the spectacle of that gallant old woman sitting there in the dusk of her long life; her mind still alert, her indestructible will to fight, to get her own way, to dominate, still alive and kicking, but trapped into irascible dependence by the treachery of her body. Louise looked at her wonderingly, trying to envisage Aunt Esther's skin with the bloom of adolescence on it; the cheeks filled out and glowing with youth; the mouth full-lipped and stretched wide in convulsive laughter all the way to Sicily.

'What are you staring at?' asked Aunt Esther sharply. 'Is my hair coming down?'

'I was admiring your shawl,' Louise replied hurriedly. 'It looks so pretty and soft.'

Aunt Esther looked at her bleakly and leant forward.

'Your shawl——' Louise leant forward too and enunciated the words carefully. 'Your shawl looks so pretty and soft.'

'Oh!' grunted Aunt Esther, 'is that all!' She fingered the shawl disdainfully. 'Hubert's wife sent it to me from Scotland at Christmas. I should think it would be more useful to her than me, shut up all the year round in that draughty barrack miles away from anywhere.'

Louise, remembering that Hubert's wife was Lady Macleven, one of Aunt Esther's grander nieces, smiled and nodded appreciatively.

'I stayed there once——' went on Aunt Esther reminiscently. 'But never again!'

'It's a very lovely old house though, isn't it?'

'What?'

Louise repeated the question more loudly.

'Hideous,' said Aunt Esther. 'Filled with antlers and stuffed pike.'

At this moment Clara came in, carrying two little batteries, which she gave to Aunt Esther. 'Here——' she said, 'I expect these are what you wanted, aren't they?'

Aunt Esther took them from her with a muttered 'Thank you' and proceeded to fit them into the little box.

'How on earth did you know?' asked Louise.

'I could tell by the ring,' said Clara laconically, 'when she jabs at the bell like that it nearly always means battery trouble.'

Aunt Esther closed the box and lowered it carefully into her bosom; she then struck herself briskly again and said, 'That's better.'

Louise rose to her feet. 'I really must go now, darling, I've got a million things to do and I have to be up at six in the morning.'

'I'm always up at six in the morning,' said Aunt Esther, 'winter or summer.'

Clara sniffed. 'Awake maybe, but up never.'

Aunt Esther ignored her and looked at Louise critically. 'You're as thin as a scarecrow, I suppose you've been reducing or some such nonsense.'

'No, I haven't,' Louise replied. 'I just don't eat fattening things.'

'If I'd been as skinny as that when I was your age they would have thought I was going into a decline and sent for the doctor.'

'You needn't worry about me——' Louise bent down to kiss her, 'I'm as strong as a horse.'

'Thank you for coming to see me.' Aunt Esther returned Louise's kiss by pecking the air. 'I fully realise that it can't be very exciting talking to a deaf old woman like me.'

'You know perfectly well I love coming to see you.'

'Fiddlesticks!' said Aunt Esther with a gleam in her eye. 'If you loved it all that much you'd come more often.' She gave a little cackle at her own wickedness. 'Anyhow send me a postcard from Bermuda if you have time.'

'I will,' said Louise feeling unequal to further argument.

'I remember the woman's name now.'

'Which woman?'

'The one at Bournemouth who told me all about it,' said Aunt Esther testily. 'Mrs Cutler-Harrison. She was rather common, poor thing, but quite amiable. If you should run into her tell her you've seen me, she might introduce you to some of her friends. She seemed to know everyone on the island.'

'She'll have to bring them all down to the airport at one in the morning, the plane only stops for an hour.'

Aunt Esther either didn't notice the flippancy of Louise's tone, or decided to rise above it. 'Good-bye then,' she said, making a gesture of dismissal with her claw-like hand. 'I don't suppose I shall be here when you come back. One more winter like this will finish me off I should imagine. And a good job too!' she added briskly.

Louise, suddenly stricken with compassion and restraining an impulse to burst into tears, kissed the old lady again swiftly and unexpectedly, and fled from the room.

(4)

'Now then.' Mrs Peverance peeled off her grey suède gloves and placed them on the arm of the sofa beside her. 'What exactly is your husband going to do in Jamaica?'

Louise shot an appealing look at Boy Sullivan who was leaning against the mantelpiece sipping a dry martini: Myra, Mrs Peverance's daughter, a pasty girl of seventeen, was sitting in an arm-chair clutching a glass of orangeade and staring into space.

'Well——' said Louise with a forced smile, determined not to allow Mrs Peverance's didactic manner to fluster her. 'It's all rather complicated really. You see, Henry – that's him, my

husband – had a little money left him last year and, as he's
never felt particularly fit in this climate after being a prisoner
of war in Malaya for three years, he decided, with two friends
of his, one of whom knows Jamaica well, to buy some
property there with a view to building a hotel.'

'Good Heavens!' Mrs Peverance couldn't have looked
more startled if Louise had announced that Henry and his
friends were planning to erect a chain of brothels. 'Where?'

'On the North shore I believe.'

'The *North* shore!' Mrs Peverance stared at her incredulously.

'Yes. Somewhere near a place called Port Maria.'

'I know it well. It's where the hurricane struck in 1944.'

'Well, let's hope that the next one will strike somewhere
quite different,' said Louise. 'Hurricanes are fairly unpredictable, aren't they? I mean you can't rely on them hitting
exactly the same place every time.'

'You can't rely on them at all,' put in Boy Sullivan
flippantly.

'A hurricane is no joke I can assure you,' said Mrs Peverance. 'When we were in Barbados, before my husband was
transferred to his present position, our entire garage was
blown into the sea.'

'It was only a temporary one,' said Myra.

'Apparently a little more temporary than you bargained
for!' Louise, gathering from Mrs Peverance's expression that
she was definitely not amused, changed the subject hastily.
'I'm terribly excited by the whole idea as you can well
imagine, never having seen a tropical island in my life. It all
sounds to me so romantic and Boy's Own Paperish. Is it true
that you can send little native boys shinning up palm trees
to get delicious green coconuts?'

'Quite true,' admitted Mrs Peverance grudgingly. 'But I
fear you won't find them so very delicious.'

'Mother, how *can* you!' protested Myra. 'They're lovely.'

She turned to Louise. 'You cut off their tops with a machete and fill them up with ice and put in gin too if you like. We did it last January when I was staying with the Croker-Wallaces – and old Mrs Croker-Wallace was simply furious when she found out – about the gin I mean – she's very strait-laced.'

'There's a family you must meet,' said Mrs Peverance. 'They own an enormous banana plantation near Port Antonio. She used to be a Crutchley you know!'

Louise managed to look suitably astonished. 'No – really?'

'Her father, old Sir Kenneth Crutchley, was one of the most famous figures on the island in the old days. They say he used to ride fifty and sixty miles a day without turning a hair. Then of course the slump came and he had to get rid of all his horses.'

'I wonder that there were any left to get rid of,' said Louise.

Mrs Peverance looked at her dimly and continued. 'He was a very remarkable man and he did a tremendous lot for the natives. They absolutely worshipped him. It was quite a common sight, I believe, to see vast crowds of them following him wherever he went.'

'How nice!' Louise, aware that her reply was inadequate, endeavoured to enhance it with a knowing wink.

'He died in 1923,' went on Mrs Peverance, 'and his widow only survived him by two years. Her eldest daughter married Adrian Croker-Wallace shortly afterwards and they had five children, all girls unfortunately but full of fun. They're Myra's greatest friends aren't they, dear?'

'Vivienne isn't bad,' said Myra. 'But I can't stand the other four.'

'Nonsense.' Her mother quelled any further signs of mutiny with a glance. 'At all events——' she turned once more to Louise. 'Adrian Croker-Wallace's mother, that's the one Myra was talking about just now, is one of the most fascinating characters in Jamaica, over eighty and bursting with energy. She became a Roman Catholic a few years ago and always says exactly what comes into her mind, but you mustn't let her intimidate you. Just stand up to her and answer her back and she'll be your friend for life!'

'I'll do my best,' said Louise repressing a shudder.

'She's an old beast!' said Myra sullenly. 'And she spits when she talks. I hate her.'

'You are not to say things like that, Myra,' said Mrs Peverance sharply. 'I won't have it.' She turned to Louise and, leaning forward a little, spoke with the steely authority of a detective trying to coax vital information from a recalcitrant criminal, 'Who is this friend of your husband's who knows Jamaica so well?'

'His name is Edgar Jarvis,' said Louise. 'He's apparently lived there on and off most of his life.'

Mrs Peverance relaxed and gave a pitying little laugh. 'Poor old Edgar! I might have guessed it. He's always getting himself involved in some harebrained scheme or other, but still——' she added charitably, 'he's as straight as a die and most amusing – we're all devoted to him.'

'I'm glad,' said Louise.

'His grandfather, old Sir Pelham Jarvis, was one of the richest men in the island. He owned thousands of acres all over the place; sugar, bananas, coconuts . . . and then of course everything went.'

'Why?'

'He died in 1911 but it had all begun to disintegrate long before that. Stephen Jarvis, Edgar's father, inherited everything but of course he was absolutely hopeless, one of those weak, head-in-the-clouds sort of men, quite irresponsible, no business sense, full of crackpot ideas and an appalling gambler into the bargain. You can well imagine that, what with various slumps and one thing and another, there was soon nothing left but a ramshackle old house up in the hills behind St Ann's Bay with no light and no water. That's where Edgar lives now.'

'It's got a marvellous view,' interpolated Myra.

'You can't live on a view,' said her mother severely. 'But there he sticks, year in year out with that wife of his and all those children – do you know her?' she asked Louise abruptly.

Louise shook her head. 'I don't know either of them.'

'She's a common little thing but quite pretty if you care for those kind of looks.'

'What kind of looks are they?' Louise felt herself becoming increasingly irritated by Mrs Peverance's illusions of grandeur.

'Flashy!' replied Mrs Peverance. 'She touches up her hair and uses too much make-up – but you will probably quite like her once you get over her accent. She's Australian I think, or South African, I can never remember which.' She smiled superciliously.

'There's a considerable difference,' put in Boy Sullivan from the mantelpiece.

Mrs Peverance ignored this and, fixing Louise with a penetrating look, said in business-like tones, 'But this hotel project of your husband's, I presume that he has gone into the whole matter very carefully?'

'Naturally he has,' Louise replied with dignity. 'He's been planning it and discussing it for ages and the whole proposition has been worked out to the last detail on a solid financial basis.'

'I'm sure I'm very glad to hear it.' Mrs Peverance spoke with such palpable disbelief that Louise longed to slap her face; conscious however that such a gesture might be a little too drastic, but determined to endure no further patronage at the expense of Henry and his plans, she rose to her feet.

'Do let me get you a fresh martini. That one must be quite scalding by now.' Swiftly taking Mrs Peverance's glass from her hand she went over to the drink table, noting, as she measured the gin and vermouth into the shaker, that she was trembling. This was all Boy's fault. She glanced at him out of the corner of her eye: he was still leaning nonchalantly against the mantelpiece and blowing smoke rings, serenely oblivious to any tension in the atmosphere and apparently still convinced that by bringing Mrs Peverance to the flat he had done Louise a signal service.

'She'll be frightfully useful to you out there,' he had said over the telephone, 'she's tremendously important socially and knows everybody and she'll be able to advise you and keep you from getting in with the wrong people. She'll also be able to put you wise about domestic problems and servants and what clothes to wear and generally prevent you from making a silly twit of yourself.' Louise looked at Mrs Peverance's hat, which was skittish and unbecoming, and at her dress, which was devoid of line and badly cut, and shook the cocktail shaker with considerable violence, at the same time running over in her mind a few of the things that she would have to say to Boy afterwards. It really was too much. She had had a nerve-racking day. What with her recurrent jitters about flying; that tedious hen lunch at Sheila's then having to say good-bye to Aunt Esther, probably for the last time, and getting herself so upset that she had left the house in Connaught Square feeling miserable and utterly depleted. So much so indeed that instead of going to see Freda and her new baby, which she had fully intended to do and would at least have been cheerful, she had had to come straight home, take a hot bath and three aspirin and lie down! And now, on top of everything else, to have to be polite to this insufferable woman and her idiotic daughter, on her last day in London, possibly her last day on earth! . . . She gave the shaker an extra shake of such force that the top came off and a stream of dry martini shot up her sleeve.

'God damn it!' she said, regardless of Myra's tender years. 'It's always doing that!'

'You were bashing it about a bit you know,' said Boy

advancing with a handkerchief which Louise accepted with a baleful look.

'Here——' she said handing him the shaker, 'give Mrs Peverance her drink while I dry myself.'

Mrs Peverance, protesting shrilly, allowed her glass to be filled to the brim. 'I really oughtn't to,' she cried. 'It's dreadfully strong.'

Louise, having dabbed at her bedraggled sleeve and wiped her wrist, gave the handkerchief back to Boy, permitted him to pour her out another cocktail and sat down again.

Mrs Peverance bared her irregular teeth in an affable smile. 'You'll like Jamaica,' she said authoritatively as though she had been weighing up all the pros and cons with meticulous care and arrived at an irrevocable decision. 'But from the social point of view you must be prepared to make allowances.'

'I always do,' replied Louise.

'We're a small community. Everybody knows everybody else and on the whole we manage to have quite a lot of fun in our own way, but of course, as in all small places, there are certain little cliques that it's as well to steer clear of.'

'I quite understand,' said Louise with deceptive meekness.

'Then there's the colour question.' Mrs Peverance assumed an air of worldly tolerance. 'That's very complicated and has to be handled with the utmost tact. I mean to say you have to accept conditions as they are and not be too surprised when, for instance, you suddenly notice that the gentleman next to you at dinner is, well – on the dark side!' She gave a metallic laugh, apparently convulsed at the thought of Louise's dismay upon finding herself in such a bizarre situation. 'Some of them are very intelligent, quite brilliant in fact, you'd be astounded at their scientific knowledge.'

'I'm always astonished at anyone's scientific knowledge,' said Louise.

'Take Dr Mellish now.' Mrs Peverance turned to her daughter for support but was greeted with a stony stare. 'He's a real Jamaican born and bred and quite definitely coloured, but my dear!——' she paused dramatically. 'To hear him talk about all the technical aspects of the atom bomb – well – it's perfectly fascinating!'

'It must be,' said Louise making a private resolve to avoid Dr Mellish like the plague.

'Then there are the De Laras,' continued Mrs Peverance. 'They're an enormous family. You're bound to run into some of them, particularly on the North shore.'

Louise, confronted suddenly with a vivid mental picture of a palm-fringed coral beach littered with De Laras, giggled. Mrs Peverance however paid no attention and continued. 'Where are you going to stay when you arrive?' she enquired, dismissing for the moment the De Laras and the social intricacies of the colour question.

'My husband has rented a small house near a place called Ora – something.'

'Oracabessa.' Mrs Peverance nodded. 'I expect they've charged him the Earth. They ask the most fantastic prices along the coast, particularly if they think you're green and don't know your way about.'

'I think Edgar Jarvis arranged it.'

'Poor old Edgar would be fleeced quicker than anyone. He has no money sense at all. He's just one of those people who drift through life, you know, thriftless and improvident, with never a thought for the morrow. I only hope that this hotel scheme of your husband's will come to something, for his sake.'

'I hope so too,' murmured Louise.

Mrs Peverance sighed. 'I always think it's so tragic to see a man like poor old Edgar; well born, carefully educated, starting off with so many advantages and yet somehow quite incapable of carrying anything through – do you know what I mean?' She looked at Louise with a pained expression in her eyes, as though she were at a loss to explain, to anyone so obviously imperceptive, such a unique psychological phenomenon. 'It's as if something vital, something essential had been left out of him entirely, as if a wicked fairy had appeared at his christening and cursed him with total lack of ambition, lack of the will to succeed!'

Louise's patience snapped; she felt suddenly overwhelmed by a surge of irrational loyalty to the wretched Edgar Jarvis whom she had never even clapped eyes on and exasperated beyond endurance by the pretentious smugness of Mrs Peverance. 'I like people like that,' she said. Boy Sullivan, detecting the change in her tone, gave her a quick look and frowned warningly, but, ignoring both the look and the frown, she continued in a bright, edgy voice, 'I find them agreeable and friendly and easy to get along with, whereas I must confess that people crammed with implacable ambition and bursting with the will to succeed bore me to extinction. They're so unrestful, so perpetually on the qui vive, so terrified that they might be missing something, so vulgar! You can hear their unsatisfied egos rattling a mile off!'

Mrs Peverance, contriving to look bewildered and shocked at the same time, opened her mouth to speak but Louise mowed her down.

'As for this Edgar Jarvis, I'm perfectly certain that I shall adore him. He sounds just my cup of tea. Henry of course is already devoted to him, but then he's known him for some time. You should just read his letters! Nothing but "Edgar says this" and "Edgar says that" – just like a schoolboy getting a crush on the head prefect!' she laughed indulgently. 'But that's typical of Henry – I don't mean about the prefect exactly, although nowadays one never quite knows, does one? I mean the whole world is becoming more and more uninhibited every day – but he's always getting violent enthusiasms for people. I can't wait for you to meet him. You'll get along like a house on fire! He's a really genuine bohemian you know – not exactly eccentric but quite definitely unpredictable. You never have the faintest idea what he is going to do from one minute to the next. And as for coloured people, he has an absolute mania for them, so you need have no fears for us on that score, our house is certain to be chock-full of them from morning till night! That negro poet that there was such a fuss about – I can't recall his name for the moment but you must know who I mean – the one who was an ardent communist and then suddenly gave up the whole thing and became a Seventh Day Adventist or something peculiar and wrote all those lovely, turgid things about the Deep South! Well – he was one of Henry's closest friends before the war. They used to go to Workers' meetings together and have a whale of a time.'

Mrs Peverance, with commendable poise, smiled emptily and proceeded to put on her gloves. 'I'm afraid he will have to modify his views a little if he wishes to be a success in Jamaica,' she said, 'particularly if he is contemplating building a hotel.'

'But the hotel is going to be exclusively for negroes,' cried Louise. 'Didn't I tell you? Henry has been studying living conditions over there very carefully and he is convinced that a really comfortable hotel, run on a communal basis of course, will go far towards solving a most pressing and urgent problem. – It's going to have a swimming-pool!' She added recklessly.

'Come, Myra,' said Mrs Peverance. 'It's dreadfully late and we shall have to hurry if we are to change and be at the theatre by seven-thirty.'

'How extraordinary to think that the next time we meet it will be in Jamaica!' said Louise blandly. 'When do you expect to be back?'

'At the end of next month.' Mrs Peverance looked Louise full in the eye; her expression was forbidding. 'I have to take Myra to Switzerland and then spend a few days in Paris.' She rose and shook hands coldly with Boy Sullivan.

'Good-bye, Major Sullivan. It was so nice seeing you again.'

'Are you flying out?' asked Louise.

'I never fly,' said Mrs Peverance.

'Mother's airsick,' put in Myra with sudden animation. 'She's sick from the moment she gets into the plane until the moment she gets out of it. When we flew to Nassau last year she had to be carried off in a stretcher.'

'That will do, Myra,' said Mrs Peverance. She offered Louise a limp hand. 'Good-bye, Mrs Goodrich.'

'Good-bye.' Louise shook it warmly. 'It was so kind of you to come, and I shall remember all you've told me.'

'I expect you will find your own friends in the island,' said Mrs Peverance in a tone that left no doubt of her personal determination not to be one of them. 'People always do don't they? At all events I wish you a pleasant journey.'

'Thank you,' said Louise.

'As you and your husband will be so far away on the North coast and as I scarcely ever leave Kingston, I don't suppose we shall find many opportunities of meeting.' Mrs Peverance's anxiety to scotch once and for all even the faintest possibility of any further intimacy was almost painful in its intensity. 'However, we must hope for the best, musn't we?' With a smile of ineffable remoteness she took Myra firmly by the arm and swept out of the room. Boy Sullivan followed politely in order to see them into the lift and Louise was left behind. She wandered about the room for a moment, seething with irritation and restraining an impulse to fly at Boy when he came back and beat him with her fists. When he did come back, however, she was sitting on the sofa lighting a cigarette with a shaking hand.

'Well!' he said cheerfully. 'You certainly bitched that little enterprise.'

'What did you expect?' asked Louise with dangerous calm. 'I've always been allergic to excessive patronage. That woman's a pretentious ass and you know it.'

'My intentions were pure. I hardly know her myself. I merely ran into her at Angie's the other day and, discovering that she was a social big shot in Jamaica, I genuinely thought it might be useful to you to meet her.'

'If she's a social big shot I'll settle for the riff-raff.'

'How was I to know you'd take a black hatred to each other on sight?'

'By just taking one clear look at her,' said Louise crossly. 'You couldn't seriously imagine that either Henry or I would be likely to form a lasting friendship with that dessicated old mem-sahib.'

'At any rate,' replied Boy equably, 'you definitely couldn't now, even if you wanted to.'

'Was I abominably rude?'

'Yes. You certainly were.'

'Oh dear!' Louise felt a pang of conscience.

'Not that it matters all that much,' he laughed. 'Poor old Henry!'

'Why poor old Henry?'

'I suspect that Mrs Peverance is a keen letter writer, that type of woman usually is, and as you made it abundantly clear to her that your husband was an eccentric bohemian, a communistic negrophile with homosexual tendencies——'

'Don't!' cried Louise, burying her face in her hands and rocking to and fro. 'It's too awful! I knew I was going too far but I couldn't stop myself.'

'He will probably be blackballed immediately from the local tennis club and cut stone dead from one end of the island to the other.'

'Give me your handkerchief again,' said Louise laughing helplessly. 'Mine's in my bag and my bag's in the bedroom and I wish I were dead!'

'As far as Jamaican society goes you already are,' replied Boy, giving it to her. 'Perhaps it would be a good idea if Henry changed his plans and built a hotel in Trinidad!'

(5)

THE taxi was at the door and Mrs Meaker had taken her luggage down in the lift. Louise went into the sitting-room for one last valedictory look around; her eyes were prickly from lack of sleep for she had been awake most of the night, and in spite of two cups of strong coffee she still felt half anæsthetised, as though only part of her brain was functioning and that part liable to pack up at any moment leaving her stranded, without volition, in a mindless trance. She wondered drearily whether, if this should occur, Mrs Meaker would have the presence of mind to lead her to the Air Terminal and deposit her in the bus, or whether she would lose her head, telephone the nearest hospital and have her carried off, mouthing vacuously, in an ambulance. The sitting-room looked, in her exhausted imagination, a little unfriendly, almost as if it resented being stared at so early in the morning or perhaps had already accepted the idea of her desertion and was placidly adjusting itself to receive the Warrilows. The Warrilows! Louise gave a sudden cry and, galvanised into action, dashed to the writing-desk to scribble a note to Grace Warrilow about the tap in the spare-room lavatory which had been dribbling for the last week and needed a new washer. Having explained that she had meant to have it fixed days ago but had forgotten and that the name and address of the plumber was to be found in the small blue house-telephone book in the top right-hand drawer, she sealed up the note in an envelope, wrote 'Grace' on it in block capitals and propped it against the clock on the mantelpiece. The clock announced that it was ten minutes past seven and her heart jumped in her breast as though someone had crept up behind her and suddenly shrieked in her ear. She turned to look at the room again, desolate and near to tears. She and

Henry had lived in this flat ever since their honeymoon five years ago, except for the three months in Ireland in 1947 when they had let Anabelle have it. The Warrilows had taken it for a year with options; they were old friends and fairly quiet in their habits so there was little likelihood of their giving wild parties and emptying Pernod into the piano and burning holes in everything. She patted the sofa cushions despairingly as though they were dumb, devoted pets who would miss her when she had gone and howl all night.

At this moment Mrs Meaker appeared in the doorway. 'All ready,' she said morosely. 'You'd better be getting a move on.'

'Good-bye, Mrs Meaker. You will clean up, won't you, and see that everything's nice and tidy?'

'Trust me,' Mrs Meaker nodded. 'Remember me to Mr Goodrich and I hope you get there all right I'm sure. The weather doesn't look too good.'

'We shall fly above the weather,' said Louise with forced brightness. 'It's a Constellation plane you know, they go very high indeed.'

'Good heavens!' Mrs Meaker looked incredulous. 'It makes me dizzy to even think of it!'

'Well – good-bye again.' Louise shook hands with her. A parting gift of three pounds in an envelope had been presented and accepted in the kitchen earlier and there didn't seem much more to say. 'I've left a note for Mrs Warrilow on the mantelpiece explaining about the tap. You might telephone Mr What's-his-name later in the morning, but if you can't get hold of him I've told her that his name and address is in my blue book.'

'All right,' said Mrs Meaker. 'Happy landings!'

Louise collected her hand-bag and book from the hall table and went out to the lift.

(6)

'PLEASE fasten your safety-belts.' The stewardess smiled as she said it, hoping to rob the sinister command of any urgent implication. She was a tall, thin girl with reddish hair and a very slight cast in her left eye; her manner was mercilessly affable and her voice was so constricted with refinement that Louise was surprised that she was able to get any words out at all. She helped, or rather assisted, Louise with her belt and retired to the back of the plane where she disappeared behind a curtain. A moment or two later, the steward, a short, tubby man with twinkling eyes and a cheerful smile, appeared through a door in the front of the plane and, taking up a stance in the centre of the aisle between the two rows of double seats, made a routine speech to the passengers. In this he explained that life-saving apparatuses, in case of sudden immersion, were to be found beneath the chairs; that there were two emergency exits marked clearly in red on each side of the fuselage; that the plane was about to take-off and would fly at an average altitude of eighteen thousand feet and would arrive in Lisbon in approximately four hours' time. He added that once they were airborne smoking would be permitted but that smokers were requested to confine themselves to cigarettes and not light pipes. He concluded by wishing everyone a pleasant flight and disappeared in the direction of the stewardess.

The aeroplane, which had been vibrating for some time while each of its four engines were switched on in turn, now proceeded to lumber slowly along the tarmac. Louise closed her eyes so as not to have to look at the actual take-off and then opened them immediately so as not to miss it. It was the take-off, she remembered with numb resignation, that was always considered to be the most perilous moment; it was

during the take-off, or just after, that engines were most likely
to 'cut out', plunging the plane nose first into the ground
where it at once exploded and burst into fierce flames. She
fingered her safety-belt anxiously and wondered just how
quickly she could release herself and bash her way out of one
of the emergency exists if, after the first impact, she was still
capable of moving at all. The plane, having reached the
furthermost end of the runway, turned round bumpily and
stopped. There was a moment's pause and a loud moaning
sound like a prolonged burglar alarm, then a sudden,
reverberating roar as all four engines went into action
together, and the plane began to move forward faster and
faster. She gripped the arms of her chair and stared, hypnotised, at the ground slipping away in streaks of grey and
gun-metal beneath the vast silver wing. After a few moments
of rapidly increasing momentum there was a sudden lessening
of sound and vibration and she saw the earth drop down. –
The stewardess touched her on the shoulder and she jumped
violently.

'Can I tempt yeow to a little chewing-gum or barley sugar?'
Louise shook her head dumbly and she passed on to the
next passenger.

The moaning recommenced and Louise watched the flaps
along the edge of the wing sliding slowly out of sight. Trees,
fields, houses and telegraph poles were by now reduced to
miniature and cars crawling along the highways looked like
small shining insects. A few wisps of cloud appeared, increasing gradually until the English countryside, the solid,
comforting land upon which she had lived and breathed and
walked for thirty-two years, was hidden from her sight. . . .
The stewardess once more made her jump by hissing sibilantly
in her ear—— 'You can unfasten your belt neow – alleow
me.' With expert hands she loosened the belt, smiled com-
passionately, and moved away. Louise leant her head back
and envisaged bitterly the calm, inevitable heroism of the

stewardess in the event of a crisis. She would be efficient, reassuring and refined to the last. 'Please alleow me to assist you to bleow up your rubber dinghy!' – 'Can I tempt you to a tayny shot of morphine?' She would, beyond a shadow of doubt, be singing 'Roll Out The Barrel' in a bird-like soprano as the plane slid finally and for ever beneath the cold grey waves.

Presently, in spite of herself, Louise felt her nerves beginning to relax; the noise of the engines was now steady and soothing and there was no sensation of movement whatsoever. It was impossible to believe that she was being whirled through the sky at several hundred miles an hour. She glanced across the aisles at a red-faced man in a Palm Beach suit methodically taking off his tie preparatory to going to sleep; when he had put his tie in the pocket of his coat and also taken off his shoes, he gave a practised jerk to the green knob at the side of his seat and, shooting himself backwards into a recumbent position, closed his eyes. Louise decided enviously that he was an experienced air traveller and without fear. Not for him the night of horror that she had endured; the continual waking up and lighting cigarettes with a shaking hand; the periodic stumblings into the bathroom for glasses of water. Not for him the graphic mental pictures of sudden crashes, searing flames; people trapped and suffocating, trampling on each other, shrieking and fighting to escape from a blazing inferno! On the contrary he had probably spent a nice bibulous evening with some business pals, perhaps clambered into bed with some accommodating lady friend, and finally slept like a top, without a pang, without a qualm, without even a momentary stab of dread that possibly this time, this particular flight, this particular plane might just be the one destined to hit the mountainside, to crash into the sea, to encounter that fatal, unexpected electric storm and disintegrate in mid-air flinging him twisting and turning grotesquely through infinities of space until the ultimate, sickening thud shattered the life out of him.

At this moment the stewardess appeared suddenly with a pillow. 'Can I assist you with your chair?' she enquired. 'We shall not be serving a meal just yet and I thought that perhaps you might like to lie back.'

'Thank you,' murmured Louise.

The stewardess twisted the knob until Louise was comfortably extended, then, placing the pillow solicitously behind her head, she smiled again, that same smile of indulgent compassion, and minced away. A few seconds later the steady hum of the engines seemed to change its tone, to become muffled and far away, then there was no sound at all, no anxiety, no piercing fears, no aeroplane, no life, no death; nothing but profound and dreamless sleep.

At London Airport Louise had been too dazed and wretched to pay much attention to her fellow passengers. They had all shuffled out together into the windy, grey morning and once in the plane they had been hidden from her by the high backs of the seats. She remembered vaguely noticing a small, yellow baby being carried by its equally yellow parents in an oblong box with handles. They had looked so utterly depressed that she had averted her eyes and banished from her mind the immediate vision of baby, box and parents hurtling down through the clouds from a great height. At Lisbon Airport, feeling calmer and clearer after her sleep and the dainty meal that the stewardess had brought her on a tray, and also deeply thankful for the ground under her feet, Louise was more inclined to look about her, to work up a little interest in her surroundings. After all, the first take-off and landing had been accomplished without mishap and there were only eight more to go including the ultimate arrival in Jamaica! Herded with the others into a dark, fly-infested restaurant, she observed a vacant table in a corner and sat down at it. A harassed waiter rushed up to her, banged a cup of coffee and a stale rusk on to the table and rushed away again and she was left alone. The yellow baby in the box was at the other side of the room; its parents leaned over it from time to time, pursing their mouths and making clucking noises in an effort to wring from it some sign of animation, but it remained comatose with its eyes shut. At the table next to hers was the man in the Palm Beach suit with a large, thick-set negro wearing a creased grey alpaca coat and trousers, a beige shirt and a green and orange tie. The negro was talking in a light, sing-song voice with a strong Welsh intonation which made it difficult for her to hear what he was saying. Perhaps, like Dr Mellish, he was expounding with scientific brilliance the technical intricacies of the atom bomb. Whatever he was talking about, the man in the Palm Beach suit was obviously exceedingly bored by it because he kept fidgeting and looking round the restaurant like a prisoner scanning the walls of his cell in the desperate hope that there might be some slab of stone that moved aside disclosing a secret exit, or that the bars of the window might have been filed through and could be whipped out with a flick of the wrist. At a further table there was a tiny, freckled nun sitting with a heavy-bosomed girl of about sixteen; the girl, whose skin was waxy and moist, looked uncomfortably hot. Sharing the table with them was a swarthy young couple who sat quite still, holding hands and staring straight before them. Probably they were just married and this was the beginning of their honeymoon. Poor Ellen and Charlie came into Louise's mind again. They had been so ecstatic, so very much in love, starting their lives together so gaily! – then that ghastly, tearing crash. She pulled herself together and took a large gulp of coffee which was so hot that it burnt her throat and brought tears to her eyes, then, after lighting a cigarette, she looked firmly at the couple again. At least they couldn't be described as either ecstatic or gay, they were just sitting there, silent and unsmiling, apparently in a trance. They both appeared to be so utterly lacking in vitality that they probably wouldn't notice whether the plane crashed or not. There was another group, further away still, over by the yellow baby, composed of three men and one lush-looking woman; they were all gesticulating a great deal and talking at the top of their lungs in Spanish or Portuguese.

Presently, irritated by the buzzing flies and the fusty atmosphere of the restaurant, Louise got up from the table and wandered out. There was nothing to do and nowhere to go. She contemplated for a moment going to the lavatory but remembering that she was on Latin territory, thought better of it and decided to wait until she got back into the plane. She strolled up and down for a little while and stared idly at a curio shop filled with straw hats and cheap jewellery, and a bookshop that had little to offer beyond foreign movie magazines, some ancient copies of *The Illustrated London News* and a few 'Penguin' thrillers. Finally she found a wooden bench in the Customs hall upon which she settled herself and watched the agitated crowds rushing back and forth under the contemptuous eyes of various officials; the porters yelling and staggering in and out with luggage of all shapes and sizes; the frantic travellers struggling to cram mountains of soiled clothes back into fibre suitcases which had been pitilessly ransacked. The noise was deafening. Everybody was talking at once. The Latin races, she decided with insular detachment, obviously regarded travel as an emotional experience of the greatest intensity. Shrill cries rent the air. Families, either arriving or departing, embraced each other violently, laughed, wept and waved their arms about with the utmost abandon. She watched with interest the entrance, through the swing doors, of a tall distinguished man in a dark suit and an 'Eden' hat. It was clear that he was someone of importance because the Customs officials greeted him with obsequious smiles and marked his expensive suitcases swiftly and delicately as though the very thought of opening them in search of contraband would be sacrilege. This having been accomplished in record time he thanked them courteously and, still maintaining his air of suave, diplomatic dignity, turned towards a group of people who had been waiting at the other side of the barrier. In a flash his studied composure fell from him and he became transformed into a screaming maniac. Three ladies in black flung themselves into his arms one after the other, emitting groans and shrieks of excitement; two young men with pock-marked faces and straw hats kissed him repeatedly, and a very small boy in a sailor suit was hoisted, gibbering, on to his shoulder. The reunion was brought to a climax by the eldest of the three ladies in black giving a wailing cry and bursting into floods of tears upon which the erstwhile suave diplomat seized her in his arms and, raining kisses on her face with such fervour that he knocked her hat on one side, led her, followed by the others screaming in unison, through the swing doors and out of sight. Louise's reflections on this curiously uninhibited display of family feeling were abruptly shattered by a raucous voice from the loud-speaker ordering the passengers of Flight 445 back to the plane.

Ten minutes later the sun-stained houses and churches and twisting streets of Lisbon lay far below her like a map flung down on to a rumpled green carpet. She unfastened her safety-belt hurriedly in order to circumvent the stewardess who was approaching her with a solicitous gleam in her eye, and breathed a sigh of relief. Take-off number two over and done with. She looked out of the window; the flaps had creaked out of sight again and the wing, like a sheet of molten silver, was so dazzling that she had to turn her eyes away and draw the curtain. She picked up the novel that Boy Sullivan had brought her yesterday as a parting present and looked at it without enthusiasm. It was called *The Seeker and the Found* and was written by a young American journalist, Elwyn Brace Courtland, who, the blurb informed her, had served with conspicuous gallantry as a fighter pilot in the war and now lived with his wife and two children on a barge in Salem,

Massachusetts. A photograph of him adorned the back flap showing him looking rather anxiously at a sheep dog. It was a strange face with wide-apart eyes and high cheekbones; his hair, which was cut in a fringe, made him look artificial, like a Dutch doll. The blurb went on to say that *The Seeker and the Found* was unquestionably the most courageous, forceful and outspoken contribution to American literature that the post-war generation had yet produced, and that the reader would be moved, repelled, fascinated and enthralled by it from the first page to the last. Louise opened it at random and read:

'Marise lay back wantonly on the rug Buck had spread for her on the sand. Her naked flesh, honeyed by the shrill sunlight, challenged his senses until his groins ached and his mouth became harsh and dry and drained of spittle like that time when he won the race at school and Mom and Pop were there and old Doc and Zelma too with her wild colt's legs and flying hair. In the blue shadows of Marise's armpits where she had shaved, beads of sweat glistened like jewels; like the silvery tinsel snow Mom used to sprinkle on the Christmas tree; like tiny sharp-pointed spears of light stabbing ruthlessly into the heart of his desire. He leant over and cupped her eager, uptilted breasts in his lean brown hand, "Christ, Kid——" he muttered hoarsely. . . .'

Louise closed the book firmly and put it down on the seat beside her. It was high time, she reflected, that Boy Sullivan took a course in psychology. First Mrs Peverance and then this! I must send it to Aunt Esther, she thought with a giggle, just as an antidote to Sir Osbert. The man in the Palm Beach suit, apparently taking her giggle as an invitation to a little chat, got up from his seat and leant over her, steadying himself by resting his arm on the chair immediately in front. 'Well,' he said cheerfully. 'So far so good!'

Louise, not wishing to appear disagreeable, smiled vaguely and nodded.

'I must say I didn't expect such a smooth flight when I saw that baby being yanked on board this morning,' he went on. 'They're always bad luck in an aeroplane, you know.'

'No,' Louise's smile faded. 'I didn't know.'

'Babies and nuns.' He looked cautiously over his shoulder and lowered his voice. 'Fortunately we've only got one nun this time. When you get a couple of 'em together it's disaster! – You're not a Catholic by any chance?' he added anxiously.

Louise shook her head reassuringly and he looked relieved.

'Not that I'm all that superstitious myself, but when you notice the same sort of thing happening again and again in the same sort of circumstances you can't help but put two and two together can you?'

'No – I suppose you can't.'

'I remember once, just after the war it was, I was flying from Montreal down to New York with a friend of mine. We'd had a few drinks in the bar and we were both feeling, well – a little gay as you might say – and just as we were about to board the plane he suddenly gripped my arm, "Harry," he said, and I could hear the panic in his voice, "do you see what I see?" I looked to where he was pointing with a shaking hand and there they were, two of 'em, climbing in just in front of us!'

'Babies or nuns?' Louise enquired with rising hysteria.

'Nuns!' he said dramatically. 'And in the middle of the night too!'

'I don't think there's any hard and fast rule about them travelling only by day,' said Louise.

'Well, I'm here to tell you that the sight of 'em sobered us up double quick pronto and we stopped dead in our tracks. "I'm not going," said Mac – my friend's name was Maclure, "I wouldn't get into that plane now not if you gave me the Koh-i-noor diamond——" '

'That's supposed to be fairly unlucky too!' murmured Louise, but the man in the Palm Beach suit was not to be deflected by any flippant irrelevancies.

' "Don't be a fool," I said. "We can't go back now. I've got a conference at nine-thirty in the morning and you've got to get the midday plane to Baltimore." "I don't care," said Mac, and I could tell by his tone that he meant it. "You can go if you like, but I'm staying here!" – and he started to walk back into the airport. I ran after him and grabbed his arm but he shook me off. I was in a fine state I can tell you, not knowing whether to stay with him or leave him behind and get on to the plane by myself. But it was him who made up my mind for me as a matter of fact. He suddenly gripped my hands and looked me straight in the eye – I can see his face now – "Don't go, Harry boy," he said, and I could feel him trembling. "If you do I shall never see you again – I feel it in my bones – I know it!" Well, that decided me. "Come back and have another drink," I said and that was that.'

He paused, and Louise, realising that the denouement was yet to come, thought it best to get it over quickly. 'What happened to the plane?' she asked.

'Crashed just after the take-off,' he said. 'We saw it happen from the window of the bar – the most terrible sight I've ever seen – it exploded as it hit the ground and in a split second it was a sheet of flame – nobody could get near it, and not a single soul survived! Burnt to a crisp every man jack of 'em!' He paused and smacked his lips thoughtfully. 'That's the narrowest squeak I've ever had in my life and no fooling. You can see what I mean about two nuns being unlucky though can't you?'

'Yes,' replied Louise dimly. 'I certainly can.'

Four hours later the plane flew in low over a coast of sombre black rocks and landed delicately at Santa Maria in the Azores, so delicately indeed that there was scarcely any bump at all when the heavy wheels touched down on the runway.

Louise unfastened her belt with a sigh of relief. One more lap accomplished; quite an agreeable lap, all things considered, apart from the man in the Palm Beach suit and he at least, upon observing her close her eyes either in appreciative horror or sheer boredom at the climax of his story, had had the grace to move away. She had dozed a little and read a little. In addition to *The Seeker and the Found* she had wisely packed *Persuasion* and *The Oxford Book of Victorian Verse* into her overnight bag at the last minute. The stewardess had served another dainty meal, the yellow baby, in a sudden access of vitality, had had a screaming fit which proved at any rate that it was alive. Nothing had happened in the heavens; no dangerous weather, no unforeseen meteoric disturbances; the plane had droned along monotonously over an endless prairie of white clouds which occasionally thinned and parted for a moment showing the flat blue of the sea far below. She had been stabbed by no sharp alarms, no sickening terrors, and the dead weight of fear that lay permanently at the back of her mind had remained obligingly dormant.

The persuasive melancholy of *The Oxford Book of Victorian Verse*, its recurrent preoccupation with the quiet grave, its nostalgic sentiment, its emphasis on gentle death, its almost smug avoidance of violence and shrill agony, had been very soothing: soothing and at the same time tantalising! Viewed from a pressurised metal tube hurtling through space at an altitude of eighteen thousand feet, the nineteenth century seemed incredibly remote and most enviably secure. How little they had to fear, those Victorians, compared with us today! Of course there were occasionally routine disasters like the Tay Bridge blowing down with a train on it, the sinking of the *Princess Alice*, and that awful fire in the Charity Bazaar, but after all, that was in Paris and so didn't quite count. True, many more people died of appendicitis than they did nowadays, and there were no anæsthetics, not in the early part of the reign anyway, but taken by and large they had had an easy time of it. They had had leisure to think and plan and get their minds into a peaceful state of acceptance. The idea of death had so much more dignity and grace. Lovesick girls went into 'Declines' and had a little calves-foot jelly and expired: poets coughed their lives away in sanatoriums and died peacefully murmuring lovely things to their loved ones. There was hardly any banging and burning and being blown to bits and torn by jagged steel.

After the man in the Palm Beach suit had gone away to embark on an arch conversation with the stewardess, she had turned to Walter Savage Landor and read:

> 'Death stands above me, whispering low
> I know not what into my ear;
> Of his strange language all I know
> Is, there is not a word of fear.'

Then Christina Rossetti, 'When I am dead my dearest, sing no sad songs for me' – and the charming bit about not seeing the shadows and not feeling the rain; and then dear Algernon Charles:

> 'So long I endure, no longer; and laugh not again, neither weep
> For there is no God stronger than death; and death is a sleep.'

'There now!' she reflected. 'What could be more comforting than that?'

The airport at Santa Maria was smaller than the one at Lisbon and a little cleaner. Once again the passengers were herded into a restaurant, but Louise, perceiving the grey sandwiches, the dirty tablecloths and the flies, rebelled and went to the bar where she discovered that she could buy a whisky-and-soda with English money. While she was sitting there sipping it, the pilot of the plane and another officer came up and ordered, she was grateful to observe, two glasses of lemonade. She glanced at the pilot's hands which were well shaped and brown and looked efficient; his eyes were very blue and he had a pleasant voice: he smiled politely at her and then went on chatting to his companion apparently in no way overwhelmed by the terrifying magnitude of his responsibility.

Some words of Tennyson's that she had read only an hour ago flashed into her mind and she repressed a giggle:

> 'For tho' from out our bourne of Time and Place
> The flood may bear me far,
> I hope to see my Pilot face to face
> When I have crost the bar.'

In due course they were all ordered back to the plane and, obediently disposing of their cigarettes, they climbed on board and strapped themselves in. The steward reappeared and gave an abbreviated rendering of his original speech for the benefit of two new passengers who were blue-black and looked furtively about them as though they were expecting some blatant display of racial discrimination. The stewardess, with painstaking gentility, gave them chewing-gum, wool for their ears and two pillows; she also strapped them in and, with a smile of ineffable condescension, left them.

Louise, warmed by the whisky-and-soda, watched the take-off with splendid calm. The plane slid off the ground and out over the black rocks and churning sea, rising smoothly and gradually until presently the clouds intervened again blotting out the diminishing land. The sky was lemon and orange in the evening light and far above, where it deepened into blue, she saw a star. She glanced at her watch which she had kept at London Time; it said six-thirty. She tried fruitlessly for a little to work out in her mind if two hours had already been lost or gained, then remembering that someone had said something about daylight saving either operating or not operating in Portugal, she gave up the whole idea and decided to eat, go to sleep, and wake up when the stewardess told her to. This, at all events, was the longest lap of the whole journey – nine to ten hours! She shuddered and hurriedly opened *The Oxford Book of Victorian Verse* at random:

> 'Let me be gathered to the quiet west,
> The sundown splendid and serene,
> Death.'

Nine and a half hours later Louise was awakened from an uneasy sleep by the stewardess hissing in her ear, 'We shall be landing in Bermuda in twenty minutes time.' She untwisted her cramped limbs, having been lying half on the seat next to her which had fortunately been unoccupied for the whole journey, and half on her own. She had a crick in her neck and the right cheek of her behind was entirely numb. There was a dim blue light in the plane and the man in the Palm Beach suit was snoring with his mouth wide open; the upper plate of his false teeth had slipped down which gave the impression that he was grinning obscenely at some private bawdiness. Louise, seizing the moment to stagger to the lavatory before anyone else was wakeful enough to get there, plunged her face in cold water and brushed her teeth. She scrutinised herself in the mirror and arrived at the conclusion that air travel, although comparatively clean, was definitely not becoming. Her face was quivering violently, not from fear this time but from the vibration of the plane, it looked wan and tired and her hair was terrible. She did the best she could with it, and after dabbing herself with some eau-de-Cologne and putting on some lipstick she went back to her seat again feeling a little better. Her watch said five-thirty and she peered out of the window expecting to see at least the vague beginnings of sunrise, but it was still pitch-dark and there weren't even any stars. The yellow baby, lolling in its mother's arms, passed her, looking far from well. Louise was profoundly thankful that she had managed to get to the lavatory ahead of it. Suddenly the stewardess switched all the lights on and the man in the Palm Beach suit woke in the middle of a loud snore and stared angrily and incredulously at Louise as though she were an unwelcome stranger who had forced her way into his bedroom. After a moment he realised where he was, snapped his teeth back, gave a sickly smile and heaved himself off to the lavatory. The stewardess reappeared and walked up and down from seat to seat collecting pillows and rugs while the steward, with a sort of flit gun, appeared through the door in the front and proceeded to spray the air with sickly-smelling disinfectant. Presently the 'Fasten your belts – No smoking' sign flashed on and Louise felt her ears clicking as the plane began to descend. She looked out of the window and saw some scattered lights in the darkness below; some of them were reflected in water and she could distinguish shadowy shapes of land and low white houses. The engine nearest to her which had frightened her dreadfully in the night by suddenly emitting jets of flame, coughed out a few sparks; there was a gentle crunching bump and she loosened her hands which had been gripping the arms of the chair in a vice and relaxed.

The waiting-room in the Bermuda airport, where coffee and sandwiches were served, was a marked contrast to the drab restaurants of Lisbon and Santa Maria. Here there were no harassed waiters, no grubby tablecloths and no flies: there were however, to her great astonishment, two women and a man in evening dress. The man was fairly drunk and a red carnation had died in the buttonhole of his white dinner-jacket. It was not until she heard the younger of the two women, who was wearing a very decolleté pink dress, urging the young man to let the plane go on without him and come back to the party, that she realised that whereas as far as she was concerned this was the beginning of a new day, as far as they were concerned it was still last night. She looked at her watch which said five-fifty-five, and then up at the clock over the door which said one-fifteen, and her heart sank. The night had already seemed to be interminable and now she was faced with the prospect of several more hours of it.

The girl in the pink dress was obviously in a state of considerable agitation; her voice was deep and hoarse and very American and she was arguing heatedly.

'I think you're mean,' she said, 'just as mean as a little old skunk. You know Lenore won't give a God-damn if you get there tomorrow or the day after. As a matter of fact she won't give a God-damn if you don't get there at all.'

'Now don't talk that way, honey——'

'It's true and you know it. – Isn't it true, Gloria?' She turned to the other woman who had bright blue hair and was sitting on the arm of a chair doing up her face.

'Isn't what true?'

'About Lenore not caring whether Elsworth gets there or not.'

'Listen, dear——' The woman with blue hair had a strong Middle-Western accent and stared at herself critically in the mirror of her compact with her head on one side. 'You've been harping on that same tried theme ever since before we got in the car to go to Marion's, and I'm here to tell you that you're driving me crackers. Why the hell can't you lay off Lenore for two minutes and shut up.'

'Lenore's a bitch and you know it.'

'All right – all right – so Lenore's a bitch – let's leave it at that.'

'I hate her!'

'All right, that's fine. You hate her. But she does happen to be Elsworth's wife and she is expecting him home on this plane tomorrow. Whether she cares or not is his problem, not yours. For heaven's sake stop belly-aching about it and let's get the hell out of here and go back to the party.'

'It won't be the same without Elsworth.'

'Oh yes it will. – Except that Marion will be a little more stinking than she was when we left, and so will everybody else, everybody but us! That's what's burning me up, just loitering about here in this glamorised toilet and not getting any place. Come on – let's go.'

'Go on, Honey – do like Gloria says!' The young man put his arm tentatively round her shoulders but she wriggled away.

'Leave me alone!'

'Now don't get mad, sweetheart – you know I'd stay if I could – but we did agree to let everything ride for a bit now, didn't we? Won't you kiss me good-bye now and go back to Marion's like Gloria said?'

'I'm sick of Gloria!' said the girl at bay. 'And I'm sick of you too – so there!'

'You know you don't mean that, honey——'

'I do too mean it!'

'Oh, for God's sake!——' said Gloria.

'And what's more – I don't ever want to see you again. I'm through!'

'Here, dear——' Gloria pacifically offered her a packet of cigarettes. 'Try one of these – they're toasted.'

The girl pushed Gloria's arm away violently, knocking the packet of cigarettes on to the floor. Elsworth bent down unsteadily to pick it up.

'And if your plane falls into the sea – it's okay by me!'

'Don't talk like that – it's unlucky,' said Gloria sharply.

The girl, abandoning suddenly all belligerence, burst into tears and flung herself into the young man's arms.

'I didn't mean it!' she sobbed. 'But don't go – not on this plane – please, please don't. Catch the next one if you like – but not this one. I had a presentiment coming along in the car – I swear I did——'

Louise, feeling suddenly sick, got up and moved away out of earshot.

Back in the plane Louise steeled herself to face three and a half hours more of dreadful night. She decided against trying to go to sleep again realising that the attempt would be doomed to failure anyway, as she had had two cups of black coffee and her nerves were strung to such a pitch of acute wakefulness that she felt she would twang like a guitar if anyone touched her.

A different steward appeared and gave his own version of the routine speech. He was rather a saturnine young man with hairy wrists. There was also a different stewardess, brisk and dumpy; altogether a tougher proposition than her predecessor. She bustled up and down distributing chewing-gum and cotton wool, with the hard, detached efficiency of an overworked matron in a crowded hospital ward.

The young American having finally shaken himself free from the girl in pink and taken off his coat and tie, settled down in his seat and was staring glumly at a copy of *Esquire*.

Shortly after the take-off the stewardess switched out the lights and the interior of the plane became blue again. Louise discovered a button which when she pressed it shed a small beam of white light from the ceiling on to her lap. She opened *Persuasion* hoping that Miss Austen's impeccable gentility would soothe her nerves and waft her away from the dangerous sky into a less agitating world, wherein young ladies and gentlemen drove about in curricles and went to Assemblies and viewed life, not in terms of speed and swift achievement and vulgar publicity, but sedately; sometimes with sly humour, sometimes even with exasperation but always, always with dignity and discretion. But it was no use, her mind, like a tired gramophone needle, skidded across the gentle attitudes and verbal arabesques and refused to hold. She read one sentence over three times without gaining any impression from it whatever: 'From situation, Mrs Clay was, in Lady

Russell's estimate, a very unequal, and in her character she believed a very dangerous companion . . . and a removal that would leave Mrs Clay behind and bring a choice of more suitable intimates within Miss Elliot's reach, was therefore an object of first-rate importance.' – With a sigh she closed the book and leaned her head against the back of the chair. Only a few more hours and this journey, this insecure, nerve-wracking and continually anxious journey, would be over. She would be on land again; solid, comforting land. Earthquakes might shake and rend it, tropical storms might flood it and hurricanes devastate it but it would remain land upon which she could walk and sit and lie without the scarifying knowledge that immediately beneath her was a void, a vast infinity of space, with nothing between her and utter oblivion but a few wisps of insubstantial cloud. There would also be Henry – dear, darling Henry! She was suddenly overwhelmed by such a passionate longing for him that her eyes filled with tears. She would lie, safe and at peace, in his arms, perhaps under a mosquito net, perhaps not – she was not sure about the mosquito situation, but at any rate she would be relaxed and happy and this exhausting, idiotic nightmare would be past and done with and she would never leave him again in any vehicle of any sort or allow him to leave her either. She rested her forehead against the window and stared out into the dark. The engine nearest to her continued to glow in a sinister way and occasionally shot out jets of blue flame. She remembered the beastly girl in pink and her hysterical, drunken babbling about a presentiment, and down went her heart again and she sat back, rigid with fear and claustrophobia and wanting to scream.

Dawn was breaking as the plane circled over the turquoise lagoons and white beaches of Nassau. It must have been raining an hour or so before because Louise noticed oily puddles on the tarmac as she stepped out of the plane and walked down the gangway. She had not slept; she had not read; she had just sat quite still for over three hours trying as much as possible to make her mind a blank, to think of nothing, to indulge in no imaginative flights pleasant or otherwise. She had partially succeeded but the effort had left her worn out and lethargic. She walked over to a sort of bungalow restaurant, the veranda of which was being swept indolently by two coloured maids. There was a tropical warmth in the air, even at that early hour; she sniffed it gratefully after the curious ozonic smell of the plane and, selecting a table by a window, ordered orange juice, coffee and eggs and bacon in the hope that solid food might mitigate the pervasive tiredness that seemed to have settled into her joints and bones and made even the powdering of her nose a major endeavour.

The rest of the passengers looking sleepy and disgruntled were dotted about at other tables. The yellow baby and its parents arrived last; the mother's eyes were puffy from lack of sleep and a bit of the father's wiry black hair was sticking out at the back like a handle. The freckled nun and the fat girl were silently devouring cornflakes and milk. The blue-black couple and the Jamaican negro, having apparently bridged successfully the subtle shade of colour that differentiated them, were strolling up and down outside and talking animatedly, occasionally baring their brilliant teeth in wide laughter. The man in the Palm Beach suit had left the plane at Bermuda and the young man in the white dinner-jacket had been met by a small, hatchet-faced young woman in green slacks, presumably Lenore, and whisked away in a shiny station wagon. There were some other people sitting about whom she failed to identify; they had got on at Bermuda and been placed up in the front of the plane beyond her vision. She ate her eggs and bacon listlessly, drank some coffee and lit a cigarette. Her watch said ten minutes to ten, but the restaurant clock blandly contradicted it by pointing to five minutes to six.

At six-fifteen (by the restaurant clock) the plane took off

again. The last lap! – Only one more landing, only one more strapping on of the safety-belt, only one more cold sweat of fear as the ground rose nearer and nearer. Louise twisted the knob of her seat and tilted it back a little, not too far as she didn't wish to sleep, but just at a comfortable angle at which she could lie peacefully with her eyes closed and count the minutes.

Presently she opened her eyes and was surprised to see that the plane was no longer flying steadily along through a clear sky but seemed to be climbing almost vertically through dense banks of cloud. She tried vainly to rise but was unable to lever herself up from her chair; she wrenched violently at the knob but it wouldn't budge. At this moment the pilot appeared through the door in the front, encased in a life-jacket and smiling charmingly. 'We are now flying at an altitude of approximately eighty-five thousand feet,' he said in a hoarse, rather drunken voice that sounded curiously familiar. 'But owing to serious engine trouble I fear that it will be necessary for you to fasten your safety-belts and have some chewing-gum.' He advanced towards Louise and she saw to her dismay that he was no longer smiling but crying bitterly. 'I had a presentiment that this would happen,' he muttered, 'I swear I did. The first moment I saw those nuns I knew that we hadn't got a chance of survival and it's all my own fault for not travelling to Sicily with Mrs Morpeth and those two lovely little girls. . . .' He leaned close to her face and she saw that his front teeth had slipped over his under-lip and that he was quivering with dreadful terror; she strained away from him and turned to the window; as she did so the engine nearest to her was suddenly enveloped in a sheet of flame and as, sick with horror, she watched it, it detached itself from the plane entirely and went spinning away upwards into the sky like a vast catherine wheel. She gave a strangled shriek and began to pummel the pilot's chest with her fists but it sank in like soft rubber as she touched it and he seized her arms and began shaking her, 'If the plane falls into the sea——' he screamed malignantly, 'it will be okay by me – okay by me!' At this moment there was a sharp jolt and she fell forward——

'Wake up, please,' said the voice of the stewardess, edgy with controlled impatience. 'We shall be landing at Kingston in ten minutes' time.' Seeing that Louise was at last awake she stopped shaking her and, with a tight-lipped smile, moved away.

Louise, feeling as though she had been dragged up by her hair from the furthermost pit of Hell, started to laugh weakly. She glanced out of the window and saw below her a range of corrugated green mountains; in the distance their colour changed to deep blue and they looked as though they had been cut out of some opaque material and gummed rather untidily on to a paler blue background. There were deep, shadowed valleys with the gleam of water in the bottom of them; little roads twisting up and down through groves of feathery bamboo and scattered clusters of straw-coloured houses clinging to the summits of the lower hills. Ten minutes' time! She dashed hurriedly to the lavatory but had to wait while one of the Bermuda passengers, a tall horsey woman in a Shantung suit, finished her ablutions at the basin and put on her rings. When at last she had gone Louise washed hastily, wrestled with her face and hair, upset about half of her bottle of eau-de-Cologne up her sleeve and returned, trembling with excitement, to her seat. The plane was sweeping lower and lower over the wide bay of Kingston. She looked down at a spit of land stretching out into the sea with behind it an immense wall of purple-grey mountains. She fastened her belt; her ears clicked, 'Please God . . .' she prayed silently. 'Not now. Don't let it crash now. Don't let it overshoot the runway; don't let it nose-dive into the sea; don't let it explode and burst into flames! – I want so very much to see Henry again – just once. I know we were married in a Register Office and not in a church and so from your point of view we probably aren't married at all, but I do love him – more than anyone or anything in the world – and love is important – you've said so often enough yourself God knows! . . .' The plane touched down lightly with an almost imperceptible bounce; the airport, with some white-clad figures standing outside it, flashed by the window and, for the last time she unfastened her safety-felt.

A little while later she was standing in a small yellowish room with a thermometer in her mouth, gazing raptly at Henry through some wire netting. A nurse with a magnolia skin and enormous dark eyes whipped the thermometer from her mouth and Louise rushed forward. Henry poked a brown finger through the netting and she clung to it tightly, trying hard not to cry.

'Well, Cockie,' he said. 'Did you have a good trip? – Were you scared?'

'Of course not,' she replied. 'I adored every minute of it!'

Star Quality

(1)

'SHE'LL do it,' said J. C. Roebuck. 'To begin with, she hasn't had an original script since *Dear Yesterday*. Also she hasn't got a man at the moment and she's in serious trouble over her taxes. Oh yes, she'll do it all right and if you feel, Ray, that you can stand the wear and tear it's okay with me but never say I didn't warn you!'

Ray Malcolm laughed. 'I'm sure I can deal with her.' He leaned forward and took a cigarette out of a massive silver box: there was an intensity, a wiry vitality about him that made his recent meteoric rise to fame as a director clearly understandable. His movements were alert and his speech decisive; his personality embodied all the requisite qualities – drive, force and authority.

Bryan Snow, who had been sitting silently for some time on the edge of the sofa trying valiantly to appear calm while the fate of his play was being discussed, watched him with whole-hearted admiration. 'I'm sure I can deal with her.' There was something so firm, so charmingly confident in the way it was said. Bryan was convinced that this dynamic, fascinating young man of the theatre would find no difficulty whatsoever in dealing with a cage full of ravening lionesses, let alone one allegedly temperamental leading lady. Ray Malcolm turned on him the full force of his concentrated charm. 'You want her, don't you, Bryan? You feel that she really would be right for the play?'

'Yes,' said Bryan, 'I do.'

'Well then that's settled. Will you handle it J.C., or do you think I'd better go along and see her first?'

J. C. Roebuck scribbled something on his telephone pad and smiled. There was a certain benign resignation in the smile. 'I'll handle it,' he said. 'I'll call up Clemson, her agent. He'll be very relieved. I don't think you'd better have anything to do with it until it's all signed and sealed: you'll have quite enough of her later on.'

'She's read the script?'

'Probably. She's had it for two weeks.'

'What about Gerald Wentworth? Does she get on with him all right?'

J.C. smiled. 'As well as she gets on with any leading man, a little better if anything. She had a swing round with him when they were in *Wise Man's Folly* a few years ago; since then they've appeared together fairly painlessly several times. I suspect that he hates her guts, but he's far too easy-going to allow her to ruffle him.'

'You do too, don't you?' Ray fired the question sharply, almost challengingly.

'What?'

'Hate her guts.'

'Not at all,' J.C. spoke blandly. 'On the contrary I'm very fond of her. I admit I did say on one occasion that I'd never allow her to appear in a theatre of mine again. That was after she'd given poor Ella Craven a nervous breakdown and driven Scott Gurney into a nursing home.'

'Scott Gurney!' Ray snorted contemptuously. 'Scott Gurney couldn't direct a Church Social.'

'But since then,' J.C. went on, 'we've kissed and made friends.'

'She's looking wonderful,' volunteered Bryan. 'I saw her in the Savoy Grill the other night.'

'She always looks wonderful,' said J.C. 'And what is more she knows she looks wonderful.'

'I've only spoken to her once in my life,' said Bryan. 'I thought she had tremendous charm.'

'She's always had tremendous charm,' said J.C., 'and she knows that too.'

Ray Malcolm quizzically raised one eyebrow a trifle higher than the other. 'You'd fall dead with surprise wouldn't you, if we got through this whole production without a single row – without a single argument?'

J.C. laughed outright. 'I certainly would,' he said. 'But before I fell dead I should have the presence of mind to give you a cheque for a thousand pounds.'

'Is that a bet?'

'Most definitely not. But it's a promise.'

'You're a witness to that, Bryan,' Ray said gaily as he rose and put on his overcoat. Then, with an abrupt change of expression he said very seriously, 'I know, J.C., that you think I'm over-confident when I say so surely that I can deal with her, but believe me, I have a very good reason for saying it and that reason is that underneath all her fiddle-faddle and nonsense I know her to be a bloody good actress. Her talent is true and clear, in addition to which she has the quality that this play needs. I know a dozen women who could play it technically as well, if not better, but none of them could bring to it that peculiar magic that she has, that extraordinary capacity for investing whatever she touches with her own truth.'

'Yes,' said J.C., a thought absently. 'She can do that well enough, but she sometimes does it at the expense of the play.'

'She hasn't been properly directed for years. Not since old Jimmy died really.'

'All right, all right.' J.C. began to show signs of impatience. 'I've said my say. I agree with you that she's a fine actress. I agree with you that she has a quality of magic that is completely and entirely her own. I agree with you that in the right part in the right play she can be one of the biggest draws in the country. I also agree with you that she has never been properly directed since Jimmy died, but where I don't agree with you is in your supposition that she ever *can* be properly directed. If anybody can do it, you can; I have a profound respect for your knowledge and your determination. But apart from her talent and her magic and her truth there is one thing that you don't know about and that I do.'

'What is it?'

J.C. sighed and got up from his swivel chair. 'She is the least intelligent, most conceited and most tiresome bitch that I have ever encountered in all my long experience of the Theatre.'

(2)

LORRAINE BARRIE's house was in a mews near Knightsbridge. It was easy to identify from quite a long way off because it was painted pale pink and had blue shutters and a blue front door. It also had window-boxes glowing with scarlet geraniums and obviously could belong to no one but a famous actress or a scene designer. Bryan hesitated before ringing the bell. He felt distinctly nervous and needed a moment or two to gather himself together. He was irritated with himself for feeling nervous although he realised that it was natural enough that he should. This was an important occasion, the first official meeting with the star who was, he hoped, prepared to lavish her talent, charm and technique on a play by an unknown playwright. It wasn't actually his first play; there had been *The Unconquered*, which had been produced the year before in a small artistic theatre in Bayswater where it had run for a week, but unfortunately, in spite of excellent press notices and a competent performance by an all-male cast, failed to achieve a West End production. This had been a bitter disappointment at the time, but the fact of its having been produced at all had spurred him on. This play, *Stones in Heaven*, was therefore his first real bid for commercial success. *The Unconquered* had been raw and autobiographical with patches of good writing in it but, apparently, little popular appeal. Nobody, it seemed, wanted to know about life in a prisoner-of-war camp. The war was over and the sooner it was forgotten the better. The intricate psychological problems, both tragic and comic, of a group of men mewed up for years in a draughty barrack in a remote German village were not considered by theatrical managements to have entertainment value. True certain critics had said that the play had strength and realism and moments of sheer nobility but the fact had to be faced that strength and realism and sheer nobility were not enough. Other ingredients were needed, most particularly love interest – or at least sex conflict. One eminent manager who had been sufficiently interested in the play to invite Bryan to lunch at Scott's had suggested the introduction into the prison camp of a female parachutist who, apart from being brave and tough, could have immense glamour which in itself would create an emotional situation acceptable to the larger theatre-going public. He had also implied that if Bryan were willing to go away to Cornwall or somewhere quiet and re-write the whole play on those lines, there would be a very good chance of popping it into the Jupiter Theatre when *Sweet Ladies* closed. Bryan, diplomatically concealing his irritation, had agreed to think about it and returned fuming to his flat in Ebury Street.

Stones in Heaven was different in every way from *The Unconquered*. It was what might have been described in earlier years as a 'drawing-room' drama. That is to say its protagonists were educated people with money who lived their lives in comfortable surroundings. The play was primarily the study of a neurotic woman whose subconscious jealousy of her husband's heroism in the war caused her to run off to the South of France with a worthless but attractive man younger

than herself. The main theme of the play was her gradual disillusionment not only with the young man who inevitably lets
her down, but with herself. In the last scene of all she leaves a
superficially gay lunch-party and commits suicide by crashing
a speedboat into a lighthouse at forty-five miles an hour. It
was, on the whole, a well-written play; the dialogue was
natural without being scintillating and the characterisation of
the husband was particularly clear. The heroine, though
neurotic and at moments tiresome, commanded enough
sympathy to justify her rather arbitrary behaviour, and if
played by an actress of outstanding personality had every
chance of charming the audience into believing in her and the
validity of her suffering.

Ray Malcolm had been right when he said that Lorraine
Barrie had the exact quality that the play needed; he was also
right when he said that, leaving aside the temperamental
excesses that had tarnished her reputation among theatrical
people, she was a bloody good actress. She was. She had been
a bloody good actress right from the beginning. Her instinct
for timing, her natural grace of movement, her gift for
expressing, without apparent effort, the subtle nuances either
of comedy or tragedy had all been part of her stock-in-trade
since she had stepped on to the stage of the Theatre Royal,
Sunderland, at the age of nine and piped, with the utmost
emotional authority, 'Oh Hubert, spare mine eyes!' Throughout her dazzling career in the theatre these rare and un-
accountable gifts, this almost incredible facility for expression
had seldom failed her. She had, with the years, acquired by
experience certain technical tricks and mannerisms, none of
which had impaired the purity of her talent. Occasionally,
perhaps, they may have obscured it, but never for long. It
always popped up again, that peculiar magic that Ray had
described, endowing a turgid, unreal play with truth; decorat-
ing a clumsy, inept comedy with such enchanting personal
arabesques that the author, on reading his press notices would

be gratified to discover that he was the wittiest playwright since Congreve. It was a little unfair of J. C. Roebuck to say that she was unintelligent; unfair and inaccurate, for she had a native intelligence where her own desires were concerned that was quite remarkable. He was also a little off true when he said she was conceited. Lorraine Barrie's ingrained convictions about herself far transcended mere conceit. Her profound, magnificent egocentricity was far removed from such paltry bathos. A mountain peak lit by the first light of dawn is superior to a slag-heap in size and shape and design but it is not conceited. Niagara Falls are unquestionably more impressive than the artificial cascade in Battersea Park but they are singularly devoid of personal vanity. It would never have occurred to Lorraine to compare herself either favourably or unfavourably with Bernhardt, Duse or Réjane. She was Lorraine Barrie and that was enough; it was more than enough – it was unequivocally and eternally right.

When Bryan finally summoned up courage to ring the bell, there was an immediate outburst of ferocious barking; the sound of smothered imprecations, further barking and footsteps in the passage, then, to his surprise, the door was flung open by Lorraine Barrie herself. She was wearing grey linen slacks, a lime-coloured sports shirt and enormous dark glasses, and she had in her hand a blue-covered typescript. 'Look,' she cried triumphantly, waving it in his face, 'you've come at exactly the right moment. I was just reading your wonderful play for the seventh time!' Before he had time to make a suitable reply, a snarling Aberdeen terrier rushed at him from between her legs and sank its teeth into the cuff of his trousers. Lorraine gave it a sharp blow with the script whereupon it yelped and retired into the hall. 'It's only excitement,' she said. 'Bothwell always goes on like that when anyone comes to the house for the first time, don't you my angel?' Bothwell, who had taken up a menacing attitude at the foot of the small staircase, growled. Lorraine shooed him up the stairs. 'Come on up,' she went on. 'My maid's out for the afternoon so we're all alone and can talk in peace. Tea's all ready except for just popping the water into the pot. You can leave your coat here or bring it upstairs whichever you like.' Bryan took his overcoat off and laid it on a chair and followed her up into a charmingly furnished sitting-room on the first floor. There was a fire crackling in the grate, in front of which was a low table with tea things spread invitingly upon it. Above the fireplace was a large painting of Lorraine herself in a wide grey wooden frame flecked with gilt. In it she was portrayed in her dressing-room staring at herself fixedly in a mirror; behind her hovered a bulky woman with sandy hair. Lorraine laughed gaily when she saw Bryan looking at it. 'It's a Charles Donovan,' she said. 'He did it three years ago. Personally I loathe it although it's supposed to be one of the best things he ever did. That's Nellie, my dresser who's been with me ever since I was at the Haymarket before the war – it's really far better of her than it is of me. Look at the way he's done the hair just on the verge of coming down and the painting of the hands and that heavenly safety-pin, it's terrifying, isn't it. I need hardly tell you that she despises it – she says it makes her look like a lavatory attendant and I've never had the heart to tell the poor sweet that's exactly what she does look like. Here, darling, have a biscuit and shut your trap.' Her last remark was addressed to Bothwell who was still eyeing Bryan malignantly and snarling. She threw him a chocolate biscuit and he disappeared with it behind the sofa.

'Now just sit down and relax' – she gave Bryan a gentle push towards a low armchair by the fire – 'while I go and make the tea. There are cigarettes in that hideous silver box: it was presented to me on the last night of *Dear Yesterday* by the whole company and they'd all subscribed their little pennies and put their signatures on it, and it really was heartrending and took me so completely by surprise that I literally hadn't a word to say; I just stood there stammering like a fool with the tears cascading down my face. If Bothwell makes a beast of himself just give him another chocolate biscuit and he'll adore you.'

She went swiftly out of the room, shutting the door behind her. Bryan obediently sat down and helped himself to a cigarette. Bothwell came out from behind the sofa, sat down by the tea-table and stared at him. Bryan said 'Good dog' automatically and stared back. Then he looked up at the picture again wondering why, if Lorraine hated it as much as she said, she had hung it in such a prominent position. It was unquestionably a good painting; it had strength and sureness but it was not attractive. The face staring into the mirror with such intensity had an unreal mask-like quality, the modelling of the features was perfect, the texture of the skin shone in the bright light shed by the two symmetrical dressing-table lamps. It was not a beautiful face in the classical sense, the nose was too formless and the mouth too big. The eyes were widely spaced and the high cheek-bones, which the artist had slightly over-emphasised, gave an impression of Asiatic exoticism which was somehow out of key. It was perhaps this that accounted for the general artificiality of the whole picture. It was clever, arresting and highly decorative both in execution and design but there was no life in it.

His reflections were interrupted by Bothwell giving a conciliatory whine and rearing himself, with some effort, into a sitting position on his short back legs. Bryan leaned forward obligingly and gave him a chocolate biscuit, which he received with a satisfied grunt and withdrew once more behind the sofa. A moment later Lorraine re-appeared carrying a teapot and a hot-water jug on a small tray.

'It's China tea,' she said. 'If you prefer Indian there's masses in the kitchen and you can have a little pot all to yourself.' Bryan rose to his feet and relieved her of the tray and was about to reply that he was devoted to China tea when she cut him short by saying abruptly, 'You know you're quite different from what I thought you'd be. I can't imagine why but I expected someone much older and dryer – in fact I can tell you now that I was really quite nervous. I've always had a dreadful inferiority complex about authors – to me there's something incredible about people being able to sit down and write plays and books. It's torture to me to have to write so much as a postcard. I'm just physically incapable of stringing three words together on paper. I suppose it's never having been to school properly and having to earn my living ever since I was tiny. I'm completely uneducated you know; I used to drive poor Doodie Rawlings quite frantic when he was directing me in *The Cup That Cheers*. He was an Oxford don, you know, with a passion for the Theatre and of course madly intellectual and he was astounded that anyone in the world could know as little as I did. He was a darling of course but frightfully twisted up emotionally and if I hadn't had a sort of instinctive feeling for what he wanted we should never have got beyond the first week of rehearsal. I remember, quite early on, going to Clemmie – that's my agent – in absolute despair. "It's no use," I said, "I can't do it. It isn't that I don't want to be directed. I do. I want it more than anyone in the world; I want to be told every gesture, every intonation, but this man, poor angel, doesn't *know* the theatre!" He may adore it; he may write brilliant essays on the Restoration playwrights or Shakespeare and God knows who but he doesn't really *know* – I mean one can tell in a flash, can't one? I remember at the very first reading of the play when we were all sitting round a table he kept on getting up and walking about and *explaining* our parts to us, it really was disaster. Finally of course Clemmie calmed me down and back I went with my heart literally in my boots and went straight up to Doodie in front of the whole Company and had it out with him. "It's no good," I said, "expecting me to give what I have to give before I've got the book out of my hand. God knows I'm willing to rehearse until I drop at any time of the day or night, but you must let me work it out in my own way to begin with. Later on when I'm sure of my words and not trying to think of a million things at once and worrying about my fittings into the bargain, you can do what you like with me. You can tear me to pieces, turn me inside out, but not yet – not yet – not yet!" ' On the last 'not yet' she struck the tea-table sharply with her left hand which caused the sugar-tongs to shoot out of the bowl and clatter into the fender: Bryan stooped down to retrieve them and Bothwell charged out from behind the sofa barking loudly. 'There I go,' said Lorraine with a gay unaffected laugh, 'over-acting again.' She handed Bryan a cup of tea. 'I don't know whether you like sugar or milk or neither so just help yourself. I made those little scones myself specially for you so you must eat them all up to the last crumb – I adore cooking but I never dare go into the kitchen when my maid's in the house, so I send her off to the movies every so often and have a real field day. Can you cook?'

'Only scrambled eggs,' said Bryan modestly.

'There's nothing in the world,' said Lorraine simply, 'more divine than scrambled eggs.' She turned to Bothwell who was once more wobbling uneasily on his hind quarters. 'You're mother's sweetheart angel pie and the cleverest dog that ever drew breath but this is definitely and finally the last chocolate biscuit you're going to have today.' She threw him a biscuit which he caught in mid-air. 'And if you go on whining and begging and making a revolting greedy pig of yourself mother will lock you in the bathroom.' She turned back to Bryan. 'He simply hates the bathroom,' she said, 'because the smell of the bath essence makes him sneeze. Where was I?'

'We were talking about scrambled eggs really,' said Bryan. 'But just before that you were telling me about Doodie Rawlings.'

'Poor Doodie.' Lorraine sighed and nibbled a sandwich pensively. 'He went back to Oxford after the play opened and

I haven't clapped my eyes on him from that day to this. Tell me about this new man that J.C. says is going to direct our play, Ray something or other; I missed the thing he did at Hammersmith and wild horses wouldn't drag me to Stratford, particularly with poor Etta Marling flogging her way through all those long parts, so I've never really seen any of his work at all.'

'I think he's brilliant,' said Bryan firmly, aware of a sudden uprush of loyalty to Ray Malcolm. 'He has a terrific personality and great charm.'

Lorraine assumed an expression of grave interest.

'But does he really *know* about the Theatre ?' she asked, 'or is he one of those artsy-craftsy boys who pop out of the Services bursting with theories and keep on doing *The Cherry Orchard*?'

'He's not a bit artsy-craftsy.' Bryan decided that the moment demanded a little diplomatic flattery. 'He was holding forth about you for ages the other day in J.C.'s office. He said that your talent was clear and true and that you had a particular magic of your own that no other living actress possessed.'

'Did J.C. agree with him or say I was a bitch?'

Bryan, taken aback by the suddenness of the question, stammered for a moment and then said 'Both' before he could stop himself. To his relief Lorraine only laughed and offered him another scone.

'J.C. adores me really,' she said tranquilly. 'He's always telling people I'm a bitch because I won't stand for any of his nonsense. As a matter of fact in many ways he's quite right, I can be dreadful when I'm driven to it and he certainly drove me to it when, not content with forcing me to do that dreadful play of Caldwell Rogers, he wished Scott Gurney on to me as a director. Have you ever seen Scott Gurney?'

Bryan shook his head.

'Well——,' Lorraine gathered herself together. 'To begin with, he isn't a director at all, he's a glorified stage-manager.

He hasn't the faintest idea of timing or grouping or tempo; He used to leave me and the wretched Company wandering about the stage and tying ourselves into knots while he sat in the stalls and dictated letters to a stenographer. Finally I couldn't stand it any longer so I went to Clemmie and said "Either he goes or I go." Then there was a terrific hullabaloo and I refused to rehearse and J.C. came and pleaded and Scott Gurney came and apologised and sent me flowers and for the sake of the company I agreed to go on with the damn thing, a decision I have never for one instant ceased to regret. It was a mouldy script from the word go and with that red-faced drunken little butcher in charge of it it hadn't a chance. Then J.C., who really ought to have known better, came bursting in to a rehearsal without so much as a by-your-leave – it was one of those nightmare days when we were working in the set for the first time – and fired Maureen Raleigh on the spot and put in Ella Craven! Without consulting me or even discussing it with me, you can imagine how I felt – there we were, four days off production in complete chaos. I'm not saying that poor Maureen was very good in the part, in fact she ought never to have been engaged for it in the first place, but what I am saying is that compared to Ella Craven she was Rachel and Ellen Terry rolled into one.' Here Lorraine paused to pour herself some more tea. Bryan, who was feeling a trifle dizzy, stumped out his cigarette and shifted his position in the chair. Lorraine waved the teapot enquiringly at him and he shook his head. 'What happened then?' he asked, feeling that some sort of comment was expected.

'What happened!' Lorraine put down the teapot with a crash. 'What happened was that Miss Craven came flouncing on on the opening night without ever having learned it properly, threw the whole play out of balance and played the end of the second act like a Lyceum melodrama. All I could do was just stand about and pray for the curtain to come down. Afterwards of course I bearded J.C. in his office and really told him what I thought of him. Then to cap everything the critics, who are always incapable of telling the difference between a good part and a good actress, gave her rave notices. I don't think I have ever been so really deeply angry in my life. After all, it wasn't myself I was thinking of, it was the play. That's where I'm such a fool, but I can't help it. I always put the play first. From the moment that woman came on the stage we were sunk; you could feel the whole thing disintegrating. It was heartbreaking. I've never quite forgiven J.C. for that, although we are outwardly as friendly as we always were; his behaviour to me over that whole production killed something in me, do you know what I mean? It isn't that one *wants* to go on nursing grievances one *wants* to make up and be friends – forget. But there are some things one just can't forget. He rang me up, you know, about this Ray whatever his name is. . . .'

'Malcolm,' said Bryan.

'He said that in his opinion he was the most exciting new talent that had appeared in the English Theatre for years.'

'He's quite right,' said Bryan, 'I'm sure he is.'

'Anyhow,' said Lorraine resignedly, 'the die is cast now. It's too late to go back. I've signed the contract.'

'I really do want to tell you,' said Bryan with sincerity, 'how proud and thrilled I am. It will make the whole difference to my play, the fact that you're playing it. I can hardly believe in my good luck.'

'Wait and see.' Lorraine, who was obviously pleased, smiled indulgently. 'I may ruin it for you.'

'You'll make it for me,' went on Bryan enthusiastically. 'You'll be magnificent.'

Lorraine leant forward and looked at him intently for a moment and when she spoke the whole timbre of her voice changed, and with it the whole personality seemed to change too. Her inconsequential manner dropped away and it was as though the light in the room had been lowered.

'I want you to promise me something, here and now,' she

said, taking off her dark glasses and fixing him with her lovely grey eyes. 'I want you to promise me that from this moment onwards you will always be absolutely and completely honest with me. I have a strange feeling that we are really friends even though we first met only half an hour ago. I have the advantage over you of course because whereas you have never known me before, I have known you. I have learnt to know you and become fond of you through your lovely, lovely play. . . .'

Bryan made a slight movement to speak but she silenced him with a gesture.

'Don't say anything for a moment, my dear, let me finish. I have never been good at saying flattering things or paying extravagant compliments, particularly to anyone whom I respect; on the contrary, it's generally my idiotic honesty that gets me into trouble and makes people hate me. I just cannot and will not lie and I want to tell you frankly now, at this first step of our adventure together, that this agonising, twisted, moving play of yours is one of the most beautiful things I have ever read, and I can only swear solemnly that I will do my best to be worthy of it.'

She flashed him a brave smile of ineffable sweetness and he was startled to see her eyes were filled with tears. With a quick, businesslike gesture she drew a green chiffon handkerchief from her waist belt, blew her nose delicately into it and put her dark glasses on again. Bryan, in an agony of embarrassment mixed with gratification, racked his brains to find something simple and appropriate to say but his mind was blank and so, smiling rather fatuously, he offered her a cigarette which she refused with a weary shake of the head. He took one himself and lit it and the silence continued. The clock on the mantelpiece struck five very quickly as though it were in a hurry and outside in the mews there was a noise of a car starting up which elicited an ominous growl from Bothwell. Lorraine, with a change of mood as sudden as a slap in the face, said,

'God damn it I forget to telephone Clemmie, forgive me a moment will you?' and reaching over to the telephone which was on a small table at the end of the sofa, proceeded to dial a number.

Bryan, thankful that the quivering emotional tension had at last been dissipated, relaxed and sat back in his chair. Lorraine at the telephone, said in an authoritative tone, 'Mr Clemson, please. This is Miss Barrie,' then, placing her hand over the receiver she hissed at Bryan, 'Be an angel and shut the window will you. That's the hell of living in a mews, one can't hear oneself think.' Bryan, ignoring hostile noises from Bothwell got up, closed the window and sat down again.

'Clemmie dear,' said Lorraine into the telephone, 'I would have called you before but Bryan Snow is here and I got so carried away talking about the script that I completely forgot what the time was. Yes, darling, of course I do. I do think you might have warned me that he was young and attractive and had a divine sense of humour. . . .' Here she smiled roguishly at Bryan and threw him a kiss. 'I expected someone middle-aged and starchy and difficult and was fully prepared to tear myself to shreds in order to break down his reserves and make him approve of me, I even made some of my special scones. . . . Yes, of course he does.' She smiled again at Bryan. 'You do approve of me, don't you?' Bryan nodded enthusiastically and she turned to the telephone again. 'What news from J.C.'s office? Have they got anyone for Stella yet? What about Marion Blake? In heaven's name why not? Well, really . . .' she bit her lip angrily and when she spoke again there was an edge to her voice. 'I've never heard such nonsense in my life, she's one of the best actresses we've got. Oh, it was Mr Ray Malcolm who turned her down, was it? I see. Who does he suggest? What! Carole Wylde! He must be out of his mind. Hold on a minute.' She put her hand over the receiver and turned to Bryan. 'Your Mr Thingamejig wants Carole Wylde for Stella.'

'Yes,' said Bryan uncomfortably, 'I know he does.'

'Have you ever *seen* Carole Wylde?'

'Only once, in *Leave me my Heart*. I thought she was quite good.'

'You can't possibly go by that, it was a fool-proof part anyway. She couldn't play Stella in a thousand years. She's far too young to begin with and with that maddening voice she'd drive people out of the theatre.'

'Oh,' murmured Bryan inadequately.

Lorraine returned to the telephone. 'Listen Clemmie, you can tell Mr Ray Malcolm from me that he'll have to think again. I couldn't possibly play that important scene in the last act with Carole Wylde; she's utterly and completely wrong for it. Yes dear, I know the critics like her and I also know she won the R.A.D.A. medal, but if she plays Stella it will be over my dead body. The part cries out for Marion Blake. I don't know whether he likes her or not and anyway I have yet to be convinced that he really knows anything about the theatre at all. Yes, all right. Of course and the sooner the better. The first reading is in two weeks' time and I must certainly meet him before that. As a matter of fact I ought to have met him at the very outset and you can tell J.C. from me that I consider it was very high-handed of him to engage a director that I've never even clapped eyes on in my life. Very well. I'll leave it to you to arrange it within the next two days. Yes, dear. Call me in the morning, I shall be in until lunch-time.'

Lorraine hung up the telephone and held out her hand. 'I'll have a cigarette now,' she said. 'Just to calm me down because really that has put me into the most terrible rage.' Bryan handed her a cigarette and lit it for her. She inhaled deeply and gave a bitter little laugh. 'It's incredible. Quite incredible!'

'I don't think Ray is all that set on Carole Wylde,' he said tentatively. 'I'm quite sure that if you talk it over with him he'll see exactly what you mean.'

'He ought to know without me telling him that Carole

Wylde in that part would throw the whole play out of balance.
That's what's worrying me really. I'm in despair. I honestly
am.'

'Please don't be,' said Bryan soothingly. 'I am sure it will
all be all right.'

'All this is quite typical of J.C.,' went on Lorraine. 'To start
with he's not a true man of the Theatre at all, he's a real-estate
agent. I swore that I'd never work for him again and I wish to
God I'd never weakened, and if it hadn't been that I fell in
love with your play the very first minute I read it, I wouldn't
have. He's as obstinate as a mule and I wouldn't trust him an
inch. He's always getting idiotic crazes for "exciting new
talent" as he calls them. Do you remember Yvonne Laurie?'

'No,' said Bryan, 'I don't think I do.'

'Neither does anyone else,' said Lorraine. 'She was one of
J.C.'s finds, one of his "exciting new talents". He dragged the
poor thing out of the Provinces, where she was perfectly
happy pottering about in small repertory companies, and
gave her the lead in that French play that Edgar Price
translated into basic Surbiton. You should have seen her got
up as a symbolic prostitute from Marseilles. Exciting new
talent indeed! She was so exciting that the play ran three whole
nights.'

'What happened to her?'

'The Old Vic of course,' said Lorraine witheringly.

'There was once talk of you doing a season with the Old
Vic, wasn't there?' said Bryan unwisely.

Lorraine shuddered.

'There certainly was,' she said. 'They've been badgering
me for years, but I'd rather die. I'm too old and too tired.' She
sighed and gazed into the fire. 'I expect I'm old-fashioned
too,' she went on. 'I've been at the game too long, I learnt the
hard way. Now everything's different. Amateurs have taken
possession of the theatre. Some of them are quite talented
I'm willing to admit, but their talent never really develops;

everything is made too easy for them. Take this Mr Ray Malcolm that you're all so mad about. How long has he been in the Theatre?'

'I don't know,' said Bryan. 'I think he ran a small repertory before the war. Then of course he was in the Army for five years.'

'I've nothing against that,' said Lorraine decisively. 'Nothing against it at all. He may be a genius for all I know. But this play you've written doesn't need genius. It has that already in the writing. What it does need is a real down-to-earth professional to direct it, a man who has all the technical tricks at his fingertips; God preserve us all from enthusiastic intellectuals like poor Doodie who have theories about acting and talk about rhythm and colour. As I said before, I need direction more than any actress living. I'm an absolute fool at rehearsals and so slow that I drive myself mad and everybody else too. In this play of yours I don't have to have the character explained to me. I don't have to be told what she feels and why she does this or that or the other. I knew all that from reading it the first time. I have always, ever since I was tiny, had that particular gift of understanding a part immediately. I have often in fact electrified authors by quite obviously knowing a great deal more about the inside workings of their characters than they do themselves. But what I do need all the time is guidance; to be told *how* to do it. Now in your honest opinion do you think Mr Malcolm can do this?'

'I really don't know,' said Bryan who was becoming a trifle irritated at Ray Malcolm continually being alluded to as his own personal property. 'I have never seen anything that he has directed. In fact I only met him for the first time about ten days ago.'

'Then we're both more or less in the same boat!' cried Lorraine triumphantly. 'We can be allies against a common foe!'

'I don't see why he should necessarily be regarded as an enemy,' said Bryan.

Lorraine laughed charmingly. 'That was only a joke,' she said. 'Actually I can't wait to meet him. And when I do I shall probably be completely bowled over by his charm, obey him slavishly and follow him about like a lapdog!'

Bryan took the plunge that he had been contemplating in his mind for the last ten minutes. 'Will you come and dine with me tomorrow night or the night after and I'll ask Ray and you can get to know each other sort of officially?'

'I should simply adore to,' said Lorraine. 'But I can't either tomorrow or Thursday. What about Friday?'

Bryan, who had arranged to go away for the week-end on Friday afternoon, hesitated for the fraction of a second and then, realising how important it was to his play that Ray Malcolm and Lorraine Barrie should meet in the most amicable circumstances possible, rose to his feet and said, 'Friday will be perfect providing that I can get hold of him. May I telephone you in the morning?'

'Done,' said Lorraine, holding out her hand boyishly. 'I shall leave it all to you. Would you like a cocktail before you go?'

'No thanks.' Bryan shook his head. 'I'm late as it is.' He paused. 'I can't tell you how excited I am. And how grateful too.'

Lorraine snatched up the script from the sofa and held it up solemnly. 'This is our talisman,' she cried. 'The token of our lovely new friendship.'

The enchanting quality of her voice when she said these words was still echoing in Bryan's ears as he walked up the mews in search of a taxi.

(3)

BRYAN, in a state of irritable nervousness, arrived at the 'Vert Galant' a full half-hour early. He had been to a film at the Empire which he had had to leave before the end. He had chosen the 'Vert Galant' after careful consideration. It was quieter than the Savoy Grill, less vibrantly theatrical than 'The Ivy' and not quite as crowded as 'Caprice'. Upon arrival he verified the corner table he had reserved by telephone two days before and sat down to wait in the bar. Having ordered himself a dry martini, he lit a cigarette and contemplated, with rising agitation, the ordeal before him. To begin with, Ray Malcolm had shown signs of petulance when he had called him up to invite him. First of all he said he couldn't possibly manage it as he was going to an opening night with Martha Field and couldn't ditch her, then he said that supper parties in public restaurants were always dangerous for first meetings on account of there being too many distractions and too much noise and that he would rather his initial encounter with Lorraine Barrie took place in some peaceful office somewhere, preferably in the morning, when they could meet on a professional rather than a social basis, get down to brass tacks and discuss the play seriously.

Finally, after a good deal of coaxing and argument, he had given in, agreed to shake himself free from Martha Field and promised to be at the 'Vert Galant' not one minute later than ten-thirty. Lorraine, on the other hand, had put no difficulties in the way. She had agreed enthusiastically to the 'Vert Galant' on the grounds that it had always been for her the luckiest restaurant in London, even going so far as to ascribe to Bryan a certain clairvoyant tact in choosing it. She might, she had added, be the tiniest bit late and so they had better start eating at once and that she would have whatever they were having when she arrived.

In due course Ray appeared in an immaculate dinner-jacket, flashed Bryan an affectionate smile and ordered himself a double whisky-and-soda.

'It was all right about poor Martha,' he said. 'She was going to a managerial party at the Savoy, so it was all quite painless. What's happened to our glamorous star ?'

'She said she might be a little late and that we were to start without her.'

'Nonsense,' said Ray. 'We will sit here and sozzle ourselves into a nice coma so that when she does arrive we shall be past caring. Tell me about your baptismal tea with her – you weren't very communicative on the telephone. Did you fall madly in love with her ? Did she fascinate you within an inch of your life, or did you find her tiresome, affected and utterly repellent ?'

'She was much nicer than I thought she'd be,' replied Bryan with care.

'Oh God,' said Ray. 'Simple, dreamy and unspoiled by her great success I suppose ?'

'Yes.' Bryan gave a conspiratorial giggle. 'But you're going to have your work cut out if you want Carole Wylde to play Stella. She hates her. She wants Marion Blake.'

'All dynamic leading ladies like having Marion Blake in the cast,' said Ray equably. 'She is dull, competent, and offers no competition. Also she's far too old for Stella.'

'Lorraine Barrie thinks that Carole Wylde is too young.'

'We'll cross that old-world bridge when we come to it,' said Ray. 'No one is actually engaged yet anyway. I am feeling benign tonight. I have seen quite a good play, reasonably well acted. I am about, I trust, to eat a very good dinner, God's in his Heaven and all's right with the world. Let's have another drink.'

The next three-quarters of an hour passed happily for

Bryan. The nervousness that had beset him earlier in the evening evaporated and he became aware of a warm glow not entirely engendered by alcohol although he had two more double martinis, and Ray two more double whiskies-and-sodas. The warmth, the sense of ease and well-being were caused principally by the knowledge of growing intimacy. There was a sweet friendliness in the air, an aura of mutual discovery, which, whether Ray was equally aware of it or not, gave a special enchantment to the occasion. One of the most glittering facets of Ray's personality was his capacity for concentrating the full force of his intelligence and vitality upon the person he was talking to. He questioned Bryan penetratingly, sometimes quizzically but always kindly about his hopes and ambitions, his war experiences and his life in the prison camp; he commiserated with him on the commercial failure of *The Unconquered*, implying with flattering sincerity that it had been far above the heads of the present-day public. He even remembered and described certain emotional scenes in the play, holding them up to the light and scrutinising them and then handing them back to Bryan embellished and made more important by his expert analysis of them. His hands were slim and flexible and he used them graphically to illustrate his comments. Bryan, who had never really enjoyed being on the stage during his brief pre-war apprenticeship in Repertory, found himself longing to be an actor again, if only for the chance of being directed by Ray Malcolm. For one moment he actually toyed with the idea of suggesting himself for the small part of Maurice in the second act of *Stones in Heaven*, but discarded it on the reflection that it would not only be waste of time but that he was entirely the wrong type for it.

Ray, at the beginning of his third whisky-and-soda, began to outline wittily and vividly his own early experience in the theatre: he recounted incidents and disappointments and jokes against himself so lightly and so gaily that Bryan was entranced. How enviable, how truly remarkable to be able so cheerfully to rise above heartbreak and despair and turn every defeat into victory by sheer force of character and sense of humour. Ray was in the middle of describing the first rehearsals of the first big success he had ever had and Bryan, enthralled, was hanging on to every word, when Lorraine Barrie arrived wearing a mink coat over a black evening dress and a spray of white gardenias.

'Never,' she announced dramatically, 'until the grave closes over me will I go to a first night again. The strain is too much and I am utterly worn out!' Ray and Bryan sprang to their feet, helped her off with her mink coat and installed her between them on the banquette. Bryan stumblingly attempted introductions but it was quite unnecessary as Lorraine seized both Ray's hands in hers, looked deeply into his eyes and said, 'At last I meet the one man I've really wanted to meet for years!'

For the next hour and a half Bryan was a comparatively silent spectator of two remarkable performances. Perhaps if he had had a little less to drink he might have been more cynically appreciative of the subtleties and overtones of the acting, more genuinely amused at this superficially suave but fundamentally ruthless conflict between two violent egos, each one inexorably resolved to charm, conquer and dominate the other. Even as it was he was fascinated most of the time, although it must be admitted that he found his mind wandering occasionally. Both Lorraine and Ray talked incessantly; the rather expensive dinner that Bryan had ordered with such care was served and devoured automatically and without comment. He reflected with a slight tinge of bitterness, as he watched smoked salmon, crême vichyssoise, filet mignon and pineapple salad vanish down their gullets, that he might just as well have ordered shepherd's pie and stewed prunes for all the attention they were paying to it. Also at the back of his mind he was aware from time to time of a little stab of sadness, of undefined disappointment. In other less hectic circumstances he might have recognised this for what it was – nothing more nor less than jealousy; not profound, not the tearing agony of outraged love, but a dim, dreary sense of disillusion. Ray, before the arrival of Lorraine, had been so true and clear and understanding. There had been a sincerity underlying his words and a certain tenderness in his voice even when he was joking and laughing at himself. There was no tenderness in his voice now. It was brittle and sharp and supremely conscious of its effects. Lorraine was radiant. Her conversation, devoted to the Theatre in general and herself in particular, was gay, ironic and devoid of the slightest trace of the imperious grandeur usually attributable to a great star. On the contrary, she was occasionally over-realistic; stripping even from her acknowledged successes the trappings of glamour and showing them up mercilessly in their true light as just jobs of work well done. Admittedly, most of the poignant little anecdotes she recounted ended with the balance of credit heavily weighted on the side of her own extraordinary perception and strength of character, but the possible monotony of gallant virtue invariably being its own reward was largely mitigated by her lightness of touch and calculated flashes of humour. Whether or not Ray was as enchanted by her as he appeared to be, Bryan was unable to decide. Even later, when they had dropped Lorraine at the corner of her mews and were sitting in Ray's flat having a final drink, he was not sure. Ray's comments on the evening were amiable but sardonic; his mood of amused cynicism seemed genuine enough but it might well be assumed in order to deceive either Bryan or himself. Bryan ultimately left him and walked home to Ebury Street in a haze of indecision. The evening had undoubtedly been of value; he had brought his director and his leading lady, the two most important protagonists of his brain-child, successfully together. The future of his play lay in their hands. By rights, he reflected, he

should be feeling elated and triumphant; this after all was the
chance he had dreamed of – a West End production under the
best possible auspices; 'J. C. Roebuck presents Lorraine
Barrie in *Stones in Heaven*, by Bryan Snow. Directed by Ray
Malcolm'. But as he let himself in with his latch-key and
walked up the dark stairs to his bed-sitting-room he was
aware of no elation at all, nothing but utter weariness and a
slight headache.

(4)

THE first reading of *Stones in Heaven* took place on the stage of
the Caravel Theatre at ten-thirty in the morning. Bryan
arrived at ten twenty-five and was immediately conscious of
the atmosphere of subdued tension that usually characterises
such occasions. Various members of the cast were standing
about chatting in low tones; one man, whom he was unable to
identify, was sitting on an upturned rostrum reading the
Daily Telegraph. The current attraction at the Caravel was a
whimsical comedy in verse called *The Last Troubadour*, which
having hovered for some months between success and failure
was now within two weeks of closing. The action of this play
took place in the banqueting hall of a mediæval castle, a setting
designed by Robin Birkett which had received enthusiastic
notices from the press but had failed to compensate for the
roguish dullness of the play. It was a built set and therefore
immovable and any company wishing to use the theatre for
rehearsals on non-matinée days were forced to rehearse in it or
not at all. The safety curtain was down and in front of it was a
table around which were placed a dozen chairs in a semi-circle.
At a smaller table sat a harassed young man with unruly hair,
dark green corduroy trousers and horn-rimmed glasses. On
the table in front of him was a pile of typewritten 'Parts'
bound in dull pink paper which he was sorting feverishly.
A working light hung from the flies betraying with its harsh

effulgence the pseudo-Gothic glories of poor Robin Birkett's decor. A large arm-chair upholstered in faded chintz, obviously a tribute to Lorraine Barrie's position as a star, was placed prominently in front of a huge open fireplace in which a papier-mâché ox was wobbling uneasily on a spit.

Bryan's arrival coincided with that of Gerald Wentworth, a florid, handsome man of about forty-five. The harassed young man at the prompt table sprang up and greeted him respectfully and a lady with a curious green bird in her hat gave a little squeal and flung her arms round his neck. No one paid any attention to Bryan so he sat down on a vacant chair, lit a cigarette and read with frowning concentration a bill from The Electrical Supply Company which he happened to find in his pocket. Presently Ray Malcolm strode on to the stage and immediately the atmosphere became so intensified that Bryan would not have been surprised if the stage manager had handed everyone oxygen masks. Ray was followed purposefully by a short thick-set young man in a camel-hair coat whom he introduced to Bryan as his assistant, Tony Orford. 'My dear,' said Tony Orford as they shook hands, 'Ray has talked about you so much that I've been positively counting the moments. This must be a great day for you; are you in a terrible tizz?'

Bryan, disliking him on sight, shook his head with what he hoped was bland assurance and before he had time to explain that far from being in a 'tizz' he was as cool as a cucumber, they were interrupted by another shrill squeal and the lady with the green bird in her hat kissed Tony Orford effusively and then turned to Bryan.

'I saw you sitting there and I wasn't sure,' she said, 'but now I *know* and if nobody is going to introduce us I shall introduce myself. My name is Marion Blake and I've read your play and to my mind it's got everything – but everything. I don't believe I've been so excited over a script since I first read *Love Child* and God knows I was right about that. . . .'

'*Love Child*,' interposed Tony, 'was my *un*favourite play of all time.'

'Be that as it may,' cried Marion Blake, 'it ran two solid years and we never dropped, even during the election.' She turned to Bryan. 'Isn't he horrid? He's always like that. So damping!'

Further revelations of Tony's character were cut short by Ray rapping a pencil on the table and announcing in a voice only faintly tinged with irritation that they would start without Miss Barrie as she was not immediately in the first scene. There was a general movement towards the chairs; the stage manager distributed the parts; Ray motioned to Bryan to come and sit next to him at the table: Bryan, with a thrill of pride, sat down. There was a brief argument between Gerald Wentworth and Ray as to whether he should read from his script or from the 'part'. In course of this Ray hurriedly introduced him to Bryan who rose to his feet and sat down again. Finally it was decided that Wentworth should read from the script. He took a chair exactly facing the table and put on his glasses. A hush descended, Ray cleared his throat and proceeded to read a preliminary description of the set. He read swiftly and concisely; the authority in his voice was unmistakable. From outside in the street came the muted noises of traffic; the Company sat expectantly, waiting for their moments to begin. The unidentified man sitting on the upturned rostrum continued to read the *Daily Telegraph*. Suddenly there was the sound of barking in the passage leading to the stage; the swing door with 'Silence' painted on it in large white letters burst open and Bothwell appeared on a leash dragging Lorraine Barrie after him. She was simply dressed in a neat blue tailor-made suit and a black hat; a fur cape hung from her shoulders and she was hugging to herself three parcels, a big scarlet handbag, a rolled umbrella and the script.

'This,' she cried gaily as she approached the table, 'is quite definitely the worst entrance I've ever made. I know I'm late and I'm bitterly ashamed. Please, please will you all forgive me?'

She looked appealingly at Ray and then smiled at the Company. Gerald Wentworth rose, kissed her solemnly and sat down again. Marion Blake, emitting shrill noises, hugged her emotionally as though she had just been rescued from a foundering liner; Bothwell snarled and yapped until Lorraine struck him with her umbrella.

'Listen, Angel Pie,' she said grimly. 'Mother only brought you to rehearsal because she was sorry for you being left all alone and you have been making a maddening beast of yourself ever since we left the house. Here, Harry!' – she beckoned to the stage manager – 'Take him to the property room and tie him up to something really heavy.' She glanced round the set. 'With any luck you might find a script of this play!' There was an obsequious titter from the Company. She handed Bothwell's lead to Harry who reluctantly took it and dragged Bothwell off the stage. Lorraine deposited her parcels on the table in front of Ray and smiled radiantly at him.

'You'll have to forgive me for all this. You really will,' she said. 'Because I *know* my first act! Not quite all of it but I can do up to Stella's exit without the book!'

'It's all right,' said Ray pleasantly. 'We were only just starting the first scene.'

Lorraine leaned across the table and patted Bryan's hand. 'Good morning, dear Author,' she said affectionately, 'this is all wildly exciting, isn't it?' Bryan gave a nervous smile of agreement. Lorraine gathered up her parcels and sat down on a small hard chair at the side.

'The arm-chair is for you,' said Ray courteously, 'Harry routed it out from somewhere or other specially.'

Lorraine shook her head firmly.

'I couldn't, darling, I really couldn't. Once I sank into that I should go into a deep, deep sleep. Laura must have it.' She beckoned to Laura Witby, a tired-looking character actress who was playing the maid. 'Take this chair, Laura dear. I absolutely insist.'

Laura Witby looked anxiously at Ray and mumbled something about being perfectly comfortable where she was. However, her timid protests were over-ruled by Lorraine, who, after embracing her affectionately and knocking her hat on one side, led her firmly to the arm-chair and forced her down into it. Lorraine, thus having established at the outset that she was brimming with democratic good-fellowship, returned to her wooden chair, deposited her umbrella and bag on the floor beside her and opened her script. The reading of the play began. In course of it Ray made occasional comments, corrected an intonation here and there and scribbled notes on a pad that lay on the table in front of him. Bryan, smoking incessantly, watched the pile of cigarette ends growing in a tin ash-tray and tried vainly to resist a mounting feeling of disappointment.

Lorraine, far from proving her boast that she knew the first act up to Stella's exit, kept her eyes glued to the script and read stumblingly, without expression; at moments her voice was so low that Bryan couldn't hear what she was saying. Gerald Wentworth lost his place several times and muttered, 'Sorry, that's me.' Marion Blake read swiftly and brightly, so brightly indeed that Ray winced several times quite openly.

At the end of the reading Ray gave a little talk to the Company. What he said was highly technical and was concerned mainly with the tempo at which certain scenes should be played. He concentrated his attention for a moment or two on Marion Blake, explaining firmly that although her reading had been clear and competent she had obviously not quite grasped the psychological significance of Stella's character. Lorraine at one point made an attempt to interrupt but he quelled her with a courteous smile and she tapped her lips chidingly with her right forefinger and relapsed into silence, passing off this minor defeat by rummaging in her bag for her compact.

Bryan, Lorraine, Ray and Tony Orford lunched together at 'The Ivy'. Marion Blake was sitting alone at a table nearby and blew them kisses repeatedly. At two-thirty they were back in the theatre again. There was no longer a semi-circle of chairs, for Harry, the stage manager, had arranged them in various formations according to the ground plan of the first act. Bothwell, who had behaved surprisingly well during the reading and only barked twice at lunch, was again consigned to the property room. The first rehearsal began.

To a layman, unless he happens to be abnormally interested in the Theatre, the preliminary rehearsals of a new play are dull in the extreme. Most of the proceedings are conducted in undertones; the actors wander about reading from parts and making occasional vague gestures to indicate that they are closing a door or opening a window. Each time a new movement is set for them by the director they stop dead and borrow pencils from each other with which they scribble hieroglyphics on their scripts. There is a staleness in the air, an atmosphere of insecurity, slowness and frustration. To the actors themselves of course none of this applies. For them it is a period of great nervous activity. Not only are they concentrated on trying to remember the words in relation to the movements but their minds are seething with secret plans and projects for effective little bits of 'business' they intend to do when they get their books out of their hands. Many of them are also beset with nightmare worries about billing, clothes, dressing-rooms and ultimate press notices. In addition they are all, as a general rule, a prey to agonising nerves. This malaise takes various forms and years of experience are likely to increase rather than assuage it. In some it expresses itself by over-emphasis; a sharp, bright, too quick-on-the-trigger efficiency: in others by a hesitant, constricted self-consciousness, and it is one of the primary duties of a good director to recognise these temperamental and psychological symptoms early and make reasonable allowances for them.

Bryan sat with Tony Orford at the side of the stage and watched intently. Ray did nothing beyond indicating an occasional movement and saying from time to time such phrases as 'Go back to your entrance' or 'Try it again from where you move down to the window'. He sat hunched up in a chair against the safety curtain with his overcoat slung from his shoulders and his hat tilted over his eyes. Tony Orford hissed comments into Bryan's ear every now and then but Bryan discouraged him by leaning forward still more intently. He had disliked Tony on sight and, up to date, had found no cause to revise his opinion. Admittedly he had been a help at lunch, having talked a lot in rather a bitchy strain and lightened the distracted gloom which usually prevails after a first reading. Ray had introduced him as his assistant but Bryan was still confused as to the exact scope of his activities. It couldn't possibly be of any great assistance to Ray that he should sit at the side of the stage whispering irrelevant and occasionally scurrilous gossip into the author's left ear.

Lorraine walked through the rehearsal with lamb-like docility. On the few occasions that Ray made a suggestion to her she merely nodded thoughtfully, scribbled something in her script and went back a few lines in order to set what he had said securely in her memory.

At five o'clock the rehearsal came to an end and the Company dispersed. Bothwell was retrieved from the property room and flew on to the stage barking wildly. When his first emotional transports had calmed down a little Lorraine produced a biscuit from her bag which she made him sit up and beg for. Presently Ray, without even a look in the direction of Bryan and Tony, went off with Lorraine and Bothwell and the door marked 'Silence' closed behind them.

'I thought as much,' said Tony laconically. 'He's going to start work on her.'

'How do you mean?' asked Bryan.

Tony began to struggle into his coat, Bryan helping him find the sleeve.

'He will drive her back to her house, dog and all,' said Tony. 'Once there, happily ensconced with a whisky-and-soda and in a general atmosphere of peace and good-will, he will proceed to tear the liver and lights out of her.'

Bryan was genuinely startled. 'But why? Do you think he didn't like the way she read? After all it was only a first run through.'

'Come and have a drink,' said Tony. 'And I'll tell you the facts of life with Father. To begin with,' he went on, as they walked up the stairs and out of the stage door, 'he will explain to her sweetly but firmly that her whole approach to the character is wrong. He will then list accurately every mannerism and trick she has ever used and tell her to throw all she has ever learned into the alley. When he has successfully asserted his dominance over her and reduced her either to maudlin tears or screaming hysterics he will inform her with almost clairvoyant intensity that she is a great, great actress with more talent in that well-known little finger than Duse had in her whole frail body. After which he will kiss her affectionately and bugger off. The results,' he added, 'will be discernible on a clear day at the beginning of the second week of rehearsals.'

(5)

THE first week of rehearsals passed without incident. Lorraine continued to be docile and accepted Ray's direction with businesslike submissiveness. The young man whom Bryan had failed to identify at the first reading continued to sit on the rostrum with the *Daily Telegraph*, only discarding it every now and then when called upon to make his one brief appearance as the chauffeur at the beginning of Act Three. Bryan was fascinated by his almost insolent lack of interest in the proceedings. Marion Blake continued to play her part with stubborn archness and, to Bryan's surprise, Ray allowed her to do so without protest. On the Thursday afternoon Ray was absent and Tony Orford took a word rehearsal. Once more the chairs were arranged in a semi-circle and the cast, in an atmosphere of controlled irritation, were forced to go through the entire first act three times, without their books. Bryan, with grudging admiration, had to admit that Tony conducted the whole business with patience and firmness. Gerald Wentworth wasted a good deal of time and energy by striking himself violently on the forehead every time he forgot a line and insisting that he had known it backwards the night before, and Laura Witby created a diversion by having a nose-bleed, upon which the stage manager produced a key, which he dropped discreetly down her back and led her to the pro-perty room, where she lay on the floor. Apart from this the afternoon was dull in the extreme.

That evening Bryan dined by himself at an oyster bar in Gerrard Street and went to a movie at the Plaza. He was feel-ing low in spirit, and the movie, a historical romance in blinding technicolor, did little to alleviate his gloom. It was raining when he came out and he had to wait in the covered entrance to the cinema for over ten minutes while the com-missionaire darted backwards and forwards between the road and the kerb blowing a whistle for a taxi. Finally one appeared, and Bryan, having given the commissionaire half a crown because he hadn't anything smaller, huddled himself into the corner of the cab and tried, as it rattled through the sodden streets, to analyse the feeling of deflated melancholy which had been gradually mounting during the last few days and now threatened to overwhelm him entirely. By rights, he reflected angrily, he should be supremely happy. His career as a playwright had taken a pronounced upward curve, everything was going well, rehearsals were smooth and orderly, there had been, to date, no turbulent moments, no nerve-shattering scenes, none of those sudden pre-production crises which he had been led to believe were fairly inevitable in the putting on of a new play. True, there were still two and a half weeks to go before the actual opening: there was still time and to spare for the battles and tears and anguish, but, even so, this sense of vague disappointment, almost of boredom, was surely unusual? There must be, lurking in the back of his consciousness, some cause for it, some acknowledged reason why, instead of eagerness, pride and pleasurable anticipation, there was nothing in his heart but listlessness and an undefined sense of unhappiness.

Having paid the taxi and let himself into his bed-sitting-room, he undressed quickly, mixed himself a strong gin and tonic and got into bed. While he sipped his drink he surveyed the room thoughtfully and decided that whether *Stones in Heaven* was a success or not he would at least get enough money out of it to be able to afford a flat. The bed-sitting-room was all right as bed-sitting-rooms go but it was small and dingy and congested with his personal possessions, none of which seemed to take kindly to it. His framed reproduction of 'The Bridge at Arles', by Van Gogh, looked out of place against the flowered wallpaper. His writing-desk was piled untidily with books and papers and was dominated by two large leather frames containing photographs of his mother and sister respectively. His mother was sitting on a garden seat wearing a pained expression and holding a cairn terrier which had moved while the picture was being taken and consequently looked like a muff. His sister Margaret, a pretty girl of twenty-five, was posed on a staircase in her wedding dress. Her expression was non-committal. On the mantelpiece together with two empty glass vases and a clock which remained monotonously at eleven-twenty, was an enlarged snapshot, framed in passe-partout, of a good-looking young man in swimming trunks holding a large fish in his right hand and pointing to it triumphantly with his left. This was Bryan's closest friend, Stuart Raikes, who had gone to Barbados after the war to grow bananas and wrote rather dull letters every month or so. Bryan missed him very much. The rest of the room was impersonal as such rooms usually are. Two of the rings were missing from the blue curtains, which made them sag unattractively, and the window rattled. Having finished his drink and smoked two cigarettes, Bryan was about to switch out the light when the telephone rang downstairs. He lifted the receiver of the extension by his bed in the forlorn hope that the call might be for him and was startled to hear Ray Malcolm's voice. In the split second before he replied, his imagination envisaged a lightning series of disasters. Lorraine Barrie had been run over on her way home from rehearsal: J. C. Roebuck had decided that the play was no good after all and cancelled the production: Ray himself had been offered a monumental movie contract and was flying to Hollywood the next day. He murmured 'Hallo' in a strangled voice which sounded as though he had been crying.

'Thank God,' said Ray fervently, 'I was afraid that you would be out gallivanting with your fine friends and I want to talk to you. Are you alone?'

'Quite alone,' replied Bryan, wondering blankly who Ray imagined was sharing his bed with him.

'It's the end of the play,' said Ray. 'Lorraine isn't happy about it and I must say I'm not either.' Bryan's heart sank even lower than it was already.

'What's the matter with it?' he asked, trying to keep his voice free from agitation.

'Well,' said Ray, 'to begin with it's too like *The Green Hat*. I never realised it until Lorraine pointed it out to me.'

'I've never read *The Green Hat*,' said Bryan defensively.

'It doesn't matter whether you've read it or not,' said Ray
with genial firmness. 'Your suffering heroine decides to "end
it all" in a big way by flinging herself into a speed-boat and
ramming a lighthouse at fifty miles an hour. Iris March the
suffering heroine of *The Green Hat* decided to "end it all" in a
big way too, only she chose a Hispano and an oak tree which
she called, with whimsical sophistication, "Harrods"! At
least you haven't called your lighthouse "Pontings".' Bryan
heard Ray chuckling to himself at this little sally and said with
undisguised irritation, 'I don't quite see what I can do about
it – it's a little late to start making major alterations now.
She's got to commit suicide somehow, hasn't she? It's the
climax of the whole play!'

'Of course she has,' said Ray gently, 'for heaven's sake
don't get upset about it. I've got a lot of ideas which I can't
possibly go into on the telephone. All I want you to do is to
think about it quietly before I say anything more, then I
should like you to come down to the country with me
tomorrow afternoon after rehearsal and we'll have a peaceful
week-end hashing it all over. It's only an hour and a half's
drive and we'll have all the time in the world – how's that?'

Bryan, aware of a sudden, quite irrational lifting of his
spirits, said, 'That will be fine. I'd love it.'

'Good,' said Ray. 'Small suitcase, no dinner clothes, just
ourselves. Until tomorrow – Good-night, sweet prince.'

Bryan heard the click as Ray hung up the receiver.

Ray Malcolm's cottage was in Kent half-way between
Maidstone and Ashford. The bedrooms had sloping ceilings,
exposed oak beams and small, low windows. There was a
minute bathroom with a lavatory adjoining it, distempered
in shrimp pink, which commanded a superb view of the Weald
of Kent and, as an added attraction for the contemplative
guest, contained a series of eighteenth-century playbills
framed in bright green. Downstairs two small rooms had
been knocked into one to make a dining-room, and outside,

a few yards away, was the living-room which had once been a stable. This was enormous with a wide open fireplace built in at the end of it. The white-washed walls were alive with theatrical implications: highly coloured engravings of dead and gone actors picked out with tinsel; large Victorian prints of crowded opera houses; and a whole series of Robin Birkett's original designs for *'Tis Pity She's a Whore*, the production of which a few years earlier had established Ray in the modern theatre.

Ray and Bryan arrived at about seven-thirty and were received, to Bryan's surprise and dismay, by Tony Orford who had come down by train during the afternoon. He was wearing a Canadian lumber-jack's shirt, maroon trousers and sandals.

'Mrs Hartley,' he said as he greeted them, 'is in a terrible tizz on account of the joint not having come for tomorrow's lunch. She also went off into a Mrs Siddons tirade about Colonel Spencer's red setter.'

'What's it done now?' said Ray irritably.

'Killed three chickens,' replied Tony. 'It is now sitting under a tree in Colonel Spencer's garden with one of the corpses tied round its neck, the idea being that twenty-four hours' worth of decomposing fowl will teach it that Crime Does Not Pay. My personal guess is that the higher it gets the more it will adore it. Like Stilton.'

Later, after Bryan had been taken to his room and shown where to wash, they all three sat round the fire in the living-room drinking whiskies-and-sodas and waiting for dinner to be announced. The daylight faded and the windows became blue in the dusk; Tony and Ray got into an argument about a review in *The New Statesman* of a recent play, Tony maintaining that the critic was a Bloomsbury highbrow whose knowledge of the Theatre began and ended with *Murder in the Cathedral* and Ray insisting that whether the play in question was good, bad or indifferent the critic had a perfect right to state his opinion of it. Bryan lay back in his arm-chair and closed his eyes; the country air, the pungent smell of wood-smoke in the room and the warming effect of the whisky were beginning to make him drowsy. His initial annoyance on discovering that Tony was in the house gave place to a feeling of benign resignation. After all he wasn't bad and had certainly gone out of his way to be friendly ever since they had met at the first reading; he was quite attractive too, if you were prepared to bridge the bewildering gulf between his appearance and his conversation. Bryan regarded him critically through half-closed eyes: the bright check lumber jacket enhanced his general stockiness, making him look as though he had just climbed off a tractor and sluiced himself down under a pump in the yard; his curly hair, which was rather too long, glinted in the firelight. It was his voice that was the trouble, Bryan decided, it was too light and high-pitched and his choice of phrase and manner of speaking were too startlingly at variance with his looks. His sense of humour was quick and destructive and essentially of the Theatre. He described with affectionate, contemptuous gusto the carryings on of famous stars and elderly character actresses. He seemed to have little interest in the younger ones. He was now re-counting gleefully some fresh details of a famous feud between Dame Laura Cavendish and Miss Lavinia Kirk, who had apparently loathed each other since they had appeared together with the late Sir Herbert Tree in the palmy days of His Majesty's; his voice and his laugh pierced Bryan's sleepi-ness like a stiletto.

'Darling Laura arrived late of course and there was Lavinia literally on the Queen's lap, my dear, nattering away as if they had known each other for years! Laura gave one look, turned bright green and would have dropped dead if she hadn't remembered she had a matinée the next day – then with a supreme effort she pulled herself together and became ze life and death of ze party, but it wasn't until after the Royalties had left that she really pounced. She churned up to Lavinia like an old Thames steamboat with her paddles thrashing the water into a frenzy. "Lavvy, dear," – here Tony imitated Dame Laura's voice – "how lovely for you to have had the Queen to yourself for such a long time. I thought she looked dreadfully tired, didn't you?" ' Tony's rendering of this with an emphasis on the words, 'lovely', 'long' and 'dreadfully' was so cruelly accurate that Ray laughed immoderately and was about to help himself to another whisky-and-soda when Mrs Hartley, a fat woman with a scarlet face, flung open the door and announced breathlessly that dinner was served.

After dinner they returned to the living-room and Bryan steeled himself against the dreaded discussion of his play which he felt was now imminent. He had lain awake most of the night after Ray's telephone call vainly endeavouring to figure out an effective way for his heroine to dispose of herself. She couldn't jump under the Blue Train because of Anna Karenina; nor could she shoot herself off-stage because of Paula Tanqueray; an overdose of sleeping tablets was too slow and would necessitate reconstructing the whole last act and inserting a time lapse of several hours. A sudden heart attack of course was always possible, if a trifle far-fetched, and there would have to be a lot of re-writing of the earlier part of the play to explain her cardiac condition. There were no ramparts from which she could fling herself like Floria Tosca and no Samurai sword on which to impale herself like Madame Butterfly. Tuberculosis was obviously out of the question, quite apart from its being reminiscent of *La Dame aux Camellias* and *La Bohème*, because, modern therapy being what it is, the whole last act would have to be transferred to a sanatorium in Switzerland. Bryan, in the still silence of the night, had worked himself into a furious rage against Lorraine Barrie. She had obviously argued Ray into agreeing with her. It was also obvious that the whole situation had been brought about merely for her to assert her idiotic ego. He had fallen asleep just before dawn and awakened at ten o'clock calmer but devoid of any constructive ideas whatsoever. Ray had said that he had some ideas of his own and so the only wise course was to wait and see what they were, and then without stubbornness or prejudice, try to do the best he could with them.

Ray settled himself comfortably on the sofa and regarded Bryan benevolently.

'Now then,' he said. 'Coats off. Shoulders to the wheel. Cards on the table.'

'Wigs on the green,' murmured Tony with a giggle.

'Shut up,' said Ray. 'This is business and we've got to concentrate.'

A long while later Bryan, utterly dazed and with a blinding headache, undressed in a trance and fell into bed. He had drunk six whiskies-and-sodas, smoked countless cigarettes and listened to his play being twisted, changed and entirely reconstructed no less than three times, each version being completely different from the other. Ray's daemonic vitality was inexhaustible and Bryan had received the full brunt of it for five hours, Tony having long since retired to bed. Now, with throbbing head and jittering nerves he lay staring at a patch of moonlight on the ceiling, regretting bitterly that he'd ever thought of writing a play in the first place and trying to sort out in his mind at least some of the drastic alterations that Ray had suggested. Finally, he gave it up as hopeless: a church clock struck three somewhere in the distance, his brain was too tired and confused to be capable of coherent thought, and so, after stumbling along the dark passage to the bathroom for a glass of water, he swallowed three aspirins, clambered back into bed and went miserably to sleep.

The next morning at eleven o'clock Tony came into his room with a breakfast-tray which he deposited on the bedside table. He was wearing a peacock-blue and scarlet sarong and the upper part of his body was naked. Bryan, who had been dozing uneasily, was startled into full wakefulness.

'It's all right, dear,' said Tony cheerfully, 'it's only me and not Dorothy Lamour as you thought. My sister sends me these things from Malaya, they're wonderful to sleep in and you can kick your legs about all night long if you feel like it without them riding up and strangling you. How did you sleep?'

Bryan hoisted himself up on his pillow and blinked. 'I don't quite know yet,' he said huskily.

'I brought you some breakfast myself because I thought that the sight of Mrs Hartley in the cold light of remorseless dawn might be too much for you.'

'Thanks very much,' said Bryan. 'I think I'd better brush my teeth.'

'But *Do*,' said Tony. 'I'll wait here and nurse you back to health and strength.'

Bryan groped for his slippers with his bare feet and stumbled off to the bathroom: when he came back Tony was sitting on the end of the bed smoking a cigarette.

'If this cigarette sends you off into a frenzy of vomiting I'll put it out,' he said obligingly. 'You'd better get back into bed and I'll put the tray on your knees.'

'Thanks very much,' said Bryan again. 'I've got a slight hangover.' He kicked off his slippers and got back into bed obediently.

'I rather thought you would have,' said Tony. 'I gave one look at the Maestro stretched out like a fish on a slab and put two and two brightly together. He's just coming to now. I suppose you sat up till all hours?'

'Yes,' said Bryan with a wan smile. 'I'm afraid we did.'

'I knew he was working up for one of his big virtuoso performances.' Tony arranged the tray on Bryan's knee and proceeded to pour out the tea. 'And so I went to bed. I suppose he re-wrote your entire script for you, played out every scene and tore himself to shreds?'

'I was the one that was torn to shreds,' said Bryan bitterly.

'You poor dear.' Tony looked at him with genuine anxiety. 'He didn't really upset you, did he?'

Bryan, valiantly resisting an impulse to burst into tears of self-pity, mumbled almost inaudibly, 'I'm afraid he did rather!'

'Drink some tea,' said Tony with practical sympathy. 'Have a stab at that sensational brown egg and relax. Meanwhile mother will give you a little kindly advice based on long experience.'

Bryan sipped some tea and, with an effort, attacked the brown egg with a spoon. Tony lit another cigarette and retired to the end of the bed again, hunched up his knees and looked at Bryan thoughtfully.

'To begin with,' he said. 'There is no need for you to be upset at all. You've written a very good play and J. C. Roebuck wouldn't have considered doing it for a moment unless he thought it had an excellent chance of success. What you've got to get into your poor fuddled head is that Ray, although he has genius as a director, is a frustrated actor. He would also give his eye teeth to write one page of creative dialogue but he can't, and what's more he knows he can't because writing is a gift and you either have it or you haven't. What happened to you last night has happened to every author of every play he's ever done. He gets carried away by his own virtuosity; his imagination, which is fantastic, works overtime and before you know where you are you have fifteen plots instead of one, an entirely new set of characters, and the whole thing looks like a dog's dinner.' Here Tony paused and patted Bryan's foot affectionately.

'I don't want you to think I'm being disloyal to Ray,' he went on gently. 'I adore him and admire him more than anybody in the world but I've been with him too long not to know his little failings and his principal one is that his own violent energy makes it impossible to let well alone. You may have had a bloody evening last night but I can assure you that he didn't; he enjoyed every minute of it. He got rid of a lot of superfluous vitality and gave himself the whale of a time. Lorraine Barrie got at him about the end of the play and that gave him a springboard. Now he's got it all out of his system and he'll be mild as a kitten until next time. What is important of course is whether the end of the play is right as it is or whether it should be altered. What do you think yourself? Really and honestly?'

'I don't know,' said Bryan. 'I'm in a muddle.'

'Would you forgive me,' said Tony, 'if I made one small insignificant suggestion?'

'Of course I would.' Bryan smiled gratefully. 'You're being very kind and very sympathetic.'

'Don't kill Eleanor off at all,' said Tony. 'Make the scene where she discovers Audrey and Stella together much stronger. Then let the audience think for a little while that she really is in such despair that she is going to do herself in, then let her pull herself together and at the end, after the cocktail scene, get all the others on to the patio for lunch and let the curtain fall on her telephoning to Robert, quite quietly with a smile on her lips and tears rolling down her face. Lorraine can do that sort of "Smiling, the boy fell dead" performance better than anyone alive. It's not so melodramatic as the way you've written it, but I think it's more real.'

There was silence for a moment while Bryan's mind sniffed warily at Tony's suggestion. There was certainly a good deal of sense in it although it would necessitate re-writing nearly the whole of the last act. He sipped his tea and was aware of a lightening of his spirits. Spring sunlight flooded the room and from outside in the garden came the clicking purr of a lawn-mower. The high-powered tension of the night before receded further and further away and he found that now, in the fresh light of morning, he could view the whole situation in clearer perspective. He looked at Tony, who, with concentrated determination, was trying vainly to make smoke-rings, and the last shreds of his initial prejudice against him vanished. He remembered with shame how at the first reading he had sneered to himself when Ray had said, 'This is my assistant, Tony Orford.' He saw now with sudden clarity how valuable his assistance must be. Tony abruptly stopped blowing smoke-rings and jumped off the bed.

'Think it all over quietly,' he said. 'And don't allow yourself to be barracked. It's your play and nobody else's. Have you finished with the tray?'

'Yes,' said Bryan, 'and I can't tell you how grateful I am. I'm going to have a shot at re-writing the last act on your lines only I really would like to go over it all with you in detail before I start it if you can spare the time.'

'All the time in the world,' said Tony, balancing the tray on the upturned palm of his right hand like a waiter. 'We'll creep away somewhere after lunch while Ray goes off into his afternoon coma and if you take my advice you won't say a word about it until you've got it done or at least clear in your mind.'

He went out of the room, closing the door after him.

The rest of the day passed without interest. Ray appeared just before lunch in a turtle-neck sweater and a tweed jacket carrying the Sunday papers bunched up under one arm and a number of play scripts under the other. He plumped the whole lot down on a deck-chair, screamed for Tony, and they all three walked down a lane to the village and had gin and vermouths in the 'local'. Ray exchanged neighbourhood gossip with the lady behind the bar, played a game of darts with three labourers who Bryan suspected would infinitely have preferred to play by themselves, laughed over-loudly when his darts missed the board entirely and generally gave a rather unconvincing performance of a country squire. Tony sipped his drink and observed the proceedings with a quizzical eye. On the way back to the house Ray squeezed Bryan's arm affectionately and said he was the most receptive and attractive author he had ever worked with. Apart from this there was no allusion made to the night before. At lunch he recounted anecdotes of the Theatre with consummate brilliance. Some of the incidents he retailed might, to anyone uninterested in the drama, have appeared to be a trifle drawn out, a little over-elaborated, but as his sole audience consisted of Bryan and Tony the atmosphere was unclouded by criticism. At moments Bryan felt a little sorry for Mrs Hartley who frequently was forced to wait for a considerable time before proffering a dish of vegetables while Ray was leading slowly but wittily to a histrionic climax. On one occasion he made an unexpected gesture with his left hand which nearly sent a sauce-boat full of gravy flying across the room; however Mrs Hartley, with a swiftness obviously born of long training, whisked it out of the way in the nick of time.

Tony's phrase 'frustrated actor' recurred to Bryan's mind once or twice but he crushed it down loyally and gave himself up wholeheartedly to enjoying the vivid play of Ray's words and the extraordinary fascination of his personality.

After lunch Ray retired upstairs with the scripts and the papers, and Tony and Bryan went for a walk. They climbed over a stile at the end of the garden and walked up a muddy path through a small wood, emerging finally on a grass plateau which commanded a sweeping view. Here, with the gentle Kentish countryside at their feet they sat down with their backs against a tree trunk and reconstructed method-ically the last act of *Stones in Heaven*. Tony talked concisely and professionally and Bryan, making notes on a piece of paper, was surprised to find how easily everything seemed to fall into place. Now, in the light of Tony's kindly but ironic in-telligence, the original ending of the play appeared to be almost childishly melodramatic. The only thing that per-plexed Bryan was the fact that neither he himself, Lorraine, Ray nor J. C. Roebuck had noticed it in the first place. At last, when the sun was low across the hills, Tony got up. 'It's tea-time,' he said, 'and the Maestro will be in a tizz and think we have run away together to start a new life. Also' – he added, 'if we stay here any longer we shall catch the Universal Complaint, if we haven't got it already.'

Bryan got up, stuffed the notes into his pocket and they walked arm-in-arm down through the wood to the house. He felt happy and relaxed and burning with ambition to start re-writing at once. Tony warned him against too much sudden enthusiasm. 'Let it simmer for a bit,' he said as they clambered over the stile. 'Type out all your notes before you start and see that there aren't any sticky passages.'

They found Ray lying on a sofa in the living-room. 'The tea,' he said laconically, 'is jet black and very cold indeed.'

'In that case,' said Tony, pressing the bell by the fireplace, 'we will have some fresh.'

Bryan, immediately aware of tension in the atmosphere, began to explain loyally that it was entirely his fault that they were late. Tony cut him short. 'Run upstairs like a good obedient author,' he said, 'and wash those pudgy little hands.'

Bryan, reflecting that it ill became the most dynamic director in the English theatre to be as crotchety as an aged spinster because someone was late for tea, said, 'All right,' cheerfully and went upstairs. When he came down again a few minutes later Ray, who had risen from the sofa and was stand-ing in front of the fire, came forward smilingly and flung his arms round him. 'Tony's just told me about the new ending for the play,' he said enthusiastically, 'and I'm genuinely thrilled with it. And if Lorraine isn't as delighted as I am I shall thrash her within about two inches of her artificial life! How long do you think it will take you to write it?'

Bryan felt a sharp stab of panic. 'I don't know,' he said. 'Probably not more than a few days once I get started.'

'You shall start tomorrow,' Ray said decisively. 'And what's more you shall stay here in peace and quiet until it's done. Tony and I have arranged it all. I'll concentrate this whole week on the first and second acts so that they're word-perfect and out of the way. Mrs Hartley will wait on you hand and foot. Tony will drive up with me tonight and come down again tomorrow afternoon to keep you company.'

'What about my typewriter?' said Bryan, aware of a vague resentment at this arbitrary rearranging of his life.

'I'll bring it down tomorrow,' said Tony, handing him a cup of tea. 'Or you can use mine – it works like a dream except for the Y, which is a little bent.'

'I think I'd rather have my own,' said Bryan a little doubtfully.

Ray laughed gaily. 'Nothing could be easier,' he said. 'You can give Tony a brisk little note to your landlady, spend the whole of tomorrow lying in the sun, relaxing your mind and contemplating your navel. Tony will arrive, typewriter and all, on the five-fifteen and you can start bashing away first thing on Tuesday morning. How's that?'

'Fine,' said Bryan, not quite certain in his mind whether it was fine or not. 'It's awfully nice of you to suggest it.'

'Nonsense,' said Ray. 'The house is here, Mrs Hartley is here; she does nothing but eat like a horse from the beginning of the week to the end. You can stay on in the room you're in now or move into mine, whichever you like. Perhaps mine would be better because the telephone is by the bed and you can call me whenever you want to.'

'Stay in your own room,' said Tony. 'That telephone cuts both ways. He can call you too and what's more he will if he suddenly feels the 'fluence' coming on – you won't get a wink of sleep.'

'You see,' said Ray, flinging out his arms in a gesture of suffering resignation, 'how this sardonic little son of a bitch tries to undermine me at every turn?'

Bryan intercepted a wink from Tony and smiled. 'I do,' he said.

(6)

BRYAN, after Ray and Tony had driven away in the car, returned to the living-room, poured himself a drink and sat down before the fire. The room, bereft of Ray and Tony's physical presence, felt stale and unco-operative and the silence was oppressive. A log crashed in the open fireplace and made him jump so violently that he spilled some of his whisky on to the brocaded arm of the sofa: he was dabbing it furtively with his handkerchief when Mrs Hartley came in to ask him at what time he wanted to be called in the morning. He said that he would like tea and toast at nine o'clock, upon which she said good-night politely and went out, shutting the door behind her. The silence closed in on him once more and he got up irritably and wandered about, regretting whole-heartedly his own weakness in giving way to Ray's no doubt well-meant suggestion that he should stay and work in the peace of the country. At the moment he felt an active distaste for the peace of the country and a nostalgic longing for the less peaceful but more familiar atmosphere of Ebury Street. The personality of the house, even when empty, was strong and obtrusive, and far from giving him a feeling of quiet relaxation, made him nervous and self-conscious. He took an early volume of the *Play Pictorial* from the shelves and returned with it to the sofa.

At all costs, he decided, he would think no more about the dreaded re-writing of the last act until he had had a good night's sleep, and if, as he suspected, it turned out that he couldn't do it satisfactorily even with Tony's help, they would just have to get on with it as it was or not do it at all. Slightly comforted by his own fatalistic defiance, he sipped his drink and turned the pages of the *Play Pictorial* and found they did little to dissipate his feeling of general futility about the Theatre and everything connected with it. Being a very early volume it contained photographs of actors and actresses long since dead, playing scenes in plays long since forgotten, sometimes by authors he had never even heard of. His attention was caught by the picture of a radiant young woman, full-bosomed and plump, lying in a hammock and smiling seductively at a slim young man in flannels and a straw hat. The letterpress beneath gave only the name of the characters they were playing, but Bryan, with a slight shudder, identified them, for he had seen them fairly recently. The slim young man was now a very old character actor who appeared from time to time in small supporting roles on the screen. The radiant young woman of thirty-five years ago was acting currently in a mediocre farce in which she played a fat comedy charwoman. He had seen her the week before last and thought she over-acted appallingly. He wondered bleakly whether or not, in her heyday, she had insisted on last acts being re-written for her and also if she had been able to coerce vital young producers into doing what she wanted them to do against their better judgement and whether or not she had had an Aberdeen terrier. Realising that the taboo subject was forcing its way ruthlessly into his mind, he slammed the book shut, turned out the lights and went up to bed. The next day it rained incessantly. He spent most of the morning elaborating the rough notes he had made with Tony the day before; in the afternoon he found a raincoat in a cupboard under the stairs and went for a walk. Tony arrived on the five-fifteen train bringing with him Bryan's typewriter as promised. He also brought with him the news that Lorraine was absolutely enchanted with the suggested changes for the last act and sent him her fondest love and a pot of caviar from Fortnum's. Bryan, warmed by this gesture, was about to telephone her immediately in a glow of gratitude but Tony stopped him.

'Write her a note tomorrow,' he said. 'Don't give way to

too much schoolboy enthusiasm. After all, it's you who are
doing her the favour, not the other way round, and it's only a
very small pot anyhow!'

The next three days were arduous. Bryan was called each
morning at seven-thirty and worked alone at his typewriter
until one. The afternoons were devoted to reading and discussing what he had written. Actually after the first plunge
the newly constructed last act took shape more swiftly and
more easily than he would have believed possible. Tony
contented himself with a few minor criticisms and suggestions
and by five o'clock on the Thursday afternoon the job was
done. After an early dinner that night they caught the eight-
thirty to London and took a taxi straight from Charing Cross
Station to Ray's flat. Bryan was in a mood of high exaltation.
An urgent and difficult task had been accomplished, and he
felt unutterably relieved and very pleased with himself. Tony,
vicariously sharing his satisfaction, was in high spirits.

'It's good,' he said with conviction as the taxi turned out of
the station yard into the Strand, 'I know it's good and I'm
pretty certain that Ray will think so too. The last bit at the
telephone is beautifully done, and if Lorraine Barrie doesn't
like it I have a very neat suggestion as to what she can do with
it.' Tony opened the door of Ray's flat with a latch-key and
Ray met them in the hall.

'Lorraine's here,' he whispered. 'I thought if Bryan was
going to read it, it would be better to get it all over in one fell
swoop.'

'I see,' said Tony, and Bryan was surprised at the tone of his
voice: it was sharp and almost angry. When they went into the
sitting-room Lorraine was standing in front of the mirror
over the fireplace and tidying her hair. She turned with a little
cry of welcome and seized Bryan's hands.

'I'm so excited,' she said. 'When Ray telephoned me and
said you'd finished it and were actually on the way up to
London I felt as though a great leaden weight had been lifted

from my mind.' She turned to Tony. 'Are you pleased with it? Is it really good?'

Tony turned away with a non-committal smile. 'Bryan's worked like a slave,' he said.

Lorraine slipped her arm through Bryan's and led him over to the drink table. 'You poor darling,' she said. 'Was it hell, torment and despair? I always think that to have to go back and re-do something you've already done must be one of the most ghastly things in the world. You don't hate me do you? I mean for feeling the way I did? I just knew when I was trying to learn it that it wasn't right somehow. I tried and tried but something was in the way. I could not get the words into my head and then suddenly I realised what it was ... I mean I felt absolutely that somehow or other she wouldn't do just that. I don't know why or how but it didn't ring true to me. *She* didn't ring true ... it was ... how can I put it? *Contrived!* That's the word! *Contrived!* How you must have cursed the day I was born!' – she laughed wistfully – 'Now you must have a drink quickly and read what you've done. I can't wait another minute. . . .'

Bryan looked appealingly to Tony, but he was talking in an undertone to Ray at the other side of the room. He felt suddenly panic-stricken. Lorraine mixed him a strong whisky-and-soda and shouted gaily to Ray and Tony. 'What are you two whispering about in that sinister way? This is the most thrilling moment. I can hardly bear it. I adore being read to anyway whatever it is. For God's sake let's all sit down. . . .'

(7)

Two weeks later Bryan drove through the empty Sunday streets to Euston Station. As he got out of the taxi and waited while a porter collected his two suitcases Marion Blake, wearing tweeds and an unsuitable hat, waved vivaciously to him and disappeared into the station. His heart sank, her smile was so assured, her wave of the hand so carefree and cheerful; obviously she was sublimely unaware that she was to receive her fortnight's notice after the opening performance on Monday night. No premonition of disaster marred her bright insouciance; she clearly had no suspicion that she had been the focal point of a nerve-shattering battle which had raged for three days and nights. The trouble had started during the first run-through in the set on Wednesday but Tony had foretold it many days before. 'Mark my words,' he had said, 'the infant Reinhardt will not stand for that vintage coquetry much longer. He never wanted her in the first place but Lorraine insisted on having her. Just you wait and see – one more coy gurgle, one more frisky exit through those French windows and ze storm she will break and ze land she will be laid waste and there will be a great wailing and gnashing of teeth.'

His forecast had proved to be dismally accurate. After the rehearsal on that fateful day Ray had called a conference in the bar behind the dress circle of the theatre. The conference consisted of Bryan and Tony and J. C. Roebuck, who had been summoned by telephone from his office. It started quietly enough by Ray announcing firmly that he had no intention of allowing the play to open in London with Marion Blake playing 'Stella'. 'It isn't that she's a bad actress,' he said with restrained fury. 'I can forgive a bad actress and occasionally coax her into being a good one. But this poor overpaid Repertory hack is worse than a bad actress, she's thoroughly and appallingly competent. There is no cheap technical trick that she doesn't know and use with cunning unscrupulousness. No prayers, no exhortations, no carefully phrased explanations will budge her inner conviction that she knows how to do it, and what is so macabre is that she's right, she does know how to do it, but she knows how to do it *wrong* – she has always known how to do it wrong. In this particular part she is sweet, tolerant, understanding and lethal.

She's a bloody murderess – she kills the character and the play stone dead with the first line she speaks.'

'I am not questioning your judgement for a moment,' interposed J.C. gently, 'In fact I agree with you, but I must, for all our sakes, deliver one word of warning.' Ray turned on him. 'I know what your warning is going to be – Lorraine loves her. Lorraine must have her in the theatre to wait on her hand and foot, to toady to her, to be a foil to her' – his voice rose – 'Of course Lorraine loves her. Any star would love Marion Blake, she's the megalomaniac's dream. She offers no competition, her clothes are catastrophic, she's a monumental bum-crawler and makes tea at matinées, but all that, J.C., is not enough for me. All I ask is a decent hard-working actress who can take direction and give the proper value to the play, and the woods are full of them. One glance through *Spotlight* and I could get you a dozen who could play this part perfectly, and here I am landed with this fifth-rate clacking soubrette just because Lorraine likes her.'

'The fact remains,' said J.C. imperturbably, 'that if you fire her there will be all hell to pay and God help anyone you engage in her place.'

'I want Carole Wylde,' shouted Ray. 'And what's more I intend to have her.'

'That,' said J.C., 'will put the lid on it.'

J. C. Roebuck, as usual, was perfectly right. It did.

On the following day Ray had sent for Carole Wylde, given her the part of 'Stella' and told her to learn it and stand by for a telephone call from Manchester during the week. This secret interview had taken place in J.C.'s office after morning rehearsal. Unfortunately, however, just as Ray and Carole Wylde were coming down in the lift they met Lorraine face-to-face on her way up to discuss some clause in her contract with J.C.: Lorraine, realising in a flash that conspiracy was in the air, had bowed icily to Carole Wylde, dug her fingers urgently into Ray's arm and swept him into the lift again and back into J.C.'s office, leaving Carole Wylde alone in the lobby apprehensively clutching the script and wondering if Lorraine's acknowledged dislike of her would prove strong enough to do her out of the job. Up in the office the storm broke and had raged and rumbled intermittently ever since. There had been tears, accusations, refusals to appear – all the routine posturings of an outraged leading lady whose dictatorship has been challenged and whose personal wishes have been ignored and thwarted.

Tony, sitting next to Bryan in a first-class compartment in the train to Manchester, gave his view of the existing situation with a certain gleeful cynicism. 'The whole thing,' he said with a giggle, 'is primarily biological and it began way back in the beginning of the world when the Almighty, for reasons best known to himself, arranged that ladies should be differently constructed physically from gentlemen. All temperamental scenes made by all temperamental female stars since the theatre was first invented have been based on that inescapable fact. It isn't of course their fault entirely. It is drummed into their fluffy little heads from infancy, through adolescence and on into adult life that they possess something unique and infinitely precious, something that every man they meet desires more than anything else. The dawning realisation that, in the theatrical profession at least, this comforting conviction is not always true flings them into paroxysms of fury and frustration. They hate the men who do want them and the men who don't and they hate each other profoundly and mercilessly. Actresses are fussed over and spoilt out of all proportion to their actual status in the Theatre. They receive cartloads of flowers on opening night, whereas the poor leading man or the author or the director consider themselves lucky if some fan gives them one carnation wrapped in cellophane. Male actors, poor swine, are never temperamental to the same extent as their female counterparts. They cannot afford to be. They can be morose, nervous, wretched, miscast and sometimes tearful but that is as far as it goes. They must not stamp or shriek or tear their clothes off and jump on them or refuse to appear because they are denied their own way over some trifle – oh dear no. They must press on gallantly, standing aside for the leading lady, presenting her graciously to the audience; they must dress in a less comfortable dressing-room, give up cheerfully many privileges their talent may have earned them, all to feed the already overweening vanity of some gifted, hysterical, domineering harridan whose every thought and feeling is motivated by sex-consciousness, treachery and illusion.'

'You make it fairly obvious that you don't care for women,' said Bryan rather tartly.

'Don't be silly, dear,' replied Tony. 'I adore women but not in what is known as "that way". Some of my greatest friends are women and they're a damn sight more loyal and sweet to me than they are to each other. Above all I love great big diamond-studded glamour stars, they fascinate me; I love watching them and foreseeing how they will react. I love all their little tricks and carry-ons; their unscrupulousness, their inflexible determination, their courage, their magnificent dishonesty with themselves and everyone else. I love and pity their eternal gullibility and their tragic, silly loneliness. Take our little treasure Lorraine Barrie. There you have a perfect, glittering example of a bona fide ripsnorting megalomania. She could only exist in the theatre or the film studios. No other career, not even that of a brilliantly successful courtesan could ever provide enough food for her ravening ego. Her basic power lies in her talent, her superb natural gift for acting. I don't suppose she has ever acted really badly in her life. I don't believe she could if she tried. That is her reality; the only reality she herself or anyone who knows her can be sure of. That is the foundation upon which the whole structure of her charm and personality rests and, believe you me, it's rock solid. Apart from it she has nothing that thousands of other women don't possess in richer measure. Her figure and looks are little more than attractively adequate. She is virtually illiterate; her conversation is adroit and empty and although she has immense reserves of cunning and shrewdness she is not particularly intelligent. Whatever genuine emotional equipment she originally started with has long since withered and atrophied in the consuming flame of her vanity. Her whole life is passed in a sort of hermetically-sealed projection-room watching her own "rushes". She loves nobody and nobody loves her. Occasionally they think they do for a little, occasionally she may think she does, but there's no truth in it. To meet she can be alluring, charming, very grand, utterly simple, kind, cruel, a good sort or a fiend – it all depends on what performance she is putting on for herself at the moment. What really goes on, what is really happening deep down inside, no one will ever know – least of all herself. Then, my boy, you pay your money at the Box Office and go in and watch her on a matinée day with a dull audience, in a bad play with the fortnight's notice up on the board and the house half full, and suddenly you are aware that you are in the presence of something very great indeed – something abstract that is beyond definition and beyond praise. Quality – star quality plus. It is there as strongly in comedy as in tragedy, magical and unmistakable, and the hair will rise on your addled little head, chills will swirl up and down your spine and you will solemnly bless the day that you were born. All this, of course, only applies if you happen to love the Theatre, and I suspect that you might learn to if you stick around a bit.' Tony paused. 'And it's no use,' he added, 'accusing me in that prim, disapproving voice, of not liking women because it just doesn't make sense. Nobody can love the Theatre without liking women. They are the most fascinating, unpredictable and exciting part of it.' He rose to his feet. 'Let's go and have some railway lunch.'

In the restaurant car, Lorraine was sitting at a small table

for two with her maid, Nora. She bowed coldly to Bryan as he
passed and flashed Tony a look of unmistakable loathing.
They moved on up the car and found two vacant places at a
table with Gerald Wentworth and Marion Blake. Bryan, in an
agony of embarrassment, squeezed Tony's arm protestingly
but it was too late. Marion welcomed them effusively and they
were forced to sit down. She was in high spirits and talked
incessantly; a spate of theatrical reminiscences gushed from
her, anecdotes of her early years in touring companies, play
titles, actors' names, trivial little scandals, vivacious
descriptions of bad 'digs' and dead and gone landladies.
Gerald Wentworth occasionally attempted a modest contribution of his own but was inexorably mown down. Bryan
and Tony lunched in anxious silence, dreading any reference
to the imminent dress rehearsal and opening night. Fortunately, Marion was so carried away by her volubility as a
raconteuse that *Stones in Heaven* was never mentioned at all
until they had drunk some strangely metallic coffee and the
usual squabble about the bill had been settled. Then she
announced in a hissing whisper that she had a terrible feeling
that poor darling Lorraine was either not well or very worried
about something. Tony quickly rose to his feet, mumbled
something about Lorraine probably suffering from pre-
production nerves, grabbed Bryan by the elbow and piloted
him back to their compartment. Once back in it with the
sliding door closed he flung himself down on the seat and
groaned. 'That,' he murmured with his eyes closed, 'was sheer
undiluted Hell. The poor beast hasn't got a clue. She's as
merry as a cartload of grigs, whatever they may be. The blow
will fall on Monday night, if not before, and she will be
caught completely unawares. The gutters will run with blood
and it will be terrible. Terrible.' He opened his eyes and
smiled wanly. 'Before that dreadful little meal I felt sorry for
her, pity and compassion were twanging at my old heart-
strings; but now – oh baby – now, after that death-dealing

monologue, that vomit-making welter of stale memories, that
soul-destroying archness, that hideous, protracted torture of
boredom, I'm glad she's going to get the sack. See? Glad,
glad, glad! And what is more I hope she suffers and remains
out of work and in dire poverty for seventeen and a half
years.' He flung himself full-length on the seat and groaned
again. Bryan threw *The New Statesman* at him and the train
rattled on.

They arrived at London Road, Manchester, at four-twenty-
five. Ray was waiting on the platform with some press reporters and photographers. He was holding, rather self-
consciously, a large bunch of red roses. He stepped forward
as Lorraine descended from the train and presented the roses
to her while the cameras clicked. She received them with a
frigid bow, handed them immediately to her maid, and swept
off up the platform without saying a word. For a moment Ray
looked nonplussed and a gleam of livid anger shone in his
eye, then he recovered himself completely, chattered and
laughed with the reporters, introduced Bryan to them and
posed casually arm-in-arm with him while the cameras clicked
and the light bulbs flashed. In the car he dropped his gay
insouciance and swore articulately all the way to the Midland
Hotel. A little while later, in his suite, he and Bryan and Tony
had tea and discussed the situation at some length. Ray was
obviously nervy and apprehensive and quite incapable of
sitting down for two minutes at a time. He strode up and
down the room with a cup of tea in one hand and a bridge roll
with watercress hanging out of it in the other. 'This is going
to be murder,' he said savagely. 'She's going to make our lives
a misery, bitch the dress rehearsal and have the whole Company in a state of jitters.'

'Don't let her,' said Tony. 'You're stronger than she is.
Take the offensive; she hasn't got a leg to stand on really. You
have a perfect right to engage or fire anyone you like.'

'Of course I have,' snapped Ray. 'I know that as well as you do. She knows it too. She's not going to compromise herself and commit herself by having a public row with me over Marion Blake. She's far too shrewd for that – she'll think up something else.'

'What will she do?' enquired Bryan rashly. Ray turned on him so violently that the teacup shot from its saucer and crashed into the fireplace.

'Listen, my poor innocent dreamer, the time has come for you to stop gurgling idiotic questions at me like Alice in Wonderland and face the facts of life. A woman of Lorraine's temperament and position with a run of the play contract can inflict torture on her director, her fellow actors, the management and the play that would make Torquemada sob with envy. Not possessing the gift of clairvoyance, being pitifully unversed in the arts of sorcery, black magic, spirit rapping, table turning, thought-reading, telepathy and crystal gazing and having inadvertently mislaid my Ouija board I am unable to tell you *what* she will do or *how* and *when* she will do it. All I can tell you is that you had better hold on to your hat, throw away your cigarette, tighten your safety-belt and prepare for a crash landing!'

'It's no use flying at poor Bryan,' said Tony. 'He didn't engage Marion Blake and you did and if you hadn't been so besotted over Lorraine Barrie and allowed her to get round you, you would have thrown Blake out on her ear after the first reading. You can rant and roar as much as you like about not having the gift of clairvoyance, but it seems to me that as far as this situation is concerned you haven't even used common sense.'

'Christ!' said Ray. 'Whose side are you on?'

'Have some more tea and calm down.' Tony smiled equably. 'You can have my cup as yours is in the fireplace.'

Ray groaned with rage and sank on to the sofa, burying his head in his hands.

'I don't want any bloody tea.'

'Come, come, dear,' said Tony taking up the teapot. 'You're getting a big boy now.'

Bryan got up from his chair by the fireplace. 'I think I'll go and have a bath and change before the dress rehearsal,' he said. 'I shall have time, shan't I, Tony?'

'As things are going now,' replied Tony, handing Ray his cup of tea, 'I should think you'd have ample time for a mastoid operation and a permanent wave.'

(8)

THE dress rehearsal, which was timed to begin at seven-thirty, actually began at ten-forty-five. The reason for the delay was a message from Lorraine Barrie that was telephoned through to the theatre at six-thirty when most of the cast were already dressed and made up. The message stated that Miss Barrie was dreadfully sorry but she was in bed with incipient laryngitis, that a doctor was in attendance and had forbidden her to speak at all for three hours and even after that only in a whisper. She would, however, make a supreme effort and be ready to go on at ten o'clock if Mr Malcolm would be kind enough to excuse her from either dressing or making up. On receipt of this, Ray gritted his teeth, dismissed the Company with the exception of the understudies and decided to concentrate on the relighting of certain scenes. Tony and Bryan sat in the back row of the stalls and watched. Bryan was genuinely worried at first about the laryngitis, but Tony soothed him.

'Keep calm, my poor duck,' he said. 'If Lorraine Barrie has laryngitis, I have curvature of the spine. I'd be willing to bet a thousand pounds to sixpence that she is at this moment sitting up in bed having a delicious little something on a tray. She is perfectly aware that from eleven o'clock onwards the stage staff work on double time. She will be ready to start just before that breathless moment; she will perform veree veree slowly for the first hour or so, then she will suddenly fling away her truss and give a full-throated magnificent performance of the second and third acts. The Company will be overwhelmed by her "Old Trouper" gallantry, applaud her to the echo and she will faint just before the final curtain and have to be carried to her dressing-room. All this will come true – it is written in the sand.'

In due course Lorraine arrived at the theatre and walked on to the stage at ten minutes past ten. Ray had finished his lighting and was sitting silently in the third row smoking. Lorraine, clutching her mink coat round her, looked deathly pale and ineffably weary. 'I am very sorry, Ray,' she said in a hoarse whisper. 'But I don't think I can go through with it.'

Ray got up and walked down to the orchestra rail.

'Why not?' he asked briefly.

'You know perfectly well why not' – her voice increased a little in volume – 'I presume that you got my message?'

'Yes,' said Ray, 'I got your message.'

'Well then. . . .'

There was silence for a moment while Ray looked at her fixedly. She gave a painful little cough.

'I think you'd better come to my dressing-room,' she said, still in a hoarse whisper, but with a note of anger underlying it. 'I want to talk to you.'

'What about?' Ray's voice rang out in the empty theatre with the sharpness of a pistol shot.

Lorraine jumped perceptibly at his tone and took a step back. She opened her mouth to speak, then thought better of it, bit her lip and opened her eyes wide instead. They filled with tears. 'Nothing can be gained by continuing this unpleasant little scene,' she said with dignity. 'You'll find me in my dressing-room if you want me.' She turned to go but Ray's voice stopped her.

'I don't want to find you in your dressing-room,' he said.

'I want to find you on the stage in exactly half an hour from now, dressed and made up for Act One. Is that clear?'

'Quite clear,' said Lorraine. 'Thank you for your courtesy.'

She walked swiftly off the stage. Ray clapped his hands loudly. 'Harry,' he shouted. 'Call the half an hour.'

Without looking at Bryan and Tony he marched up the aisle in the direction of one of the exit doors. Tony was up like a flash. 'Stay where you are,' he hissed urgently to Bryan. 'That was a brief but famous victory. From now on he's going to need help.'

Bryan gloomily lit a cigarette and watched them both disappear into the lobby.

At ten-forty-five the curtain rose on Act One. A handful of people had appeared in the auditorium. The resident house manager and his wife and a large girl in a pink beret, presumably their daughter; the four walking understudies, who spent their time before the curtain rose eating sandwiches from a paper bag; Madame Nadia, a Russian Jewess who had made Lorraine's dresses, with her two assistants, and the actor who played the chauffeur in Act Three, who was made up and concentrating on the *Sunday Times* crossword.

Tony and Ray had returned five minutes before the rehearsal began and were sitting together in the front row of the dress circle. Bryan remained alone in the tenth row of the stalls, a prey to bitter melancholy.

Tony's prediction that Lorraine would play the first act slowly proved to be painfully accurate. Not only did she play it slowly but almost entirely inaudibly, in fact it would be an exaggeration to say that she played it at all. She merely walked about like an automaton and made no effort whatsoever. This naturally paralysed the action and reduced the rest of the cast to a uniform flatness with the notable exception of Marion Blake, whose professional vivacity was nothing short of terrifying.

When the curtain fell it rose again immediately and the cast stood about in various attitudes of despondency, waiting for Ray to make his way from the dress circle and give them their notes. Lorraine waited patiently with the others. Ray strode on to the stage, gave them their notes briskly and told them to get ready for the second act. He neither spoke to Lorraine nor even looked at her. She went off with the others and he, after a short consultation with the stage manager, returned to his seat in the dress circle. Tony popped his head over the rail and beckoned Bryan to come up and join them. Bryan stumbled up the dark staircase feeling utterly miserable and playing with a half-formulated decision to go back to the hotel, pack his bag and catch the midnight train back to London. To his surprise he found that Ray and Tony were quite cheerful and drinking neat whisky from a large silver flask. They offered him a swig which he accepted eagerly.

'So far so good,' said Ray complacently.

'Good!' Bryan looked at him in astonishment. 'I thought it was awful.'

'From your point of view of course it was awful,' said Ray, patting his knee reassuringly. 'But as far as mechanics go it was perfectly satisfactory and that's all I'm worried about tonight. If we can get through the whole play once without any waits or hitches we're all right for tomorrow.'

'But what about Lorraine?'

'That remains to be seen,' replied Ray. 'She won't walk through like she's doing tonight with an audience, you know. . . .'

Bryan shook his head glumly. 'I don't think she'll open at all,' he said.

At that moment the stage manager appeared at the side of the circle and groped his way along the front row towards them; the expression on his face was grim.

'Mr Malcolm.'

Ray turned swiftly. 'What's the matter, Harry?'

'Miss Barrie wants to speak to you in her dressing-room.'

'Here we go,' said Tony. 'Up the Barricades.'

'Shut up, Tony,' said Ray sharply. He thought for a moment. 'Tell Miss Barrie that I will come to her dressing-room at the end of rehearsal.'

'Miss Barrie wants to see you now, otherwise she says she won't go on for the second act.'

'I see,' said Ray. 'An ultimatum.'

'She's in a bit of a state, sir,' said Harry. 'Trembling like a leaf.' Tony took a swig at the flask. 'I'll bet the hell she is.'

'I think, sir,' said Harry tentatively, 'you'd better go and see her and get it over with. It's waste of time going on as we are – the whole Company's upset and nobody knows where they're at!'

'Harry's right,' said Tony. 'The time has come for a show-down. Grasp the nettle danger and have a bash.'

'I'll be God-damned if I'll be dictated to,' said Ray through clenched teeth.

Tony sighed. 'That comes under the heading of naughty pride and this is no moment for personal considerations. We've got to open tomorrow night. So far you've been in the right but if you refuse to see her when she asks you to you'll be putting yourself in the wrong.'

'All right,' said Ray decisively. 'We'll all three go. Come on, Bryan.'

'Include me out,' said Tony. 'She hates me like poison anyway. I'll stay with my thoughts. The thoughts of Youth are long, long thoughts and there's still a little liquor left in the flask.'

'Is it really necessary for me to come?' asked Bryan apprehensively.

'Certainly,' said Ray. 'You're the author, it's perfectly in order for you to be there. After all, the fate of your opus is hanging in the balance, also I like a witness on these sort of occasions. Come on. . . .' He grabbed Bryan by the arm and started off with him along the front row.

'Good luck, girls,' shouted Tony after them. 'The honour of St Monica's is at stake.'

Ray knocked on Lorraine's dressing-room door. After a slight pause, Nellie, her dresser, opened it and ushered them in. Lorraine was sitting at the dressing-table staring at herself in the glass; she was wearing a man's dressing-gown of dark blue foulard with white polka dots. Bryan immediately remembered the painting over the mantelpiece in her house when he had gone to tea with her and met her for the first time. She turned and indicated the chaise-longue with a weary gesture. They sat down on it in silence.

'Wait outside, Nellie, dear,' she said huskily. Nellie went out, heavy with doom, and closed the door after her. Lorraine offered them a cigarette-box with remote politeness. 'I'm afraid I haven't got a light.'

'I have,' said Ray. She took one herself and Ray produced a small gold lighter and lit hers and his own. Bryan noticed that his hand was trembling.

'Now then,' Lorraine spoke as though the effort were draining her to the dregs. 'I asked you to come to see me because I just can't go on like this any longer. I can't work under these conditions; this atmosphere of mistrust and suspicion and hatred is breaking me completely. I want you to be as honest with me as I intend to be with you. Let's put our cards on the table and try – for the sake of the Company and Bryan's play – to find a way out.'

'Willingly,' said Ray. 'How is your laryngitis?' There was no cynicism in his tone, no trace of irony; he merely asked the question plainly and simply.

Lorraine looked at him long enough for her eyes to brim over with tears, then she turned her head away.

'I haven't got laryngitis,' she said. 'I only said I had because I had to think of something to explain why I couldn't rehearse. What I am suffering from is far worse and far more dangerous than laryngitis. I don't think you quite understand, Ray, what the effort of creating a new part means to someone like me. After all, you are still – from the point of view of professional experience – fairly young in the Theatre. With me it's different. It has been the be-all and end-all of my life ever since I was a small child. I need help and encouragement and understanding every step of the way. I can't concentrate, I can't – how shall I put it? – come to life unless I am happy and relaxed and know that my director is on my side, rooting for me, willing me to succeed. God knows it isn't hard work I mind; I welcome it, I adore it, I'll work until I drop. The play comes first, that is my creed. It always has been and I have never deviated from it for one instant. But this situation is new to me, something I have never experienced before – this deadly remoteness, this strange, twisted cruelty. Don't think I'm blaming you entirely, Ray, I know you were in the War and war can do terrible things to people's minds. But I'm appealing to you now from my heart; this is a cry for help because I'm lost, utterly lost and I don't know where to turn. . . .' Her voice broke and she gave up all pretence of controlling her tears and, burying her head in her hands, she sobbed helplessly.

Ray rose to his feet, stubbed out his cigarette in an ash-tray and put his arm round her shoulder.

'Snap out of it,' he said. 'There's a good girl.'

Lorraine pushed his arm away, firmly and without petulance. 'I don't want to be babied,' she said in a muffled voice. 'You still don't understand. You merely think that I'm making a scene.'

'Well, you are really, aren't you?' said Ray with an attempt at lightness.

Lorraine dabbed at her streaming eyes with a face towel and turned on him. 'You're a very clever man, Ray,' she said bitterly. 'Very clever and very talented but you have no heart, my dear. And you'll achieve nothing real and lasting in the theatre without it.'

'Are you accusing me of lack of consideration to you as a director?'

Bryan detected an undertone of exasperation in Ray's voice.

Lorraine smiled wanly and shook her head. 'Not as a director,' she said. 'I have found working with you extremely interesting, you have great talent and a brilliant mind, but...' She gave a little frown as though the words she needed were eluding her. 'You'll probably think I'm affected and tiresome when I say that I want more than brilliance and talent. More, and yet less at the same time. I know I'm expressing myself badly and that you are probably laughing at me inside, but I must say what I feel however incoherent and foolish it sounds; I must say honestly what is in my heart even though you and your Tony what's-his-name do discuss me and mock at me behind my back.' Ray made an attempt to protest but she lifted her hand and silenced him. 'Please let me go on. I don't want this to be a quarrel or even an argument, I merely want to state my case. I'll be only too pleased to listen to whatever you have to say afterwards.'

Ray heaved a sigh of resignation. 'Very well,' he said, 'state away.' Bryan, acutely embarrassed, bit his underlip. That 'state away' was a mistake. Lorraine, however, gave no indication that she had noticed it.

'My case is this,' she said simply. 'I am lonely and frightened and completely bewildered. I don't know what I have *done*! Before rehearsals and during the first two weeks we were close, you and I. We were growing day by day to like each other and respect each other more, then suddenly, without warning, everything changed. I put out my hand trustingly as a comrade for your help and support when the path was difficult and you were no longer there, you had withdrawn. I'd watch you and Tony – and Bryan too...' She paused for an instant and looked at Bryan reproachfully, 'come into the theatre and go out of the theatre, I sometimes heard you laughing together in the stalls – I know how tremendously amusing Tony can be – but I was never included in the jokes. I am sure I was the butt of many of them. I was shut out, left stumbling along in the dark alone. I tried to reason with myself, to tell myself that it was imagination and silliness but it wasn't and I knew it wasn't; my instincts never lie to me and I am too honest with myself not to face the truth at all times however unpleasant it may be. Why did you suddenly change towards me, Ray? Was it my fault? What did I do, what did I say? It couldn't have been because I was slow and sometimes stupid at rehearsals, even you are theatrically experienced enough to know about that. Was I uncooperative? Did I offend you in any way? If I did I swear it was unintentional – for God's sake tell me and let's make an end of it.'

Tears sprang to her eyes again but she dashed them away with the back of her hand and rose to her feet.

'Don't you understand?' – her voice took on a stronger, deeper note. – 'Are you both so blind and lacking in perception that you don't realise one thing and that is that I *love this play*! I have lived with it for weeks, for months really, ever since I first read it. It has been part of me night and day, waking and sleeping, and now, because of something strange, something sinister that is beyond my comprehension, I have lost my way to it, I can't do it – I can't – I can't – I can't!'

She sank down again sobbing on to the stool in front of her dressing-table and once more buried her face in her hands. Ray shot Bryan a quizzical look and shrugged his shoulders. Bryan, feeling that somebody must do something, got up and went to her. 'Don't cry like that, Lorraine,' he said. 'Please don't cry. You're wonderful in the part, far, far more wonderful than I ever hoped anyone could ever be. Please don't be upset.'

Lorraine seized his hand and pressed her wet face against it.

'Thank you, Bryan,' she said brokenly. 'Thank you at least for understanding a little.'

Bryan looked at Ray in the mirror. He was taking another cigarette from his case and lighting it.

'Is that all?' Bryan's blood congealed at the coldness of Ray's voice. He felt a tremor go through Lorraine. She lifted her head and looked Ray in the eye.

'Yes,' she said. 'That's all.'

'Are you sure that you've been quite honest in this . . . this "case" you've presented?'

Lorraine met his gaze unwaveringly. 'Absolutely honest,' she sighed. 'But I realise already, only too clearly, that you haven't believed me.'

'Dead right,' said Ray briskly. 'Not a bloody word.'

'I see.' Lorraine rose with dignity. 'Then there is nothing more to be said.'

'On the contrary.' Ray got up and went towards her. She quailed a little and sat down again. 'There is a great deal more to be said. . . .'

'For God's sake, Ray,' cried Bryan, 'let's not go on about any of it any more and finish the rehearsal.'

'Shut up,' said Ray with some ferocity, then he turned again to Lorraine. 'You graciously said a little while ago that you would be only too pleased to listen to whatever I had to say afterwards. In that, as in everything else you have said, you were inaccurate. You will not be at all pleased to listen to what I have to say and it's this. Never in all my limited experience of the theatre have I seen such an inept, soggy and insincere performance as that you have just given in this dressing-room. Every gesture and every intonation was ham and false as hell. And, if I may say so, your improvised script was lousy. You are *not* lonely, or lost or bewildered. You are *not* honest with yourself or with anybody else, you never have been and you never will be. You don't give a good God-damn whether I've changed towards you or not. All you're upset about is that you have been thwarted, denied your own way over a comparative triviality and that is more than your overblown ego can stand. You sent for me to see you because, having deliberately wrecked the rehearsal, sent a phony message about mythical laryngitis, mumbled through the first act, thereby throwing the whole Company for six and utterly destroying Bryan's play which you assert you love so much – having achieved all this unnecessary tension and chaos, your well-trained professional instincts probably warned you that you were going too far, so you sent for me in order to declare a temporary truce. You longed for a nice satisfying scene ending up with all of us in tears and me soothing you and comforting you and telling you you were the most glorious, God-given genius the Theatre has ever known. Then we should have billed and cooed our way through the rest of the rehearsal – which incidentally is just as important for you as for the rest of the cast – and once firmly established on a sickening kiss-and-be-friends basis you would immediately have set to work again insidiously to win back the point that you lost at the outset, and that point is that Marion Blake should continue playing "Stella", for which she is too old and entirely unsuited, and you've wanted her in the cast from the first for one reason only, because she is a good foil to you and is shrewd enough to allow herself to be your off-stage toady and bottle-washer!'

'How dare you!' Lorraine's voice was shrill and she was shaking with fury. 'How dare you speak to me like that. Get out of my room.' She rose impressively but Ray pushed her down again on to the stool; she made an attempt to strike his hand away but missed. He towered over her threateningly and Bryan noticed a vein throbbing in his forehead.

'Keep quiet!' he shouted violently. 'I haven't finished. . . .'

'Get out! Get out! Get out!' Lorraine screamed and in a frenzy of rage jumped up and smacked his face so hard that he staggered back and fell on to the chaise-longue. Bryan made a movement to intervene, but she pushed him back and advanced until she was standing over Ray with blazing eyes.

'I'll teach you to insult me in my own dressing-room, you tawdry fifth-rate little amateur' – she spat the words venomously into his face. – 'The most brilliant, dynamic new director my foot. Do you think I haven't met your sort before, camping in and out of the theatre with your giggling boy friends! Who the hell gave you the right to throw your weight about and attempt to tell experienced actors what to do and what not to do? Get out of this room before I have you thrown out. Go and peddle your insipid artsy-craftsy theories to some cheap summer repertory theatre where they'll be properly appreciated. Go and do *Uncle Vanya* in drapes at New Brighton. Go and breathe new life into Shakespeare at the Cotswold Festival of Dramatic Art, but get out of my sight!'

At this moment a diversion was caused by the door opening violently to admit Marion Blake, who bounced into the room, attired in an Alice-blue satin wrapper with some cheesecloth swathed round her head and carrying a tortoiseshell hairbrush. With a piercing cry she flung herself between Ray and Lorraine. 'Don't, don't, don't,' she wailed dramatically. 'The whole theatre can hear you and I love you both!' She flung her arms round Lorraine, who pushed her away. Ray, seething with rage, rose to his feet.

'That, Marion,' he said icily, 'is entirely irrelevant. You are fired anyway!' With that he strode out of the room, slamming the door after him.

An hour or so later Bryan walked along the grey, wet, cobbled street to the hotel. Immediately following the scene in the dressing-room Ray had dismissed the rehearsal and disappeared with Tony. Bryan, having extricated himself from the hysteria raging in Lorraine's room, had been buttonholed and questioned by various members of the Company.

Gerald Wentworth had given him two large gins in a tooth-glass and he now felt dizzy in the head and utterly wretched. He walked, aching with nerve strain and weariness, through the deserted lobby of the Midland, got into the lift, exchanged mechanical 'good-nights' with the liftman who had one arm, staggered along the long dreary corridor, let himself into his room and fell on to the bed in tears.

(9)

At nine o'clock the next morning Bryan was awakened by the usual saturnalia of breakfast trolleys bumping and rattling along the corridor. For a brief moment he lay staring at the ceiling and trying sleepily to account for the leaden feeling of depression that was weighing on his spirit. He had been dreaming deeply and his mind was confused. Then, with sudden clarity the memory of the night before came back to him and, with a groan, he staggered into the bathroom, sponged his face with cold water and brushed his teeth. He went back into the bedroom and drew aside the curtains; the day was grey and a steady rain was falling. He watched, abstractedly, an elderly man in a mackintosh running through the puddles after a tram, but the tram quickened its speed and the man had to give up and return to the pavement. Bryan returned to bed. This was the day, the great day he had been living for, the first important stepping-stone of his career. Tonight people from all over this grey city and the suburbs beyond would be getting into trams and buses and private cars to come to the theatre to see Lorraine Barrie in *Stones in Heaven* by Bryan Snow. What they would actually see would probably be a notice pinned into the Box Office stating that owing to the sudden indisposition of Miss Lorraine Barrie there would be no performance. A day or two later the papers would announce that the play had been indefinitely postponed. The story would eventually get out that there had been quarrels and scenes and disunity but by that time nobody would care. Nobody beyond the actual people concerned. Bryan, with tears of self-pity pricking his eyelids, reached for the telephone and ordered, in a hollow voice devoid of emotion, China tea for one and rolls and marmalade.

An hour or so later when he was lying in the bath, trying in his mind to compose explanatory letters to his mother and sister, Tony came in cheerfully and sat down on the lavatory seat.

'Your door was not locked, dear,' he said. 'Which only goes to prove that you are an incurable optimist and open your arms wide to life. It also shows a refreshing ignorance of L.M.S. hotels. Why, you poor, foolish, heedless creature, *anything* might happen to you with all these lusty cotton-manufacturers pounding up and down the corridors. I really don't know whether to slap you or kiss you.'

'Please don't do either at the moment,' said Bryan, sponging his head violently. 'I'm feeling bloody miserable.'

'I know.' Tony lit a cigarette and flipped the match into the bath. 'Lorraine won't appear; the play won't open; we shall all go back to London defeated and humiliated. All is lost, there is no hope anywhere. . . . Isn't that what your poor storm-tossed mind is telling you?'

'Yes, it is,' said Bryan gloomily. 'And it's probably right at that.'

'Rot,' said Tony. 'I am your Fairy Godmother and all I have to do is wave my wand, which up to now I have been unable to locate owing to the cold weather, and all will be well.'

'What are you talking about?'

'I won't keep you on those well-known tenterhooks any longer.' Tony grinned benignly. 'J. C. Roebuck has arrived. He came up on the midnight. He and Ray have been having breakfast together and they are now closeted with La Belle.'

'Do you really think there's any chance of her appearing? After last night?'

'Elemental, my darling little Watson.' Tony sprang up and kissed him on the forehead. 'There never has been the slightest question of her not appearing. I could have told you that last night.'

'Well, it's a pity you didn't,' said Bryan, getting out of the bath and reaching for the towel.

'I couldn't. Really I couldn't.' There was genuine contrition in Tony's voice. 'I had a terrible time with the Maestro and it lasted for hours. Then when I'd finally got him to bed and stoked him up with Seconal, it was too late.'

'What makes you so sure, anyway?'

'No actress of her position and reputation could afford not to appear just because she'd had a row with her director. It would be breach of contract to start with. Also, that sort of thing just doesn't happen. If she had stuck to her illness story she might have worked it, but she'd have had to produce a doctor's certificate. But believe me, she's never had any intention of not appearing. All she wanted was to establish a nice cosy atmosphere of chaos, make everyone uncertain and wretched, get her own way over Marion Blake, and then bounce on to the stage as though nothing had happened.'

'If that's true,' said Bryan, stamping into the bedroom, 'she's a tiresome bitch, and deserves a bloody good hiding.'

'For God's sake pull yourself together, old man,' said Tony. 'You can't talk like that about a woman.'

'All right,' said Bryan, throwing a shoe-tree at him. 'You win.'

At five-past seven that evening Ray, Tony and Bryan took their places in the box nearest to the stage; a small passage at the back of it led to the pass door. The theatre orchestra was playing brassily a selection from *Glamorous Nights*. The large auditorium was already nearly full. The day had passed without incident beyond the fact that J. C. Roebuck had insisted upon Lorraine and Ray declaring a formal armistice. In the afternoon, after an uneasy lunch in the restaurant, Ray had returned to bed and Tony had taken Bryan firmly to the pictures, in order, he said, to calm his nerves. They saw a newsreel which showed several dead bodies being taken from a train wreck, some violent army manœuvres in the United States exploiting a new flame-thrower, a famous boxer being carried from the ring streaming with blood and an admiral's wife launching a new destroyer in the pouring rain. Then came an admonitory 'short' issued by the Ministry of Health which portrayed, in revolting detail, the inevitability of food-poisoning. After this there was a trailer of the next week's attraction which, peppered with alliterative adjectives, showed a man being shot in the stomach, a mother weeping over the body of her dead baby, and a plane crashing into a stormy sea. After this came an exquisitely acted but rather tedious picture about a psychiatrist who committed suicide. Tony had slipped his arm through Bryan's as they stepped out of the cinema into the drizzle.

'Nothing,' he said, 'can hurt us now.'

They had just had time to get back to the hotel, change and have a sandwich and a drink in Ray's suite, and here they were. Bryan shot a quick glance at Ray who was absently turning the pages of the programme. He seemed perfectly calm and, if anything, a little bored. He had made no reference whatever to last night's scene in the dressing-room either during lunch or while they were having drinks before the show. In fact he had not mentioned Lorraine Barrie or the play at all. Bryan wondered anxiously what he was really thinking, whether he was expecting success or failure, whether he minded one way or the other. Tony was peering over the edge of the box at the audience.

'You will be interested to know,' he said to Bryan, 'that Mrs J. C. Roebuck has elected to wear silver lamé with a large red rose tucked into that fascinating hollow between her bosoms. The whole idea was a grave mistake!'

At this moment the overture came to an end and the house lights went down. Ray patted Bryan's knee kindly.

'Here we go,' he said.

After a few minutes, when Lorraine had made her entrance, been duly applauded and embarked on her first scene with Gerald Wentworth, Bryan's nervousness began to ebb away. She was obviously in complete control and playing with consummate charm and authority. She looked younger and more attractive than he had ever seen her look before; every gesture, every movement she made, was exquisitely graceful and exquisitely right. For the quarter of an hour that the first scene lasted Bryan was spellbound, and when she made her exit and the whole audience applauded, he closed his eyes with a feeling of infinite relief. Tony pressed a cigarette into his hand.

'Don't go to sleep yet, dear,' he said. 'It gets better later on.'

Marion Blake made her first vivacious entrance through the french windows, and Ray groaned audibly. At the end of the first act the applause was good. The three of them went quickly to the office where the house manager, an amiable little man with a scarlet face, was waiting for them.

'So far, so good,' he said, effusively. 'Now, what shall it be? Scotch, gin, sherry or tea?'

'All four,' said Tony.

The manager laughed delightedly. 'Mr Roebuck is coming up in the next interval,' he said, proudly. 'We're old friends, you know. We were together at the Royal years and years ago before it was a cinema, long before your day, Mr Malcolm. But old J.C.! What a man! He hasn't changed a bit!' He poured the drinks and handed them round. Bryan sat on the edge of the desk and felt himself getting nervous again. He wished he was back in the box. At last the second act bell went. The house manager, still talking volubly, ushered them out.

During the second act there was less tension in the box. Ray relaxed and whispered comments to Tony, who made notes on a pad with a pencil with a small electric bulb on the end of it. Bryan sat in the corner of the box nearest to the stage and concentrated on the performance. There were no technical hitches, except at one point during a scene between Marion Blake and Lorraine when the light brackets over the fireplace began to flicker in and out distractingly. Ray writhed with irritation and murmured, 'Sweet God!'

Tony giggled, and said in a hoarse whisper, 'Don't worry, it's only the head electrician giving Marion Blake her notice in Morse!'

At the end of the act Bryan, feeling unequal to facing further conviviality in the manager's office, went back-stage and sat for a while in Gerald Wentworth's dressing-room. Gerald Wentworth had taken off his coat and was sitting at his dressing-table having a cup of tea.

'They seem to be liking it,' he said, 'but of course they're missing all the finer points. That bit, for instance, when I'm waiting for the telephone to ring and playing with the paper knife – went for nothing! In London, you see – they'll eat it up!'

'You're giving a wonderful performance,' said Bryan gratefully. 'So sure and so steady.'

'That's my best act,' Gerald Wentworth sighed. 'The whole part goes to pieces in the last act. Not that it's your fault,' he added hurriedly. 'I know that Lorraine and Ray bullied you into re-writing the end of the play, but if you want my candid opinion, it was better as it was. Of course I see Lorraine's point. If we'd played the original version she'd have been off-stage committing suicide for the last ten minutes of the play. As it is, she finishes on the stage by herself with the telephone. I'm not saying, mind you, that she doesn't do it beautifully, nobody can smile through her tears better than she can. After all, she made her first great success in *Sheila Goes Away* doing precisely the same scene – not as well written, of course, but the same idea – and she's done it in different ways ever since. Did you ever see her in *Winter Wind* at the Strand?'

'No,' said Bryan. 'I'm afraid I didn't.'

'More or less the same situation all over again, except that there was no telephone on account of it being Victorian. But there she was, crinoline and all, giving up her lover and going back to her husband with a gay smile and a breaking heart. You've never read such notices. Old Agate – God rest his soul – compared her with that French actress that there was such a hullabaloo about.'

'Bernhardt?' suggested Bryan, hopefully.

'No, dear boy, not Bernhardt.' Gerald gave an indulgent smile. 'One of the other ones.'

'She's giving a magnificent performance tonight, at any rate,' said Bryan.

'Slow in the first act.' Gerald scrutinised his teeth in the mirror. 'But she always takes time to build. I've played with her enough to know all her little tricks.'

The assistant stage manager rapped politely on the door, and said, 'Beginners act three, Mr Wentworth.'

'Only one more river to cross,' said Gerald, mechanically, as Bryan left him.

As he passed Lorraine's dressing-room door it opened and she came out. Bryan's heart fluttered with terror at meeting her face to face after his unwilling participation in last night's drama, but she smiled serenely at him and, linking her arm with his, walked with him on to the stage.

'How are you enjoying your baptism of fire?' she said.

'Very much indeed,' Bryan stammered. 'You're absolutely superb. The audience adore you.'

'Lot of cods' heads,' she said, contemptuously. 'We ought to have opened in Edinburgh!'

When the curtain fell on the last act there was an outburst of cheering from the upper parts of the house. Bryan, whose fingers had been tensely clutching the plush edge of the box, relaxed his grip and sat back. His throat was constricted and there were tears in his eyes. Ray and Tony were both applauding with wholehearted sincerity. The curtain went up and down again, disclosing various members of the Company bowing to the audience and to each other. When Lorraine walked on alone for her star call the applause and cheers were thunderous. The curtain fell and rose again on the whole Company standing in a row with Lorraine in the centre. Ray had definitely decided that neither he nor Bryan were to take a call and so, after a number of curtains, Lorraine, with a warning look at the stage manager, stepped forward and held up her hands graciously for silence. The noise died away. She made a brief and charming speech beginning with the tactful statement that Manchester audiences were well known to be the most receptive and intelligent in England. She acknowledged gratefully the splendid performance of her old and valued friend, Gerald Wentworth. Applause. 'That gay and versatile comedienne, Marion Blake.' Tumultuous applause.

('That,' hissed Tony, 'was unwise from every point of view.')

Then she made a charming reference to Bryan and said how proud she was to be appearing in a first play by such a promising young author. Bryan flushed and felt a little dizzy. She finally said, with touching simplicity, that neither she herself nor any of the cast could have achieved anything without the sensitive guidance of the most brilliant young director in the theatre of today – Mr Ray Malcolm. She shot a swift glance up at the box and finished up by thanking the audience once more and wishing them good-night.

The house lights came up, the orchestra played 'God Save the King', during which Bryan stood rigidly to attention and stared at a lady wearing maroon satin in the opposite box.

'Come on,' said Ray. 'We'd better get it over with.'

'I shall come, too,' said Tony, with a giggle. 'I dote on family reunions.'

They went through the pass door and on to the stage. Lorraine was standing in the centre of a group of people who were congratulating her effusively. Ray broke through their ranks and, taking Lorraine in his arms, kissed her. There was a little murmur of indulgent appreciation from the onlookers. Lorraine stepped back from Ray's embrace, then, taking both his hands in hers, she looked wistfully in his face.

'Were you pleased?' she said. 'Was I a good girl?'

'You were beyond praise,' said Ray, with complete sincerity. 'You gave the most lyrical, moving performance I have ever seen.'

'Thank you,' she said, her eyes filling with tears. 'Thank you, Ray, for everything.' She brushed away her tears with her hand and gave a gallant little laugh. 'And when I say "everything" I mean "everything". You've taught me so much, so very much, my dear.'

'This,' said Tony, sotto voce to Bryan, 'is where we came in.'